BEFORE
I
WAKE

JULIAN FOSTER

DEDICATION

This book is dedicated to my sister Tiffany R. Conway for asking, "Where's the second chapter at?" Without you, this novel would have been another one of those things that I started and never completed. Thank you for reading my first draft and encouraging me to finish the story. Thank you for the reassurance that the story and I were both "good enough."

ACKNOWLEDGMENTS

I would first and foremost like to thank God for blessing me with the gift of creative writing and for furnishing all the right obstacles and shortcomings that always and inevitably led me back to it. I would further like to take this opportunity to sincerely thank God for all the failures, heartbreaks, disappointments, and all the "losses." They MADE me and because of them I am stronger, I'm wiser, and I'm better.

I am sincerely hopeful and optimistic that at the end of this journey, I will be thankful and humbled to finally know and understand why "everything else" never worked out. I thank You for Your grace, patience, blessings and favor in sparing my life and my freedom as I traveled blindly and recklessly down a path towards self-destruction.

Thank You for granting me the time and space necessary to get over me, in order to get where I needed to be. Through the darkest, loneliest nights, I always knew deep down that You were not finished with me yet and on the beach of my life there is a long trail of footprints. Thank You for carrying me. Thank You for protecting me from myself and unlike so many others, thank You for never giving up on me! #AmazingGrace

See: Job 1:12

Secondly, I would sincerely like to give thanks to Nina Alvarez, an amazing editor who is officially the first professional in the industry to believe in my ability and talent. I greatly appreciate all your time, knowledge, expertise, and, most importantly, your patience. I jokingly referred to you early on as being the Yoda to my Luke and I can never thank you enough for your insight, honesty, and for challenging me along the way when necessary. I am thankful now that I listened to your advice and trusted your judgment in this field (even when I strongly disagreed with things). I know now that you were trying to bring the best out of my writing and I definitely feel as though I have grown as a writer because of it. This has been a long process and I cannot tell you how thankful I am that you saw this through with me from beginning to end. You are a very valuable resource and I look forward to working with you in the future.

Now I lay me down to sleep,
I pray the Lord my soul to keep,
If I shall die before I wake,
I pray the Lord my soul to take.

- classic 18th century children's bedtime prayer

ONE

"WHOOP THAT BITCH'S ASS!" Ke-Ke heard a female voice coaching her from the sidelines through an inhale of weed smoke. Her mouth filled with the metallic taste of blood as she slammed Kya into the large green dumpster that sat outside of the "old-timers'" bar.

Ke-Ke knew in her heart that fighting in the street was just as much about showmanship as it was about a unanimous victory. So no matter how tired her body felt and how her head throbbed from the first few punches Kya had managed to land (*before she was ready*), she had to make it look like she was in control and using as little effort as possible. It was an art form that Ke-Ke had all but perfected from her early years on the playgrounds of elementary school and junior high.

She tore into Kya, taking advantage of the fact that she knew she was stronger, hip-tossing her to the ground with a move that she had learned in the YMCA judo classes she had been forced to attend with her mother when she was "too young" to stay home alone.

They were encircled by the hood regulars, who always loved a good takedown and responded in an intoxicating chorus of "Ooh" and "Oh shit!" that hung in the air like a black haze of evil encouragement.

Ke-Ke began to take full control of the fight. She climbed on top of Kya and began pounding her head into the sidewalk like a mad woman. She was taking punches to the face but the punches were having no effect on her. She felt the burn of anger in her chest overcome her whole body with a heated rage as she straddled Kya's waist and let loose with a barrage of left and right punches that painted Kya's face with blood.

She had gone into blackout mode and felt any thoughts of compassion slip away as a darkness overcame her that would only be satiated by seeing Kya's limp body bloody, unconscious, or dead.

"Stupid-ass bitch!" Ke-Ke spat, to punctuate her punches that were now finding their mark with ease. Kya flailed helplessly beneath, her body weakened. Ke-Ke ripped a part of the girl's weave out and threw it in the air for the crowd's approval. Suddenly she felt a finger slip underneath the strap of her thong panties and begin pulling. The whistles and comments were enough to let her know that the attention of the male spectators had momentarily shifted. She slapped the hand away and began to get up and straighten her clothes.

"Don't fucken put your hands on me, nigga!" she snapped as she focused her attention on one of the crowd members who just laughed and slapped hands with the man next to him. His friend wore a hoodie and smoked a Black & Mild cigar. They grinned at her like teenage boys who had found a hole to look through in the female locker room. Ke-Ke rolled her eyes and hid the fact that it had turned her on a little bit and that she secretly received the gesture as a twisted compliment, like when the old-ass men that sat outside the barbershop would say "mmph" when she was walking home on her way from school.

"Oh, that bitch getten up! It ain't over!" she heard someone say as she spun around to see Kya cursing and wiping the blood off her face.

"Stay yo' ho-ass down!" Ke-Ke screamed as she pounced on Kya again with fear in her insides, wondering how much she had left in her and if Kya could find the strength to keep fighting. She delivered a few more punches to the side of Kya's head that sent her back to the ground. She could feel a strong set of hands attempting to pull her off of Kya but she wrestled away. She straddled Kya once again and ripped off her sequinned, spaghetti-strap top, then pulled the girl's skirt and panties down to her knees and then completely off.

"Daaaaaaaamn!" she could hear niggas screaming behind her in unison like they were part of some ghetto gospel choir. She threw Kya's clothing in the air and heard them rip as hands grabbed in a frenzy to catch them like hyenas tearing away at a fallen zebra.

"Now what, bitch!" Ke-Ke boasted as she beat her chest like she had seen King Kong do in the movies when she was little. The looks and laughter of the crowd were more than enough to dissolve any inner feelings that she may have gone too far as Kya struggled to her feet and tried to cover her pierced nipples.

Ke-Ke could feel an arm wrap around her and begin to pull her away. She watched Kya make a half-hearted run of shame as niggas in the crowd chased after her, snapping pictures on their cell phones. Some laughed and smacked her naked ass while others tried to catch glimpses of her body while they followed her route back to her grandmother's house.

"Told you not to fuck wit me, bitch!" Ke-Ke screamed at the top of her lungs, knowing that Kya was too far away to even hear her. "Ugly pussy-haven-ass bitch!" she continued, playing to the crowd "Yo' shit look like meatloaf!" she yelled, as an older nigga from the crowd shook with laughter. She looked around to see niggas tossing Kya's weave back and forth like it was a football and one nigga had even put the straps of Kya's panties around his ears and was wearing them on his face like a surgical mask. Overexaggerated laughter filled the air and Ke-Ke couldn't help but bask in the antics that followed the scene she had created.

Her body was tired and sore and she was out of breath, but she wasn't going to let them see her sweat. She talked shit and acted like she was ready to go another round if she had to. Ke-Ke only half-turned as she felt hands massaging her shoulders and slowly pushing her through the crowd of satisfied onlookers. "I told y'all my bitch was a beast!" She recognized Cry's voice behind her and smiled as she was escorted to the black Infiniti Q45 that was parked across the street, shining in the sunlight. Cry was a hood "block star" and was famous for hustling, fighting, shooting, and doing anything a nigga could or would do. "Bitches don't really want it!" Cry continued as she ushered Ke-Ke to the car, opening the door for her and closing it behind her.

She had always seen Cry around and watched her like she was a movie star but, before today, all Cry had ever said to her was, "Whatsup" if she passed her in a corner store or walked past her on the block. The fact that she had obviously gained her approval and attention excited Ke-Ke. She told herself, "Don't say nothing stupid!"

She could hear Cry talking shit as she walked around the front of the car to the driver's side but couldn't make out what she was saying. Cry fell into the driver's side and steered the luxury sedan down the Ave in one fluid motion. Ke-Ke glanced down and noticed her powder blue and grey #13 Jordans working the pedals. They matched her Ralph Lauren polo shirt and the band on her watch. The face of the watch was surrounded by diamonds that sparkled violently when the sunlight struck it at a certain angle. She steered the car with one hand in silence and glanced at people on the street as if she were looking for someone. Ke-Ke had never seen a woman act as confident as Cry did and had secretly admired her for years. She was always dressed in some exclusive shit that led Ke-Ke to believe that she must have regularly made trips to NYC to buy clothes. She had seen Cry wear outfits and shoes that she had never on anyone else.

She glanced down at Cry's Jordans again and wondered how she had managed to get them in those colors. Ke-Ke's mind drifted off into a partial fantasy where she envisioned Cry calling Michael Jordan on her cell phone and demanding that she needed his shoes in "these" colors and he would have them made and shipped to her door. For some reason, she didn't see it as being out of the realms of possibility. Cry's name rang bells all over the city.

"It's about time you shut that loudmouth bitch the fuck up!" Cry crashed through Ke-Ke's crystal fantasy like a raven on fire. "She been runnen around this bitch for weeks, speaken on you!"

Cry produced a sandwich bag full of Sour Diesel, the most potent form of weed to hit the West Side in years, from a compartment underneath the steering wheel. She handed the bag to Ke-Ke with a cognac wrap for her to roll up. Ke-Ke tried to act normal as she reached in the bag and broke off enough to fill a blunt. She pulled it apart and smiled as she took note of the brownish orange hairs that wormed their way through the green buds. "That's that fire, right there!" Cry informed her, but Ke-Ke was all too familiar and impressed with the quality already. She had only seen it in dime bags that she got off the block here and there, and never in such a large quantity. She wrapped the bag up and handed it back to Cry as she wondered what it was like to always have more than enough of what you wanted and needed. This was everyday life for Cry and Ke-Ke had to remind herself that, at best, she was just visiting.

"Light that shit, why you holding it?" Cry asked impatiently when Ke-Ke finished rolling the blunt and was drying it with the lighter.

"My bad," Ke-Ke responded, kind of embarrassed, and lit the blunt, took a puff, then handed it to Cry.

"You gotta handle yo' business out here, or it will definitely handle you!" Cry preached in a distorted voice as she held in the weed smoke. Ke-Ke just nodded coolly, like she agreed and understood, while her insides did flips. She felt like she had just gotten a record deal, or won the lottery. She tried to soak in all the details of this encounter, from Cry's dark, rich complexion that looked as if God hand-picked the color then slowly and carefully poured it all over her body, to her perfectly manicured fingernails. She took quick glances like snapshots so Cry wouldn't notice and ask her what she was looking at.

"That bitch really thought I wouldn't bring it to her!" Ke-Ke finally said back, after a few awkward moments of silence. She took the weed that Cry handed her and tried to appear as if she was comfortable. She pulled down the visor and examined herself in the vanity mirror. "I'm still fine though," she joked, as she kissed at her reflection playfully.

"Yeah, you straight," Cry answered with a smirk on her face as she pulled to a stop in front of the liquor store. "I'll be back," she said and got out of the car and crossed the street. Ke-Ke watched as she slapped hands with the dude that always stood there and sold bootleg DVDs that never played clearly when you got them home.

Ke-Ke reclined in her seat a little bit and looked up through the moonroof at the sky above. She cracked the window and laid her head on the headrest and suddenly felt a throbbing sensation from one of Kya's blows while the weed smoke, mixed with the smell of the leather interior, was making her sick to her stomach. She took deep breaths as various thoughts invaded her mind all at once. *Niggas is natural-born actors and actresses*, she could hear the words of her uncle echoing in her head out of nowhere. She smiled at the memory of him, her Uncle James who had been killed in prison—some said by the guards—but the family was never able to get to the bottom of it and nobody was ever charged in his death. He'd had a million of those little sayings. When she was younger, Ke-Ke used to think he was just crazy, but as she had gotten older, the sayings would come back to her and fall into place.

She started to feel the guilt begin to form and grow. She really hadn't wanted to fight Kya. They had been the best of friends ever since Number Four School, where they both had gone to elementary. Kya never would've humiliated her like that if the fight had gone the other way.

She let her eyes drift to the right and settle on an old graffiti mural that adorned the brick wall across from the corner store. The chipped and faded paint seemed to be a part of the overall beauty and message of it. The faces of Malcolm X, Martin Luther King Jr, and Harriet Tubman. She had remembered who they were because the hallways of her last school had been named after them. They seemed to be staring directly at her with sadness and disapproval in their eyes. Ke-Ke found herself trapped in that moment. She knew Cry would bounce her out of the car in a heartbeat if she tried to speak on it, so she buried her self-resentment in the cloud of smoke that was filling the car.

Exhaling, Ke-Ke thought back to what had caused the whole dispute between her and Kya in the first place.

Ke-Ke, Kya, and Trish had been shoplifting in Stacey's, an upscale department store in the suburbs. The item most coveted by girls their age at the time were sexy G-string or thong panties, the shortest skirts they could find, and anything that was see-through, revealing, or tight. Ke-Ke remembered stealing a cheerleader-type skirt that was so short that when she sat down at school, her bare ass made contact with the cold chairs. She giggled to herself as she remembered getting up at the end of the period and seeing her cheek prints were still visible.

This particular time, the three girls had loaded up and were heading out of the store when they were confronted by store security who quickly escorted them to the back of the store, passing the nosy-ass, paying customers who looked, shook their heads, pointed, and whispered. The trio sat on a bench in the dungeon-like office as the security guard asked them for identification and began to fill out a stack of paperwork for each one of them. He took their oversized purses from them and one after the other dumped piles of risqué lingerie on the desk in front of them. Ke-Ke and Kya played hard, but Trish broke out in tears and begged the man not to call the police or her mother.

"Are you wearing anything under your clothes?" the security man asked in a professional tone, but Ke-Ke and Kya had already read the look in his eyes.

"Hell naw! These shits are mine!" Kya responded first, as she lifted up her denim skirt to reveal her lime green bikini panties that she had stolen from another store a month earlier. "Y'all don't even carry these," she continued as she spun around slowly to give him a good look.

The middle-aged man could only stutter, "Oh... okay, okay," but didn't take his eyes off of Kya. Ke-Ke followed Kya's lead and unzipped her jeans to reveal that she wasn't wearing any underwear and went even further, informing the man that she rarely did. Trish took the hint finally and revealed lacy boy shorts that she had managed to order online with a stolen credit card her aunt had let her use.

Then she pulled up her tank top to show him that she wasn't wearing a bra.

The security guard's face was bright red and he leaned back and asked with a sick smile on his face, "Why should I let you girls go?" The girls looked at each other. Within seconds all three of them were naked, dancing in front of him, making their ass cheeks clap together and grinding on his lap, like he was someone who they found irresistible. He called Ke-Ke over and asked her to play with him while he watched Trish and Kya. Ke-Ke still cringed at the thought of it. "Nasty muthafucka!" she spoke out loud to herself. But ten minutes later, they were on the bus on their way back to the hood. No jail, no nothing.

"We rocked that old man's world! He probably wanna leave his wife!" Trish laughed and spoke too loud for them to be on a bus full of people. "He couldn't even close his mouth!" Kya laughed as she used one of the stabilizing bars as a stripper pole, spun around it and slapped hands with Trish. "We probably could've kept that shit if we had asked him!" Ke-Ke added, as she remembered trying to forcibly get her thoughts off what she had been forced to do to free them. The three of them laughed and joked through the shame that they were all feeling and vowed to file it away as one of the many "crew secrets."

Six months later, Kya had gotten drunk and high at a party and was trying to get the attention of Dub, a young drug dealer from the East Side that everyone said looked like Allen Iverson. Dub had already expressed his interest in Ke-Ke so to gain pole position, Kya leaked the whole story of how Ke-Ke had gotten "all nasty" with the security man while she and Trish had only danced.

Kya had done her dirty and over a nigga. Ke-Ke comforted herself with the thought that the ass-whooping was justified.

"You good?" Cry was back in the car, looking over at Ke-Ke as she closed the door.

"Yeah, I'm straight," Ke-Ke answered while she tried to act like Cry hadn't scared the hell out of her. She had gone so deep into her thoughts that she didn't even notice her making her way back to the car.

"I got you a present," Cry said as she pulled a lime green G-string out of her pocket and threw it on Ke-Ke's lap. Cry had recovered the panties as a souvenir.

Ke-Ke ran them through her fingers and shook her head. "That nasty bitch still wearen these same panties!" she said out loud before she could catch herself.

"Let me find out!" Cry laughed and looked over at Ke-Ke with a confused look on her face. Cry shifted the car into drive and took a right turn onto Jefferson Avenue, driving slow with the windows down and the music bumping. Ke-Ke looked in the bag Cry had handed her and saw a large bottle of coconut Cîroc and another smaller bottle of Remy Martin.

"Money Mayweather!" she heard someone call out as the niggas in front of the store rolling dice had noticed her in the car and were still clowning, throwing air blows and laughing hysterically. Ke-Ke added to their antics when she threw the panties out of the car window and watched as they picked them up, sniffed them, and then acted like they were fainting on the sidewalk. Ke-Ke couldn't help but bust out laughing as the comic relief chased away her guilt and better judgment.

Cry was yelling out the window in agreement with the crowd that was still lingering from the fight and Ke-Ke felt like the snow princess on a float in a holiday parade. She waved at a couple of people and blew kisses, knowing that by tomorrow it would be old news and she wouldn't be able to live off of this fame forever.

The next thing she knew, Cry was nudging her, "Wake up, bitch, you at home!"

Ke-Ke sat up, shocked to see it was dark outside. The last thing she remembered was drinking the coconut Cîroc mixed with pineapple juice in a parking lot, talking to Cry and smoking weed. She wondered how long she had been asleep.

"You not a weed smoker, huh?" Cry asked with a smile on her face.

Ke-Ke could only shake her head and mumble, "Not that Sour. I ain't used to that!"

She crawled out of the car. She felt ashamed of herself for how she had passed out in front of Cry like that but tried to play it off.

"I'll call you tomorrow," Cry said with a grin on her face as she inhaled what looked like a freshly rolled blunt.

"Aiight," Ke-Ke answered as she turned and tripped on the curb on her way to the house. She could hear Cry laughing behind her as she honked the horn and pulled off.

Once inside, she climbed what seemed to be a mountain of stairs to her room and collapsed on her bed, kicking her shoes off onto the floor. She reached down and noticed that her pants were unbuttoned and her zipper was pulled down. She froze for a minute, somewhat stunned. She knew Cry swung that way, but had she tried her while she was passed out in the passenger seat? Images flew through her mind of Cry kissing her on the neck and face while she played with her pussy. She shook at the thought of it and dismissed it as paranoia from the weed. Cry wouldn't do her like that.

Would she?

That uneasy feeling circled in her sea of thoughts like a hungry tiger shark until she passed out again.

TWO

"KE-KEEEEE! KE-KE! KETASIA MONTIQUE! If you don't answer me, I'ma come up there and beat yo' little hot ass!"

Ke-Ke woke up to the sound of her mother's footsteps stomping up the stairs. She turned over to find her standing at her door with her arms folded in her work uniform.

"What, Ma?"

Her mother flicked on her bedroom light and it tap-danced on the tin roof of her pounding headache.

This bitch! Ke-Ke only dared think to herself, as she shielded her eyes from the two exposed lightbulbs in duct-taped sockets directly above her bed. She sat up on one elbow and tried to mentally prepare herself for the flurry of insults that her mother could string together at a moments notice.

"So you fucken wit dykes now?" her mother asked with a sick sarcasm in her voice that Ke-Ke knew meant that she already knew and no amount of explaining would make her believe any different.

"Ma, what are you talken about? Cry is my homegirl... that's it." She rolled her eyes and collapsed back onto her bed, wondering how long it would take her mother to spread this rumor to everyone she came in contact with. She pictured her sister in her room down the hall pretending to mind her own business while she soaked up all the gossip.

"That's why when you got out the car, your pussy was hangen out for the entire world to see?" Her mother grossly exaggerated details with such skill that if you didn't know her, she would have you questioning what really happened yourself.

"Ma, I fell asleep in the car, I unbuttoned my pants. That's a crime now?" Ke-Ke's head was throbbing as she rubbed her temples and her eyes adjusted to the lights. The thought of her mother peeking out the blinds just to have ammunition to use against her pissed her off, but she didn't dare mention it. She'd have to endure the whole "This is my fucken house" speech.

"Whatever, bitch!" her mother's voice snapped back and threw Ke-Ke's thoughts into outer space. "All I know is you better get ya shit together cause you ain't fixen to be not goen to school, unemployed, AND eating pussy under my roof! Get yo' ass up cause I don't even want you in my house while I'm at work. Ain't no tellen what you'll have jumpen off in here!"

"Ma, I—"

Her mother cut her off. "Get up, bitch, and I ain't given you no money, so don't even waste that coochie-smelling breath to even ask. You better get it how you usually do."

Ke-Ke's head was now spinning from the early-morning sneak attack. She regretted coming home at all last night. She rolled on her side and swung her feet around to the floor. She entertained the thought of waking up at Cry's to find three of Cry's fingers deep inside her pussy and how that would have been a consequence that she could have lived with if it meant she wouldn't have to hear her mother's mouth.

She forced herself to her feet and quickly picked an outfit from her closet then headed for the bathroom. "Bitch!" she said under her breath as she passed the stairs that her mother had just gone down and slammed the door to the bathroom behind her.

Fifteen minutes later she had finished her shower and was in the mirror clawing through her hair with her fingers. The pink rinse she had put in was growing out. She decided that she would have to scarf it today as she reached for one of her silk head wraps and tied it in one of her signature styles that more often than not led people to believe that she had worn it for fashion reasons and not as a Band-Aid.

"Bitches still gonna hate!" she said as she admired her profile in the mirror, but was interrupted by a knock on the door.

"Ke?" she heard her younger sister Misha's voice whisper from the other side of the door.

"What?" Ke-Ke answered in a way that sometimes made her sister abandon her attempts to pry into her business, ask questions, or beg her for money.

"Open up," Misha knocked again to confirm that she was not going to retreat anytime soon.

Ke-Ke swung the door open with disgust in her voice, "What, little girl?" She glared at Misha with her crazy look, hoping she could punk her little sister into leaving her alone.

You fucken wit girls now?" Misha asked with her eyes stretched wide and her mouth open. She had that stupid look of shock on her face, as always, when she heard something she shouldn't have or got busted trying to pull off one of her many failed capers.

"Bye!" Ke-Ke grabbed Misha's forehead and attempted to push her out of the bathroom.

Misha pushed past her sister's hand and forced her way into the bathroom with her.

"Okay, okay! You fucken crazy!"

Ke-Ke closed the bathroom door and finished drying off as she watched her sister put the seat down on the toilet and prepare for story time. Ke-Ke purposely dropped her towel and admired her naked body in the mirror in one last attempt to run Misha off.

"Uggh!" Misha responded on cue as she covered her eyes but still watched Ke-Ke through the small spaces in between her fingers.

"Don't hate, bitch!" Ke-Ke laughed as she walked toward her sister then spun around like she was on the runway of a fashion show in Paris. She knew deep down that Misha envied her shape and wished that her body had developed in the way that hers had within the past couple of years. She paraded around the bathroom and rubbed her body seductively, watching her sister cringe as she watched.

Ke-Ke had a slim shape and what some had called a walnut complexion that darkened with hints of red depending on how long she stayed in the sun. Her uncle had told her that they had Seminole Indian in their bloodline and she had always taken this to mean that she was a warrior who could never lose a fight. She had small but perky and noticeable breasts and could go without wearing a bra if she wanted to. She had learned early on, though, that a silky, colored bra strap exposed at the right time was more than enough to hold a nigga's attention when she wanted it to. Not to mention that her nipples seemed to poke through most of her tops with the slightest breeze or any sudden drop in temperature—and the *wrong* niggas seemed to always be around when they made their public appearances.

Her most treasured body part though was her P-booty that even made her mother jealous. She could remember her saying, "Bitch, that's just baby fat! You better enjoy it while it lasts!" She had worn a denim cat suit for Christmas that had her male cousins saying, "If you wasn't my cousin..." She was too young at the time to understand what they were talking about but figured it out quickly after she wore the outfit to school and had to pry hands off of her ass the entire day as she walked the halls between classes.

After being satisfied that she had thoroughly disturbed Misha and that she still wasn't going to leave her alone, Ke-Ke grabbed the white stretch pants that she had dubbed her "Wonder Pants" and carefully slid them on. They had earned the name because countless times in the past when she had worn them, niggas would wonder whether she had on any panties or not. They usually didn't have a problem asking her either. When they did, she would flirtatiously answer, "You want me to have panties on?" then she would follow their eyes and laugh as she left them holding their crotches in exaggerated admiration saying shit like, "Damn, girl!" as they called after her or chased her down. That type of shit would make her day, especially when they were grown men. The thought that she could make their dicks hard without even touching them made her feel like the most beautiful woman alive. Their reactions and comments never got old and had prompted her to steal the pants in every color she could find them in.

She straightened the band around her waist and shook her legs to allow the thin material to settle in the crack of her ass. She put on her bra, an orange lace demi-cup style, and clamped it in place behind her back with ease as her sister stared in amazement. Finally Ke-Ke pulled on the Lycra top she had selected to complete the outfit and adjusted her breasts to make sure that the print from her nipple ring was noticeable.

Ke-Ke replayed the whole conversation in her head from the day she came home with the piercing and remembered how it ended with her mother making some off-color comment about her "dancing for dollars" as being her only possible career choice because of a half-inch piece of jewelry.

"You a ho!" Misha had seen enough of her sister's daily preparation and stomped out of the bathroom and slammed her bedroom door.

"Haaaater!" Ke-Ke laughed as she spun in the mirror to admire how the pants hugged and clung to her figure like a second skin. She walked back to her room, just in time to see her phone vibrating and blinking on her bed.

"Hello?" Ke-Ke answered with her sexy voice and a fake Brooklyn accent, thinking it had to be some nigga that she had given her number to.

"Whatever, bitch! You ain't sexy!" a familiar female voice answered through the phone. "I gotta lick, bitch. Come through. These niggas got bread too!" It was Trish, reporting like she was on the six o'clock news.

"Aiight, give me a sec, you know I'm wit it." Ke-Ke smiled, knowing the issue of how she was going to get her hair done and put minutes on her phone were instantly solved.

Trish and Ke-Ke had maintained a "down for whatever" type of relationship over the years that could fill a book with secrets and stories that would shock and amaze most. Whatever they did stayed between them and more times than not they would end up with a decent amount of money, weed, a ride, or whatever else they were in need of at the time. Whatever happened was always an adventure with twists and turns and the two had made many memories together, some of which they wouldn't even discuss with each other. She took one last, long gaze in the mirror as she put on her bubblegum-flavored lip gloss and kissed at her reflection, grabbed her Dereon leather, and hit the front door, but not quick enough to miss her mother's goodbye joke sing out from the kitchen, "Something strange for a piece of change!"

"Fucken bitch!" she answered after the door was closed. She could still hear her mother laughing loudly from inside of the house. She jogged down to the sidewalk, reached in her pocket, pulled out a loose cigarette that had gotten crushed, repaired it, and began to smoke as she walked down the block.

She had reached the corner in less than a minute and turned onto Reynolds Street as she tried to mentally prepare herself for the upcoming festivities at Trish's house. She went through her routine of smiling a lot and complimenting and developing fake answers to questions, like where she lived and what was her last name. The goal was to make them fall for you without letting them know that, if it wasn't for the money, most times, you wouldn't even be talking to them.

The technique usually worked liked a charm. Niggas were so fucking stupid, especially if their dicks were hard! Just stroke their little fragile egos and you had them every time! She could almost see a hologram of the lady she had heard that from in the salon where the older women talked shit, told stories, and passed on "wisdom."

When she reached the next corner, Pam and Butt Naked were standing on the corner, trying to catch a date. Reynolds was known as a minor league ho stroll where ten dollars would buy a man a story that he more than likely would not admit to later on. Most of the females that worked the strip were crackheads, wearing dingy clothes that were too small for them, and were engaged in an ongoing competition with each other called "who has the most tread left on the tire." They openly argued and came to blows over the occasional car or two that pulled over and honked.

Pam and Butt Naked were the dynamic duo of crackheads and their legend was as notorious as it was endless. Butt Naked had been so named years ago by niggas in the hood. She was famous for stripping off every stitch of her clothing and running up and down the street, into a store, or performing whatever ridiculous, unbelievable acts the person paying desired. Ke-Ke remembered the time some years ago, when niggas in the Gateway projects had created a diving competition and Butt Naked and some other crackheads were jumping off of the Ford Street bridge into the dirty river water below while niggas stood on the grass and held up makeshift scorecards and laughed.

Ke-Ke almost laughed out loud at the image of Butt Naked climbing out of the water with her stretch-marked stomach, sagging titties, and grey pussy hair running back up to perform another "Olympic dive" for twenty dollars. She let it be known far and wide that if you had some extra money and needed a cheap laugh, find Butt Naked, she would do it!

Pam on the other hand, was her handler and "manager" of the corner. She made sure that the price was right for the entertainment and kept renegade crackheads from across town away from their prime real estate.

Ke-Ke would usually cross the street to avoid the wholesale begging that would ensue once she was spotted. "You got a cigarette, or a quarter, or a dime? When you gonna do my hair? You wanna buy a..." and on and on and on. After all that, they would try to soften her up with a compliment on how good she was looking that day or mentioning God in some out-of-context way.

She used to feel bad for them, especially when she found out that Pam had actually been the baddest bitch in her high school. She had heard from her mother that she was the best looking, had the best shape, and how all the boys followed her around or wanted to carry her books. The story was she could make a man do whatever she wanted to and in her early twenties had cars and a house, all paid for and maintained by her "man friends." Pam still had a cute face, compared to her competition, but the years of drug abuse had taken a very noticeable toll on her.

Ke-Ke thought back to a time when she was younger and she was in the store waiting for her sub to be made. Two older men had entered the store to play lottery when Pam walked by the front of the store. "There go Pam!" one said as he tapped his friend on the arm. "Yep, old Pam Grier they used to call her, didn't they?" the two laughed and the one went on saying, "Yeah, that bitch wouldn't give a nigga the time of day, back in high school. Now if I ride by, she be beggen to suck my dick!" The two laughed again and slapped hands. "And I let her too, sometimes! Ol' funny-acting bitch! Payback is a muthafucka though!"

Ke-Ke remembered how, all at once, they noticed her standing there and tried to clean up their act. "Oh, excuse me, young lady, how are you today?" She just grabbed her sub off of the counter and left without speaking.

She hadn't ever been really close to Pam or anything, but it was just the thought of how they spoke of her, like they were kicking her when she was down. She told the story to her mother when she had gotten home and her mother just shook her head and said, "That's how it goes." From that day on, Ke-Ke always felt a tinge of sadness when she would see Pam getting in and out of cars or escorting some man into the alley on the side of her building.

Thoughts and feelings that she would usually keep to herself she had one day allowed to slip in a conversation with Pam.

"Don't feel bad, girl! Shit, we all the same," Pam had stated with a huge grin on her face that Ke-Ke couldn't understand. "Yeah, girl, you just like me." Pam clapped her hands with a smile, but kept her eyes on the passing cars. Ke-Ke remembered thinking this bitch done smoked her brains out.

"I ain't no fucken crackhead!" Ke-Ke blurted out before she could even catch herself. She stood there and waited for Pam to take offense.

"Naw, boo, you ain't no crackhead. But you addicted just the same! See, I smoke crack and I have for years and probably will until the Good Lord takes me away from here. It runs me, it runs my life, and I jump in and out of these cars and do whatever I gotta do to get it. You..." Pam continued, "You addicted to glamour! Always getten your hair and nails done, buyen clothes and shoes, racen up the block to put minutes on your phone. I be seeing you. Shit, I was just like you! All for what, Ketasia?"

Pam always took license to call her by her real name since she had lived down the street from her ever since she could remember. Her voice was calm and soft and her words were spoken slowly and with purpose, like when her grandmother was trying to drive some important point home to her or one of her cousins.

"You spend every penny that comes through your hands on a whole bunch of shit that if it does make you happy, it's only for a little while!"

The truth entered Ke-Ke's ears and settled in her stomach like hot stones. "Shit, you ain't even goen to school no more from what I can tell. A big dressed-up dummy!"

The words hit Ke-Ke like a punch in the face.

There was a moment of silence while Ke-Ke stared into Pam's eyes, trying to figure out what to say or what to think. "So work it, work it, Ke-Ke!" Pam made a dancing motion as she spoke with a smile that she made vanish like a magic trick before she spoke again. "While that ass is still tight and them titties still perky!"

Ke-Ke remembered the anger she felt. She had wanted to knock Pam out that day but felt paralyzed at the same time. Pam must have seen it and she had an answer for that too. "You can fight me all day long, Ketasia, but you can't fight the truth. Even you know that shit."

Pam had smiled, sighed, and slowly backed away, leaving Ke-Ke with tears running down her face. Ke-Ke never forgot that day that she had been humiliated by a crackhead. She felt overcome by different emotions as she walked away, but the words weren't what had hit her the hardest. For a moment, she had actually caught a glimpse of her own reflection in Pam's glassy, bloodshot eyes, and at night sometimes when she closed her own, that image would come back to haunt her.

She never spoke to Pam again after that day, but every time she hit the corner, Pam would have something slick to say, to remind her of that conversation. Ke-Ke would just speed-walk with her head down and try to turn the next corner and pretend that she hadn't heard her. *Don't ever let em know they getten the best of you*, she would remember her uncle's words and allow them to coach her through those moments and deafen the sound of Pam's voice.

Ke-Ke took the shortcut, a path that wound behind a row of boarded-up houses that was littered with beer bottles, used condoms, blunt wrappers, and empty crack baggies. If you could stomach the visuals and the smell and dared chance the more-than-frequent occurrence of stumbling across a female on her knees in front of a man with his pants pulled down, then you would choose to take "the chute" as it was called in the neighborhood. The chute saved a walker a good five minutes and spilled out onto Jefferson Avenue through two large bushes that kept its existence a secret. Ke-Ke exhaled as she walked the narrow dirt path as a memory from seventh grade chased away the sound of Pam's voice.

She was in seventh grade and had taken a health class taught by the school nurse. The class snickered and joked through pictures of male and female sex organs and their scientific definitions and functions. Ke-Ke usually walked home with a group of kids that lived around her and they would stop at the store on the way home and play-fight the whole way, with the chute marking the tail end of their journey.

The group had just entered the chute through the large bushes and were making their way down the path when one of the boys began taunting her, saying, "Ke-Ke gotta bald pussy!" as the other boys in the group burst out laughing and pointed their fingers at her. "She ain't got no grown woman *public* hairs!" he carried on, misnaming what they had just learned fifteen minutes earlier.

"It's pubic hairs, you dumbass!" Ke-Ke remembered saying as she hit him with her book bag and started to chase him.

But he was too quick. The damage had already been done and within moments the four boys were taunting and chanting together like they were in the stands of a basketball game. "Bald pussy, bald pussy, bald pussy!" They laughed, pointed, and ran circles around Ke-Ke as she walked and swung her book bag wildly, trying to hit them as they passed in front of her. Without thinking, she stopped and said, "I can prove I ain't got no bald pussy!" and watched as the boys stopped chanting and joking like someone had pushed the pause button on a DVD player.

"Prove it! Prove it! Prove it!" they all demanded with smiles on their faces and excitement in their eyes.

Ke-Ke remembered feeling stuck. If she didn't show them, "Bald Pussy" would be her new name at school and there was NO WAY she could live with that. She dropped her bag on the ground and began to unbutton her jeans as she glanced around the chute for someone coming. Ke-Ke remembered their eyes wide with excitement as the boys watched her hands while she pulled her zipper down.

"See!" Ke-Ke had offered as she showed the front of her panties, thinking that would be enough as anyone could clearly see the print of her short, tangled, black hairs through the thin white material of her panties.

"We can't see shit!" she remembered Banger saying as he kept shoving barbecue potato chips into his mouth.

"You can tell!" Ke-Ke demanded and stretched the front of her panties against the hair beneath them, so her critics could get a better view.

"Nope, still can't see shit!" he said again, shaking his head with a mouth full of chips. "Pull them shits down! And we gotta count to three!" He explained the rules as if he had seen this on a game show somewhere. Ke-Ke looked behind her and over their shoulders and sighed as she pulled the front of her panties down and waited for their count. "One... t-t-t-t...," the boys stuttered to stretch the time.

"Fuck y'all, I proved it!" Ke-Ke let her panties snap back into place, zipped her pants up, and grabbed her book bag.

Years later she figured out that they had just played a game with her to get her to show her pussy to them, but it was too late to do anything about it. She smiled as she thought about how, to this day, she could be on the Ave hanging out with her girls or walking to the store and one of the four boys would remember that day at the sight of her and whisper "Bald Pussy" and they would share a smirk. "What the fuck he say?" one of her friends would ask, but she would never tell them what it was all about.

Ke-Ke made it through the bushes at the end of the chute and was standing on the sidewalk, waiting for traffic. She checked herself for leaves as the doorway to the chute was known to leave its mark on your clothing. Leaves and small branches would stick to a person's clothes without them knowing, prompting someone to ask, "You just came through the chute?" as the frustrated person was left to wonder how many people hadn't said anything to them about it.

She crossed the street and walked into the corner store, now only about a half a block away from Trish's house. *I can't fucken wait to get my own place,* she thought as she bought two Kingpin wraps, Laffy Taffy, and a Boone's Farm Fuzzy Navel. She was on her way out of the store when she felt a hand grab her arm and spin her around. "I saw you rollen around on the ground wit that girl the other day wit ya ass hangen out!"

It was Burned Up Fred. He was a drifter type who did odd jobs in corner stores for extra money. The hood called him "Burned Up Fred" because he had splotches of light skin on his face, neck, and arms and people said he had been burned in a house fire when he was a baby. The truth was it was some skin condition that was too hard for Ke-Ke or anybody else to pronounce so Burned Up Fred was the name that stuck.

Ke-Ke sucked her teeth at him, as she snatched away from his grasp. He ALWAYS had part of the story or less and was known for telling a fucked-up account of countless things that happened in the neighborhood.

"That's all you saw, right?" Ke-Ke rolled her eyes as she looked at him with disbelief and pity.

"That's what I saw when we rode by," he answered as he shrugged his shoulders and smiled, knowing that he didn't really have the whole story. "I be tellen y'all about all that fighting in the street," he said as he pointed one of his discolored fingers in Ke-Ke's face. "A hard head makes a soft behind, girl" he smiled and winked in a way that made Ke-Ke uncomfortable as she remembered stories of how Fred had tried to pay a few girls from her school to sleep with him.

"What the fuck ever, Fred!" she responded and turned to walk out the door. She thought of something quick before she pushed the door open. "You ever think maybe I *WANT* my booty soft?" She looked Fred directly in the eyes, so she wouldn't miss his reaction. The look on his face and the dirty grin confirmed to Ke-Ke that the rumors were true. Fred was a pervert. She walked through the door and let it slam behind her, shaking her head.

"Whatup, bitch?" Trish called out from her porch with her arms stretched out, grinning from ear to ear. Ke-Ke walked up the steps and sat on one of the wooden chairs, still thinking about the look on Fred's face and wondering how grown men ended up that way. "Heard you was wit Cry last night! Whatsup wit all that?" Trish started as she steered Ke-Ke's thoughts into a new territory.

"Don't start, ho!" she answered as if it were a reflex. She was annoyed that Trish made her think about her mother again. She reached out to take the blunt Trish was holding. She had learned the previous summer *If you don't ask, Trish won't pass.*

"Shit, ain't no shame, girl. If you wit the licky-licky, then you wit the licky-licky!" Trish stuck her tongue out and flicked it up and down with lightning speed. She gyrated her hips as if she was being pleasured until Ke-Ke shot her a "For real bitch, I'm not fucken wit you!" look and Trish changed the subject.

"And I *hearrrrrd* you finally banged Kya's ass out!" Trish stated in a voice that begged to hear details. Ke-Ke smiled. News in the hood traveled faster than the Internet. She knew the game. Act like there was nothing to tell and Trish would sweat her even harder for information.

"Yeah, I had to give her the business, real quick." Ke-Ke threw out a scrap. She made sure to keep her voice sounding laid-back and nonchalant, like it was no big deal. "What's good wit today, though?" Ke-Ke skillfully changed the subject, not knowing how long she would be able to hide her enthusiasm about the fight with Kya.

"Oh, you ready to trick, bitch?" Trish said, sticking her tongue out again. She had that wild look in her eyes that she only got when something major was about to go down.

"Hell yeah, I need this money!" Ke-Ke answered as she handed the blunt back to Trish. "A bitch broke as hell out here!" she finished as she coughed, enjoying how the weed made her feel like she was weightless. "I hope you didn't call me over here just to pop off." She stared at Trish with a serious look.

Trish and Ke-Ke had been partners in crime for a long time and they had their own advanced slang. "Popping off" was a term that they developed in the year and a half that they both had actually attempted high school. The girls at the school would wear plastic colored bracelets that all stood for different sex acts. The black ones meant straight sex, the pink ones meant head, and on and on down the spectrum. The boys would attempt to pop the bracelets off the girls' wrists and, if they were successful, the girls had to perform whatever sex act the color dictated. The girls that actually carried these acts out and took it seriously were given the name "pop offs" and the term evolved to mean any girl that was down to fuck for little or nothing.

Ke-Ke and Trish had developed rules to popping off that, in their own way, were an attempt at taking some of the power away from the boys who expected that the girls would be trying to date them after the sex act. That rarely, if ever, happened and more times than not left a few girls in the bathroom or locker room crying their eyes out.

The rules were as follows:

1. MEET A NIGGA.
2. SMOKE WIT A NIGGA.
3. FUCK A NIGGA.
4. FORGET A NIGGA.

It was all for fun, recreation. Tricken, on the other hand, was all business: basically, when you were approached by a nigga you weren't really feeling and you required him to "pay to play."

"Well, check it! I met these niggas on the chat line." Trish started to tell the story but was cut off.

"Here we go," Ke-Ke said and looked over at Trish like she was crazy. She thought by now, with all the things that they had been through, that Trish would know better. Niggas always talked monster shit on the chat line and in the end never showed up, or showed up looking less, driving less, spending less, being less. Just downright WORTH-LESS.

"No, no, wait!" Trish waved her hands and tried to plead her case, knowing already what Ke-Ke was thinking. "These is older niggas. They talken straight business. Cash and carry!" Trish watched the expression on Ke-Ke's face and coughed from the weed until tears formed in her eyes.

"How old?" Ke-Ke shot back, as this situation got worse and worse in her mind. She didn't mind tricken but she DID have standards and she knew from prior occasions that Trish couldn't even spell S-T-A-N-D-A-R-D-S. Too many times she had left Trish behind because the scene had become too wild for her. Trish would do it all. Literally!

"They just older," Trish answered in a low voice that led Ke-Ke to be even more suspicious. Trish passed the weed back and opened the Boone's Farm, then sat back to hear Ke-Ke's reaction. When Ke-Ke said nothing, she continued, "I be tired of young niggas. They talk too fucken much! Don't know how to keep they mouths shut!"

Trish knew Ke-Ke would agree with that logic at the very least.

"True!" Ke-Ke responded on cue. "Then they wonder why they can't get they dicks sucked," she added and Trish spit out the wine laughing and slapped her hand.

"Word, though!" they said in unison. It was their trademark saying that always strengthened their bond.

Trish grabbed a rag out of the house and began to clean up the wine she had spit out as a black Lincoln truck with Mississippi license plates pulled up in front of the house.

"That's them!" Trish whispered as she nudged Ke-Ke.

"Oh, hell naw!" Ke-Ke said in disbelief as she looked back at Trish. "Them niggas look like they in they sixties!" she said under her breath.

Trish held her finger to her mouth, like she was shushing a child. She then rubbed the tips of her fingers together to symbolize cash. Ke-Ke could only roll her eyes and then close them completely as she shook her head in disgust.

"Whatupwityallguhls?" the driver asked as he smiled from ear to ear and made his way onto the porch with his friend. Ke-Ke dropped her head and made a sneak glance at Trish, thinking *these niggas geechie as fuck too*. She took large gulps of the wine and tried to focus her mind on how badly she needed her hair done and minutes on her phone. She wondered if she could even go through with this one though. The image of a gold-tooth-wearing, geechie ass, dirty old man sweating on top of her turned her stomach.

Trish greeted them like she had known them for years and invited everybody into the house. Ke-Ke had already begun her mental trick of removing herself from her body. She managed to smile and laugh at their corny jokes as she struggled to understand half of what came out their mouths in long, jumbled, connected words.

After twenty or thirty minutes, Trish escorted one of the men back to her bedroom and turned and gave a nervous smile towards Ke-Ke before she closed the door.

"Sowhatupwityou.. lilbit?" the man she had named "Geechie Dan" asked her as he scooted closer to her on the couch. Ke-Ke, all at once, wished she had bought something stronger to drink.

"Shit!" Ke-Ke answered as coldly as she could, hoping that this was the one man in the world that could actually read a female's body language. The rest of what he said, she tuned out. She prepared her body to go numb as she had done so many times in the past.

He started feeling on her chest and was out of his clothes in a second when he realized that she wasn't going to resist him. Ke-Ke slowly reclined on the couch, sliding off her beloved Wonder Pants that now actually made her wonder what the hell Trish had gotten her into.

Ke-Ke glanced at his body and a chill ran through her body as she noticed the grey and black cluster of hairs that spread from his chest to his shoulders and down his arms. She couldn't help but notice his hooked-to-the-left, raggedy-looking dick. She closed her eyes and told herself that she just wouldn't look. But the worst of it all was the fact that he smelled like Bengay. Her insides were screaming.

She decided that she couldn't even face this nigga, so she quickly got up and positioned herself doggy style, hoping he would take the hint. He was definitely going to have to settle for back shots. She could hear him mumbling something about her being flexible or sexy or whatever. She closed her eyes and imagined it was the R&B singer Usher behind her.

Ten minutes later, Geechie Dan was still behind her pumping, making weird noises and sweating all over her back. She felt like his hooked dick was going to knock one of her ovaries out. She winced in pain and tried to reposition herself to relieve some of the discomfort she was feeling. Nothing was working. The worst part about it was that he was mistaking her body language and movements for pleasure and he began pumping harder and faster, while his nails dug into her hips. For some reason, her argument with Pam came back to her mind and she could feel the tears about to burn in her eyes again, but she snapped back to reality when she noticed that Geechie Dan had stopped and was now trying to stick his dick in her ass.

"Hell no!" she yelled as she reached behind herself and swatted his dick away like it was an insect. He laughed it off as he leaned down and kissed her cheek. She thought she was going to die as the hairs on his chest made contact with her bare skin like a damp sweater. "Just hurry the fuck up!"

She had run out of patience and was tired of not being able to speak her mind. She looked out of the corner of her eye and noticed Trish and the other man standing in the doorway with matching shirts on while Trish massaged his dick. She focused on the shirts, confused. They said "Jackson Family Reunion."

She began to get that sick feeling in her stomach that she only got when she was scared or embarrassed. She glanced up at Trish's face and was about to say something when Trish began to explain that her family reunion was in town and that the two men were her uncles from Mississippi.

Trish had set this all up for Ke-Ke to get a train run on her by her nasty-ass uncles. "You ain't shit, bitch!" were all the words Ke-Ke could find to say as she slipped her pants back on and looked for her shirt. She was so mad, she could feel her heart beating in her head. She kept looking back and forth at the faces in the room around her, hoping to God one of them was going to say "Gotcha!" or "You got punk'd!" The man in the door with Trish waved his hand and headed back into the room. He said something to Trish about Ke-Ke, but she was too mad to even care what he had said.

"She get down!" Trish responded in a twisted effort to defend Ke-Ke.

Trish came into the front room and knelt down by the couch next to her. Ke-Ke was fumbling with her shirt and adjusting herself when she noticed that her titties had popped out of her bra, thanks to Geechie Dan. She focused her attention and anger on Trish after she had slid her shirt back on. "Girl, you gonna get paid! I promise!"

Trish tried her best to convince her, but as always seemed to be missing the whole point. "I promise I ain't gonna tell nobody! Just do it as a favor... for me! I done already told them that you would be wit it!" Trish pleaded like a little kid begging for candy in a grocery store checkout line. Geechie Dan placed his hands on Ke-Ke's shoulders and whispered, "Wegon'begentle... lilbit... tell huh, Trish! Ain't we gon be good?"

Trish nodded slowly as Ke-Ke jerked from his grasp. "Do this as a favor for me Ke. I got you back, *ANYTHING* you want!" She was really begging now. Then Trish leaned in and whispered in her ear, "They was always gentle with me."

Trish's words hit her ear in a whisper that somehow felt like a slap in the face. She glared at Trish with disgust and pity. *This brainwashed bitch had been molested by these nasty-ass niggas and now that they were tired of her, they had her recruiting new pussy.* The thoughts and questions dangled and danced in her head like puppets on strings, while her shock and disbelief worked the wooden controls, bringing endless animation to the painted, wooden characters below.

Ke-Ke stood up, speechless, as she took a final glance at Trish, who still believed that she had actually done her a favor. She thought about beating Trish's ass right there but realized that she was outnumbered. She didn't want to risk being jumped and raped as the visions of Trish's sick ass helping her uncles hold her down played in her head like a bad movie. The anger burned within her at hundreds of degrees as she thought of at least slapping Trish and then making a run for the door, but the thought of "Captain Hook Dick" gaining unauthorized access to her asshole formed ice cubes that sizzled into warm puddles and stuck to her skin in a cold sweat. Plans like that never went the way you envisioned them; she would have to live to whoop Trish's ass another day.

"Where the fuck's my money at, nigga?" is all Ke-Ke could say as she finished tying her shoes.

"Hereshawty," Geechie Dan said as he reached for his pants, still playing with himself.

"Don'twannittob'noproblems," he mumbled in his connected words. Ke-Ke snatched a wad of bills out of his hand before he could begin counting it out and speed- walked to the door.

"Ya need to lemme eat a slice," he tried one more time as his eyes glanced down towards Ke-Ke's pussy like he could see through her pants.

"Y'all some sick muthafuckas!" Ke-Ke screamed, loud enough for everyone in the house to hear. She slammed the door and ran down the steps of the porch, her whole body shaking with anger, as she made her way towards the chute.

Everybody plays the fool... sometimes, she could hear her uncle's voice singing.

"Shut the fuck up!" she said out loud to no one. The hot tears streamed down her face as she stomped up the sidewalk.

THREE

THE NEXT MORNING Ke-Ke was up early with plans to go to the hair store and then to the salon. She had wrestled with the thoughts of what had happened the night before at Trish's house and knew she would have to stay busy in order for them not to eat away at her for the whole day. She was dressed and out of the house before her mother could even get a chance to harass or insult her. She slammed the door, hoping her mother would think someone was breaking into the house. Ke-Ke smiled as she visualized her in a robe, creeping down the stairs in a momentary state of fear, as she ran down the steps to the sidewalk.

She hit Reynolds Street, rolled her eyes at Pam, and turned the corner, but still heard her comment, "She's a movie star!" which was followed by loud laughter that echoed and chased her around the corner. Ke-Ke stopped at the store and was relieved to see that Fred wasn't seated in the stool next to the pop coolers. She bought two Kingpin wraps and continued her trek to the hair store while she looked for anyone that might be selling weed early in the morning. She reached in her pocket and lit the half blunt that still remained from her bath the night before then checked her phone for missed calls and texts. Twenty-two missed calls! She scrolled through the text messages first.

G-NICE: WHY CAN'T WE MAKE A MOVIE?

What the hell is this nigga talken about? She stared at the screen, thinking she had missed part of the message or it had gotten cut off. G-Nice was a nigga she had fucked with last summer and from time to time would still smoke weed with. He was wearing on her nerves though, because he never wanted to give up any money and she had started to bump his calls and ignore his texts.

The next text was from Cry.

CRY: DAMN GIRL, CAN'T TURN MY BACK ON YOU! THAT'S WHY YOU WAS SO TIRED!

Now Ke-Ke was really confused. She tried to make sense of the two messages and wondered if they were related. She scrolled down through her messages and saw text after text she had received from niggas on the Ave that said everything from "Encore!" to "Let me find out!" followed by LOL, SMH, and smiley faces. What the fuck was going on?

Ke-Ke stopped walking and thought as hard as she could but wasn't coming up with anything. She searched her brain for something she may have forgotten, or some secret that she might have told in front of the wrong person. She started to walk again and then froze.

Trish had taped her!

Ke-Ke's hands shook with rage as she fumbled through her purse, looking for her favorite pink box cutter. She sprinted to Trish's porch and was pounding on the door as hard as she could without hurting her hand. "Open the door, bitch!" Ke-Ke screamed. "I'll kick this muthafucka down!" She began kicking the lower part of the aluminum screen until it was dented and the torn screen panels had fallen out. She could feel nothing but rage when she dropped her purse and prepared herself to kick the door as hard as possible.

"She ain't home! She said she was goen to get her hair done! It's too early in the morning for all that noise and shit!" Trish's next-door neighbor had opened up a second-floor window and was glaring down at Ke-Ke with an orange shower cap on her head. Ke-Ke glared back at the oversized woman in the window. She picked up her purse. *Pick your battles*, she heard her uncle's voice say.

She decided that she would catch Trish at the salon. She walked in a trance down the block towards the hair store as she imagined snatching Trish from underneath one of the hair dryers and beating those large green rollers off of her head one by one.

Ke-Ke reached the doors of the hair store and was still on fire as she swung the door open and struck the large Christmas bells that hung from the ceiling. She headed straight for the human hair rack, selected the color she wanted, and then picked out the hollow gold earrings she always used to make her new look pop. They were cheap and would change colors if you didn't coat them with clear nail polish, but she loved the different designs they came in. And from a distance they looked expensive.

She had everything she had come for and was walking towards the checkout when she passed the lingerie racks and saw a sign that advertised glow-in-the-dark thongs. She picked out a pair that turned pink and put everything on the counter, next to the register. The young Arab cashier scanned and bagged her items, but stopped at the panties and gave her a look. "Damn, I'd like to see you in these," he spoke through a thick accent.

Jackpot! Arab men might smell funny, but from all the stories she had heard they kept cash and they were more than willing to pay for some pussy. They bought clothes, paid rent, and in some cases had bought girls cars. She had to play this right. "Yeah, when?" Ke-Ke flirted back and smiled, changing her whole mood and demeanor in seconds, a talent that had made the school district write her mother letters saying that they thought she had ADD and "other emotional issues."

She ran the panties through her fingers on the counter and waited for him to make the next move. He smiled and nodded his head towards the fitting rooms that separated the hair items from the rest of the store that sold clothing, boots, and shoes. "Why not now?" he suggested as he stepped from around the corner and walked Ke-Ke to the fitting rooms.

Ke-Ke winked, grabbed the panties off of the counter, and followed his path through the racks full of merchandise. Ke-Ke stepped into the fitting room and closed the curtain. She was glad that she had not worn panties that day. She slipped out of her sweat pants and stepped into the underwear, pulling them up slowly. When she turned to adjust the panties in the mirror, he had slipped into the fitting room behind her. She could feel his hard dick through his jeans and moaned as his firm grip massaged her tits while he sucked on her neck. She wondered through her butterflies if he was really going to try and fuck her right there in the fitting room while the store was still open. His fingers slipped into the front of the panties as she tried to remember whether anyone else was already in the store.

He had dropped to his knees, pulled the front of her panties to the side, and was licking her pussy before she could stop him. She gasped for a moment and regained her composure, "Later for all that!" She pushed his head from in between her legs. Teasing had always been a specialty of hers and she was relieved that he had gotten up smiling, staring directly into her eyes.

"My name is Ahmed."

Ke-Ke was starting to find his accent cute. "Let me get you my number."

He disappeared from the fitting room, closing the curtain behind him. Her thoughts went back and forth as she wondered whether she should've played a little harder to get. He *DID* work in a hair store and more than likely had ass thrown at him all day.

Ke-Ke returned to the counter after she had gotten herself together. She noticed an older woman talking on the phone and wondered if she had been sitting there the whole time. She turned to face Ahmed and told herself not to worry about it, when from behind her, she heard the woman saying, "Jesus, Lord... these children," she only half-spoke into the phone as Ahmed cracked a smile and glanced over at her with an embarrassed look on his face. Ke-Ke grabbed her bag and took his number that he had scribbled on the back of a party flyer. She winked at him, rolled her eyes at the old lady, who was still staring at her, and walked out of the store, happy that Ahmed hadn't charged her for the earrings or the panties.

She just mad ain't nobody tryen to eat her wrinkled-up shit! She laughed as she called a cab and directed them to her next stop for the day: Queens, the only hair salon she had gone to for as long as she could remember.

Ke-Ke stared out of the cab window, watching the activities on West Main Street, as she thought about Ahmed. She half fantasized as to what would come of the meeting and thought at the very least he would make good "head-bread" material. Kya and Ke-Ke had made up the name for men who didn't fuck but just ate pussy and paid for it. She stopped herself from laughing out loud at the thought of all the niggas that said they didn't eat pussy. What she had learned over the years was that many of them were content with doing that and that alone. An older woman in the salon had taught them years ago, "For every nigga that won't, there's three niggas that will!"

The cab pulled up in front of Queens Salon and the brakes made a screeching noise as the late-model Chevrolet Caprice came to a stop. Ke-Ke had felt herself dozing off twice. It wasn't even twelve o'clock and already she had a pounding headache and desperately needed another blunt to calm her nerves. She had learned in school that weed wasn't supposed to be addictive, but she found herself having to eat penny candy at times to fight off the cravings. She handed the cab driver the nine-dollar fare that was blinking in red on the dash and stepped out of the car.

Once she had stepped in the door and saw no signs of Trish in the styling chairs or under the dryers, she exhaled, slipped her box cutter back in her purse, and looked for the only person she would allow to touch her hair.

"Heyyy girl!" Tiff, her hairdresser and part-time street psychiatrist, stepped from the back, removing surgical gloves she used when she was applying dye to someone's hair. Tiff was a Florida girl who would NEVER let you forget it, but had relocated up north to be closer to her brother and other family. She had lived a life and a half and Ke-Ke loved coming to the salon to listen to her stories and get her unsolicited advice on things. Tiff embraced Ke-Ke like she was family as Ke-Ke handed her the bag of hair and quickly recalled the style she had seen on a music video that she wanted Tiff to recreate for her.

Tiff was always dressed to kill. She had on a pair of form-fitting leather pants that complimented her fat ass and a matching pair of high-heeled boots with a gold heel. Ke-Ke smiled as she examined her outfit. She looked like some R&B singer straight off of BET. Ke-Ke would often joke with her about borrowing some of her ass for the weekend. They would both get a good laugh off of that and Tiff would always say, "Girl, if I could I would, but I don't think you want *these* problems!"

Ke-Ke was reminded of the time Tiff had told her she had worked the "shake clubs" in Florida and looked up at the picture above her station that was proof that she had made plenty of money as she posed next to a money-green convertible Mercedes-Benz with white leather interior. She had acquired that and a condo by the beach at the young age of twenty. Tiff would say, "I would collect married niggas like baseball cards back then!" and laugh until the tears swelled in her eyes.

"Have a seat, girl. I'll be with you in a minute." Tiff nodded at the small waiting area furnished with leather couches, a table full of hair magazines, and a large flat-screen television that only played stories, talk shows, and music videos. Ke-Ke sat down and picked up a *Vibe* magazine and tried not to let the smell coming from the manicure stations make her head hurt worse than it already did.

A few minutes later Tiff had called her back and she was getting her hair rinsed, shampooed, and conditioned. She enjoyed the pampering she got at the salon almost as much as she did the conversation. Tiff would massage her head with the sprayer and warm water and Ke-Ke would close her eyes and think, *this is better than sex... almost!* The feeling was interrupted too soon when she was placed underneath the dryer and the thought of all the text messages forced their way back into her head like police raiding a drug house.

"You seen Trish today?" she asked Tiff from across the room.

"Naw, she don't come here no more," Tiff answered her without looking at her. "Ever since I cursed her ass out bout my sixty dollars! Bitch always sayen 'I got you, I got you,' and you already know I ain't never 'got' so she had to get the fuck on!"

The shop erupted in laughter. Tiff had a way of making EVERYTHING funny, even when she was upset. Ke-Ke took her turn in Tiff's chair and relaxed. She was confident that Tiff would work her magic on her and she would again be the baddest bitch in the hood.

"So what's goen on with y'all?" Tiff asked with her eyebrows raised. She had read through Ke-Ke and knew there was a reason behind why she had asked about Trish.

"I don't even wanna get into it, girl!" Ke-Ke answered, hoping that Tiff wouldn't pry. Tiff sighed and cocked her head to the side as she spun Ke-Ke around in the chair to face her.

"C'mon, bitch, spill it! You know that's half the reason you come here, to lay it on momma, so don't catch a case of the tight lips now!" She spun Ke-Ke back around and rubbed her shoulders. "You know I don't judge you," she added, for extra encouragement. Tiff knew how to get Ke-Ke to open up about anything. She should've been a homicide investigator.

Ke-Ke began to tell the whole horrid tale, making sure to keep her voice low, so the other women couldn't make out what she was saying. When she finished, Tiff spun her around in the chair and mouthed the words, "Get the fuck outta here!" while Ke-Ke looked her straight in the eyes and nodded to confirm that the story was all true. There was an awkward moment of silence before Tiff said, "Damn, I guess you never know what a person is dealing with... damn! But you know you shouldn't have put yourself in that position in the first place! I woulda made that bitch spill the whole script before I had even went over there."

"Don't preach to me, Tiff, my head is already killing me!" Ke-Ke said and rolled her eyes.

"I ain't gonna preach to you. I know how you don't like nobody tellen you nothing anyway!" Tiff planted an overexaggerated kiss on her cheek that made her jump.

"C'mon wit them wet kisses, Tiff," she wiped her face off like a little kid.

"Don't wipe it off! You losen all the love!" Tiff joked as her gold teeth showed through her lips. "You remember what I told you about that lifestyle before?" Tiff asked as she pointed one of her rat-tail combs in Ke-Ke's direction.

Ke-Ke sighed as she remembered the day in the salon that Tiff had gone off on the way she and her friends were living.

"Y'all young bitches don't know y'all pussies from pound cake these days! The problem is, y'all really think y'all are getten somethen from these niggas and y'all ain't getten shit! When I was out there, we used to break a nigga. Send him back to his wife, his girlfriend, or the bitch he lived with on E with a bunch of excuses and a story to tell. Y'all bitches today take forty or fifty dollars. These niggas got it so good up here they give you what they can afford! When I said 'show me the money,' I meant show me ALL the money! I had what you called subsidized pussy."

Tiff stopped and laughed. "I slide up and down wit a nigga depending on his income. And trust me, baby... I never hit the ground! What the fuck is a hundred dollars from a nigga that's making a couple hundred thousand a year? See, y'all little whores don't know nothen about that type of clientele, chasen after these niggas sellen dimes off a half-pound of weed and pushen a Honda wit wheel covers on it. Not even rims! Wheel covers on the bitch and these little hos will be in the middle of the street fighten barefoot and pregnant, pullen each others' hair out, shedden blood for a sorry-ass broke nigga who probably across town at the same time, fucken another dizzy-ass bitch down to her feelings."

The words shot out of Tiff's mouth like she was an assault rifle. Her audience in the salon stood up, slapped hands, and said "Amen." Ke-Ke remembered that sick feeling in her stomach and resented Tiff for blowing her up in front of the whole shop.

"Y'all bitches need to get it together up here!" Tiff was on a roll. "Let me ask you something: how you call yourself 'getten a nigga' when you don't even know if he got and what he got in the first place? I be hearen y'all talken about how fine a nigga is, how you like his braids, 'he can dress,' and all that bullshit. Cute don't pay the muthafucken rent! These niggas up here work for a year and use tax return money, get a settlement, or they parents got a little paper on the low. They take they raggedy ass to the car auction, buy a seized Lexus for four or five thousand, put some Walmart rims on the bitch, and y'all bitches line up to suck his dick like it's inscribed and made of gold!"

Women were bent over in their chairs, laughing at Tiff. "Y'all better learn game. The next time you get in one of these bum-ass nigga's cars, check the year on the registration sticker, then check the mileage. Be slick about it and you'll know when a nigga fronten in some used hand-me-down luxury car that was probably underwater somewhere before he bought it. Bet y'all will ration the pussy then! You'll stop all this 'down for whatever' fucken y'all be doen!"

Tiff knew she had her audience just where she wanted them and went for the kill. "Look, this is all I'm sayen: the shit y'all think y'all getten is nothing. A nigga up here ain't gonna break himself for no broad. There's too many of y'all out here fucken for steak subs and a bag of weed! They done fucked the game up! I feel like this: if it's nothen to him, then why should it mean somethen to me?"

Tiff shrugged and looked around the room, as if she was waiting for an answer. "Why y'all act like they doen so much for you? Y'all ready to give your all to a nigga who, at the end of the day, ain't got nothen and wouldn't give you shit if he did. What the fuck is a bag of weed and McDonald's?"

Tiff had stopped talking long enough to allow some of the other women to share their own testimonies. Then she took center stage again. "I'll be damned if a nigga jump up and down in my velvet walls for an hour and some change, sweat all over me, mess my hair up, probably break a few of my nails, and then take me to the drive-through and drop me off!" She stood there for a minute with her eyes bulging and her head tilted to the side, like she always did before she said her signature, "Shiiiiiiiiiiiit!!!!" as she stomped her feet for dramatic effect.

Ke-Ke remembered that feeling of being publicly humiliated. The truth always seemed to hurt, especially when it was coming from Tiff.

"You done, guhl!" Tiff said in her deep Florida accent that she could turn on and off at will while she tapped Ke-Ke on the shoulder and snapped her back to the present.

She climbed out of the chair and stretched her legs. "How much?" she asked as she looked over, but Tiff had disappeared into the back room and was just returning with her coat and an oversized Gucci purse. Ke-Ke could only smile as she thought about the day that she would have her shit together like Tiff did.

"C'mon, guhl! I'll take you back to the hood!" Tiff smiled, waving her car keys. They walked out of the salon into the afternoon sun. Tiff pointed her keys and pushed a button while Ke-Ke watched in awe as the taillights flashed and the engine started on a pearl-white Jaguar.

"You got a new car, Tiff?" Ke-Ke asked, unable to hide her smile of approval.

Tiff just looked over at her with a grin and winked. "Everybody don't fuck for free!"

Ke-Ke rolled her eyes, but couldn't keep the smile from stretching across her face. She opened the car door by the chrome handle and sat down in the soft leather. "Tiff, I'm fucken haten right now!" she admitted as she closed the door and glanced around the interior. There was light wood grain that accented the dashboard, shifter, console, and surrounded the stereo and navigation system, then broke through the leather at the top and bottom of the steering wheel. The car smelled like a tropical fruit as Ke-Ke noticed the air freshener clipped to the air vents with an orange liquid in it. The car was sporty, sexy, and classy, which matched Tiff perfectly.

Tiff got in the car, pushed a button, and the glass moonroof slid back and allowed the sun to beam in. The stereo came on and Tiff steered the sedan down the block while she bobbed her head and sang along.

Ke-Ke noticed a picture below the stereo of Tiff with three boys. "I ain't know you had kids, Tiff?" she said as she looked at the picture in her hand closely. "What's his name?" she asked, pointing at the oldest boy.

Tiff waited until she had stopped behind a truck at a light before she looked over and answered. "That's DeAndre. He's away at school right now. That's my dude right there!"

Ke-Ke stared at the picture a little longer. "He fine! He could *get it*! I'd wear him out, Tiff, don't bring him up here!" Ke-Ke warned playfully.

Tiff looked over at her like she was crazy. "That might not go the way you plan it, he got *MY* blood in his veins, remember?" She smiled and looked over at Ke-Ke, who was still staring at the picture like it was a piece of priceless jewelry.

"You can drop me off at my cousin's house. I ain't seen her in a while," Ke-Ke said as soon as they had made it back to the West Side. The car seemed to float down West Main Street. Ke-Ke noticed that she didn't feel the bumps in the street like she did when she rode with other people. Thoughts of Cry crossed her mind as she remembered feeling the same way in her car, watching how people stopped and stared at the Jaguar as it crawled through the streets like a predator in search of prey. She felt like a celebrity again and the stereo played the soundtrack of the music video she was shooting.

Tiff turned a couple of corners, honked and waved at a few people, then pulled up in front of Ke-Ke's grandmother's house. She reached into her glove box and handed Ke-Ke two airplane bottles of Remy Martin. "I got these when we was out in California a couple of weeks ago, but I ain't gonna drink em." Ke-Ke looked at the bottles in her hand and smiled. "And don't worry about your hair this time, it's on me," she said as she slid her sunglasses back on. "Remember what we talked about, girl!" Tiff pointed her finger then leaned over and gave Ke-Ke a hug. "If you don't remember anything else I told you, remember this: what you do affects everybody around you. Your mom, your sister, the man you choose to love, and even your kids. Your reputation reflects on them too. What I'm sayen is, think about what you doen and how you liven out here cause the money is gone in a second, but a nigga can say he fucked you forever."

Ke-Ke could feel her words in her chest. "But you the one that said pussy is power and..." Ke-Ke tried to defend herself but was cut short with a wave of Tiff's hand.

"Yeah, girl, but with great power comes great responsibility." Tiff quoted words that Ke-Ke had heard in school, but she couldn't remember what famous person had spoken them.

She nodded and dropped her head and thought about how much she hated her life. She could feel the tears starting to form in her eyes as she hugged Tiff but only felt the arms of her own frustration and guilt hugging her back. Tiff gave her a kiss on the cheek and Ke-Ke grabbed the bottles of Remy and stepped out of the car. She could feel Tiff watching her as she made her way to the front steps of the house. The thoughts swirled in her head and formed questions that she didn't have the answers to. *Wisdom seems like a riddle to a fool.* Her uncle's words came through her head and framed her feelings and thoughts like an oil painting.

She stood on the porch in a daze as the conflicting feelings pierced her mind and made her heart feel heavy. She glanced back at the street, but Tiff was gone.

***

Ke-Ke pounded on the front door, she knew more than likely that her cousin Ti-Ti was in the house "multitasking." Ti-Ti would be watching TV, blasting music, talking on the phone, posting pictures on Facebook, and burning some food on the stove, all while she was waiting on her nails to dry. Ke-Ke remembered the time Tre, one of her ex-boyfriends, had been showing naked pictures of her to his boys. She had texted the pictures to him the night before when she was in the shower. Ti-Ti was all nonchalant about it like, "Shit, girl, fuck it, that's free advertisement! Shit! More dick for you! I mean it ain't like you got a fucked-up body or somethen....*oh shiiit, shiiit, shiiiiit! Goddamn, nigga!*"

Ke-Ke could only smirk as she remembered hearing a dude laughing in the background. That bitch had been fucking the whole time they were on the phone! Then had the nerve to be like, "Whoooo! Had to get that... ok girl, I'm outta breath, but I'm back, now what was you sayen?"

Only Ti-Ti! That bitch was special. After that, Ke-Ke would just hang up the phone when she suspected that Ti-Ti was "too busy" to have a conversation.

Ke-Ke knocked on the door again and then on the window as well, hoping that it would be enough to get Ti-Ti's attention. She cracked open one of the bottles of Remy and waited. She was about to turn around and leave when a black Escalade pulled to a stop in front of the house.

Ti-Ti emerged from the passenger side with a huge smile on her face and two shopping bags from the mall.

"Gimme some!" were the first words out of her mouth as she spied the bottle of Remy in Ke-Ke's hand like a hawk.

Ke-Ke rolled her eyes and handed her cousin the bottle. "Now gimme some," she said back to Ti-Ti after she had taken a few sips.

"Gimme got shot by that nigga named Hell Naw!" Ti-Ti laughed at her own stupid joke, then opened the door, letting Ke-Ke walk into the house in front of her. "Don't say I never did anything for you," she smiled as she closed the door behind them and took another sip from the bottle. Ke-Ke walked into the family room, opened the second bottle of Remy, and collapsed on the plastic-covered couch.

"Your hair look cute. Who did it? Tiff's loudmouth ass?" Ti-Ti asked as she finished off the bottle and slammed it down on the wooden table by the door. Ke-Ke nodded and remembered to sit up on the couch so she didn't mess the back of her hair up.

"Oh my bitch, I got somethen to show yo' ass. Don't hate either!" Ti-Ti said as her faced filled with that overexcited look that had made teachers say on more than one occasion that she was hyperactive. Before Ke-Ke knew it, Ti-Ti had dropped her bags and was struggling to pull her tight jeans down.

"Bitch, what the fuck you doen? Don't nobody wanna see your ashy ass!" Ke-Ke held her hand over her eyes in protest.

Ti-Ti stopped what she was doing and extended her middle finger in Ke-Ke's direction. "You gonna wanna see this!" Ti-Ti said as she stepped out of her jeans completely.

Ke-Ke looked and noticed a thin white line that began just below her belly button. "Bitch, you got a tattoo?" she asked, as she squinted to make out what she was actually seeing. Ti-Ti paused and then pulled her panties down to her thighs. Ke-Ke just stared in shock as she took in the whole masterpiece. Ti-Ti had a lollipop stick tattooed just below her navel that led down to her trimmed pubic hair, which was dyed white with green polka dots like the Blow Pop suckers with the gum in the middle. Ke-Ke shook her head and stared back and forth at this ghetto work of art and then up at Ti-Ti's smiling face. Her pubic hair was even cut into an oval shape to make the look even more authentic.

"Yeah, bitch, don't hate. I got that sour apple for a nigga now!" Ti-Ti said as she glanced down and pointed at her pussy with pride.

The "coochie calling card" was common among females on the West Side of the city. It referred to a tattoo that associated a girl's pussy with something, usually candy. Ke-Ke had seen everything on girls in school, from paw prints to the "slippery when wet" road sign, to her homegirl who had a cat tail that wrapped around her belly button like a question mark and ended where her pubic hairline began. Ke-Ke had decided at one point that she was going to get a pack of Skittles pouring down into her pubic hair, so she could tell a nigga to "taste the rainbow," but a girl in her math class stole the idea after she had told her about it. Her latest idea was a pack of Now and Laters cause a nigga could eat her pussy now and later! She laughed in her head at her own brilliance but kept the concept a secret until she had enough money to actually get it done.

Ti-Ti, as usual, had taken the trend to a whole new level of ignorance though. "Dumb ass, now you gotta keep your hair dyed and trimmed in that shape or that shit gonna look a hot mess!" Ke-Ke stared at Ti-Ti, hoping that her words would make her little cousin feel some sort of regret.

Ti-Ti jumped around in circles with her panties still around her thighs cheering. "Hate. Bitch. Hate... I love it! Hate. Bitch. Hate... I love it!"

Ke-Ke covered her face and shook her head. This was an all-time low, even for Ti-Ti. She took another sip of Remy as she wondered how many people Ti-Ti had dropped her pants in front of.

"Girl, if you don't put your clothes on..."

"What the hell y'all doen down here?" Neither one of them had heard their grandmother coming down the stairs. The old lady moved like a ninja. "Y'all on that freaky-deeky stuff up in my sanctuary? Y'all gotta take that somewhere. This house is blessed! Ain't no Sodom and Gomorrah up in here!"

Ti-Ti jumped and had her pants back on in a half second. "Sorry Grandma, I was showen Ke-Ke a scar I had."

"Mmmmhmmm!" their grandmother answered. She never believed a word Ti-Ti spoke to her. "Look to me like your little fast ass was tryna give Ke-Ke some of your scar down there!" she said with a curious smile as she glanced back and forth at her granddaughters.

Ke-Ke rolled her eyes and sank down into the couch. Great, another gay rumor had been born and would be floating around the family in no time. This Thanksgiving all eyes at the table would be on her and Ti-Ti, the suspected "kissing cousins." She could hear her Aunt Ruby now: "You gotta watch them two. They'll go somewhere and get it on!" And there would be nothing you could say to get that out of her head.

Their grandmother returned from the kitchen and came into the living room spraying Lysol and praying loudly. Ke-Ke shot Ti-Ti her look of death. Their grandmother hummed some hymn and when she finished, looked them both up and down, grabbed her purse, and announced, "I'm off to Bingo!"

She backed up towards the door slowly watching both of them suspiciously. "Y'all get them urges again, pick up that Bible over there. Don't be stanken up my house! I come back and my house smellen like corn chips and sweat, I'll know what's goen on! I ain't nobody's fool!"

Ke-Ke sat shocked for a minute as she wondered whether her grandmother really believed that. "C'mon Grandma! You know that ain't true," she pleaded with her. Their grandmother paused, looked at both of them over the rim of her glasses, then burst into laughter. She blew them a kiss and was out the door.

"Dumbass!" Ke-Ke threw the empty bottle she had hidden between her legs and narrowly missed Ti-Ti's head as she took cover in the kitchen. "Stop hiding, bitch, and let's go to the store! I want a beef patty," Ke-Ke yelled in the direction of the kitchen, where Ti-Ti was waiting her out.

Ti-Ti stuck her head out of the kitchen and waved a freshly rolled blunt as a peace offering. "You gonna really need a beef patty after this fire I copped from cross town." She waved the blunt in her finger tips, like she was feeding seals at the zoo.

Ke-Ke crossed the room, grabbed the blunt from her hand, and the two headed for the basement, the only place in their grandmother's house where they could smoke and get away with it. "It smells like mothballs and mildew," Ke-Ke stated the obvious. She glanced around the basement at the broken pool table and labeled boxes everywhere. "Grandma's a hoarder!" she decided out loud as she remembered to check her phone.

Ke-Ke stared at her phone in a rage as she noticed ten more missed calls and twice as many text messages. She scrolled through them and read comments from different niggas around the hood with messages that said things like "click click" and "Hey Paris Hilton. Get at me when you're not recording!" followed by more smiley faces and "LOL." She shoved the phone back in her pocket and looked over at Ti-Ti, who had lit the blunt and was opening the window to let the smoke out. The last time they had smoked in the basement, their grandmother had complained of something smelling funny coming through the vents.

"Yo, you heard some shit about me?" Ke-Ke asked, testing the waters. Ti-Ti was her cousin and all, but if someone had told her something and swore her to secrecy, she knew Ti-Ti wouldn't tell her shit.

Ti-Ti poked her lips out and cocked her head to the side, her own personal way of letting you know that she was "thinking." Then she snapped her fingers and said, "Hell yeah! I knew it was somethen that I had to tell you! You remember your little fling with G-Nice?"

Ke-Ke nodded slowly, already knowing what was coming. "I just seen that nigga at the mall. He gonna ask me am I in the movie-making business like my cousin, talken bout he might wanna make a double feature with us AND he willing to pay!"

Ke-Ke just shook her head. This shit had spread like wildfire. "What the fuck is that nigga talken about? He wouldn't tell me. He just walked off laughing! Bitch, what the fuck you do now? You made a sex tape that got out?" Ti-Ti asked with a sneaky smile on her face.

Ke-Ke grabbed the blunt and looked out the window. "Fuck it, bitch, this is what happened." Ke-Ke spilled the whole story as her cousin sat across from her, hogging the weed but listening intently to every detail. When she finished, Ti-Ti laughed uncontrollably.

"You thirsty-ass bitch! You fucked an old-ass man!? You know they give you worms, right?" Ti-Ti laughed between coughs and ended up on the basement floor gasping for air with tears in her eyes. "Damn bitch, when you say 'down for whatever,' you really mean that shit!" She laid on the floor as her whole body shook with laughter. "Aaaaaaand it's on tape, so you can't even deny the shit!" Ti-Ti shook her head and started wiping the tears from her face.

"Fuck you!" Ke-Ke spat and kicked her cousin in the leg. "Bitch, you suppose to be on my side in this shit!" But she couldn't stop Ti-Ti from laughing even harder as she rolled a safe distance away from her. "Get it all out, bitch, and come the fuck on! I'm hungry as hell!"

She watched as Ti-Ti dusted herself off and used an old bike to climb to her feet. "Okay... okay... I'm good! I'm sorry, girl!" she apologized in her little-kid voice and gave Ke-Ke her innocent look, with her lips poked out.

"I ain't got time to whoop your ass, just come the fuck on and shut the fuck up wit all the jokes! You sure as fuck ain't no nun around this bitch!"

They walked halfway to the store in silence. Ke-Ke knew her cousin had a head full of jokes but dared not say them. They crossed the field and walked around the laundromat to Jefferson Ave, the main strip where everybody hung out, hustled, showed off cars, drank, smoked, plotted, sold dreams, and told lies. They crossed the street and saw the normal cast of characters: Jaymo, Jerks, Fifty, Gates, Naps, Esco, Banger, Stacks, Bungee, and a bunch of other niggas talking on cell phones too loudly, smoking weed, and rolling dice. When the crew noticed Ke-Ke and Ti-Ti, they tapped each other and applauded with huge smiles on their faces.

"Damn, all these niggas done seen that shit already? You famous, bitch!" Ti-Ti said as she tried to spin the situation in another direction. Ke-Ke could feel her anger go from zero to one hundred in two seconds.

"Y'all niggas don't ever get none, that's why y'all so excited!" Ke-Ke snapped at them as she walked in the store, pushing them out of the way. She waited to hear a comment about the age of her "co-star," but to her surprise, no one mentioned it. She made it to the back of the store and ordered fried gizzards and a beef patty, picked up a fruit punch, sat it on the counter, and waited for her food to be done. She put her head down on the counter and wondered what she had done in life to deserve this level of humiliation.

She looked up just in time to see Ti-Ti rush into the store with that sneaky smile on her face that had made her notorious in the family.

"Yooo... here that bitch come though!" Ti-Ti whispered in her long drawn-out tone as she pointed towards the window. Ke-Ke looked over the bags of chips that blocked most of the window and saw a familiar jacket and then a face she had been waiting to see all day. Trish!

She instinctively went to the back of the store, found her blade at the bottom of her purse, and waited. She figured Trish was just coming to the store to get a blunt, and she was right. When Trish stepped into the store, Ke-Ke crept up one of the aisles behind her, box cutter in hand, and tapped her on the shoulder. Trish turned around, but before she could speak, Ke-Ke had run the razor across her face three times.

"Payback's a muthafucka, you inbred bitch!" Ke-Ke screamed as Trish ran towards the door and stumbled outside. She held her face and looked back at Ke-Ke shocked while the blood began to gush through her fingers.

"Oh, shit!" she heard from the crowd outside of the store. The man from the grill was bringing her food to the front of the store, unaware of what had just happened. Ke-Ke grabbed the food, dropped her money on the counter, and then held her index finger to her lips as she stared directly into the eyes of the female cashier. The woman nodded quickly with a look of terror in her

51

eyes as Ke-Ke bolted out of the store. "C'mon bitch, we out!" she pulled the back of Ti-Ti's coat and half dragged her as they ran across the street, around the laundromat, and out of sight.

By the time the two had gotten back to their grandmother's house, both of their phones had rung at least a dozen times. *Those nosy-ass niggas just saw what it was. What the hell they got questions for now? She fucked me and I fucked her back! Basic shit!*

When they got into the house, she noticed Cry's number pop up on her screen and she answered the phone. "Whatup," she said in the coolest tone she could manage. She wanted it to appear like everyday business and not like she was celebrating the shit. She had always figured that it made her look harder to the outside world. Ti-Ti laughed at her performance as she went through cabinets in the kitchen.

"Yo, I been trying to get at you! I ain't have shit to do with that the other night. My hand to God! I had left you in the car to catch a few sales and that's when that bullshit happened!" Cry's voice was urgent but still smooth and calm.

Ke-Ke was lost, but she answered, "I just ate that bitch food in the store, don't worry about it!" She opened her bag and turned the television to the Kardashians.

"Who, Troi? You ain't beat that bitch. That bitch like two of you!"

Ke-Ke felt like Cry was speaking another language. "Why you talken about Troi? I'm talken about Trish," Ke-Ke said as she sat up on the couch and muted the television.

"You don't know?" Cry asked in a voice that sounded like she was whispering.

"Know what?" Ke-Ke was tired of feeling like she didn't know what was going on in her own world.

"Hold on, where you at?" Cry asked.

Ke-Ke gave her the directions to her grandmother's house and waited, trying to figure out what she was missing. Twenty minutes later, Cry's green sport Infiniti pulled up in front of the house and she was chirping the alarm. Ke-Ke watched in admiration. Cry seemed to change cars like they were clothes. She opened the door and without saying anything else, Cry asked, "Where your computer at?"

Ti-Ti pointed to the computer in the corner and they all walked across the room.

"What the fuck is goen on?" Ke-Ke asked, unable to take the suspense any longer. Cry just shook her head as she pulled out a USB cord and connected her phone to the computer.

FOUR

ON THE SCREEN an image popped up of Ke-Ke asleep in the passenger seat on the same night she had fought Kya. There was movement and she could hear voices whispering. The driver's side door opened and someone got into the car. It was Troi. Troi was a neighborhood girl that was openly gay and had been named "Troi the Boy" by her high school classmates. Ke-Ke watched in horror as Troi put her hand up her shirt and underneath her bra, groping her titties and kissing her neck. Troi unbuttoned and unzipped her jeans and was rubbing her pussy and visibly working her fingers in and out of her. The person holding the cell phone was directing her actions and laughing. A small group had formed and they could clearly hear people saying, "Daaamn!" and cheering Troi on.

Ke-Ke's disgust turned to horror when she noticed that her body seemed to be responding to Troi. She was moaning and grinding her hips in her passed-out state.

"Oh shit, I look like I'm wit that shit!" Ke-Ke said as she pointed at the screen. "I was passed the fuck out!" she protested as she glanced up to see if her words were having any effect on what Cry and Ti-Ti were seeing.

Troi continued to feel on her as she lifted her shirt and bra, exposing her titties to the camera, then winked as she licked circles around Ke-Ke's noticeably hard nipples. You could hear a voice in the crowd cheering, "Get that pussy, Troi, turn that young bitch out," followed by more laughter. Troi began licking lower and lower, past Ke-Ke's belly button.

Tears began to form in Ke-Ke's eyes as she stared at the screen in shock. Troi struggled to pull Ke-Ke's pants down, but they were too tight and she didn't have enough room in the car to maneuver. Troi worked around it though, by ripping the string off one side of her panties and sticking her tongue in Ke-Ke's crotch. Ke-Ke remembered all at once that her panties had been ripped, but she thought they had popped on their own because they were cheap.

"Ohhhh!" a few voices chimed in together, as they watched Troi through the window. There was more laughter and comments and Ke-Ke struggled to try to make out the voices, but she couldn't. Then a voice warned, "Yo, Cry's coming back!" and you could see Troi pull down Ke-Ke's bra and shirt, close her pants without zipping them, and dart out of the view of the camera, closing the door behind her. The image jumped up and down and nothing more could be made out but what sounded like running and then more laughter until the video clicked off.

Ke-Ke sat on the couch with her face in her hands. She could hear her own heartbeat as she fumed. "Yo, we gonna jump that big bitch!" Ti-Ti said as she walked around the living room, pounding her fist in her hand.

Ke-Ke couldn't even think that far ahead. She was paralyzed by embarrassment, anger, and doubt. The thoughts made her feel like she was underwater with weights attached to her ankles that kept pulling her deeper and deeper into a cold and unfamiliar abyss. She couldn't get the image of how she had reacted to Troi's touch out of her head. *Am I fucken gay?* she thought as the image kept replaying itself, like her brain had an automatic repeat button. She couldn't deny that she had been aroused. Did that mean she had liked it?

A drunk mind speaks a sober tongue. The words of her uncle floated into her head and taunted her spirit. She had always been one to say that girls that said they were drunk were really just hos that wanted to do whatever they ended up doing in the first place. She knew she couldn't use that as an excuse, especially not in front of Ti-Ti. She slid her hands away from her face slowly and stared blankly off into space.

"Yo, we gonna ride on that half-a-man-ass-bitch!" Ti-Ti kept shouting and looking over at Cry and Ke-Ke for their approval.

"You know if I had been there, I wouldn't have let that happen, right?" Cry finally spoke after she had unhooked her phone and put the cord back into her pocket. "Keep it one hundred though, you was kinda acten like you was into it." Cry shrugged as she sat on the table and looked confused, like she was really trying to figure things out for herself.

Ke-Ke's mind was flooded with different thoughts. She finally realized what all the calls and texts had really been about. She played the whole scenario out in her head, how all the gay rumors would start and how people would say she knew she was being recorded and didn't care, because "she was a freak like that."

Ke-Ke sat in a daze, knowing that the talk and the rumors could follow her for a lifetime. Ti-Ti still got teased for pissing on herself when she was in kindergarten. Niggas never forgot shit.

Ke-Ke finally got the strength to look up at Cry and say in her most sincere voice, "I don't even remember that. I *DEFINITELY* didn't think it was Troi, even if I *was* going along with it!"

She stopped as she realized that her argument wasn't helping her situation at all as Cry half-smiled, cocked her head, and asked, "So you thought it was me?"

Ke-Ke just shook her head and exhaled. "I don't know what I thought, *if* I thought anything."

The conversation was interrupted as Cry's phone rang. She said a couple of "yeahs" and "naws" and hung up the phone. "I gotta pick up my baby from my mom's house. I forgot it was Bingo tonight," she said as she stood up and walked towards the door. She turned and saw the blank look on Ke-Ke's face and walked back over to her. "I'm gonna hit you up later, aiight?"

Ke-Ke slapped her hand and noticed how Cry held onto her hand longer than normal before walking away.

"Yo, let's shoot that bitch!" Ti-Ti suggested once she had closed and locked the door behind Cry.

"Shut the fuck up!" Ke-Ke shot her that look that said, *I know you ain't gonna do shit.* She fumbled through her purse, knowing that Ti-Ti didn't have the heart to shoot a squirrel with a BB gun. Ke-Ke opened her hidden pocket in the purse and found the black and gold card she was looking for. She grabbed her cell phone, checked the battery life, then ran up the stairs to her grandmother's bedroom and slammed the door. She took a deep breath while she fought back tears and dialed the contact number on the back of the card.

"Queens!" a familiar voice answered the phone.

"Hey Tiff, this Ke-Ke," she held the phone and waited to see if Tiff would recognize her voice. Tiff did hair for everybody and she knew she couldn't have possibly been the only Ke-Ke.

"Ohhh heyyyy, lil' miss sex tape! You ain't tell me about your *new release* when I dropped you off."

Ke-Ke's mouth fell open as she tried to figure out how Tiff lived across town and had already heard the news.

"Oh, so you already know?" Ke-Ke asked when the initial shock of Tiff's comment wore off.

"Girl, I just found out on my way back here. Some niggas was watching it on they iPhone at the corner store. Girl, you really need to be more careful bout where you go layen your head."

Ke-Ke felt a lecture coming so she decided to get to the point. "Well Tiff... I was thinken, you think that makes me gay?"

She braced herself for the answer, but all she heard through the phone was, "Aaaaahahahaha" for a good twenty seconds.

"This bitch talken bout she think she might be gay now!" Tiff announced to the shop. Ke-Ke could hear the scattered laughter in the background and once again she was the center of attention at the shop and wasn't even there. She felt herself about to get mad at Tiff and thought about hanging up the phone, but she was learning Tiff never really meant any harm. She had a big mouth and any man, woman, or child would be a fool to think that she wasn't going to use it.

"Whooo! Okay, girl, I swear you gonna be the death of me!"

Ke-Ke held the phone and waited patiently for Tiff to pull herself together. "Bitch, if *anything*, you are bi!" Tiff started. Ke-Ke got comfortable and prepared herself for the long speech to come. "How you be out there fucken like a jackrabbit and don't know nothen about sex, guhl?" She was using her Florida accent for this episode.

"What you mea—?" Ke-Ke started to ask but was cut off. Tiff was on a roll like butter, as she always said, and Ke-Ke knew she would have to wait to get a word in.

"Look, bitch, sex is mental. And stimulation is... stimulation!" Tiff repeated and pronounced the word slowly.

"Mmmhmm, preach," Ke-Ke could hear someone playfully giving Tiff a witness in the background. She had to smile at the way the people in the salon always encouraged and supported Tiff's rants.

"Child, yo' body was responding to the STIM-U-LA-TION." She slowed it down again, more for dramatic effect than for Ke-Ke's understanding. "Not to get too nasty girl, but if you turn off the lights, a tongue is a tongue and a mouth is a mouth."

Ke-Ke didn't have time to figure out if she agreed on her own. She heard someone in Tiff's congregation catching the Holy Spirit or the HO-ly Spirit, she couldn't tell the difference.

"I'ma tell you how I know," Tiff sighed on the phone and Ke-Ke could tell she was going deep into her archives for one of her greatest hits.

"I was in love with this married nigga back home," Tiff began her story with a sigh. "It was good for a while, but I was young and dumb. He was talken about how he was gonna leave his wife and take me around the world on his yacht and so on and so on. We was gonna live out our days together in a different country each year, so he said. Now I know this nigga married but he had boosted my head up *GOOD*! I mean he had my little ass *OPEN*." Ke-Ke could tell she was remembering her old feelings by the way she said it. "Plus he had money out the ass. He owned a club and at the time his brother played for the Dolphins. Anyway! He called himself creepen wit my best friend at the time. I came home from school early and saw his truck parked in the driveway. Something told me to park on the street and I did. I wasn't thinken nothen too crazy at first cause sometimes he would be in my bed asleep, waiting for me to come home.

"I walk up the driveway and happened to peek in the kitchen window, and *giiiiirrrl!* This nigga had my best friend bent over the sink, just a-pumpen and a-sweaten. I went into shock. They must've forgot the window was cracked, cause I hear this nigga say some shit like, 'Yo' pussy tighter than Tiff's, you gonna make me leave that bitch!'"

Tiff had lowered her voice to mock the sound of a man's voice. "This bitch talken about, 'That's what I want, daddy, just me and you, me and you!'"

Tiff made her friend sound like a cartoon character and Ke-Ke smiled without laughing as she held the phone.

"I don't know where I got the strength not to kick in the door and go fucken crazy, but I'm glad I didn't because what I *did* do was twenty times better!"

Ke-Ke noticed that the salon was completely silent and she was sure that everyone in attendance was hanging on to Tiff's every word. "Chiiiiild! I was hotter than four fat bitches in a Neon wit the heat on!"

The women broke their silence and all Ke-Ke could hear was loud laughter and clapping.

"I was crushed though! I'm *tellen* you! I had planned my life wit this nigga, had already named our children and EVERYTHING! Girl, I drove around for like an hour just thinking! That bitch, her name was

Peaches, was only living wit me cause her mom had kicked her out when she got a new boyfriend. I called myself bein a good friend to the bitch. She gonna fuck my nigga in my house over my sink and get away with it? Hell to the muthafucken nawww!"

Ke-Ke could tell Tiff was getting worked up just remembering the time and she braced herself for the finale.

"So I end up at my homeboy Lionel's house. He gay, but that's my boy. He was the one that taught me how to braid hair. That Lionel is crazy as hell though!" Tiff laughed as she spoke on her old friend. "I tell him the story and girrrl, that's when the world-famous move called the Fifty-Fifty Fake Out was born."

Ke-Ke was finally able to get a word in. "What the hell is that?"

Tiff only laughed at the question. "I almost don't wanna tell you, because you'll probably try to use it, but I will anyway. It's your birthday, girl! I'm gonna tell you what we did and then you'll know what it is." Ke-Ke could hear Tiff snapping her fingers as she rhymed her words.

"The first part takes *A LOT* of mental strength. I went back home, walked back into the house like I usually do and acted like I never saw nothing. I went upstairs and this nigga was in my bed asleep! Now, I'm knowing why this nigga is always so tired and it's burning me up inside, but I gotta hold it together. I can't get all crazy and blow up on him like I really, really want to. I just kiss him on the cheek like I always do and ask him if he had seen Peaches. He of course gonna say, 'She was gone when I got here.'"

Tiff did a man's voice almost too well, Ke-Ke thought as she shook her head.

"So I goes and takes a shower and come out and tell him I gotta surprise for him. I tell him I rented a Jacuzzi suite at the Wyndham Hotel. I show him this see-through cat suit I had picked up at the mall on my way home. I told him tonight was the night that I was gonna give him what he had been beggen me for for the last six months. That nigga got dressed so quick, had his keys and was like, '*C'mon!*' I hadn't even finished getting dressed.

"I gotta go to the bathroom, hold up!" Tiff put the phone down and Ke-Ke could hear her heels clicking across the floor as she walked away. Tiff knew she had everybody in the salon, and Ke-Ke on the phone, in the palm of her hand. She always picked the worst possible time during her stories to take an impromptu intermission.

"Awwww bitch, you be doen that shit on purpose!"

Ke-Ke laughed as she heard someone in the background speak what she had already been thinking. "Bitch, you ain't Terry McMillan. Why the hell you got us all *Waiting to Exhale*?"

Ke-Ke could hear the laughter and then more comments as she waited for Tiff to come back to the phone and wondered how long she could hold her audience's attention before they really turned on her. She knew Tiff was a professional storyteller and she had never seen her lose an audience completely, no matter how much they complained about her stalling and fucken wit their heads.

A few moments later she could hear Tiff taking center stage again, saying, "Sorry y'all, when you gotta go, you gotta go!" in her innocent voice.

"Bitch, you probably went in there and stood in the mirror for two minutes just to keep us waiten!" somebody challenged Tiff. "Now finish the damn story. I wanna hear this Fifty-Fifty shit!"

"Okay. Okay. So where was I?" Tiff stretched the intermission as long as she possibly could without getting hair brushes thrown across the room at her. "So we get to the hotel, I pull out the key card and tell him the champagne was already on ice, waiting for us. That nigga grinnen from ear to ear. Y'all shoulda seen him! We get up to the room, I close the door, turn the lights out, and immediately drop down to my knees and start sucken the *hell* out his dick! I mean, I got him up against the wall, scratching and moaning. I'm licken his balls and *all,* girl!" Tiff spared none of the details.

"Mmph! Damn girl, go ahead!" Ke-Ke could hear someone say, like they appreciated Tiff's honesty.

"Then I tell him I thought about it and I had come to the conclusion that wasn't nothen wrong wit the whole threesome thang as long as I knew he was all mine. Now mind you, the room is pitch black. I tell him I have a friend that will be joining us and that I'll be right back, but in the meantime, enjoy! So he says 'hell yeah' and my friend comes out of the bathroom and starts to suck his dick. He was moaning like a farm animal, talken about, 'I love you so much for this gift, baby!'

Ke-Ke held the phone, trying to figure out *how was this shit a punishment?*

"Girl, I waited good till I knew he was about to bust that nut. Then I flicked them lights on and asked him, 'Baby, is his mouth tighter than mine?'

"He just looked all confused, blinking and shit, blinded by the light as I sat there and clicked picture after picture with my digital camera. Girl, he looked at me, then looked down in time to see Lionel wiping his mouth. The look on his face was *PRICELESS* and I got the pictures to prove it!" Tiff laughed. "I grabbed Lionel's hand and we ran like hell out that room before that nigga's shock could wear off and he could even begin to get mad enough to react.

"See, me and Lionel had gotten the room earlier and he stayed behind. When we got there, he just waited for his cue and *PERFORMED!*" Tiff snapped her fingers again to punctuate her words. Ke-Ke had almost dropped the phone in disbelief. She couldn't even believe that the story was true, but she knew Tiff wasn't a liar.

The salon had filled with all sorts of comments like, "Girl, you know you wrong for that one."

"STIM-U-LA-TION," Tiff said again, bringing the story full circle. "In the dark, or in your case *knocked out*, a tongue is a tongue and a mouth is a mouth! You getten all this, girl?" she asked Ke-Ke, who hadn't been able to utter a word while she was digesting Tiff's story.

"Daaamn, you grimy, Tiff!" is all Ke-Ke could say as she imagined how that nigga must've felt about himself afterwards.

"His wife was tryna press charges on me and everything," Tiff continued. "Talken about I ruined him forever and I ain't have to go that far! Shiiit, he'll think twice before he fuck wit somebody emotions again... if he fuck wit anybody. I heard he still goen to counseling or therapy for that shit to this day!" Tiff said it like she heard he had gotten a new job.

"What you do wit the pictures?" Ke-Ke heard someone ask. "You just kept them for yourself?"

"Now y'all know me better than that!" Tiff laughed and clapped her hands.

"What you do?" Ke-Ke asked.

"I guess you know. I printed them bad boys out, went to Kinko's and got copies, and the night before I moved a few towns over, we posted them on his club, on telephone poles, buildings, benches, cars parked outside of his club, and everything else we could find. Shiiit, he wasn't getten off *that* easy!" Tiff detailed her death move like it was nothing.

"Damn bitch, remind me not to piss you the fuck off!" someone said in the background, which was followed by another loud round of laughter. Ke-Ke was still in shock.

"Look, I gotta go, girl. It's getten close to closing time," Tiff said quickly.

Ke-Ke was about to answer when Tiff spoke again, "Watch what you do and be careful who ya screw! Well, in your case, watch what you do and STAY AWAKE to know who you screw!" Tiff laughed at her own quick wit. "And Ke-Ke, one more thing," Tiff whispered like she was getting ready to tell her a secret. "Always remember... STIM-U-LA-TION." Tiff laughed hysterically and hung up the phone.

That fucken bitch is crazy. Ke-Ke looked at her phone, trying not to smile, and finished wiping the tears off of her face.

I love her.

FIVE

KE-KE STARED OUT THE WINDOW for a minute as her mind processed the conversation with Tiff. She tried to force herself to feel better about the situation with Troi, although she knew that half the hood wouldn't even understand the insight that Tiff had shared. What they saw and heard was usually all they knew and all they cared to know.

She got herself together and left the room as it was before she entered, to prevent being interrogated by her grandmother. By the time she got downstairs, Ti-Ti was asleep on the couch with videos blasting on the television. Ke-Ke grabbed the remote, turned the sound down, then headed into the kitchen to see what kind of food she could find to take with her on the walk home. She grabbed two pieces of leftover fried chicken, wrapped them in a paper towel, threw away the empty Remy bottles, and headed for home.

She slammed the door and sped down the front steps, laughing at the thought of scaring the shit out of Ti-Ti. She walked down the street, eating the chicken and throwing the bones on the sidewalk as she went. The thoughts of Troi and the video crept back into her mind as she wondered who she would pass on the way home and what they would have to say about it. She thought of what she would say and how she would try to spin Tiff's logic into her comments in a way that wouldn't make her look like she was just trying to cover things up or make excuses.

When she hit the corner and was about to hit the alley that led back to Jefferson Ave, a grey Yukon Denali with chrome rims and grey center caps that matched the paint job pulled over in front of her. She walked on the sidewalk, trying to seem unimpressed. One of her uncle's sayings coached her through the moment: *Sometimes the best way to get something is to act like you don't want it.* Those words had proven to be true for Ke-Ke on several occasions, although she had never taken the time to think about how or why it worked so well.

The truck honked its horn as Ke-Ke passed the passenger side window and was almost in front of the truck without breaking her stride. She smiled at how well her tactics seemed to always work in for her. She walked back to the passenger side of the truck, trying to make it seem like she was looking for someone she already knew. The key to the game now was to look more confused than anything as she squinted and tried to see through the tinted, passenger side window.

The window slid down to reveal the driver. It was Ahmed from the hair store.

"Get in," he said as he hit the power lock control on his side of the vehicle without even looking down. She smiled like she was happy to see him and climbed in the truck.

She glanced around the interior and noticed TVs in the sun visor and dashboard. The seats were custom, diamond-stitched white leather and suede with grey trim. His name, "Ahmed," was stitched in a cursive font on the headrests, and the polished dark wood grain crept through the cabin like branches from a rosewood tree that was planted somewhere under the hood. The scent of a man's cologne that Ke-Ke couldn't remember the name of danced in the air and had a calming effect on her. As she reclined, she felt like she was high.

"You don't look like the type that walks anywhere," he finally spoke after he had pulled away form the curb and driven a half block.

Ke-Ke rolled her eyes and said, "I do what I gotta do when I gotta do it. I'm a survivor, can't be depending on some nigga to do shit for you!" She spoke her well-rehearsed speech effortlessly. Ti-Ti and she had developed it and other responses when she spent the night over her grandmother's house. They were both sure that the phrase would be heard by a nigga as meaning, "I'm not impressed by your money."

Ahmed just laughed and kept driving, leaving Ke-Ke to wonder if he had seen through the smoke screen.

"You live alone?" Ahmed asked after there had been a moment of silence.

"Turn right here," she instructed him as she realized that Ahmed didn't even know where she lived. "Naw, I live wit my moms right now," she answered, wondering if she had her own apartment, would she have been up to entertaining him anyway.

They pulled to a stop at the corner and Ke-Ke watched Pam climbing out of the passenger side of an old Cadillac. She was happy as hell that the windows were tinted on the truck. Pam wouldn't be able to catch a glimpse of her and have something smart to say about it when she saw her again.

The feeling of anger surged through her for a moment as she remembered their conversation and was forced to see the similarities in their situations at that exact moment. She pushed the feelings aside though as she compared the vehicles they were riding in. She thought to herself, "I ain't riden in a beat-up Cadillac wit a piece of wood where the back bumper should be, bitch!"

Ahmed turned onto her street and Ke-Ke admired how his blinker formed an arrow in his sideview mirror. She told him which house was hers and he pulled to a stop and shifted the truck into park. Ke-Ke studied the blinds in the front windows for movement, knowing that her mother and sister were both nosy as hell.

"Well, maybe we could chill sometime. You know, do somethen different."

His words went in one ear and out the other as Ke-Ke cut him off: "You got my number."

She opened the door and hopped out of the truck before he could speak another word. She walked to the house, without looking back. *All that money and no fucken game! I know he didn't think he was gonna get no pussy wit that weak-ass convo!*

She laughed at his approach. That whole "do something different" line and a trip to Applebee's would have the average bitch ready to marry a nigga. Besides, they had already crossed the line when they met it was too late for him to try to play the timid gentleman role. They both knew what he wanted and the fact that he hadn't been aggressive enough was a definite turnoff. She hated being around men who wanted her to take control.

She laughed again as she thought, if he only knew how close he was. She played the ride home with her own alternate ending in her head, where Ahmed had offered her some weed and said he was taking her to his house to "watch a movie." That kind of convo would've probably led to her feet facing the ceiling and the movie watching them. He was a rookie!

When she got to the porch, she noticed he was still watching, so she bent all the way over slowly to pick up the newspaper that was wrapped in a blue plastic bag. He would call, he would DEFINITELY call.

"Still fucken them drug dealers, huh?" her mother's words hit her before she could even close the door. "I guess you'll learn when your pussy falls off!" her mother continued with a laugh as she walked up the stairs with a basket of laundry she had folded on the couch while she was spying.

Ke-Ke didn't have the energy to respond and went into the kitchen to see if anything was cooking. She rolled her eyes as she noticed the orange light beaming on the Crock-Pot. One of her mother's world-famous Crock-Pot delights: miscellaneous meats seasoned and left to cook all day while she went to work. Nobody but her mother would touch the creations, and Ke-Ke was left to wonder many nights whether she was trying to starve her and Misha out.

She leaned against the counter and thought back to happier times. She remembered back when they were younger and their mother would do anything for them. She had two or three bikes, more than enough clothes. Birthdays and Christmas were unbelievable. She remembered Nintendo game systems and Easy-Bake Ovens and all the other toys and board games that they got as soon as they asked for them. She remembered all the activities that she was involved in—from dance to karate to track—and her mother never missed a game, concert, or a meet. She was so good to them that the other kids in the neighborhood wanted her to be their mother too.

What had happened to her?

Kent.

Kent was her mother's boyfriend of about four years now and everything had gone downhill since he entered the picture. Kent was a supposed-to-be-ex-crackhead who was usually out of work and still lived with his mother. Ke-Ke and Misha had believed for the longest time that he was still on drugs and just hid it from their mother, or that she knew and just acted like she didn't. Ke-Ke felt like her mother put up with his bullshit because she was scared that he would leave her like their father had. She was afraid to be alone.

Whatever the reasons, life had ceased to be sweet when he had come into their lives. Ke-Ke had overheard Kent telling their mother she was doing way too much for them and that they were spoiled rotten. He also preached some pseudo-Muslim prison faith that he had convinced their mother to adopt.

Ke-Ke remembered the time he had taken their mother's car, like he always did, and come back to the house two days later. Ke-Ke had crouched down in the dark kitchen and waited for him to walk in the door and BAM! She smacked him across the head with the big black frying pan that had been sitting on the stove. The blow knocked him unconscious. She remembered running back up the stairs to her room thinking that she had killed him. The nigga was so high though, five minutes later he was walking up the stairs, whistling, the bucket of chicken he had bought under his arm and blood dripping from his head like nothing had happened.

Kent was famous for taking the car and disappearing for days. He would "borrow the car" and leave her mother walking to work in the dead of winter. Ke-Ke and Misha would have to walk to school and miss any practices or rehearsals they had scheduled because they had no way to get there. Her mother would just let him get away with it.

"He's sick," she would say any time they would question her fucked-up choice of mate.

There were times when she would get sick of it though and Ke-Ke and her mother together would walk all over the hood, looking for her car. Ke-Ke seemed to always be able to find him, so eventually it led to Ke-Ke just being sent out alone to find him and bring him home. She remembered how young she was, going into these crack houses to find Kent in a corner with his eyes looking like they were going to pop out of his head. She even remembered the time she had found him in a house and he wouldn't get up and leave until she lifted her coat up and spun around in front of the man that was selling drugs out of the house. She could still hear that nasty, fat black dude sucking his teeth and nodding at Kent with a smile on his face. "She right, Kent. We might could work somethen out."

A couple of years later, she put it together that it had nothing to do with her showing off what she had learned in dance class. Kent had offered her to the man for drugs. Ke-Ke had never told her mother because she didn't want to go through the mind games adults played with kids—the one where they try to convince you that what happened or what you saw wasn't that at all. That it was something else. She had dubbed the tactic "The

Magic Trick" and learned at a very young age that her mother was the queen of pulling a rabbit out of her ass whenever the reality of a situation was too hard for her to deal with or explain.

Kent was so low that he would go to members of their family and tell whoever answered the door that he had been sent there to get money for gas or some other bullshit and swindle money from Ke-Ke's aunts, uncles, and one time even her grandmother. The shit wouldn't even come out until they all came together for a holiday dinner. Ke-Ke would look at her mom when it was brought up and expect her to be embarrassed, but all her mother would say was, "Y'all know he got a problem," and continue eating after she changed the subject.

Their mother had sold herself and her kids out for a fucken crackhead.

"Get yo' ass off the counter, people gotta make food there!" her mother yelled as she entered the kitchen. "I don't know what you call *yourself* bein in deep thought about, probably the fucked-up color you gonna dye your hair next!"

Ke-Ke hopped off of the counter and left the kitchen before she caught another flashback that would surely give her the strength to curse her mother out. She climbed the stairs to her bedroom behind her and fell face first onto her bed.

SIX

TEN MINUTES LATER she head a tapping on her door, right before she was about to fall into a deep sleep.

"Can I come in?" Misha asked from the other side of the door. She had been cursed out enough in the past to know better than to barge in.

"What do you want?" Ke-Ke answered, half asleep.

Misha slowly pushed the door open with her eyes closed, feeling around with her hands outstretched in front of her like she was blind.

"Girl, what the hell do you fucken want?" Ke-Ke laughed, thinking that Misha walking into the room during one of her previous sexual escapades had probably scarred this little girl for life.

"I need a perm," Misha half-stated and half-asked as she sat down on the bed next to her.

Ke-Ke rolled over, looked at the ceiling, and said, "Then go fucken get one!" knowing that it wasn't a real solution to her sister's problem.

"I can't go. Mom won't let me walk to the store this late!" Ke-Ke already knew that was coming.

"I got seven dollars for you if you go." Misha sweetened the deal. She had learned that the magic word with Ke-Ke was "weed," not "please."

"Word?" She sat up and snatched the money out of Misha's hand, counting it to be sure that there would be enough for her to cop a bag of green on the way back home.

"Where you get this money from?" Ke-Ke asked while she checked to see how her ass looked in the mirror.

"I got my sources, I got my ways!" Misha busted into a routine she and her friends had come up with while they were waiting for step practice.

"Whatever, bitch, I find out you fucken and I'm gonna tell Ma *AND* beat ya little ass." Ke-Ke punched her in the shoulder, changed into a pair of sweatpants, grabbed her jacket, and ran out of the house.

She walked up the street, knowing that her little sister was probably raiding her underwear drawer at this very moment. She had heard Misha asking her mother for bikini-cut underwear and her mother would always respond, "Who's gonna see your panties anyway? Why you need sexy panties?"

She shook her head at how insensitive her mother could be. The truth was, for a young girl, the locker room during gym class could be a brutal place. Girls would poke fun at other girls for wearing "grannies" or not having a developed body, or whatever else they could find wrong with you, from a birthmark to a scar on your body. Ke-Ke thought back to that being the reason she and her crew had started shoplifting in the first place. She knew Misha had been dipping in her drawer for about a month now, since her swimming unit had started in gym. She knew the feeling of having to hide your cartoon panties while the other girls stood around in silk or lace bikini matching sets and took their time getting dressed.

Ke-Ke almost laughed out loud when she remembered the day a few weeks ago that Misha had left the bathroom door cracked, wearing a pair of Ke-Ke's panties and looking at herself. "Them bitches gonna *haaate,*" Misha sang to herself in the mirror. Ke-Ke just shook her head and went to her room. It was just one of the many things that she let her little sister believe that she was "getting away" with.

She hit the corner, happy to see Pam's smart ass wasn't out that night to harass her. She focused on getting to the store, thinking that after she bought the olive oil perm her sister preferred, she would probably have to put it in for her too. That would cost that little heifer five more dollars!

She approached the lights that beamed off the roof of the corner store where she was now close enough to recognize the shadowy figures that stood in front of it. She prepared herself for more comments about her video and made her way to the door.

"Whatuuuup!"

She turned to see Lee, her first real boyfriend, the one she had lost her virginity to.

"Oh shit!" Ke-Ke hugged him and smiled like they were still together. "I thought you was locked the fuck up," she said.

She tried to act like she wasn't excited. Lee had been the only nigga she had told *everything* to and the only nigga she had ever really felt one hundred percent safe around. They had kind of grown up together, so he knew all about her home life and things had just naturally progressed into them dating and messing around. He had too much trouble controlling his baby's mama though, and Ke-Ke had cut him off due to all the drama she was catching from some twenty-one-year-old female she didn't even know.

"Naw, I beat that shit," he answered as he spoke about his gun and drug charges that had made the newspaper the summer before. "Whatsup wit you though?" he asked as he did the elevator eyes thing men did and checked out her body. "When we gonna get up and get it in?"

Ke-Ke pulled out her cell phone to exchange numbers with him. She could stand some good dick again, plus Lee ate pussy like it was fried chicken. She hugged him again as he mumbled something about having to go put some "work in" and walked in the store with a smile on her face.

"My bad," said a tall, light-skinned nigga that had run into her when the door swung open.

"You good," Ke-Ke said in her sexy voice, smiling as she noticed the thick gold chain and medallion that was hanging from his neck.

He spun and watched her walk away while Ke-Ke added a twitch to her walk to keep his attention. She found the perm kits located in the back of the store.

"Damn, girl!" he said, holding the door in one hand and looking back at her like he had forgotten everything that he was getting ready to do.

Ke-Ke turned and smiled as she knew her thin sweatpants were slightly wedged, revealing the exact dimensions of her ass as she walked. The trick was to act like you didn't know or were too busy to realize how it looked. She had made niggas damn near wreck their cars before.

This nigga was no different. She had frozen him in time. He smiled and made his way through the door but he never took his eyes off of her.

Ke-Ke selected the olive oil perm in the green box and headed for the register, paid the Arab, and told him to turn the bullshit music off as she left the store.

When she crossed the street, she saw Bungee and wondered if he would come off a bag of weed for seven. She put on her "you know I love you" routine. He complained and made a comment about broke-ass niggas but agreed to the deal. She kissed him on the cheek and turned to walk home when—

BOOM! BOOM!

SEVEN

THE SOUND OF GUNSHOTS RANG OUT LIKE THUNDER. Ke-Ke ducked down by a car and spun around to see Lee in midair before he landed in the middle of the street on his back. She stared in shock as his shadowy figure shook uncontrollably in the dim lights of the corner store.

A car screeched off and turned the corner wildly as Ke-Ke caught a glimpse of the dude she had bumped into when she had entered the store. He was holding a chrome handgun and pacing back and forth. The lights danced off the chain and his gun as he screamed at no one, "I told y'all I wasn't wit that shit!" He stood there for another moment then made a panicked dash up the street, hit the alley, and was gone out of sight.

Lee lay in the middle of the street, moaning and rolling from side to side, his heels digging into the street like he was trying to stand up. Ke-Ke felt like everything was in slow motion as people jumped from their porches and ran towards the intersection.

"Yo, Lee got hit! Call 911!" somebody screamed at the Arab from the store, who was now standing in the doorway. He stared down at Lee, squirming in the street in front of him. He disappeared into the store and reappeared holding a cordless phone while others pulled out cell phones and placed frantic calls of their own.

"Stay down, dog!" people were yelling from both sides of the street. Ke-Ke noticed how nobody seemed to want to get to close to Lee. A half circle seemed to stop fifteen feet from where he was lying. Lee kept rolling and made gasping noises. He still seemed to be trying to struggle to his feet.

"Fuck!"

Ke-Ke looked around to see Jaymo smashing his bottle of Hennessy on the sidewalk while the crowd seemed to thicken by the second and she could hear people saying things like "That nigga done!" and "He got hit wit a cannon!"

Ke-Ke could hear the sirens coming in the distance, as she watched Lee's movements begin to slow down. He was making a wheezing sound like he couldn't breathe and his body convulsed and writhed in pain. She knew deep down that he wasn't going to make it.

The police pulled up first, screeching to a halt, just a couple of feet from Lee's body. The ambulance arrived minutes later. Ke-Ke could only stare as she watched the police walk around Lee's bleeding body as he jerked and gasped for air. She watched in amazement as they made no effort to perform CPR or any other procedures. They just circled and looked down on him like he was a dog in the street that had been hit by a car. The ambulance workers took their time as well, lifting Lee's lifeless body onto a stretcher and rolling it towards the back of the ambulance.

When they opened the doors, it was like a spell had been lifted on the crowd and the scene turned frantic as people rushed towards the stretcher and began trying to talk to Lee and check his condition. Ke-Ke realized all at once that she had been holding onto Bungee's sleeve the whole time as he pulled away from her while they approached the ambulance as well. She managed to touch Lee's arm before he was lifted into the van but was forced to look away when she noticed the tears on his face and the glazed look in his eyes.

"Everybody, step the fuck back!" the police were yelling now and pushing people away. "Back on the sidewalk!" they ordered as she watched one of them remove his can of pepper spray and begin to shake it in an overly dramatic fashion. "Let them do their job!" he spoke again as he continued to shake the spray as a nonverbal warning. Ke-Ke walked back to the sidewalk, knowing that they would find any excuse to spray someone and carry them off to jail. The ambulance sped off, headed for Strong Memorial Hospital, just as back-up police officers arrived on the scene and jumped out of their cars with their batons already extended.

"So, what happened out here tonight, guys?" A short police officer with gloves on canvassed the crowd. Ke-Ke watched as everyone in the crowd grew silent. "Let me guess, nobody saw nothen?" The officer smiled and nodded as he faced a sea of black faces that stared back at him with disdain. He shook his head and turned off his flashlight.

"Okay, great, less paperwork for me. It's your fucken friend, not mine!" He shrugged and performed a military about-face then headed back to his patrol car.

"Fuck you! Punk muthafucka!" somebody yelled out from the crowd. The officer nodded and performed a mock salute then climbed back into his car and pulled off.

"Them bitches don't give a fuck anyway!" a girl next to Ke-Ke said. "They just want to lock another nigga up."

Ke-Ke stared at the spot where Lee had been lying just a few minutes before and tried to make sense of everything. His blood stained the street in dark circles and glistened in the headlights of the parked patrol cars.

She turned to walk home with her opposing thoughts clashing in her head like cymbals. She knew the code was "Never talk to the police" and she had never had a problem with following it until now. She wrestled with her own emotions and thoughts that were telling her to go against everything she had ever learned and known. She thought about calling Crime Stoppers and leaving an anonymous tip with the dispatchers, but the possibility that it probably wasn't so anonymous and the thoughts of how the police would probably arrive outside of her door after they had traced the call chased the idea out of her head. She rationalized by telling herself that she hadn't really known what had happened anyway and it seemed to calm the swell of emotions in her chest for a while.

Ke-Ke walked and looked around the neighborhood that had been considered one of the worst in the city for years and all at once came face-to-face with the reality that maybe she was part of the problem. Knowing things meant keeping secrets and those secrets were the bond that connected everyone she knew. The people that didn't know didn't need to know, even if it meant justice had to go without being served her pound of flesh. She forced herself to believe that Lee would understand. He would understand how she could watch him get murdered and keep her mouth shut.

Her uncle's words flew threw her head on cue, as they always did: *And the band played on.*

"Ketasia! What the hell happened up there?" Misha and her mother were on the porch with their robes on, talking with Pam. Pam hadn't even been up there, but Ke-Ke could hear her mouth a block away saying, "It was a drive-by! Niggas came from cross town! I told y'all that gang shit was getten out of control around here!"

Pam carried on as she swung her arms around and tried to draw as much attention to herself as possible. Ke-Ke walked past the three of them and into the house without saying a word. Her mother came into the kitchen moments later after she managed to pry herself away from Pam.

"Bungee got shot?" she asked with a head full of misinformation that had been fed to her by Pam.

"Lee got killed," Ke-Ke managed to speak after a few moments of just leaning against the counter and staring off into space.

"Who shot him?" her mother asked after a few "Oh my Gods" and "Jesuses."

Ke-Ke could only shrug and respond, "Some nigga." She tried to look tough like the streets had stolen her innocence years ago and she really didn't feel anything—the same way everybody else on the block acted when something tragic happened. She hadn't mastered the art of stopping her tears though, and they flowed from her eyes against her will.

When they got upstairs, Misha brought the box perm, a towel, and her combs into Ke-Ke's room and sat on the floor with her back against the bed.

"You washed this shit?" Ke-Ke asked her as she sat on the bed with Misha in between her legs, like their mother had done with both of them when they were younger. She ran her hand through Misha's hair and shook her head as she noticed its damaged condition and the way that Misha had burned some of her edges out with the hot comb. "Your hair ain't never gonna grow!" she warned Misha as she dumped the contents of the box perm onto her bed.

The doorbell rang and Ke-Ke guessed right when she figured it was Kent. He, in the last year, had supposedly cleaned himself up, managed to get a job as a janitor at the local high school, and had even bought his own car. Ke-Ke recited the list of "accomplishments" by memory as she had heard her mother recite them to anyone who would listen countless times. She didn't give a damn what her mother said though, Kent was at best a functioning crackhead who kept his dark crusades a secret now because he had his own personal crackmobile to disappear with.

She could hear her mother whispering something to him, which prompted Kent to walk past Ke-Ke's bedroom rapping, "Niggas in the hood be poppen/niggas in the hood be droppen!" He danced and threw fake gang signs with his hands while her mother laughed hysterically in the hallway behind him.

"Shut the fuck up, crackhead!" Ke-Ke screamed, slamming the door in his face.

"He was just tryen to cheer you up!" her mother called out from the other side of the door. She thought everything that man did and said was so funny. Ke-Ke couldn't stand the sight of him or the sound of his voice. She had even tried to get her father to beat his ass once by telling him a bunch of lies, but as usual her father didn't come through.

Afer letting the white pasty substance sit in Misha's hair, she was at the bathroom sink washing it out when the phone rang. She could hear her mother getting up and coming to the door. "Y'all daddy on the phone," she called out in her trying-to-be-sexy voice that Ke-Ke and her sister were all too familiar with. Ke-Ke smiled at the sound of her voice, knowing that her father had game and that her mother would get back with him in a heartbeat, no matter how much she tried to deny it. She put the towel on Misha's head and went to get the phone, wondering what excuses he was going to make up this time for not sending her the new cell phone he had promised her.

"Hello," Ke-Ke sighed as she tried to get the rest of the white relaxer off of her hands.

"Hey girl, how are you? Your mother told me that your boyfriend just got killed."

Ke-Ke just rolled her eyes, thinking about how big her mother's mouth was. "He wasn't my boyfriend, Dad," she responded, knowing that it didn't matter what she said, her father for some reason still believed whatever their mother told him.

Ke-Ke walked back to her room and sat on the bed and prepared herself for the one-sided conversation in which her father would talk about himself. He was a career military man, a drill sergeant posted in Germany at the time. "Your dad got money, your dad got all these young girls chasing him... et cetera, et cetera."

She would just half-listen to this middle-aged wannabe playboy who was still trying to get over on females with his hazel eyes and his "I can buy you the world" game.

She didn't like to admit it, but she enjoyed hearing from him. Through all the half-truths, he had single-handedly opened her eyes to how big the world really was. She loved to hear about different places and people and their ways of life. He had lived everywhere at one point or another and always had a story. She would usually have to endure a half hour of nonsense for him to get to what she really wanted to hear, but she told herself it was worth it. Ke-Ke would close her eyes, listen to her father's voice, and visualize the beaches, the people, the open-air markets, the buildings, the statues, or whatever else he was describing. Her mental passport was stamped with his lies and empty promises, while her heart paid the fare for the journeys. She convinced herself it was a fair trade.

Misha never liked to speak to him long, if at all, and Ke-Ke would find herself on the phone with him for hours at a time, listening to his tales, experiences, and conquests. She remembered the story of how he had left them, as told to them by their mother every time they talked, and it was usually enough to snap her back to reality and demand something from him as a way of making up for it.

The story their mother had told them was that she had met their father at Midtown Plaza when she was young. She worked at one of the retail stores and he was a security guard (at the time they were called "Red Coats"). They met and began dating and before long she was pregnant. Their father had joined the military and their mother moved to Texas with him and stayed in the on-base housing. Ke-Ke remembered very little about the time, except that they had a Suzuki Samurai jeep that they had traveled in all the way to Texas.

The story split in two at this point. Ke-Ke's father said that their mother never cooked or cleaned. He said that they argued about it and that their mother just wanted to go out and party all the time, not be a mother and a wife.

The story their mother told was that their father, while on duty in Hawaii, had met another woman. He picked up and left her for the other woman, who he eventually married. She and Ke-Ke stayed in the military housing as long as they possibly could before they were kicked out and Ke-Ke's grandmother had to send money so they could catch the train back to New York.

Ke-Ke tried, but could never imagine how she would've felt if a nigga had done her like that. The two of them, with Misha in her mother's belly, struggled while her father was in Hawaii having the time of his life. He never looked back and he never sent money until Child Support forced him.

There were times, as she got older, that Ke-Ke thought maybe there was more to the story. She tried to pick up bits and pieces that her mother might've left out over the years, but they never did seem to materialize and that puzzle stayed incomplete. Her father had always vehemently denied their mother's story, but Ke-Ke had grown to believe it due to what she had grown to know about him. He had been married three times and every time she turned around, he was in a new part of the world with a new female that was "his baby."

She remembered the time that her mother forced her to go live with him a few years back. They would be in the grocery store and he would be trying to pull every woman with two legs and a heartbeat. He swore he was so fine and that no woman in the world could resist his charm. He was married at that time too. She had guessed that he figured his daughter was too young to put two and two together.

His wife at the time was some extremely materialistic, half-this-half-that broad (of course that made her "exotic") who wore too much makeup and was always blinking like she was constantly trying to get contacts to settle in her eyes. She had two sons that Ke-Ke hated, and her father did flips to make this bitch happy. She had told him repeatedly that the bitch was just using him, but of course, he never listened. Her father bought her an Escalade that she crashed into a tree within a month and was demanding another. Ke-Ke used to laugh to herself thinking if that bitch had stopped all that goddamn blinking, she would've seen where the fuck she was going!

She stayed with them for about four months until she had gotten caught skipping school. She had come out of her room not knowing that her father was still home and he had grabbed her by her throat and thrown her across her bedroom. She remembered fighting back, punching him in his face, and how he looked so mad when he said, "You're going back or I'm gonna fucken kill your little ass!"

He drove from Maryland to Rochester, New York, the same day without stopping.

Three years later he had moved to Germany on military business. He decided to stay. Of course, he had met another female. He left his wife, her sons, and the dog back in military housing to await divorce papers. They would have to fend for themselves.

Some things never changed.

"What happened to my phone, Dad?" She cut her father off mid-sentence as the anger rushed through her body on the high-octane fuel of her memories.

"Oh, I didn't forget, I'm waiting for my money to be exchanged." Blah, blah, blah was all Ke-Ke heard after that.

She had long before credited him with her attitude towards men. She never saw them as permanent fixtures in her life and on more than one occasion had been told she was like the dude in a relationship. Ke-Ke could "fuck and get up" with the best of them. Her mother called it arrogance and said she got it from her father. "He thought he was too hot for TV too!" she had told Ke-Ke a million times.

She listened to her father's bullshit for another ten minutes and then attempted to hand the phone to Misha who waved her hand as she always did, refusing to take it. She never had any words for him unless she *desperately* wanted something that their mother would not get for her. He usually didn't come through anyway and she would be back to her silent treatment routine with him.

It was a vicious cycle.

***

THE NEXT MORNING Ke-Ke awoke late to find that her mother hadn't kicked her out of the house before she left for work. She took it as a sign that her mother had really felt bad about what happened to Lee. She had become skilled in reading her mother's nonverbal communications over the past few years. It seemed like when her mother lost her mind for Kent, she had lost her ability to speak as well.

She removed her T-shirt and walked naked to the bathroom, figuring she had the whole house to herself, for a few hours anyway.

"Ugh!" she heard Misha's voice call out behind her.

"Bitch, what the fuck you still doen here?" Ke-Ke spun around with her heart still racing.

"Ma said I could stay home wit you... and you... you got your nipple pierced?" Misha pointed with her eyes wide with amazement. "You a ho!" She slammed her bedroom door, leaving Ke-Ke in the hallway holding her breasts with her tongue out. She had perfected the fine art of either grossing her sister out, making her jealous, or both.

"I'm tellen Ma too!" Misha yelled through her door.

"She already knows, bitch!" Ke-Ke laughed as she walked into the bathroom and closed the door.

She knew that the only reason her mother had left Misha behind was because she figured Misha would be her eyes and ears while she was gone. Ke-Ke smirked to herself in the mirror while she brushed her teeth. Little did her mother know that Misha could be bought and sold for the price of a steak sub.

She ran her bathwater and was putting in the last of a scented body wash while she tried to remember where she had stolen it from.

"Ke-Ke, come get the phone! It's your trick-ass cousin!" her sister's voice tore through the serenity of the moment. Ke-Ke walked out of the bathroom still naked to further disgust Misha. She took the phone and listened to Ti-Ti talk while she pinched her nipples and made a kissing gesture with her lips poked out at Misha.

"You sooo fucken nasty!" Misha said as she pushed her out of the room and closed the door.

"Is you listening to me, bitch?" she heard Ti-Ti ask through the phone.

"Yeah, bitch, damn!" Ke-Ke answered, already annoyed.

"Soooo was you out there last night or what?" Ti-Ti had asked the question three times.

"Yeah, I was out there tryna cop some weed from Bungee when that shit went down." She eased herself into the hot bathwater as she spoke.

"You know what that shit was about?" Ti-Ti asked like she already knew the answer to her own question.

"Naw, they was just standing there and the nigga got to busten!" She prepared herself for the long, drawn-out "Ti-Ti Version" of events that was sure to come. The warm water embraced her body in a steaming hug.

"Yo, check it. I heard they was tryen to rob a nigga for his chain at the store. They ain't have no pistol, so one of them niggas gave Lee one of the BB guns, ya know the ones that cock back and look real as shit?" She waited for Ke-Ke to answer.

"Mmmmhmmm." She already knew where the story was going. She remembered when Gates, one of the younger niggas from the hood, had caught her and Kya walking back from the store. He pulled out the BB gun and pulled back a part of it, making that all too familiar clicking noise. "Aiight bitches, strip!" Ke-Ke could remember the feeling of her whole body tensing up with fear as she stared back and forth at the gun and the masked face that was holding it. She remembered her hands trembling as she slowly reached down and began to unbutton her jeans. Kya was already standing on the sidewalk in her panties pulling her shirt over her head when Gates busted out laughing and pulled the ski mask down to reveal his smiling face. "This shit ain't real! Y'all bitches can't tell?" He fell against the abandoned house they were standing in front of and handed the gun to Ke-Ke for her to look at. Ke-Ke could remember the gun having weight to it and was shocked to see that it looked and sounded so real. There was a part in the back that popped out to load BBs and when you pushed it back in, it made an authentic clicking noise, like you had loaded a round in the chamber of a real gun.

"Fuck you! You a straight asshole!" She could still hear Kya's voice cursing as she pulled her shirt back on and picked her pants up off the sidewalk. Gates just laughed and pointed as she fumbled with her jeans.

"You was shook!" he managed between laughter, as he held onto the porch and pulled himself back to his feet. "You got some pretty-ass titties though! And I like them purple panties! I shouldn't have said nothen! Both y'all would've been butt-ass naked out here!" He exploded into laughter all over again.

"You woulda had to shoot me!" Ke-Ke remembered lying, wondering if Gates had noticed her fear. Gates pushed up on Kya that night and got her number with a few apologies and some exaggerated comments about her panties. Two months later he was running around the hood, telling everyone that her pussy stank, and niggas on the West Side avoided Kya for almost a year until the rumor wore off.

Ke-Ke always knew that the gun would get somebody in trouble. She imagined the police would end up shooting one of them over it. The stories grew as it passed from one person's hands to the next. Someone was robbed, pistol-whipped, or was made to do something humiliating due to that gun on too many occasions.

"Well, anyways, they handed it to Lee and he was like, 'I'm gonna get that nigga wit this bitch.'" Ti-Ti spoke in a dude's voice to make her story more entertaining. "They stepped to the dude, whoever he was and was like, 'Give it up!' I heard Lee accidentally squeezed the trigger and when the nigga heard that click and seen it wasn't real, he pulled out a hammer for real and was like, 'No! You give it up!'"

Ke-Ke sat in the tub, rolling her eyes as her cousin changed the tone of her voice and told the story like it was the gospel.

She caught a flashback of what Lee looked like after he had gotten shot and the way he was rolling in the street in pain, unable to breathe.

"Yo, you can't be playen games out in these streets like that!" Ti-Ti recited the saying, as if she was the first one to speak it.

"That shit is so fucken crazy!" Ke-Ke said after she had played the whole event out in her head like a sitcom rerun. "That nigga coulda bought his own fucken chain!" she said, half in anger and half in pain. She knew that Lee, although accepted as a hood regular, had two parents who worked and was spoiled as shit. Lee would show up with different outfits, coats, and boots and act like he had hustled for all of it, but his parents gave him money every week and he was more of a "weekend warrior" when it came to the streets. He started getting in trouble when he felt like he had something to prove to niggas.

Ke-Ke placed the hot rag on her face and let Ti-Ti's voice play like background music. She thought about how Lee had taken tests for her in school and even did her homework for her in record time, just so she would be allowed to go out bowling or to the movies. Lee was a smart dude who got mixed up in the street and, like so many others, got caught up and didn't make it out in time.

"Hellooooo..." Ti-Ti's annoying voice interrupted her thoughts again.

"What?" Ke-Ke answered, snatched from her memories like she had been asleep.

"You comen over to braid my hair or what, bitch?"

She knew that Ti-Ti knew that she was off in La-La Land.

"What the hell you want your hair braided for? You don't even wear braids out." Ke-Ke put the phone on speaker and began to wash herself.

"Bitch, I'm getten a sew-in! Are you not listening to anything I'm saying? You need to stop smoking so much weed, Ms. ADD!" Ti-Ti spoke with mock concern in her tone.

"Aiight, I'll be there. You better have some weed too!" She hung up the phone, stood up, and rinsed the bubbles off her body. She stepped out of the tub and checked her hair in the mirror as she wrapped herself in one of the good towels her mother didn't like them to use.

"Ke?" Misha called through the door.

"What do you want, little girl!" Ke-Ke said to piss Misha off.

"Y'all gonna kill Troi?" Misha asked, her voice shaking.

"What?" Ke-Ke flung the bathroom door open and looked at Misha like she was an alien.

"Tamera said that you and Ti-Ti suppose to be riden on her sister and y'all..."

"Misha, where the fuck you be getten this shit from?" Ke-Ke asked, cutting her sister off, surprised that she knew anything about what was going on. She had forgotten that one of Misha's friends, Tamera, was Troi's little sister.

"Get the fuck outta here wit that bullshit, Misha!"

She walked to her bedroom and slammed the door.

"Well, can Tamera come over?" Misha asked in a voice that sounded like she was getting ready to start begging.

"Misha, I don't give a fuck! I'm goen out anyway, just don't fuck nothen up!"

Ke-Ke pulled one of her wifebeater undershirts from her drawer and cut it in half to finish her outfit. She was going for the "around-the-way girl" look today. She selected a pair of low-rise jeans that she had trimmed to fit even lower and looked for the right kind of thong to complete the look. She went through the drawer but couldn't find the ones with the "diamonds" that ran along the straps. She started to confront Misha about them, but the thought of wearing something after it had been in someone else's ass stopped her in mid-stride. After going through the whole drawer, she eventually found a pair that still had the tag on them. They were black silk with little silver handcuffs holding the side straps together. She shook her head and smiled at her luck. She had never worn them and Misha hadn't found them yet. She slipped them on and sprinkled her body with baby powder.

The jeans and underwear combination was sexy as long as she was mindful of how and where she sat down. Too much ass cleavage hanging out was trashy. She threw on her half-shirt and thought about piercing her belly button as she stared at her reflection. Wrapping a long-sleeve T-shirt around her hips, she ran down the stairs, just as the doorbell rang.

"I hear you!" she yelled as the bell rang three times in a row before she could get to it. She opened the door to find Tamera standing sideways as if she was posing. Ke-Ke looked her up and down. *Damn, this little girl is the same size as me!* Tamera was obviously one of those early bloomers and, if it wasn't for her childish ways, she could easily have been mistaken for a woman in her early twenties.

"My sister say she gonna see you!" Tamera informed as she walked in the door, smacking her overly glossed lips.

"I ain't hard to find!" Ke-Ke answered quickly as she stepped out onto the porch and looked back at her.

"I ain't tell her where you stay, only because my girl lives here!" Tamera stated further, referring to her loyalty towards Misha.

"Bitch, I don't give a fuck! Tell her! Draw a map! Tell that man-bitch to Google me! I don't give a fuck," Ke-Ke answered back in rapid fire as she made her way to the sidewalk. *I can't stand that little dusty bitch!* She lit a cigarette and headed for her grandmother's house.

Deep down, her heart went out to Tamera though. Tamera had been exposed to a lot more than she should've been at her age and up until recently her entire wardrobe had been a collage of Troi's old, outdated clothes and shoes. She started hanging with Misha and it wasn't long before their mother wouldn't let Misha go to her house because of the way she would smell when she got back. She had even carried roaches back after one sleepover party. Ke-Ke and her mother had coined the phrase, "Don't bring any funk or friends back!" and said it every time Misha left the house with Tamera. They would laugh themselves sick at Misha's expense. The only reason Ke-Ke tolerated her was because the girl could and would bang. She would fight in a heartbeat and Ke-Ke felt like maybe Misha would stop being such a punk if she spent more time with a rougher girl.

Ke-Ke walked, smoked her cigarette, and thought back to the time she had busted into the bathroom expecting the worst when she heard Misha and Tamera whispering in the bathroom. She stopped dead in her tracks at the sight of Misha standing in the shower, naked from the waist down, while Tamera was on her knees with a pink disposable razor sculpting her first landing strip.

"What the hell is y'all doen?" Ke-Ke had yelled at both of them like they were her kids. Misha just stood there with that dumb-ass look on her face that she always got when you asked her to think. Ke-Ke remembered teasing them, calling them dykes as she closed the door and ordered them to hurry up. Less than a week later Misha broke out with a rash. Her mother noticed her uncontrollable itching of her "girly parts" and forced Misha to show and tell what she had allowed her friend to do.

Misha ended up having to go the doctor and she prescribed a special skin cream to stop itching and irritation. Ke-Ke shook her head as she took the blame for that one too. "She gets these dumb-ass ideas from watching and listening to you!" her mother had said as they walked through the pharmacy, waiting for their number to get called.

The memories of her little sister's exploits entered her mind one after the other like episodes of a sitcom. The image of Misha in the basement sitting on the washing machine in a bra and panties brought a smile to her face.

"What the hell are you doing now?" she had asked as Misha jumped and almost fell.

"Tamera told me to sit on the washing machine and something would happen," Misha explained, with the same dumb look on her face. Ke-Ke remembered pulling her off the machine and putting her laundry in.

The confused look on Misha's face was worth a million dollars and Ke-Ke never had the heart to tell her that the washing machine was supposed to be on.

***

She managed to make it to her grandmother's house in record time. She was surprised that she had not gotten a car to pull over and the offer of a ride by some nigga, but the hood was kinda slow that day. The only attention she had gotten was from some broke-ass niggas in the alley rolling dice and some drunk dude in the chute who was missing teeth that made some old-school comment that had to do with jelly and jam. Older men always spoke in riddles. You could spend an hour trying to figure out what they were trying to say.

Ti-Ti was on the porch, talking loud on the phone to someone when she walked up. She figured her grandmother had told her to "Take all that noise outside."

"Yo, here Ke-Ke go now. Let me call you back, aiight?" she heard Ti-Ti say as she got closer to the house. "Yo, why Troi tried to press me on the Ave today?" Ti-Ti spoke in her overly dramatic way.

"For real?" Ke-Ke said as she sat down and waited to hear the rest of the story.

"I was like, bitch, we gonna smoke yo' dyke ass." Ti-Ti filled in the blanks for Ke-Ke as she made gun gestures with her hands. "I told that bitch we got access to mad hardware, we goons and we ain't scared to put in that work!" Ti-Ti smiled and nodded like the story ended with her punching Troi in the face, but it hadn't.

"Why the fuck you talk so much?" Ke-Ke sighed and walked into the house, disgusted at how Ti-Ti had escalated a situation that she wasn't even sure herself how she was going to resolve.

"I ain't no punk! I ain't backen down. I'ma ride or die bitch, that's why!" Ti-Ti patted her chest to emphasize her point. Ke-Ke turned her head and caught a glimpse of her grandmother in the kitchen, smiling and shaking her head at Ti-Ti.

"Seems to me that you are a run or die bitch!" Their grandmother laughed as she walked through the living room and up the stairs.

"I wasn't running from her, Grandma! She acted like she was gonna hit me with her car, so I *JOGGED* through the alley to get back here so I could call my troops!"

Ke-Ke smiled at her grandmother as she winked from the top of the stairs. "Yeah, all at once you decided that you needed a little exercise, huh?" Their grandmother laughed again then walked away.

Ke-Ke walked into the living room, sat on the couch, and waited for the plastic to stop making noise underneath her. "I don't know why you out there talken all that big shit. We ain't got no guns!" She half-waited for a response before she continued. "I ain't no punk but you starten a war and you *KNOW* Troi's guns go off!" Ke-Ke felt the need to tell Ti-Ti something that she should have already known.

"We can get some. It's nothing! All I gotta do is call one of my niggas!" Ti-Ti spoke as if she had done it a million times in the past.

Ke-Ke sat on the couch, staring up at Ti-Ti and imagining a world where Ti-Ti actually got her hands on a gun. "The point is, Troi gets down like that on a regular and you know it. I don't know why you would try to make her feel like we are coming for her on that level. Shit, I don't know why you would tell that bitch we was coming at her at all, so she could be expecting something!"

She stared up at Ti-Ti again, wondering if any common sense was beginning to sink in. Ti-Ti just gave her a defiant look and began chanting the lyrics to a song, "I ain't never scared, I ain't never scared," as she bounced her shoulders up and down and licked the blunt she had just rolled. Ke-Ke sighed and pulled out her phone when she felt it vibrating in her pocket.

"Hello?" she answered, still irritated with Ti-Ti.

"Yoooo," Cry's voice came through the phone like music. "I heard y'all talken gun play wit Troi? You gangsta now, boo?" she asked with a playful tone in her voice.

"That's this bitch!" Ke-Ke pointed across the room as if Cry was standing in the room with them.

Ti-Ti raised her hand with the blunt and stuck her tongue out like she was holding a winning scratch off ticket. "Bang, bang! Chalk Em South gang!" she said, loud enough for Cry to hear her through the phone.

"Who dat? Ti-Ti's silly ass?" Cry asked as she laughed.

"Yeah, the one and only!" Ke-Ke rolled her eyes and tried to focus her attention on something else in the room.

"You at her spot, or she at yours?" Cry asked. Ke-Ke noticed how Cry seemed to never want to talk on the phone for too long.

"I'm over here wit her dumb ass. I gotta braid her hair. She call herself, getting a sew-in tomorrow." Ke-Ke looked back over at Ti-Ti who was still bouncing up and down and mouthing song lyrics to herself.

"Damn, a sew-in? Where she getten bread from?" Cry didn't wait for an answer. "Tricken ain't easy, I guess!"

Ke-Ke laughed, knowing that Ti-Ti would be asking her why as soon as she hung up the phone. "I'ma come through though, I got somethen for you, aiight?"

Ke-Ke nodded, "Aiight, I'ma be here!" She hung up the phone and laid back on the couch.

"What the fuck you was laughen at?" Ti-Ti asked. Ke-Ke turned her head just in time to see her grandmother coming back downstairs and held her finger to her lips as a warning to all the cussing that Ti-Ti had been doing while Grandma was upstairs out of earshot.

"What y'all up to now?" their grandmother asked with one eyebrow raised.

"Nothen," they both spoke at the same time as their grandmother looked back and forth at the two of them suspiciously the way she always did.

"I know what that means... Somethen is up!" She studied the two of them and cocked her head to the side, using her telepathic powers to read into the situation. She was usually dead on, or so close that Ti-Ti had started calling her "the gypsy lady" behind her back.

"We just chillen, G-Ma," Ti-Ti tried to throw her off. "Ke-Ke about to do my hair for tomorrow, that's all," she said with an innocent smile on her face.

"Mmmhmmm," their grandmother said as she slowly shuffled into the kitchen, watching them. Ke-Ke tried to mentally prepare herself for one of her famous lectures, but she stayed in the kitchen humming and partially singing a church hymn that Ke-Ke couldn't recognize.

Ti-Ti waved the blunt at Ke-Ke behind her back and nodded towards the front door. They both made their way to the porch before their grandmother could reenter the room. Once on the porch, they both relaxed and resumed their previous conversation. They sat and talked about the neighbors for a minute and were about to take a walk to smoke the blunt when Cry pulled up in front of the house. Her car gleamed and reflected everything around it like it was made from mirrors. The passenger side window slid down and she made a motion for Ke-Ke to come to the car. "Ask her if we can ride and smoke," Ti-Ti said as Ke-Ke walked down the steps towards the car.

Cry steered the car with one hand and glanced around the neighborhood as she drove. Ke-Ke noticed how she seemed to watch everything and everybody so effortlessly. She reminded her of one of those lions on the animal channel that sat and watched over their domain. They always looked strong and in control, even when they weren't doing anything.

"The streets is talken," she said after she had turned a few corners, then reached over her shoulder to take the blunt from Ti-Ti.

"Yeah, I heard that shit already," Ke-Ke responded as she glanced at the old men playing checkers in the front yard, while a rusty barrel grill smoked behind them.

"The shit is, Troi and her little crew believen *everything* they are hearen and they taken that shit to the head!" Cry informed them as she inhaled the thick smoke and blew it out of her nose. "She been on the Ave all day talken about she waiten to see you in the worst way, she got heat for you, and all types of wild shit." Cry reported the severity of the issue without any emotion in her voice.

"That bitch trippen. I ain't said nothen about no damn guns. I ain't really spoken on that shit since it happened!" Ke-Ke pled her case. The thought of the recording rushed back into her mind like an ice-cold tide before she had even realized it. The feelings of confusion and humiliation resurfaced within her as she took the blunt from Cry's hand. She inhaled and wrestled with her thoughts while Cry pulled down

Iceland Alley and then into a parking lot that faced the busiest part of Jefferson Avenue. They sat in silence watching the hood regulars go in and out of the store, catch weed sales, argue, laugh, and talk shit.

"These niggas don't even give a fuck that they put cameras up." Ke-Ke spoke her thoughts out loud as she referred to the police department's initiative to put surveillance cameras up on every block in high crime areas. "They be sellen right in front of them muthafuckas, like they ain't on or somethen. What, they think they don't work?" She remembered her mother complaining about how expensive the cameras were when she was on the phone and how taxpayers should've had a say in whether they wanted to pay for them or not.

"Niggas don't give a fuck," Ti-Ti sang from the backseat, as she cracked the back window to let some of the smoke out of the car.

"Yo, there she go!" Cry tapped Ke-Ke to attention as Troi and two of her friends came around the corner.

"Peep this." Cry turned the car off and cracked her window so they could pick up some of what Troi was saying.

Ke-Ke watched as Troi slapped a few hands and was looking up and down the block like she had lost something. Troi spoke to the crowd of niggas rolling dice in front of the store. She waved her arms and then lifted her flannel shirt to reveal her pistol. She walked away and Ke-Ke could hear her clearly when she said, "Bet that shit. Bet that shit! That's my fucken word!" before she turned and cut through the gravel parking lot that separated the store from the bar.

"That bitch talken cash shit!" Cry smirked, started the car, and pulled out of the parking lot and onto the Ave. Ke-Ke watched the reactions on the faces of people as they stood with their eyes wide and covered their mouths to try and hide the smiles on their faces. "I gotta see that shit!" she could hear someone say as she sped by undetected behind the tinted windows of the car.

"Niggas always wanna see somebody get fucked up!" Ke-Ke said as she tried to visualize how this situation was going to end.

She felt betrayed by some of the niggas that had known what was going on and hadn't told her anything. The same niggas that had cheered her on and sang her praises a few days earlier, and a few of the same niggas that had blown her phone up tryen to fuck her when the recording went public, were now all secret and silent. She knew in her heart that she could walk around that corner right now and niggas wouldn't warn her or anything. They would just wait for Troi to show up so they could say, "Yo, I was there. Troi shot the shit out of Ke-Ke's dumb ass." All niggas ever wanted was a show and something to talk about; they could give a fuck about loyalty.

The truth sank to the pit of her stomach and settled at the bottom like a hundred jagged boulders.

EIGHT

CRY STOPPED THE CAR in front of their grandmother's house and turned the music down with the volume control on the steering wheel. She turned around and asked Ti-Ti if she could give her a minute alone with Ke-Ke. Ti-Ti sucked her teeth, rolled her eyes, and got out of the car. "I got you on this bullshit though!" Cry said.

Ke-Ke watched as she pushed the AM button on her stereo, put her hazard lights on, and shifted the car into neutral. Ke-Ke heard a sound that reminded her of a toy robot she had gotten for Christmas one year as the dashboard rose in front of her like a small elevator that revealed a hidden compartment. She saw two stacks of money, still in their paper bands, a Ziploc bag with a large white rock in it the size of those big chocolate chip cookies her mother used to buy her at the mall, and a chrome pistol with a pearl handle.

Cry reached over her and removed the pistol and a clip that sat next to it that Ke-Ke hadn't even noticed. She shifted the car back into park and turned the hazard lights off and the compartment sunk back into the dash as quickly as it had appeared. "Close ya mouth," Cry laughed. Ke-Ke couldn't even hide the amazed look on her face. She wanted to ask Cry to do it again but didn't want to sound like a little kid. She glanced over as Cry turned the clip over and counted the bullets. She slid the clip into the bottom of the pistol and turned sideways in her seat to face Ke-Ke.

"This shit look small, but it's a .38. This shit right here is the safety." She pointed at a small lever that flipped up and down and revealed a red or green circle, depending on which position it was resting in. Ke-Ke listened carefully as Cry explained how it worked. She showed Ke-Ke how to chamber a round and then how to remove the round from the chamber. She removed three bullets from the clip and showed Ke-Ke how to load it without leaving her fingerprints on them. Ke-Ke's heart beat with excitement as she absorbed all of the information and paid attention to every word that came out of Cry's mouth.

"Your turn," Cry said, and handed the gun to Ke-Ke. "Get it ready," she ordered. Ke-Ke fumbled with the clip, but managed to slide it into place; she pulled on the slide and chambered a round.

"It's ready," she said, hoping she had done it fast enough.

"Do it again," Cry said as she smiled and watched her.

Ke-Ke released the clip and pulled the slide to let the gold bullet pop out of the top of the gun. She grabbed the bullet with her shirt and pushed it back into the top position in the clip.

"Now?" she asked as she looked up at Cry. Cry nodded and she repeated the action of sliding the clip back into the gun and chambering a round.

Cry reached over and covered the gun. "Is it ready? You should be able to tell without looking." Her hand covered the part that showed whether the green or the red circle was showing. "Do it by feel," she coached, but still Ke-Ke was drawing a blank.

Cry placed her thumb on top of Ke-Ke's and positioned it over the safety switch. "There's up and there's down." She moved the lever up and down using Ke-Ke's finger. "Think of it like this. The lever is a mouth. When it's up it's kissing your lips, and when it's down, it's licking your pussy. One is good, but the other is even better!"

Ke-Ke felt a tingle through her body as Cry spoke the words softly while their hands were touching over the cold piece of steel. "So all you gotta decide is if you want your pussy licked or not." Cry clicked the lever back and forth several times then said, "Now look at me." Ke-Ke looked over at Cry and their eyes met and locked on each other.

"Is it ready?" she asked Ke-Ke again. Ke-Ke felt the lever, not wanting to mess up again. "Remember where do you want a mouth the most? What gets you off makes the gun go off." She licked her lips and smiled as she spoke the words but never broke her stare.

Ke-Ke clicked the lever in the opposite position without even thinking. Her heart was beating out of control and she could feel beads of sweat forming on the back of her neck.

"It's ready," she answered with confidence.

Cry glanced down at the gun and nodded. Their eyes met again, but Ke-Ke looked away.

Cry shifted back in her seat and faced forward. She adjusted her stereo and reached over to slap Ke-Ke's hand. Ke-Ke stuffed the gun down the front of her pants and made sure it wasn't visible. She opened the car door and climbed out.

"Hold it down," Cry said before she closed the door completely.

"I got it," Ke-Ke answered and stepped onto the sidewalk. She watched as Cry pulled off and turned the corner and tried to adjust herself as the gun was weighing down the front half of her panties.

"What the fuck was all that shit about?" Ti-Ti hopped off the porch with an attitude. "She had to kiss you goodbye? I already know she likes you!" Ti-Ti spoke her observation like she was certain it would get some sort of reaction.

"What-the-fuck-ever, bitch! Mind yours!" Ke-Ke rolled her eyes at Ti-Ti to throw her off her scent. They walked into the house and were surprised to find that their grandmother had been looking for them.

"Where y'all two shoot off to that quick?" she asked them with a look of concern on her face.

"We just rode out real quick," Ti-Ti answered from her pocket full of stock answers that always sounded fabricated.

"Y'all move too fast." She looked at both of them while she spoke. "It takes time to get it right. It takes time to get anything worthwhile." Ke-Ke listened to her grandmother every time she spoke, even though she didn't always agree with what she was saying. There was something enchanting about the way she spoke. She was always calm and steady about her approach, and her words had a weight to them that Ke-Ke could never explain. "Y'all always runnen around here and jumping there, gone with this one, then gone with that one. What y'all in a rush to see? What y'all rushing to do?"

Their grandmother paused as if she was really waiting for an answer.

"Grandma—" Ti-Ti tried to cut her off, but she had already warmed up.

"It's my turn, child." She cut her eyes at Ti-Ti and that was enough to make the girl close her mouth and sit on the couch next to Ke-Ke.

"Y'all in a rush to be all up in a man's face. Well, let me save you the trouble. Half the time the sex ain't worth nothing and the man attached to it is running a distant second."

Ke-Ke and Ti-Ti both smiled and tried to hold in their laughter.

"See, y'all think y'all invented sex. Y'all think I'm old and I don't know what y'all be up to. I just don't say nothing! Figured I'd let you learn a few things on your own cause Lord knows y'all don't listen to nobody no way. I'm starten to wonder if y'all slow and just ain't never gonna get it. Y'all two ain't figured out nothen yet?"

Ke-Ke and Ti-Ti both sighed in unison, but they knew from experience to keep their mouths shut. Protesting and arguing would only prolong their grandmother's Tyler Perry moment by at least another half an hour. "I done heard both of you bragging about how good y'all 'stuff' is!" She pointed back and forth at them as she looked down at them. Neither one of them had the courage to look her in the face. Ke-Ke wondered how much their grandmother really knew and how long she had been eavesdropping on their conversations when they thought she wasn't paying them any attention. "Oh yeah, I listen to *EVERYTHANG* that goes on in my house! You don't like it... hit the road, Jack!"

Ke-Ke watched as her grandmother momentarily focused her attention on Ti-Ti. "Ti-Ti be talken bout she got that 'wet, wet' and you talken bout yours 'catch on fire' or something. Whatever y'all be sayen, child, please!" Their grandmother leaned against the wall laughing, while she shook her head and looked back and forth at them. "I got a question though." She paused and gathered herself then walked back and forth in front of them like she was performing a stand-up comedy routine. "If what y'all got is so good, why the boys leave just as soon as they get it?"

The words hit Ke-Ke like a blow to her stomach.

"Ti-Ti, I heard you on the phone saying you got that 'snapper' down there. Well, how come you ain't been hooked yet?"

Ti-Ti just put her head down and scratched the back of her neck. She didn't have anything close to an answer for her grandmother.

"I may be old-fashioned and half-crazy to y'all, but in my day, 'good cooking' kept a man where he was. Ya feel me?"

Ke-Ke always thought it was funny when their grandmother tried to use their slang as she threw her arms out, like she was a rap artist, to accentuate her point.

They both nodded their heads to let her know that they were still listening. "Y'all just rush and run and run and rush. It takes time to get it right! You have to learn from your experiences and stop becoming them. It takes time to bloom. That's why the good Lord created seasons! These men y'all deal with is fools too!"

Ke-Ke sat back on the couch and got comfortable as she realized this was going to be one of her grandmother's longer sermons.

"I don't know nobody wit good sense that wants to eat fruit before it's ripe. They must be starving." She had always been good at saying one thing to mean another. "Y'all two need to slow down, because when it does become your season, y'all two gonna be 'Old News' and 'Damaged Goods'!" She pointed at them individually as she assigned them their new names. "In my day, the men that worked the grove took the good apples home, and the damaged ones..." Her voice trailed off as she stopped, laughed, and wiped her hands on her apron. "The damaged ones they threw around at each other, played with them for awhile, but in the end, they left them on the ground or fed them to their horses!"

They watched as their grandmother walked away, humming one of her spirituals and chuckling. "Yes, Lord..." she mumbled something else, but Ke-Ke couldn't make out what she had said. She pictured men in an apple grove, throwing rotten apples at each other.

Ti-Ti nudged her and snapped her out of her daze.

"So we apples now?" Ti-Ti asked with a confused look on her face as she shrugged her shoulders.

"C'mon," Ti-Ti said as she got up and headed for the stairs. Ke-Ke climbed the stairs and followed Ti-Ti to her bedroom. "She think she T.D. Jakes or some shit now. I told you not to buy her those tapes for Christmas!" Ti-Ti fell onto her bed and glared over at Ke-Ke like it was all her fault.

"Whatever," was all Ke-Ke could muster as her mind still tried to untangle the meaning of the apple grove analogy their grandmother had described to them.

Ti-Ti turned on the TV and the stereo with a remote control she had heavily taped to hold in the batteries. She stood in front of the mirror and pulled the front of her pants down to examine the "art" that vandalized her pubic region. She danced seductively and rubbed her breasts in the mirror before she spun around and asked, "You goen to the reggae concert?" Ti-Ti hit the floor and performed a raunchy dance as she looked over her shoulder.

"If I can get some money for an outfit," Ke-Ke answered as she cleaned the comb out over the garbage can and watched Ti-Ti's performance out of the side of her eye.

"I'm getten my shit made. It's a bodysuit!" Ti-Ti hopped to her feet and kept dancing. Ke-Ke nodded, as she knew that Ti-Ti would use *any* excuse to be in public damn near naked. The year before she had worn a yellow fishnet tube dress with orange lace panties and a bra underneath. The outfit was topped off with yellow patent leather knee-high stripper boots that matched a patent leather half-jacket that, of course, she wore unzipped and hanging off of her shoulders. Ke-Ke laughed as she remembered telling her that she looked like an X-rated superhero that caught villains, fucked them unconscious, then called the police. Ti-Ti and her friends had let it *ALL* hang out for that concert and then had the nerve to wonder why niggas kept grabbing on them.

"If I can find some money, I'll definitely go," Ke-Ke said as she recalled how she had gotten so high that night that she didn't remember half of what happened. She had woken up on the floor next to Ti-Ti's bed missing a shoe, her hair a mess. She had found her panties in her purse and she smelled like a pound of weed.

"How you want me to do this?" she asked Ti-Ti as she grabbed a chair and waited for her to stop dancing in front of the mirror.

Ti-Ti got up from the floor where she was doing a split and walked like she was a supermodel over to where Ke-Ke was standing. Ke-Ke could hear her mother's voice in her head when she claimed that Ti-Ti had a chemical imbalance of some sort and she caught herself starting to believe it could be true. She was always in her own world where she seemed be having so much fun, far away from any sort of reality. "I don't know. Shit, you the future hairdresser!" Ti-Ti answered as she sat in the chair. "Make me beautiful" she said in a voice like she was royalty.

Ke-Ke rolled her eyes, knowing that this was a huge waste of time. In a week the sew-in would look like hell, as Ti-Ti was known for not taking care of her hair. She then of course would blame it on her for not putting her braids in right, or not using enough grease, or something else that had nothing to do with how it ended up looking.

She started braiding Ti-Ti's hair. She decided not to tell her about the gun that was in her pants. She was glad that she had chosen baggier clothes that day and had tied the long-sleeve shirt around her waist so the back of the shirt covered the front of her pants like an apron. "Where you get the money for a sew-in anyway, bitch?" Ke-Ke asked after a few minutes of listening to the radio in silence.

"I got fans, girl! You know that." Ti-Ti snapped her fingers in the air. "They do favors for me and I do favors for them."

Ke-Ke left it alone, knowing that she wasn't going to get a straight answer. She dared not enter the dark and twisted world that was very much Ti-Ti's sex life.

She finished the braids and waited while Ti-Ti checked them in the mirror. "It's straight!" she said with a smile as she gave Ke-Ke an exaggerated hug. Ke-Ke pushed her away and made sure that her scalp was greased, knowing that Ti-Ti couldn't be bothered.

The two of them were leaving the room when Ke-Ke felt the gun slip down her leg and hit the floor with a thud. Ti-Ti spun around before she could grab it.

"Ohhh shiiit!" Ti-Ti said as they both stared at the chrome gun that was resting on the floor against Ke-Ke's foot.

"Shut the fuck up," Ke-Ke whispered before Ti-Ti got all loud and out of control.

"You got the hammer?" Ti-Ti closed the door and stared down at it with amazement, like it was a big dick.

"You don't never tell me shit!" She pouted as she reached down and picked it up.

Ke-Ke managed to see that it was on safety before Ti-Ti began posing in the mirror like she was a Charlie's Angel. "Take a picture," she demanded as she handed Ke-Ke her cell phone. Ke-Ke took the phone and snapped the camera as Ti-Ti struck one dumb pose after the other.

"What y'all doen up there wit that door closed?" their grandmother called up the stairs and interrupted the photo shoot.

"Nothen!" they answered at the same time. Ti-Ti tossed the gun back to Ke-Ke like she had never laid hands on it. Ke-Ke put it back into her pants and tried to make sure it was secure as possible. They ran down the stairs where their grandmother stood with her arms folded and a look of distrust on her face.

"You getten ready to go?" she asked as the two passed her at the bottom of the stairs like she was a police officer.

"Yeah, in a minute," Ke-Ke answered in the most innocent voice she could come up with.

"Good, cause we gonna pray as a family before you leave."

Ke-Ke sighed and cocked her head when their grandmother turned her back, while Ti-Ti rolled her eyes and made gestures like she was stomping her foot then made like she was going to punch her in the back of the head. Ke-Ke had to put her head down so she wouldn't laugh and give her away.

They joined hands in a mini circle as they had usually done only before a big family meal an their grandmother prayed over them:

> MAY THE LORD
> WATCH BETWEEN ME AND THEE
> WHILE WE'RE ABSENT
> ONE FROM ANOTHER.
> AMEN.

She looked over at Ke-Ke, squeezed her hand, then winked. "Prepare a table for my enemies..." Her eyes pierced Ke-Ke but still had that soft loving glow that was always present. "Revenge is the Lord's," she finished.

Ke-Ke could feel the warmth of her grandmother's love wash over her entire body. At that moment, she realized that her grandmother must have had an idea what was going on, but for whatever reason, she wasn't going to intervene. She was "giving it to God" as they had both become accustomed to hearing her say.

NINE

"I'm gonna walk Ke to the corner, Grandma," Ti-Ti said as she put on her coat and sat on the couch to slip on her Timberlands.

"You do that baby, and y'all be careful." She looked back at Ke-Ke and smiled before she disappeared into the kitchen.

"Let's go," Ti-Ti said as she walked past Ke-Ke and out of the door. Ke-Ke followed her and closed the door behind them, still wondering how their grandmother seemed to know or have an idea about *everything* whether you told her or not.

She walked down the front stairs slowly, as she didn't want the gun to fall out of her pants again. She turned around and looked back at the house before she took the gun out and pulled the slide back to chamber a round. Then she slipped it back into the front of her pants.

"We here, bitch!" Ti-Ti yelled out like Troi could hear her from wherever she was lurking.

"Shut yo' ass up!" Ke-Ke smacked Ti-Ti in the back of her head. "You be tryen to start shit all the time! This whole shit is your fault anyway!"

Ti-Ti stumbled from the blow and ducked as she anticipated more.

"Me?" she pointed to herself, when she had gotten out of arm's reach of Ke-Ke.

"Yeah you!" Ke-Ke pointed in her direction to make sure Ti-Ti would have no more doubts about who she was speaking of. The two of them walked the rest of the way to the corner in silence. Ti-Ti reached out to slap her up, but Ke-Ke grabbed Ti-Ti and hugged her cousin like it was the last time she was going to see her. She left Ti-Ti standing on the corner and didn't look back.

Ke-Ke walked the rest of the blocks on high alert for Troi or any of her crew. She had never been on edge like this and her skin prickled with a strong anxiety. At the same time, the thought that she had the hardware to protect herself empowered her and she started to realize why men loved guns so much. A feeling of security began to surround her like a blanket. Her mind bounced back and forth among what had happened between her and Cry in the car and the feelings she had felt, her grandmother's prayer, and that image of black men in an apple grove somewhere. The thoughts carried her down the street in a dreamlike state and before she knew it she was around the corner from her house.

Pam was on the corner in plain view with her posse of crackheads when Ke-Ke turned the corner, but she was too busy trying to flag down a car to notice her. She made her way to the house thinking that if Pam had said the wrong thing to her, she probably would've popped her ass. The gun was a license to not take shit from anybody and she all at once found herself dying to use it or at least pull it out on somebody and see their reaction. She walked up the sidewalk, relieved to find that her mother's car was not in the driveway.

"Misha!" she called out as she walked into the kitchen to see if there was anything worth eating. Misha and Tamera ran down the stairs laughing, joking, and bumping into things on their way.

"Aiight girl, I'ma holla at you!" she heard Misha say as she walked Tamera to the door. Ke-Ke caught a glimpse of her before the door closed and shook her head. *That girl was way too young to have an ass like that!*

Ke-Ke put together a turkey sandwich and headed up the stairs while Misha followed and began her game of twenty million questions. The girl always wanted to know every move she made. Ke-Ke would find herself at times making up stories to entertain her and to get her out of her face. Misha was like her live-in groupie, even though Misha would choose death over admitting how much she really looked up to her.

"What you and Ti-Ti was doen?" she asked as Ke-Ke tried to close the door on her. Misha had mastered her own defensive tactic for that maneuver and ended up in the room with her.

"Nothen girl, damn! Why you so fucken nosy?" Ke-Ke would never admit that she, at times, liked the way her little sister would hang onto her every word with her eyes wide and mouth open. The phone rang and Misha went to answer it as Ke-Ke kicked her door shut behind her and sat on her bed, looking around the room. She rested her eyes on the back of the door, knowing that it would pop back open at any moment and Misha would want to finish her interview.

Ke-Ke stared at the back of the door while she ate the sandwich and waited for the inevitable. She lay back on the bed and stared at the ceiling when it hit her that something was missing from the back of her door. She sat back up. The Dereon leather that her aunt had brought her back from the city was gone. Ke-Ke was the first person to have that coat in the hood and the only one to have it in that color scheme. It had made her famous on the Ave the year before and she treasured it, even though she didn't wear it that often anymore.

"Misha, where the fuck is my coat at?" she yelled through the closed door to her room. She got up off the bed, ready to smack the hell out of her little sister for taking something from her room without permission.

Misha came back in the room with her hands in the air, like she was being held at gunpoint. "Wait, wait, you said I could wear it once in a while, remember?"

Ke-Ke's anger level subsided as she remembered she had told Misha that, but couldn't remember why. "Where's it at, Misha?" She held out her hand, expecting for her to go to her room and get it.

"I let Tamera wear it home. I'm gonna get it back tomorrow at school. She ain't have nothen to wear and

111

her mom wasn't coming back to pick her up," Misha explained, trying to make her sister feel the sense of urgency that she had felt for her friend.

"That was my fucken coat, Misha! How you gonna give *MY* shit out? You always given shit to that little dusty bitch. This ain't the fucken Salvation Army!" Ke-Ke walked over to her window and looked out, as if Tamera would still be in sight. She walked back to her bed and sat down, glaring at Misha and trying to think of more ways to insult her stupidity.

"I'ma get it back tomorrow, Ke!" Misha looked like she was getting ready to cry.

"With or without the roaches, bitch?" Ke-Ke stared a hole through Misha's face. Deep down she felt sorry for her. It really wasn't about the coat; it was about people taking advantage of her. She could never find the words to make Misha understand though. Her heart was too good. The only thing that kept her from jumping on Misha was the fact that it was half her fault for not noticing it when Tamera left.

Ke-Ke sat on the bed, shaking her head, thinking that she had to stop smoking so much weed. "Y'all caught me sleepen," she said as she looked back at Misha. She got a kick out of the way Misha would jump every time she spoke.

"Ohh shit!" Ke-Ke stood up as a thought struck her all at once. She pushed Misha out of the way and flew down the stairway in a second.

"What?" Misha called out behind her. "I told you I'd get it back tomorrow." Her words trailed off as Ke-Ke grabbed a coat out of the downstairs closet and was out the door. She sprinted up the block and hit the corner without slowing down.

"Run, Forrest, ruuun!" she heard Pam yell out and laugh behind her. She didn't have time to think about Pam as she bolted down the street and hit the alley that led to the Ave. She reached down, surprised that the gun was still secure in the front of her pants and hadn't fallen out of her panties. She slowed down a little, managed to wrestle it out, and slipped it into her coat pocket. She had almost reached the end of the alley when she heard a loud BANG! echo through the air. She made it to the Ave, now completely out of breath, and squinted to see three blocks down in the dark. She was too late.

A siren rang out and she looked across the street to see a police car parked in the darkness in the driveway of an abandoned house. They sat there and did paperwork when they were bored or called themselves spying on people. The car skidded onto the Ave and screeched to a halt in front of the store. Ke-Ke jogged down the sidewalk, trying to stay unnoticed as she tried to get closer to the scene. She took cover in a doorway and put her hood up when she had gotten a half a block away from the crowd. The lights flashed wildly off the buildings as she could hear voices saying, "Yo, that shit is fucked up!" as they talked on cell phones and crossed the street to avoid the police presence.

That's when Ke-Ke noticed Troi across the street, talking loud and fighting with the police. They slammed her up against the car and then bent her over the hood, while they wrenched handcuffs on her wrists. "Fuck that bitch! I did it! I told y'all niggas I was gonna light that bitch up!" She kicked wildly but was no match for the officers who shoved her head into the backseat of the patrol car and slammed the door.

Ke-Ke glanced back at the crowd that was slowly starting to break away from the front of the store and was finally able to catch a glimpse of Tamera on the ground in her coat with the hood still over her head. Her body lay motionless while a dark puddle grew underneath her and trickled over the curb into the street. Ke-Ke dropped her head.

"Damn!" she said out loud. She looked back at the patrol car, where Troi was banging her head up against the window, still screaming like a madwoman. Police cars flooded the Ave from every angle and turned it into a light show. Officers spoke in small circles in the middle of the street, began taping off the scene, and redirected traffic down Bartlett.

Two officers returned to the car that held Troi and began to pull away from scene. Ke-Ke took off her hood and stepped underneath the closest streetlight so Troi could see her when they passed. Troi looked like she had seen a ghost. Ke-Ke could see the confusion in her face as their eyes locked.

When the car was out of sight, she put her hood back on and walked back towards the alley. She stuffed her hands back in her coat pockets and felt the cold steel in her pocket and felt stupid for getting that close to the scene with it still on her. She stuffed the gun back into the front of her pants and adjusted her coat.

"Prepare a table for my enemies!" Ke-Ke whispered the words that came out of nowhere as she stared up at the night sky. She took a long deep breath and felt a warmth come over her body as she remembered the look in her grandmother's eyes.

"Revenge is the Lord's."

TEN

MISHA DIDN'T BELIEVE ANYTHING that Ke-Ke was trying to explain to her until their mother burst into the house screaming.

"Tamera got shot on Jefferson! Where the hell is Misha?" She slammed the door and was up the stairs before Ke-Ke or Misha could answer her. She exhaled heavily and fell against the wall when she saw Misha sitting on the bed in Ke-Ke's room. "Why the hell did y'all leave this house, when I told you earlier to stay your asses here!" She made a motion towards Misha, but Ke-Ke intercepted her and held her arms.

"Ma, Misha was here the whole night!" She could feel her mother's body relax as she let her go.

"Well, she could've been! I've told her to stop hangen wit that little fast-assed girl! Always bringen roaches over here and shit!" Their mother cursed Tamera's name a few more times and then turned to leave the room. "I saw the trucks out there, it's probably already on the news," she said as she walked away.

Ke-Ke and Misha walked to her bedroom and watched as she changed the stations and stopped on the news. "Channel 10 news reports a fatal shooting on the city's West Side that is reportedly being called a mistaken identity murder," Janet Lomax spoke from the colorful news studio. "Deanna King reports." It switched to a reporter holding a microphone on Jefferson Avenue, with the crime scene and police cars in the background.

"Thanks, Janet. I'm here on Jefferson Avenue where a young girl was shot earlier today. She was rushed to Strong Memorial Hospital but has been pronounced dead. The story we are getting is that her own sister reportedly shot her. The suspect was apprehended at the scene. She is a young woman by the name of Troi Andrews. She has been charged with involuntary manslaughter, reckless endangerment, possession of a prohibited weapon, and additional drug charges. We are being told that she was in possession of crack cocaine at the time of the arrest."

A mug shot of Troi flashed across the screen.

"Terrible," Janet responded from the studio. "Now you say the victim is her sister? Was there some sort of family feud or..." Janet's voice trailed off.

"No Janet, it had been reported that the suspect Troi Andrews mistakenly shot her sister. All we know right now is the tragedy seems to have stemmed from a conflict over an underground movie or recording of some sort. Police are trying to speak to witnesses but are getting very little information at this time."

Ke-Ke listened intently to the story, knowing that someone had been talking to the police for them to know that much.

"Wow!" Janet responded as the camera shot switched back to her sitting in the studio and the picture of Deanna became a small square in the corner of the television. "Tragic, extremely tragic situation. Thank you, Deanna," Janet said as the small square that framed Deanna disappeared from the screen.

Misha was inconsolable. She sank to the floor in a corner of their mother's bedroom kicking and screaming. Ke-Ke tried to help, but her mother waved her away and wrapped her arms around Misha. Ke-Ke glanced back at the television where they had moved on to sports. She decided to leave the two of them alone and headed back to her room, the sound of Misha's screams ripping her heart to shreds.

She fell back on her bed and stared at the ceiling as the thoughts crawled through her mind like long-legged spiders. The feeling of being blessed and lucky and the feeling of guilt played a high-speed game of ping-pong in her conscience. She was still in too much shock to keep score. She watched, helpless, as they volleyed for domination.

Ke-Ke knew that Misha would be a mess for a while. She listened as she tried to speak through her sobbing about how it was all her fault while her mother tried to convince her otherwise. Ke-Ke and her mother had always tried to shield Misha from the realties that took place in the neighborhood that surrounded their two-story rented home. They would always find creative ways to explain things or outright lie to her to keep from having to explain something. But Ke-Ke always knew that the approach would do more harm than good. One day something like this would happen and the crystal bubble that they had created for Misha would crash into the pavement of reality—a cold, hard ground littered with blunt tobacco and empty bottles of cheap whiskey. A place where innocence was a weakness that got exploited, and happiness was sold in little plastic bags. The fantasy had to end one day.

Ke-Ke listened to the noises coming from the other room with the same discomfort as the time she had listened at the door when Ti-Ti lost her virginity. She thought back to science class when they had to watch movies of a snake shedding his skin and babies being born. The pain that shattered Misha's world was just part of life that she had to experience by herself at one point or another. Ke-Ke could hear her mother as she tried to say something that would calm Misha down and stop the pain, knowing deep down that no words could explain that kind of pain away.

Later that night, after Misha had cried herself to sleep, Ke-Ke stood in the doorway looking down at her. A tissue was still balled up in her hand. She glanced around her sister's room that was filled with stuffed animals that didn't really exist and dolls that spoke and took you on adventures. Misha's whole life had been a fairy tale that she had believed and Ke-Ke felt a lump form in her throat when she thought of how tomorrow Misha would wake up and not believe in magic or unicorns anymore.

She scanned the room until her eyes rested on a board game that Misha had loved to play when she was younger. The box was full of color and had pictures of smiling kids holding candy and skipping around. An elf held an oversized candy cane, smiling as he invited and guided children through this mystical place where they could dance with a gingerbread man and eat all the candy they could find. She shook her head as she looked back and forth at the board game then at her little sister curled up on top of her pink blanket that had a large fairy stitched onto it. She felt her own tears beginning to swell in her eyes as she remembered how she had been yanked from that world years ago and into the real one forever. She watched Misha sleep and wondered how and if she would survive in a world where a fairy was a nigga that walked funny and Candy Land...

"Candy Land is a muthafucka!" She whispered the words aloud before she clicked the light off and walked out of the room.

ELEVEN

THE NEXT DAY WAS A SUNDAY. Ke-Ke awoke, surprised to smell breakfast being cooked. She figured she had to be dreaming, because their mother never made breakfast unless Kent had spent the night.

She got up and walked to the top of the stairs but didn't hear her mother talking to anyone. He must be on his way, she thought, and returned to her room and collapsed on the bed. She was almost back to sleep when her mother knocked and then opened the door.

"Girl, get up and come eat," her mother spoke in a light-hearted voice that Ke-Ke remembered from her childhood years. Ke-Ke felt her hand slap against her leg when she didn't respond.

"What?" she asked as she turned over.

"Get up! And put some clothes on too. I don't know how y'all girls walk around wit a string goen up y'all ass!"

Ke-Ke turned over in time to catch her mother give her the "you nasty" look. Ke-Ke played like she was sticking her hands down the front of her panties and pleasuring herself. She stuck her tongue out and moved her hips in a circular motion.

"The niggas love it though," she said as she winked up at her mother. "I'ma get you some for Kent," she teased as her mother stood in the doorway with a disgusted look on her face.

"Hmmpf." She walked off. "If he need a piece of string up my ass to turn him on, I guess he gonna have to just stay turned off."

Ke-Ke listened as her mother walked down the hall mumbling, knocked on Misha's door, then walked in and closed the door.

Ke-Ke sat up with a smile on her face as she thought back to when she was living with her father and he had told her about her mother entering "hot body" contests when they lived in Texas. Her father described a carefree person that Ke-Ke had never had the pleasure of meeting. She would own the stage and no female in the area could hang with her. She had won contest after contest, and Ke-Ke could only vaguely remember trophies next to the television when she was a lot younger. "Yeah, yo' momma was hot in the tail too. She won wet T-shirt contests and everything when she was younger. I used to have pictures, but I threw them all away by now."

Ke-Ke could remember the smile on her father's face as he told the stories. They were hard to believe, but Ke-Ke figured that there were too many details for even her father to be making the stories up. He told of how she was offered to be in a rap video but turned it down because she was too afraid of her mother seeing her on TV and disowning her.

Ke-Ke loved hearing the stories of how her mother acted during the happier times in her life. She rarely got to see her cut loose and really have a good time. She seemed to stay mad and was always cursing about one thing or another and usually ended up taking whatever her issue was out on her and Misha.

One time when she was in Maryland still living with her father, she remembered looking through his drawers for money and came across an old stack of pictures underneath his socks. She flipped through them and there was her mother, on stage in a string bikini, dancing between two other females. She laughed to herself whenever she thought of those pictures, but never had the nerve to confront her mother with the evidence. Her grandmother had told her years ago that, "Every woman has her own little bag of secrets," and over the years Ke-Ke had learned that the phrase was definitely true. The secret was something that she cherished. It reminded her that her mother was human and had been young once too.

Ke-Ke climbed out of her bed with a smile on her face, knowing that she would forever hold a few cards that her mother never even knew she had. The woman could scream, preach, yell, and talk shit all she wanted, but the pictures told the story of someone who wasn't perfect after all. The story of a woman twho had learned lessons the hard way, as she had so often criticized her daughters for doing. The story of a woman who was no stranger to showing a little skin or having a "piece of string" up her ass.

Ke-Ke walked towards her mirror and turned around, looking over her shoulder at how the silk fabric disappeared in between her ass cheeks. She put on her sweatpants, thinking that back in the day she would've given her mother a run for her money. "Haaater!" she yelled down the hallway before she ran down the stairs, but her mother didn't respond.

In the kitchen, she was shocked to see her mother's signature breakfast buffet. Grits with cheese and butter, fried ham, scrambled eggs, home fries with pieces of bacon in them, flaky biscuits with strawberry preserves, and corned beef hash sat in bowls and platters in the middle of the table. She sat down at the table, amazed, and tried to remember the last time she had seen her mother put a meal together like this one. Her mind drifted against her will: "Kent must've fucked the dog shit out of her last night!"

She reached for the orange juice before the images flooded her mind and scarred her for life. "That damn Viagra!" she said out loud, not realizing her mother had come down the stairs.

"What?" her mother asked.

"Uh... nothen, Ma!"

Ke-Ke prayed silently that she wouldn't push the issue. The two sat at the table, passed food, and existed in a silence that had become all too familiar over the past few years.

"And why you do that to your friend?" her mother finally broke the silence.

"What?" Ke-Ke asked hoping that it didn't lead to an argument.

"Trish, that's what! Twenty-six stitches. Does that sound familiar?" Her mother held her cup of coffee and rolled her eyes as she spoke.

"Ma, she tried to play me, she..."

"So you scarred that girl for life cause she tried to *play* you? You act like you was raised by a pack of wolves." Her mother gave her a look like she was a stranger in her house.

Ke-Ke sat back in her seat and sighed heavily, knowing that her mother would never listen to anything she had to say.

"I don't know where you get that street mentality bullshit from. You know her people was talken about pressing charges against yo' wannabe-thug ass." Her mother raised her voice as she relayed the news. "And I ain't about to be housen no felon! I'm getten real tired of your bullshit, Ketasia. You know that could've easily been you or your sister layen face down in the street last night. You know she *loves* to wear your clothes and do *everything* you do. Did you think about that when you was beefen wit that she-male lunatic? Your shit is starten to hit too close to home and I'll be damned if you endanger me or your little sister."

She spoke the words as if she had given them a lot of thought or written them down. "It's bad enough you got every drug dealer in the neighborhood stopping by every ten minutes. People think we runnen a whore house around here or somethen."

"Ma, they don't be drug dealers..."

"They don't have jobs!" her mother cut her off again. "How a nigga drive a fifty-thousand-dollar truck and ain't got no job?"

Ke-Ke stopped herself from smiling when she figured it must've been Ahmed from the hair store that she was talking about.

"Ma, he works at the hair store!" Ke-Ke defended him.

"Hair store? He works at a crack house that sells hair... maybe!" Her mother laughed at her own joke. "Girl, I was born in the morning, but not this morning! Ain't enough weave in the world could buy a truck like that!"

Ke-Ke just shook her head and covered her face with her hands as she felt a headache coming.

"Since he got so much money from selling hair, you tell him that from now on you need rent money, cause I'm going to start charging you rent to stay here," her mother announced. "Sixty-five dollars a week, and that don't include food."

"Ma!" Ke-Ke tried to protest, but her mother raised her hand and turned her head, the universal sign for, "I'm not trying to hear it."

"You *need* to find another place to live too, cause if the police come knocken on my door, I'ma turn yo' ass over like a pancake. You'll be right back in that place you was before, what they call it? Yeah, Lick Em Academy" She laughed and clapped her hands at the unofficial name for the girls' correctional camp that Ke-Ke had already been to twice for incidents at school.

Ke-Ke glared at her mother as the anger rose in her. There was no way in hell she was going back to that place.

The center for at-risk youth, as they called it, was a place that stank all the time and was either too hot or too cold. She remembered going through intake and having to strip off her clothes and bend over in front of the guards. She could still feel the dingy uniform on her skin that was too tight and too short. The male guards were famous for making inappropriate remarks and violating their privacy. Ke-Ke had talked to a girl that had been there almost a year and she told the story of being in the shower and turning around to see this nasty fat guard they had named "Cheeseburger" feeling himself through his pants. She had reported the incident in writing, but no one believed her word over his.

Then there were the girls who were too fast and didn't mind the attention and advances. Ke-Ke thought back to how certain girls were let out of the quads at night and she could hear music and sexual noises coming from somewhere off in the distance. The girl would return to the quad smelling like weed and alcohol and usually had a bag full of candy bars to show for it. They were given larger portions at mealtimes, longer phone calls, and other gifts that really didn't amount to much. They called themselves the "P-Girls," the "P" standing for pimp, and they really believed that they were beating the system.

That place was where Ke-Ke learned that there were grown-ass men that wouldn't hesitate to get some young pussy if they could get away with it. She had learned how to use that fact to her advantage over the years. The P-Girls reminded her of something Tiff had always told her: "Don't be out here taken hard dick and bubblegum!"

Ke-Ke and a couple of the other girls in her quad had vowed that they would only fuck a guard for their freedom and nothing less. She thought of Tonya, a girl she had met the first day she got there. "Shit, I'd fuck the Twinkies out of Cheeseburger if he offer to open that gate!" They had all laughed themselves to sleep off that one.

But Ke-Ke's smile disappeared as she remembered the time at dinner when they served hot dogs. She hungrily ate hers. When she came back to the table to wait to be dismissed, she looked around and realized nobody else had touched their hot dogs. Later that night, when she heard muffled moans and groaning after lights out she figured out why. All around her it was "Ohh shiit" and "Daamn!" as bunks squeaked while the girls worked the hot dogs like sex toys. She had to resort to wrapping her head with her pillow in order to fall asleep that night.

The next day she thought about how the girls had already become institutionalized when they went for breakfast and joked about their "visits from their boyfriends." They traded fake stories that entertained and sounded real over boiled eggs and burned toast. But Ke-Ke ended up kicking herself for not knowing enough to save her hot dog too.

Misha coming downstairs with her eyes still red and irritated interrupted her memories and thoughts of the place.

"Hey, girl." Their mother got up and gave Misha a big hug. Misha whispered something and sat down at the table, grabbing a plate. She watched her mother's mouth move as she tried to get inside her little sister's head, but her thoughts were already working on solving her new dilemma. She needed money for rent or her own place, clothes, and a hairstyle for the upcoming concert. She decided that her best bet was to call Cry, hoping that she could put her onto a hustle or something.

So much was going on that Ke-Ke had forgotten about something that now tied her stomach into knots. She tried to come up with ways to justify, postpone, and forget, like she had done in the past, but nothing was working. The thoughts made her heart feel black and she didn't even know if she had the strength to go through with it, but she knew something had to be said and done. She couldn't just leave things the way they were.

TWELVE

KE-KE WAS UP IN HER ROOM, sitting on her bed, trying to decide what to wear for the day. She picked her phone up and checked for messages. Ahmed had called six times. Her bend over at the door trick always kept them coming back, no matter how much attitude she gave them. She picked out her outfit for the day: a pair of jeans that she had torn the back pockets off of and shredded with a razor all the way up to the belt loops. The washing machine had done the rest of the job and she always made sure to wear a bright pair of boy-short panties that would be clearly visible through the frayed material. She was getting out of the shower and putting on her homemade moisturizer, a combination of cocoa butter and baby oil, when Misha knocked at the door. This time she opened the door and let her in without cursing her out or telling her to leave.

"Where you going?" Misha started in with her questions. "Can I go with you? Ma trying to drop me off at Grandma's house and I don't wanna go," Misha half-begged and half-asked, like she already knew what the first answer was going to be.

"Not this time. I got some business to handle today," Ke-Ke answered her without looking up and kept rubbing the lotion on her legs until her skin started to shine.

She finished then glanced up to see that Misha had already walked out of the bathroom mumbling, "Something strange for a little change."

"What you say, Misha?" Ke-Ke surprised her with the question.

"I ain't say nothen," Misha stuttered and disappeared into her room.

Ke-Ke closed the door to the bathroom and inspected the quick shave job she had given her "girly parts" in the shower. She usually tried to cut a design into the hair that remained above it, but she didn't have the patience for all that today. She rubbed the lotion around the reddened area, hoping it wouldn't itch too bad when it started to grow back; that feeling was enough to make a girl want to let an afro grow between her legs.

She had heard women at the salon talk about waxing, but it sounded too painful. She laughed out loud as she remembered Tiff being against all of it. "Now, I might mow the lawn a little, IF it's a special occasion... but I keep somethen down there! Y'all bitches crazy! Shiit! A nigga just gonna have to run through the jungle if he wanna get to MY lake!" She had the women in stitches all over the shop with that one. "Shit, a nigga that's into that make me think he like little girls or somethen. Y'all better watch these niggas!" she warned the ladies as she put on her serious face, but they were still laughing uncontrollably.

She stood in front of the mirror, dropped her towel, and replaced her hoop nipple ring with the barbell piercing with the blue "diamonds" at either end. She picked it out reluctantly after the man at the shop told her that it wasn't recommended to start with hoops.

She went to her closet and picked out a half-shirt that had been styled to look like a football practice jersey. The shirt was white with the number one painted on the front and back and was mesh from the shoulders down to the elastic band that hugged her ribcage. She decided to wear the jersey with no bra so that the ends of the barbell piercing would poke through the holes "by accident." She completed her outfit with a pair of knock-off high-heeled Gucci boots, grabbed her phone, and headed for the front door.

Ke-Ke passed her mother on the stairs and felt her nudge her and almost knock her off balance, but she caught herself on the handrail. "Ma, damn!" Ke-Ke said, looking up at her mother who continued to walk up the stairs like she hadn't done anything.

When she got to the top of the stairs, she turned around like she was some kind of pimp and spoke in a deep voice, "Bitch better have my money!" She burst into laughter, clapping her hands, and disappeared from the top of the stairwell in the direction of her bedroom. Ke-Ke couldn't help but smile at the joke as she walked onto the porch. She never understood how she could despise and love that woman at the same time.

The walk went fast, as it always did, when you dreaded what was going to happen at your destination. She thought back to when she was younger and her mother had promised her a spanking for whatever she had done while they were out. They could be hours from home, yet it would only seem like minutes before they were home and the ass-whoopings began! The flip side was if you had to go to the bathroom, whoever was driving took forever and managed to hit every bump and traffic light on the way. The mysteries of life, she thought, as she entered the corner store.

Five minutes later she was standing in front of Trish's house. She looked both ways up the street before climbing the steps and knocking on the door. There were a few noises, then Ke-Ke could hear someone shuffling towards the door and fumbling with the deadbolt locks, the chain, and then the doorknob. Ke-Ke bowed her head as the door creaked open.

"Oh, whatup Ke?" Trish sounded nervous. Ke-Ke was actually surprised that Trish hadn't slammed the door in her face when she saw who it was.

"Um... hey!" was all she could think to reply without having the strength to lift her head and look Trish in the face.

"You ain't still mad, are you? I mean, you got me back. You got me back good too."

"Naw girl, I just came by to say..."

"You ain't gotta say nothen. Come in." Trish interrupted her apology and held the door for her. Ke-

Ke followed Trish into the dark house and lifted her head to see Trish turning on the lights and the television before she sat down on the couch and revealed her heavily bandaged face. Ke-Ke paused as she took in the visual of what she had actually done to her friend but tried not to stare and make Trish feel uncomfortable at the same time.

She sat on the couch and pulled out the blunt and some weed she had found in her sock drawer. Ke-Ke was getting her words together in her head when she was distracted by a glossy red binder that was sitting on the coffee table on top of the magazines.

"What's this?" she asked as she picked up the binder and opened it.

Trish exhaled and sighed. "It's my portfolio."

Ke-Ke opened it and saw color and black and white pictures of Trish wearing different outfits with different backgrounds.

"Portfolio?" Ke-Ke tried to act like she wasn't struggling with the word as she stared up at Trish with a confused look on her face.

"I was going to be a model, Ke. I never told y'all because my auntie always said that when you talk about things, they never happen. I was just picked by this agency in New York City. I was supposed to be leaving next month." Her voice trailed off into silence. Ke-Ke just stared at Trish with her mouth open. The reality and guilt chorused in her mind and the notes pounded away at the depths of her heart. She turned the pages of the album and felt a numbness come over her body. She turned page after page and felt the lump develop in her throat, knowing that she held another person's hopes and dreams that would never be realized. Images of Trish on a runway in Paris flashed through her mind and Ke-Ke felt as if the book would turn to ashes in her hands at any moment.

"It's not your fault, Ke," Trish broke her train of guilt-ridden thoughts. "I done did a lot of dirt out here to people. Remember when I cut that bitch up at the carnival two summers ago? I guess I had it coming..."

"That wasn't your fault, Trish," Ke-Ke attempted to console her friend.

"Yeah it was. I didn't have to take it that far. I *always* take shit too far," she said as she patted the bandages on her face instead of scratching. "I been goen to church a little bit and you know, what goes around comes around. I was stupid to think I would get away with that shit, or anything I ever done for that matter. Everything always catches up to you."

Trish's voice sounded weak and defeated as she spoke with the wisdom of a woman twice her age. Ke-Ke laid back on the couch and fixed her eyes on Trish, wondering how everything she had done would come back around to her.

"Even the shit I did to you, Ke. That shit was fucked up. I should've never put you out there like that with my people. They some nasty motherfuckas anyway!" Trish just stared off in space like she was remembering every wrong she had ever committed. "My biggest mistake was thinken that I was really gonna make it out of this bitch, believing in some fucken dream! I was born and raised in the hood and I'm probably gonna die here. It's just how shit works for people like us."

"That shit ain't true, girl." Ke-Ke felt angered by her friend's defeatism, even though deep down she knew she felt the same way. Somehow it always stung when someone said it out loud.

"I ain't goen nowhere now," Trish said as she changed the channels, trying to find something to watch. "I don't blame you though, Ke. I honestly don't have no hard feelings towards you. Can you believe that I thought I was gonna be in movies and shit? I was fucken trippen." Trish laughed aloud at herself and the sound flew across the room and pieced Ke-Ke's heart like daggers.

"Stop that shit! You can be whatever the fuck you wanna be, Trish." Trish just shook her head and smiled.

She reached over for the blunt that Ke-Ke had been holding in her hand since she had walked in the door.

They smoked in silence for a few moments before Trish confessed, "I used to smoke to get high, now it's the only thing that helps the pain from these stitches."

Ke-Ke struggled to find the best way to apologize to Trish and to let her know that it was her fault and that she was still beautiful and she could still live out her dreams, but she didn't know how to begin. Apologizing had never been something she was good at and her thoughts locked into a jumbled ball as she tried to figure out what to say first. The two sat in silence, passing the blunt back and forth and watching cartoons.

"The good part about it though," Trish finally broke the silence, "my people got insurance on my face right after I signed that contract. I'm about to get paid!" Trish raised her hands above her head and danced like it was just as good as being selected as a Victoria's Secret model.

"You need to save that shit for college, girl." Ke-Ke gave her the best advice she had probably ever given anyone in her life.

"Shiit, fuck that! I'm getten a car, some clothes, a pound of weed and shit... I don't even know what else... I can't wait!" Trish looked over at Ke-Ke like she had the bandages on her face. "You trippen!"

The two talked off and on for another hour. Eventually Ke-Ke looked over to see Trish had fallen asleep. She flipped through Trish's portfolio and shook her head. She never knew her friend could take such beautiful pictures. She looked over at Trish asleep in the chair, then quietly gathered her things and left the house, making sure the door didn't slam behind her. She lit the half-blunt that was left as she walked up the sidewalk, unable to fight her tears anymore.

The fact that Trish had no hard feelings somehow seemed to make things even harder to process. She stopped walking and looked down at the ground, wiping the tears off her face as she remembered she hadn't even been able to find the nerve to apologize. She parted the bushes that led to the chute and heard her grandmother's words, "Sometimes an apology ain't nothen but an insult."

THIRTEEN

KE-KE WALKED IN A HALF-DAZE, smoking weed and trying
to get her head together. She thought back to when she
was younger and went to church with her grandmother.
She had been an usher, sang in the choir, played the
drums, and at one time considered herself to be "saved."
The memories and images circled in her head like the
billows of smoke she exhaled. That time seemed so long
ago. What had happened to her in the past few years
even she didn't understand. She used to enjoy listening
to the sermons, worshipping, catching the Holy Ghost,
clapping and singing along with the rest of the
congregation. Then there was the feet-washing
ceremony. She had always liked the ritual, because it
always made her grandmother so proud. She had
learned that it was supposed to be a humbling
experience, in which you selflessly serve your fellow
man. Those days she would leave church and her
grandmother would make her feel ten feet tall, telling
her how she would be blessed for not allowing her pride
to stop her from assisting another child of God.

When she was younger, she had actually been
afraid to sin. Now it seemed like she sinned in her sleep.
The street became a blur as her mind carried her back to
the only time that she had felt more like a demon. She
was skipping school with her then-boyfriend Red. They
were at his house watching TV and realized that they
didn't have a blunt or papers to roll the weed they had
gotten from his brother. Red said he had an idea and
went to his closet and came out with a dusty Bible. He
ripped a few pages out of it and rolled the weed in them.
Ke-Ke remembered the chill that ran through her body
and not really wanting to smoke it, but she didn't want
people to think she was soft or a Jesus freak. She could
clearly remember Red holding up the weed as the pages

burned black announcing, "This is how I get closer to God," as he coughed and everyone laughed. She had never talked to him again after that day and had prayed a million times, asking for forgiveness for her actions. The thought of that day still made her shiver and she still found herself wondering what the penalty was for such a blasphemous act.

A month or two later after the incident she had told her grandmother the story, of course putting it into the context of, "I got this friend, right." She had wanted to know if she was going to hell or not without having to personally confess. When she finished, her grandmother took both of her hands, looked her in the eyes, kissed her on the forehead, and said, "God knows your heart, baby."

That chain of thoughts ending with what her grandmother had told her back then began to bring a sense of calm over her. But she had become an entirely different person in the years that followed and through it all she began to doubt if God could still see her heart the way He did back then.

Ke-Ke was close to the corner of Reynolds when she heard a horn honk. "Yo, that weed must be the bomb! It got you walking alone and talking to yourself!" Cry was laughing at her from behind the wheel of a white Infiniti Sedan. Ke-Ke knew that her lips would move as she was working through things in her mind. Her mother used to tell her that she was going crazy.

"Naw, I was just zoned out!" Ke-Ke played it off, feeling embarrassed.

"C'mon, let's ride out." Cry said, the smile still on her face as she clicked the automatic locks. "You ain't goen crazy on me, is you?"

"Naw, I just got shit on my mind," Ke-Ke said as she got in the car, closed the door, and sank down in the soft leather seat. "I was gonna call you in a minute anyway, you must've heard me thinking about you." Ke-Ke used the joke that she had heard her mother use a million times when she was on the phone. She handed the rest of the blunt to Cry and waved her hand to signal that she could kill it.

"So what's good wit you?" Cry asked as she handed her the bottle of Remy Martin that she had been holding in between her thighs.

"I need some paper. My mom's tryna charge me rent. I need to get my own place and I'm tryna get to that concert, but a bitch is too broke." Ke-Ke recited her list of woes like they were lyrics to a song.

"You broke?" Cry said with her eyes wide as she coughed off of the weed. "How the fuck you broke with that ATM machine in between your legs?"

"You know how it go." Ke-Ke shook her head, embarrassed again as she wondered what Cry was thinking of her. "I know you got spots. Put me on in one of them. I ain't gonna fuck nothen up." Ke-Ke threw the suggestion out, half-expecting it to be shot down in mid-air.

"Oh, now you wanna hustle?" Cry said as she fell back into her seat with a mock look of surprise on her face. Ke-Ke watched as she threw the rest of the blunt out the window.

"I don't know about that one, you ain't got no experience in the game and I don't want you to fuck my money up, cause then we gonna fall out over some bullshit." Cry looked her straight in the eyes as she spoke.

"I ain't gonna fuck nothen up. I need this. My mom is gonna kick me out for real. Plus I just need to start maken some steady paper anyway." Ke-Ke pleaded without trying to sound weak. She started thinking that Cry was going to leave her hanging on this one. Cry nodded as she twisted another blunt she had removed from the console in between their seats. She nodded in silence and exhaled heavily as she stuck the blunt through the small slits in one of the air vents.

"Why you don't just fuck wit my cousin and them Get Money Bitches over there? I mean, stick to what you know and what you been doen." Cry spoke with a hint of concern like she was a ghetto guidance counselor.

Ke-Ke played with the thought in her head even though it wasn't what she had wanted to hear. The Get Money Bitches did get some serious money, it just seemed that they went through too much to get it. They were a loose-knit group of young, good-looking girls that posted themselves on the computer websites and charged by the hour for their specialized "services." Professional whores, managed by an extremely overbearing older woman named Shantelle, that had become too comfortable with being called and received as such, as long as you paid them while you were doing it. They traveled the country but usually landed in New York City, Atlantic City, Philadelphia, and Las Vegas.

Ke-Ke recalled the time she had gone to the house that they worked out of, which was owned by Cry's cousin Shantelle. The girls had no shame and no matter who came in the house, they walked around in skimpy underwear or various other states of undress, smoked weed, and talked sex for all to hear. She remembered a girl named Cat, a lead girl, counting a stack of money she had gotten the night before from "doing a party." She was a short, thick girl with large butterfly wings tattooed on her ass cheeks. She was known for performing a dance move that made it look like the butterfly was flapping its wings. She swore it had made her an overnight celebrity with her customers and her phone never ceased to vibrate and chirp on the table as she licked her thumb and slowly counted through the large stack of bills.

"I could use that kind of paper though," Ke-Ke said, with her mind still fixated on the stack of large bills that sat on the table in front of Cat. "I be tired of asken niggas to let me hold something. I need to get my own shit." Ke-Ke glanced over at Cry, figuring that she would appreciate her logic.

"I'm just sayen for now. I'm gonna try to put you on in the next week or so, but just so you don't be on 'E' until then." Cry spoke as if she would have considered doing the same thing if she was in her position, but Ke-Ke knew better.

"Aiight, for now," Ke-Ke promised herself aloud. She was determined not to get pulled into the lifestyle forever. She had never understood how the Get Money Bitches had become so comfortable with being called out of their names on a regular basis. It was almost as if they had sold their souls. They rode around the neighborhood for the next couple of minutes in silence while Ke-Ke tried to convince herself that it wouldn't be that bad and ran through a mental check list of things that she would definitely *not* do no matter how good the money was.

"Yo, I gotta go change," Cry said as she pulled up to a stop sign. Ke-Ke nodded and half-smiled as she had remembered seeing Cry three different times in one day, each time she had a new outfit on and was driving a different car. What the average person wore to the club or to a concert was everyday clothes for Cry, and she seemed to have an endless supply. Ke-Ke imagined that Cry had a huge walk-in closet at her house where butlers waited with outfits they had laid out for her approval or disapproval. Cry would nod and the outfit would be tailored to fit her on the spot or she would wave her hand and the outfit would be burned. Ke-Ke smiled at her ability to make little movies out of everything in her head.

They pulled up in front of a four-bedroom, brick-faced home in the 19th Ward, the "good part" of the city where a former mayor had lived. You rarely heard about any crime there and people who lived there announced it with pride. Ke-Ke climbed out of the car, still drinking the Remy and looking around. She had never known anyone who lived in that area, although she remembered her mother driving her and her sister to the neighborhood on Halloween because she said it was safer. The neighborhood seemed so much quieter, with kids playing on the manicured lawns, no crackheads, and no one standing on the corners of the crisp white sidewalks. Ke-Ke looked around, half-expecting the gingerbread man from Misha's game to come skipping around the corner at any moment. *A few minutes can make a world of difference.* Her uncle's words shot through her head and, all at once, she knew what he had meant.

Ke-Ke followed Cry up the driveway and noticed the black Infiniti parked behind the house next to an old-school Chevy with large chrome rims on it. The car was painted a candy-apple red and had a black convertible top; it looked to be straight out of a rap video. "That's yours too?" she asked as Cry unlocked the side door that led into the house.

"Yeah, that's me, I'm still waiting on the digital dash to come though," she said, like Ke-Ke had asked her about a pair of shoes. "You can go check it though!" Cry said with a smile as she pushed a button on her keychain and the doors of the Chevy clicked and rose into the air as if the car was getting ready to take flight. Ke-Ke walked slowly over to the car with her mouth wide open. The interior was white leather with red stitching that matched the paint job. She got closer and noticed the carpet was the same color red, with embroidered floor mats that read "Cry" in cursive letters. The car had a large chrome grill matching the rims that made the car look like it was smiling. Ke-Ke looked up and noticed the wood grain steering wheel and two small stuffed animal pit bulls that dangled from the rearview mirror.

"That shit hard, right?" she heard Cry walk up behind her. Ke-Ke just shook her head and continued to look around the interior of the car like she was stuck in a dream. "When I get the dash put in, it'll be over wit!" Cry said as she pointed to a hole in the dashboard where the speedometer and gauges were supposed to be.

"Damn!" was all Ke-Ke could say, as Cry pushed the button on the keychain again and the doors swung down and clicked back into place. Ke-Ke had only seen doors open and close like that in magazines or on TV and had heard that they came from a car, but she couldn't remember how to pronounce the name of it.

"C'mon," Cry said, and Ke-Ke turned and followed her into the house. She looked around to see which window the air conditioner was sitting in but couldn't find one. The front room of the house had a plush white carpet with black designs that bordered it where it met the walls. There were porcelain Dalmatians that sat in the four corners of the room and a black leather sectional with oversized ottomans that took up the back portion of the room. Ke-Ke slid off her shoes, stepped onto the carpet, and noticed a large waterfall that changed colors that hung on the wall like a painting. She looked up to see a ceiling fan with glass blades, spinning slowly. "Damn!" she caught herself saying out loud. Cry came into the room holding two glasses and a Red Bull energy drink. Ke-Ke walked over to the couch and sat down as Cry clicked the remote and the sixty-inch flat screen that was mounted on the wall came to life.

"This shit is like *Cribs*!" Ke-Ke couldn't hold it in any longer. Cry just smiled at the compliment and nodded. The room vibrated with sound as Ke-Ke noticed the surround sound system with small speakers that hung from the ceiling like surveillance cameras in a department store. Cry flipped through the channels and stopped on BET. Ke-Ke felt a warmth in her chest like she did when she was falling in love. She leaned back on the couch and basked in the luxury while she secretly imagined that this was her house and the group on the music video was performing a private concert for her.

"I gotta take a shower," Cry said as she put her drink down on a glass end table that doubled as an aquarium full of black and white fish. Ke-Ke watched as the small bubbles rose in the tank from a bed of black and white stones at the bottom. "Watch whatever you want," she said as she stood up, handed the remote to Ke-Ke, and walked up the carpeted stairs. Ke-Ke couldn't keep her eyes from glancing around the room and taking mental pictures of what looked like little trees in glass bowls and the mirrors that were cut into artistic patterns on the walls.

She wondered how it would feel to live like this all the time. She imagined inviting her mother over to dinner, just so she could kick her out the moment she said something that she didn't like. The thought made her smile as she inhaled the weed and blew the smoke out in perfect circles.

"Yo, come check this," Cry called from upstairs, making Ke-Ke jump. She laughed as she put the blunt in the ashtray. Ke-Ke ran up the stairs divided by a landing that forced you to change directions. She got upstairs to find Cry in the shower with the bathroom door open. "Check them outfits on the bed. Which one you think I should wear?" Cry yelled out over the water and the music that was coming from the bathroom.

Ke-Ke walked into the bedroom. It had a black carpet with a large brown design that looked to be Japanese writing. Ke-Ke had seen that kind of writing on tattoos of girls she had gone to school with but never understood how people really knew what they meant. The comforter on the bed seemed to be made of a soft brown leather that matched the design on the floor with black fur that ran around the edges. There were two lifelike porcelain Rottweilers that stood guard at the foot of the bed and the mirrored closet doors shared the same design as the carpet. Ke-Ke glanced up at the dresser, where two samurai swords sat in a stand in front of the mirror.

She looked down and saw what Cry was referring to: a dark blue jean outfit with Carolina blue Jordans and next to it a pair of black jeans with a yellow long-sleeve Polo shirt with the matching black and yellow Air Max sneakers. "This bitch got clothes for days," she thought as she inspected the sneakers that appeared as though they had just come out of the box. She glanced over to the closet that was cracked open on one side and noticed the stack of shoe boxes and told herself that Cry must buy her shoes like doughnuts: by the dozen.

"What you think?" Cry startled her as she walked into the room behind her.

"Shit, they both tight!" Ke-Ke admitted without hesitation. She had given up on trying to sound reserved around Cry, who obviously had too many surprises.

"I wasn't talking about that," Cry said slowly. Ke-Ke turned around to see Cry standing behind her completely naked and still dripping from her shower. She followed her pointing finger and noticed that she had her pussy pierced with a gold ring and an AK-47 charm dangling from it. Ke-Ke's mouth dropped as she admired the piece of jewelry. Cry walked to her dresser and began looking through a drawer with a smile on her face.

"That shit is hot!" Ke-Ke said, thinking there was no end to the exclusive items that Cry owned. She always managed to have something that no one had ever seen before and it obviously didn't stop with clothes and cars. She watched as Cry pulled out a pair of pink girl briefs, the kind that were designed to look like men's underwear. Cry had a body! She wondered why she had never noticed it before. Probably because Cry had always worn clothes that were oversized. Ke-Ke found herself stealing glimpses of her shape out of the corner of her eye.

Cry spread lotion over her body and Ke-Ke watched as her light brown complexion began to shine. She was beautiful! Her tight skin formed a golden fabric that gave way to the muscles that flexed underneath it as she moved. Ke-Ke had begun to stare so hard that she hadn't noticed Cry was watching her through her reflection in the mirror. Ke-Ke looked away, instantly embarrassed, and gave Cry her privacy.

She had turned her attention back to the outfits on the bed when she felt Cry's hands around her waist and then felt them slowly rising up underneath her jersey shirt, cupping her breasts and gently pinching her nipples. Ke-Ke felt her heart skip, but for some reason, didn't feel the urge to pull away. She felt her body tense up as Cry's tongue found her neck as she whispered, "Just relax for a second, Ke."

Her hands were strong but so soft at the same time. Ke-Ke exhaled and let out a moan as they massaged her breasts and Cry began to gently kiss then suck on her neck. Ke-Ke could feel her jersey being pulled over her head and wondered if it was the weed that was stopping her from putting up any resistance. Ke-Ke felt like she was under a spell. She slipped her arms out of the jersey, threw it on the floor, and stood topless in front of Cry and completely at her mercy. She felt Cry's lips against hers and her hand on the back of her neck, gently preventing her from pulling away. Ke-Ke tasted her tongue as it entered her mouth and persuaded her own tongue to engage in a slow, circular dance. She felt herself giving in more as Cry slowly pushed into her and made her walk backwards towards the bed behind them.

She slid her hands down Cry's back and the softness of her skin made her heart beat even faster. Ke-Ke had never been with a woman and she fumbled as she licked down Cry's neck and began sucking on her nipples, but Cry stopped her. She lifted Ke-Ke back to her standing position by her chin and whispered, "Let me handle this, okay?" Ke-Ke could only nod as her heart raced and she felt Cry's hands unbuttoning her pants and then unzipping them. She could feel her firm hands rubbing her in circles while she licked and kissed her bellybutton. A moment later her pants and underwear were gone and she was lying on the bed with Cry's head in between her legs.

"Oh shit," Ke-Ke's own voice surprised her as she looked down. Cry's tongue seemed to magically find all the right spots to stroke, lick, and suck. She was grinding her hips into Cry's face faster and faster as she felt her tongue sink deeper and deeper inside of her. Cry was gripping her ass and pulling her into her mouth with both hands. The feeling was surreal. Ke-Ke felt like she was flying. She couldn't stop herself from squirming and moaning out loud. Cry knew what the hell she was doing.

"Ohhhh shiiit!" Ke-Ke screamed as Cry worked three fingers in and out of her. Ke-Ke felt herself tensing up as she convulsed on the bed uncontrollably. "Awwwww!" She gritted her teeth and clasped the comforter in her fist, feeling like she was on a rollercoaster. Her body shook again and tingled with pleasure. She struggled to catch her breath, as her chest heaved and she locked her hands around the back of Cry's head.

"Mmmmmm," Cry finally moaned herself. Ke-Ke shook at the touch of her hands as she rubbed her stomach then reached up to pinch her nipples again. Ke-Ke managed to sit up on one elbow and looked down to see that the leather comforter was drenched underneath her. She remembered all the times she had seen a woman react like that in the movies and always thought they were faking. Ke-Ke just stared back and forth at the bedspread and Cry's smiling face while she tried to stop herself from shaking.

"Didn't know you was a squirter," Cry joked as she slapped her on the sides of her ass. "You a woman now," she said as she stared into Ke-Ke's eyes.

Ke-Ke could only smile as she collapsed on her back and wondered how long it would take her body to stop tembling.

FOURTEEN

CRY LEFT THE ROOM and came back moments later and lay next to Ke-Ke on the bed. They both stared at each other in the reflection of the mirror above the bed and smiled at each other.

"So is this suppose to mean somethen now?" Ke-Ke finally found the nerve to ask when she felt Cry running her fingers through her hair.

"What you want it to mean?" Cry answered the question with a question. She ran her hand up and down Ke-Ke's thigh and let it rest on her ass.

"This shit is so crazy," Ke-Ke said as she stared up at herself in the mirror and searched her rattled mind for an answer.

"We ain't gotta make it all complicated, boo, it is what it is!" Cry spoke, almost too nonchalantly for Ke-Ke's liking.

The words stung, as Ke-Ke remembered all the times that she had really liked a dude then realized after sex that it was all he had wanted from her. She felt a deeper connection with Cry though. The way she touched her like she knew how it felt, instead of being too rough or rushed, the way that men were. The way she seemed to focus on bringing pleasure out of her instead of forcing it onto her. She thought about how everything felt right and how she had enjoyed every moment of it and didn't have to give instructions or guide her. There seemed to be a balance of confidence and sensitivity in her touch that Ke-Ke couldn't find the words to describe. She lay on the bed, staring up at herself while her thoughts and emotions formed a tangled web around her. She had never been touched like that before, but she also knew that Cry had more bitches than the niggas she dealt with, so she knew the "sucker for love" routine would not go over well.

"I gotta get this money though!" Ke-Ke sat up and noticed her pants and underwear in a ball across the room.

Cry sat up on the bed beside her and looked down at her pussy with a smile. "That's a pretty muthafucker there!" she smiled and blew a kiss, before she got up and started getting dressed. Ke-Ke laughed and caught one last glimpse of her ass before she pulled up the black jeans she had set out to wear. They both finished dressing without speaking, but before they walked out of the room Cry pulled her towards her and kissed her.

"Dammit, man!" Ke-Ke smiled and stared directly into her eyes. They walked down the stairs holding hands. When they got to the door, Ke-Ke turned to Cry, "Yo, keep this on the..."

Cry put her finger to her mouth. "What happens between us, stays between us," she whispered and hugged Ke-Ke. "You can trust me," she said before they walked out of the door.

Ke-Ke felt in her heart that she could, but had to make sure so there were no misunderstandings. They walked to the car like two friends that were hanging out for the day. No one seemed to notice that a few minutes earlier the earth had moved.

A half hour later Cry was turning on Shantelle's street and slowed the car to a stop in front of the large blue house that the Get Money Bitches had made famous, or notorious, depending on who you asked. Cry handed Ke-Ke the rest of the blunt they were smoking and said, "Yo, just do what you gotta do for now. I'ma put you on in a minute. I got you!"

"Aiight, don't forget about me though!" Ke-Ke said as she looked over at Cry, wondering if she would switch up on her like niggas did after they had gotten what they wanted.

"I got you," Cry smiled. "Matter of fact, hit me up later tonight. I'll come get you." Ke-Ke gave her a half-hug and stepped out of the car, feeling reassured. Cry honked and pulled off as Ke-Ke walked up the steps, through the enclosed porch, and knocked on the door.

"Hey, girl! Cry said you was comen! It's about time you got down wit the team. You know we get it." Shantelle swung the door open and greeted Ke-Ke. She held the phone to her ear and reached for the blunt.

"Hey, girl." Ke-Ke spoke with less enthusiasm, already beginning to feel nervous. She liked Shantelle, but she thought that at times she was too loud and talked too much. She was definitely not a person that you ever wanted to know anything bad about you because she would tell it now and deny it later. Ke-Ke had witnessed that firsthand.

She walked in the house past the cluttered front room that had a couch full of niggas, including Shantelle's son, who were smoking, drinking, and playing Xbox.

"Damn, y'all can't walk around? We got money on this shit!" her son Levon complained.

"Shut the fuck up, Von!" Shantelle answered quickly. "This is my goddamn house! You and your friends can get this game and the loose change in your pockets that y'all *CALL* money and get the fuck out!" Shantelle barked in one breath.

Ke-Ke just raised her eyebrows and quickly passed into the other room with a smile on her face. She did admire how Shantelle ran shit.

"Whatever, man!" she heard Levon say in a low voice. Ke-Ke smiled wider as she thought of how he made sure to mumble that shit. He knew his mother could go round for round all day long.

"C'mon in here, girl," Shantelle walked through what was supposed to be a dining room that had no furniture and into the kitchen. Ke-Ke followed her and was surprised when she saw that it had been temporarily converted into a hair and nail salon. Girls were everywhere, straightening, flat ironing, and curling hair. They were around the table doing nails and using a mirror above the stove to apply makeup.

"This is Co-Co, Raven, Envy, Ashley, Asia, and Cookie," Shantelle stood in the middle of the room and introduced everybody as she pointed. Ke-Ke waved and smiled, but she could feel the girls looking her up and down and trying to find reasons not to like her. "We got a party to do at the firehouse. You wit that?" Shantelle asked more to confirm what she already knew.

"I'm wit it," Ke-Ke nodded and followed Shantelle down a short flight of stairs into the basement. Shantelle had outfits and accessories hanging from the ceiling in plastic bags, like she ran a dry cleaning business. Ke-Ke walked around looking at everything from jean suits to kinky nurse and maid costumes that still had the price tags on them. She looked down at the floor to see high-heeled boots and shoes displayed in their shoe boxes, organized by size and color.

"I'd say you was an eight if you didn't have all that ass. What you wear, a twelve?" Shantelle looked her up and down.

"I can fit a ten, if it's the right designer," Ke-Ke responded with a smirk. She loved it when anybody complimented her shape.

"Okay, if you say so. Just pick whatever you want. I keep a steady supply coming in from the garment district every month. Them Italians do me right! Just know, if you wear it, you bought it!"

She winked and pointed at Ke-Ke before she walked towards the back of the basement and came back holding a leather body suit covered in zippers. Ke-Ke looked at the outfit, trying to figure out which way was up.

Shantelle laughed loudly and said, "Oh, this my *dominatrix* suit. I get my hustle on too!" She reached into a pocket attached to the leg and pulled out a whip. "They call me Momma Chocolate when they've been bad," she said as she cracked the whip with a devious look on her face. Ke-Ke couldn't stop herself from laughing.

She searched through the endless sea of garments that were packed tightly together for something that would look cute on her. She had narrowed it down to two outfits when the rest of the girls came down the stairs in a herd. Ke-Ke watched as the girls went to different parts of the basement and retrieved outfits that they had hidden earlier. She stood and watched the girls' selections as shock ran through her entire body.

The girl named Co-Co had on a tan, sheer thong. She slid on a pair of leather-looking cowboy chaps that matched it and an ultra-sheer button-down blouse with no bra. She tied the blouse in a knot above her belly button and said, "I'm ready," as she jogged back up the stairs with her bare ass exposed for the world to see.

"Get em, girl!" she heard Shantelle laugh as she clapped in approval when Co-Co reappeared in the kitchen.

Envy had selected a sheer black one-piece that looked like a swimsuit. Ke-Ke sighed to herself. At least someone was going the conservative route. Just then Envy spun around to reveal that there was a gold chain that ran through her ass cheeks in the back. Ke-Ke could only stare and wonder how uncomfortable that had to feel, no matter how cute it looked. She finished her ensemble with a black trench coat and was back up the stairs.

Raven and Ashley yelled that they were ready from the kitchen and Ke-Ke hurried to decide on an outfit. She looked at the denim outfit in her hand just as Shantelle was making her way back down the stairs behind her. "Bitch, is you going to church or to sell some pussy?" she asked from the bottom step while she held what was left of Ke-Ke's blunt in her hand.

"I..."

"I got y'all," Shantelle cut her off, shaking her head. She selected two paper-thin cat suits and handed the pink one to Asia and the powder blue one to Ke-Ke.

"Y'all first timers can go as twins!" she said and headed back up the stairs. Asia and Ke-Ke looked at each other, shrugged, and got undressed.

Ke-Ke stood in front of the full-length mirror next to the washing machine and examined herself. She shook her head and adjusted the suit, noticing that there were circles of fur around the wrists and ankles. The suit hugged her whole body in a delicate, thin material. She had tried to wear it with her panties, but they seemed to bulge underneath, so she and Asia decided to go without any. Ke-Ke pushed the blue diamonds of her nipple piercing through the thin fabric to complete her look.

"That's hot! It almost matches." Asia stood behind her in the mirror, smiling. Ke-Ke smiled and tried not to look uncomfortable as the material crept and settled into places that only her bathwater had ever touched. She looked at the front and tried to readjust it, but the material just settled back into place, leaving absolutely nothing to the imagination. This was definitely one of those days that she was glad that she shaved her pussy on a regular basis.

"This is my first time," Asia whispered behind her, like no one knew her secret. "The other girls are already cliqued up. Can you watch my back tonight?" Her voice trembled as she asked the question.

"As long as you watch mine," Ke-Ke answered as she continued fixing her hair in the mirror. Ke-Ke turned around to see Asia holding up her hand to high-five her.

"Wonder Twins?" she asked playfully, with one of her eyebrows arched upwards.

"Wonder Twins," Ke-Ke played along, hoping Asia didn't get them both into some shit that they would both regret.

***

"Heyyyy, now that's what the fuck I'm talken about!" Shantelle clapped and announced their presence to everyone in the house. "Get em, girls!" she coached as she smacked Asia on the ass and playfully flicked at Ke-Ke's nipple ring. Envy and Co-Co even smiled and commented on how cute they looked, while Ashley and Cookie just rolled their eyes. Cookie wasn't coming to the party because it was that time of the month, so Ke-Ke mentally excused her, but Ashley was just a hater. Shantelle handed them both trench coats and informed them that their ride was on the way.

"Now when y'all get there, don't be acten all shy and scared and shit! These men gonna pay they money and they want what they want, so give it to them. Ain't none of y'all bitches virgins, so ain't no need to get there and start playen the church girl. Spread them legs and get that bread! Give up that ass and get they cash!" Shantelle paced back in forth in the kitchen, yelling orders like a drill sergeant and clapping her hands loudly. Ke-Ke looked around the room and saw the other girls nodding and smiling, some of them mouthing Shantelle's words as she spoke them.

"I'ma get mines with or without you hos!" Envy announced as she rolled her neck and held up her freshly painted nails to slap up Co-Co.

"Word! Don't make me get mine *AND* your money too!" Co-Co laughed and took a large sip from her half-empty bottle of Hennessey. Ke-Ke felt Asia squeeze her hand and knew that she was letting the other girls intimidate her. She squeezed her hand back to let her know that what they had promised each other was still in effect.

Shantelle walked around the kitchen and continued her pep talk, like they were a football team at halftime. When the word came back to the kitchen that their ride was there, Ke-Ke was almost ready to put her hands in with the other girls and yell, "BREAK" before they departed. The girls gathered their things and began walking towards the front door and Ke-Ke noticed how a few of the girls let their trench coats fly open to tease when they walked past Lavon and his friends, who had paused their game to watch the parade.

"Y'all better get that money!" Shantelle had stepped onto the porch and was still coaching as they stepped out into the cold night air. The breeze took Ke-Ke by surprise until she remembered how much she wasn't wearing underneath the trench coat.

"Hey, ladies," Cadillac Drake greeted them as he opened the back door to the limousine. Cadillac Drake was an old school hustler. Some said he was a pimp and others said he was just a car thief. He was one of those hood-famous personalities who was known for owning and driving four or five limousines that he kept on display in his front yard and driveway. The story was that he used to travel to Canada and Atlantic City and steal the vehicles, brough them back home, and began the process of changing registrations so that the cars all legally appeared to belong to him. How he had survived so long without arousing closer attention from the police department was beyond everyone's understanding. He could be seen driving up and down the Avenue in one of his fleet of limousines honking, waving, and talking shit out of the driver's side window day and night. He had fallen on hard times recently or was smoking (according to the rumors) but whatever the case, he had started renting out his limos and driving for weddings and funerals and other special occasions to make extra money.

Ke-Ke stepped into the car with Asia behind her and was relieved when she saw the interior. There were mirrors on the ceiling, sectioned off into twelve squares, a wet bar with brandy and champagne glasses hanging upside down above it, and a flat screen television that appeared to be suspended above the bar and glass stemware.

"Damn, this shit aiight. I ain't know they looked like this on the inside." Ke-Ke heard someone speak her thoughts out loud.

"Yeah, you know old people keep they shit up," she looked down in time to see Ashley agreeing with the comment.

"Ladies, the bar is open!" Drake announced proudly as he closed the door and the interior track lighting began to dim.

"Oh shit!" Envy leaned over Co-Co to inspect what the bar had to offer.

"Damn gril! Your fucken lush ass would be all over that shit," Co-Co complained as she straightened her coat.

"You daaaamn right! I gotta get right in order to do pink dick!" Envy pulled out a bottle of Jack Daniels and a cheap bottle of champagne. Ke-Ke caught the comment and realized that she hadn't even thought about who they were going to entertain. She had never slept with a white boy and had always considered it "uncooked meat." She and her friends had always joked that they liked their meat well done, or at least medium-rare.

She motioned to Envy to hand her a glass, thinking that she better get as saucy as possible so she could stomach what was to come.

Drake drove the car with precision and there were times that Ke-Ke and the other girls had to look out of the windows to see if they were moving or not. The car seemed to glide through the streets. A few turns and they were in the middle of downtown and Ashley and Co-Co were standing up through the moonroof, waving and giving the finger to people standing underneath the many bus shelters that lined main street on both sides.

"Get ya broke ass a car, nigga!" she heard Ashley yelling at some niggas that tried to run over to the limo and get her number. "I don't do buses, boo!" she said as she ducked back into the safety of the limo, blowing kisses with her middle finger extended.

"Fuck you, bitches!" Ke-Ke heard a nigga's voice yell, but the rest she couldn't make out over the girls laughing and talking shit.

JULIAN FOSTER

"Finish your drinks, ladies. We are around the corner from your final destination," Drake called out over the intercom as if he were a tour guide. Ke-Ke had to laugh at how he took himself and his "business" so seriously.

"Oh hell naww! We gotta make a toast before we go up in this muthafucka!" Envy said as she handed out the glasses to everyone in the car. She poured a double shot of Jack Daniels in all of the glasses then slipped the bottle into her purse. "Lift em up, bitches!" she ordered as Ke-Ke and Asia scooted forward and touched glasses with the rest of the girls.

"What the fuck is we toasting to?" Co-Co asked, visibly annoyed by the ritual.

"This toast is to pussy and all the tricks in the world willing to pay for it!" Ashley blurted out of nowhere. The girls erupted into laughter and downed their drinks in unison. Ke-Ke looked over and saw that Asia was trying to sip her drink and snatched it from her.

"This is how you do it." She took the shot to the head and handed the empty glass back to an astonished-looking Asia.

"I can't drink like that," Asia confessed as she placed the glass back on the bar, her face turned up.

The girls were climbing out of the limo when Raven turned to Ke-Ke and Asia and said, "Y'all don't have no thin skin in here. They can call you names, but they will never call you broke!" She slapped both of their hands and hopped out of the car, adjusting her trench coat.

"What's that supposed to mean?" Asia whispered in Ke-Ke's ear.

"I don't know, girl. Just be ready for whatever when we get up in there," was all Ke-Ke could say.

The two of them got out of the car with the help of Drake and followed the girls towards the firehouse. Ke-Ke noticed that the garage doors were all closed and the fire trucks were not visible from the outside like they usually were. She braced herself and thought that this would probably be one of those nights that she remembered for the rest of her life. She secretly wished that eight fires would break out all over the city at that very moment so she could get out of the situation and save face at the same time. She glanced over to her left and noticed Ashley looking her up and down, smirking.

"Bitch, this the big leagues. Don't get scared now!"

FIFTEEN

"HELLLOOOOO, MY JUNGLE BITCHES!" A redheaded, freckle-faced fireman with no shirt on answered the door, already holding his crotch and jumping up and down.

"See what I mean?" Ashley turned and whispered at Ke-Ke and Asia with her eyebrows lifted and a sneaky half-smile on her face.

"Yeah, well us jungle bitches feed off green, so I hope you got it or we will have to go graze someplace else!" Envy answered so quickly Ke-Ke didn't even get the chance to process what he said and get offended.

The girls walked in past the fire trucks and up the stairs where about ten to fifteen men waited like a pack of hungry wolves for their "dark meat" to arrive.

"Turn that bullshit off!" Ashley shouted, referring to the hard rock music that was blasting as she and the other girls removed their coats. Ke-Ke and Asia both nervously removed their coats and stood as far to the back of the group as they possibly could. Ke-Ke glanced around the room quickly and noticed a stage built around the fire pole, blocking access to the lower level. The opposite side of the room had a table filled with food and bottles of liquor complete with a silver platter that displayed a pile of weed. She settled her eyes on the large bottle of Remy Martin that sat unopened on the table. She knew that she was going to need plenty of that to get through this evening.

Co-Co handed one of the men a CD and the mood changed as the stereo started to play a song by Trina and Trick Daddy.

"Gentlemen, I brought you chocolate for dessert!" the obnoxious man with no shirt on announced to his coworkers. The men clapped and cheered and Ke-Ke could tell by their flushed faces that half of the men were already drunk. For the first time in a long time, she felt a nervousness pass through her body, like when she was younger and came across a stray dog. They had no security. What if these drunk-ass men just decided to take the pussy and not pay them shit? This was a fucked-up situation, she thought, as she felt Asia grabbing her hand and squeezing it again.

"Why don't y'all shake them fat asses for us!" he continued as he smacked Co-Co on the ass and held onto it like his hand had gotten stuck. The girls entered the room and spread out, making it impossible for Asia and Ke-Ke to hide in the back anymore. Ke-Ke took Asia with her to the bar area and poured two double shots into plastic cups, with no chaser. They watched as Envy, Ashley, and Co-Co took to the stage like professionals. They were surrounded by the firemen in no time and the money started to fly through the air.

Raven joined them at the bar and said, "Y'all just look at it like a hookup party. If you get picked, you go to the back, do what you do, and come back up front for more!" She pointed at a huge curtain that hung behind the stage. Co-Co had wasted no time and was already escorting the redheaded, loudmouth fireman and one of his friends behind the stage. Ke-Ke observed how the men already had their money clenched in their fists before they disappeared behind the curtain. Raven poured her drink and went back to the other side of the room. She sat on the circular couch in between two men and winked.

Ke-Ke stood by the bar with Asia and glanced around the room. She felt relieved that they hadn't been harassed yet, but she also felt like they weren't going to get paid if they didn't figure out a way to get into the mix. She glanced back over at the couch and saw Raven smiling at them as one man stood over her, dropping twenty dollar bills while another sucked her titties and another rubbed her pussy. The look on her face said that she was enjoying every minute of it. Ke-Ke had lost count at two hundred dollars and looked away while she started to formulate a plan for her and Asia.

"Look, if we act like we into each other, that's less we gonna have to do wit these nasty-ass muthafuckas! You wit it?" she asked Asia. She looked over and noticed the look of horror on her face.

"Oh... okay, you think that will work?" Asia stumbled over her own response. She pointed towards the stage and they both watched in shock as Ashley and Envy danced completely naked, each of them with a man's face in between their legs. The other men stood around watching and throwing money as Ashley pointed to men in the crowd and said, "You next, muthafucka!" Envy held onto the pole with her arms extended and bent over while one of the men dropped his pants and slid inside of her. "You can't handle this pussy, muthafucka!" she yelled as she struggled to keep her balance while he thrust himself into her wildly.

"Damn!" Ke-Ke said out loud as her mouth dropped. She wondered to herself what happened behind the curtain if all of this was going on in the open! She poured another drink and tried to act like she wasn't really surprised.

"See what I mean?" Asia asked, and Ke-Ke looked down and saw the plastic cup shaking in her hand.

"C'mon girl," she said as she took Asia by the hand and led her to the far end of the couch, where Raven was entertaining three men at the same time.

"Go with this!" Ke-Ke took the cup out of Asia's hand and kissed her, shoving her tongue into her mouth before she could react. She rubbed her titties and moaned, watching out of the corner of her eyes to see if anyone was paying attention.

"Whoooo!" Two men that were watching the show Envy was putting on came over like moths to a flame. Ke-Ke smiled to herself, as she had never figured out what drove men crazy about girl-on-girl action. They crowded around her and Asia on the couch and Ke-Ke could feel the bills falling on her head. She slipped the catsuit off Asia's shoulders and began licking her dark nipples and rubbing her pussy. She slid down to the floor on her knees, in between Asia's legs, and pulled the suit down to her waist. The thin material made a ripping noise that seemed to excite their audience even more. Ke-Ke aggressively began to lick Asia from her belly button up to her nipples, while she massaged her pussy and felt the moistness in between her legs. The plan was working, in more ways than one!

The firemen screamed and dropped money. Ke-Ke closed her eyes after she had counted four hundred dollars in fifty-dollar bills that landed on the couch next to them. She licked back up to Asia's ear and whispered the amount. Asia just gasped and whispered, "I want your phone number."

Ke-Ke smiled as she worked her tongue back down Asia's body. She ripped the rest of the cat suit off of her as the men that circled them cheered and slapped hands. She felt uneasy when she noticed that it seemed to get darker and she wondered how many men were crowded around them, but knew that she couldn't stop the show. She licked up Asia's thighs and noticed the short, straight hairs on Asia's trimmed pussy. She didn't know if she could go that far and was relieved to hear Raven's voice. "Take that dick, girl!" she coached, but Ke-Ke couldn't see her through the crowd of men that had gathered around them. She looked up to see that one of the firemen had pulled his dick out and Asia had damn near swallowed it whole!

So much for the shy routine, Ke-Ke thought as she continued kissing Asia and laughed in her head. So far she hadn't been touched and Ke-Ke knew that she had to step her game up to keep it that way. She licked down to just above Asia's pussy hairs and thought that would be enough until she heard a chant begin. "Do it! Do it! Do it! Do it!"

Ke-Ke rolled her eyes and pushed Asia's legs apart, sticking her tongue inside Asia's pussy. Asia moaned and grabbed the back of her head, forcing Ke-Ke's face into her. The crowd cheered louder as they watched Asia's reaction. Ke-Ke could feel the bills sticking to the sweat on her back, so she convinced herself that she was eating oysters as she tried to mimic the moves Cry had put on her earlier. She licked Asia's pussy up and down as the imaginary list of what she wouldn't do burst into flames in her head. She felt Asia's thighs tighten around her head and her body began to shake. "Eat that egg roll, bitch!" She felt a hand smacking her ass and she moaned and wiggled it to play along.

Then the inevitable happened. Ke-Ke felt strong hands around her waist and someone trying to position her body. She felt a little secure knowing that she still had her cat suit on and that it had to be taken off from the top. The moment of security died a horrible death as she felt the thin material being torn off of her as the audience roared and she felt the cold air hit her exposed ass. She knew she was in too deep and had to roll with the situation whether she wanted to or not. She moved out of the middle of Asia's legs and prepared to be the center of attention in her own solo show.

She felt something cold being poured on her and looked back to see the man that had ripped her suit was pouring beer all over her and smacking her ass. She turned back around and started making her ass clap on her knees, as she buried her face into the cushions of the couch. The money kept falling and stuck to her skin. She could feel his hands rubbing her pussy in a rough motion from underneath before he inserted two of his fingers. She lifted her head and fake-moaned, which sent the crowd into another frenzy.

Ke-Ke put on her best acting routine, moaning and moving her head like she couldn't get enough of him. She looked back to wink at him when she saw that he wasn't using his fingers at all. He was thrusting himself into her and talking shit about it too!

"Take this dick, you black bitch!" he shouted as he smacked hands with his friend. He was sweating and out of breath in less than a minute, as he gripped her ass and pumped like he was doing damage. "You love this white cock, don't you baby?" he asked as he went into jackhammer mode and slammed into her with everything he had.

Ke-Ke put her head back into the cushions to keep herself from laughing. She hid her smile as she looked back up at the ceiling and got her act on. "Yes, yes, I love this white cock!" she screamed as the crowd of men hooted and clapped. She couldn't believe that his dick felt like fingers as she moaned and begged for mercy.

"Ohhhh shit, you bitch!" Ke-Ke felt him jerking and having spasms behind her as he pulled out of her and she felt the warmth of his climax land on her ass. "Damn, that's some good pussy!" he gasped as he fell back onto the floor with the rest of the men laughing and cheering. Ke-Ke stood up and noticed two other men unzipping their pants. They both made a move towards her, but she pushed them back, telling them that she had to clean up before round two.

Asia was now lying on the couch with a dick in her mouth and a man thrusting and grunting in between her legs. She was a champ the whole time, Ke-Ke thought as she walked towards the bathroom past Raven, who was now bent over the back of the couch, begging some cocky, middle-aged man to show her "who was boss." She winked and smiled at Ke-Ke as she walked past.

Ke-Ke made it to the bathroom and pulled out the money that she had managed to stuff down the legs of what remained of her catsuit. She counted it as quickly as possible and was surprised when she counted out seven hundred and fifty dollars! She had been out there less than a half an hour!

She checked her reflection in the mirror and smiled as she quickly washed herself off in the sink and examined her outfit. There was no way she would be able to salvage it and she felt herself getting pissed off at the fact that she would have to pay Shantelle for a piece of clothing that was no longer wearable.

She peeled the rest of the suit off her sweaty, beer-soaked body and started rubbing the lotion she had found sitting on the sink all over herself. Ke-Ke stashed the money in a Crown Royal bag she had stolen from the bar on her way to the bathroom and looked for a hiding place. She decided on the vacuum cleaner bag and turned to look at herself in the mirror again. "Get that money, girl!" she mouthed to her own reflection as she slipped on the blue sandals she had picked out to match her outfit and walked out of the bathroom butt-ass naked.

"Damn, girl!" she heard one of the men call out from across the room by the couches. He was standing over Asia, but Ke-Ke had all of his attention. She held up one finger, telling him to hold on and walked back to the bar and fixed herself another drink. Co-Co joined her, covered in sweat, naked and smiling.

"I see you get comfortable quick! You shoulda been given an award for that acting job you did!" They both laughed and toasted with their plastic cups. "C'mon over here, you *gotta* ride the seesaw!" Co-Co said as she yanked Ke-Ke by the arm and led her across the room to where the stage was built around the pole.

"Give my bitch the seesaw!" she demanded as she clapped and tried to hype people up. The girls applauded and laughed, while Ke-Ke was directed to stand in the middle of two firemen. She looked around, confused, as she watched the one behind her get on his knees. When she turned around she noticed that the one in front of her was on his knees too. Ke-Ke felt them grab her arms—one had her wrists and the one behind her grabbed just above her elbows.

"It should be called the waterslide, because you gonna be all wet by the time you get to the bottom!" Ashley shouted out as the other girls burst out into uncontrollable laughter. All at once the fireman in front began eating Ke-Ke's pussy and just as she tried to adjust to the feeling the one behind her placed his face in between her cheeks and began licking her asshole.

Her mouth dropped as she grabbed a handful of hair on the one positioned in front of her. She gritted her teeth and shrieked, "Shiit!"

When she opened her eyes she realized that she had been lifted into the air. The higher she went, the deeper their tongues plunged into the depths of her. Ashley was right, because she was only halfway back down when she climaxed and rocked back and forth in between their faces. She had forgotten all about her fear of being dropped as her body shook like an electric current was running through it.

They put her down and she was glad that Co-Co was standing there ready to catch her, because her legs were Jell-O. Co-Co half-carried her to one of the chairs nearby and laughed as she whispered, "Can you believe they just paid YOU for that shit?"

Ke-Ke looked over at the faces that she had just gotten off of and shook her head as they smiled and celebrated. "Whoo! Another satisfied customer! Who's next?"

Ke-Ke reached for Co-Co's drink. Her legs were still shaking and she was trying to catch her breath after getting off of the ride of her life. She was still trying to pull herself together when Co-Co leaned over and whispered, "The part that kills me is knowing that they gonna go home and kiss they wives with them mouths."

Ke-Ke spit out the drink, trying to hold back her laughter, as the two firemen looked over and cheered louder. She played the image out of a middle-aged white woman kissing her husband before he left for work and tried to imagine the face she would make after she wondered what that funny taste in her mouth was. The thought made her laugh until her stomach hurt and more than paid the cost for all the names they had been called that night.

She decided that she would earn the rest of her money from dancing and borrowed a garter from Ashley and made her way to the pole. She danced like she was back at home in her bedroom, alone in front of her mirror, blocking out the fact that she was in a room full of people that were watching, screaming, and making comments. She could feel strong hands groping her body as her garter was filled with bills. She swung around the pole and opened her eyes to see a fat fireman looking up at her with a hand full of folded-up bills. She bent over and placed his head in between her titties and shook them, like she had seen strippers do in videos. When she stepped back, she smiled when she noticed that he had dropped at least half of his money on the stage in front of her. She gave him a kiss on the cheek as she collected the money and headed to the bathroom to deposit it in her private stash. Easy money.

As she walked away from the stage area, Ke-Ke glanced over to check on Asia and noticed that she was hard at work, bouncing up and down on some blond-haired man's lap who was calling her all kinds of "Asian bitches." She smiled at Ke-Ke when she passed and Ke-Ke blew her a kiss before disappearing into the bathroom.

With the door closed behind her, Ke-Ke quickly sprinkled water from the sink all over her and deposited the wet bills in the vacuum. She was checking her reflection in the mirror as she tried to count all of her own rules that she had broken for the night when she heard a knock. She figured it had to be one of the girls, so she pushed the vacuum into a far corner and opened the door.

"Hey!" she was almost shocked to see the fat fireman from the stage standing there smiling and sweating.

"Hi, I wanted something special, if you don't mind," he stuttered nervously looking around as he spoke, like he didn't want anyone to hear him.

"What you want, some of this pussy?" Ke-Ke asked as she let her hand fall down in between her legs. She watched as he touched himself through his sweatpants and hoped like hell that he would come on himself before she actually had to touch him.

"Um, maybe um... I can come in?" he asked in a low voice as he looked over his shoulder to see if anyone was watching them. Ke-Ke hesitated and looked around the room behind him, then agreed, figuring that he was the type that couldn't fuck in front of other people. She could see him as the one that they all made fun of and a feeling of pity fell over her. She closed the door and before she knew it, he had taken his clothes off and was lying on the floor, flat on his back.

"Damn, you ready, huh daddy?" she laughed as she looked down at him.

"Could you dance over me?" he asked in his low voice with the wad of bills shaking in his sweating hands.

"Okay, baby!" Ke-Ke agreed, now feeling that he was the harmless, shy, nerdy type. She stood with a leg on either side of his waist and began dancing slowly to the music that she could hear playing through the bathroom door. She looked down and saw his face turn a bright red as he breathed heavily with his hands gripping his dick as he pleasured himself shamelessly.

"Work that dick, daddy!" she coached him as she bent down and bounced her ass off of his stomach. She stood back up figuring that it wouldn't be too long now and walked forward so that when he looked up all he could see was pussy.

"You like that view, daddy?" she asked as she stood over his face and looked down at him. He nodded and then whispered another request that Ke-Ke was sure that she had heard wrong.

"What you say, baby?" Ke-Ke asked, still trying to play the dominant role and be sexy at the same time. He whispered something again but Ke-Ke was sure that she must be hearing this man wrong. She got down on her knees with her pussy inches from his face and asked him again, "What you say?"

"If it's too much for you that's okay," he said as Ke-Ke realized all at once that she had heard him right the first time. "I'll pay you extra for it, just... just don't tell anyone." He reached over and produced a larger wad of twenty-dollar bills from his balled-up sweatpants.

"What do you want me to do, baby?" Ke-Ke asked as seductively as she possibly could, like she still wasn't sure what he had said.

"Could you, would you mind...?" he stuttered as his hands shook with the bills in them and he sweated like they were in a sauna. Ke-Ke squinted and smiled at him, making a hand motion that told him to come out with it.

"Could you pee on me?"

Ke-Ke looked at him and then looked at the wad of bills. She could see the embarrassment overcome him as his face turned red again.

He lay there, shaking and gripping the money. His eyes bulged as he looked up at her waiting for an answer to the question he had struggled so hard to ask.

SIXTEEN

KE-KE STOOD WITH HER LEGS APART AND EXHALED SLOWLY. She felt the warmth running down her legs and tilted her head towards the ceiling as the feeling of relief came over her. She worked her neck in circles in an attempt to feel even more relaxed before she looked down and exhaled again deeply.

"Ke-Ke, I gotta use the bathroom!" she heard Misha knocking and whining through the door.

"Misha, use it downstairs!" she yelled back at her. The warm water from the shower seemed to be having more of a soothing effect on her than ever and she wasn't going to let her little sister ruin the moment. She adjusted the showerhead and sat down in the tub, letting the water fall down on her like a hot rain. Lathering her body with the body wash she had gotten from the store earlier that morning, she played the festivities of the night before in her head. She looked over at the Crown Royal bag stuffed with bills on the bathroom floor, and wondered exactly how much she had actually walked away with after giving Asia a cut and paying Shantelle for her outfit.

The girls had decided to leave the firehouse at around three in the morning, all except for a couple who chose to sleep over. Ke-Ke felt relieved that she had made it through the whole night without having to suck any dick and had only been asked to fuck twice. She celebrated that victory in her head with a smile on her face as she watched the body wash turn into a thick, white foam. She wiped her forehead with her washcloth and then laid it across her face and sighed.

Thoughts and scenes from the night before flashed through her mind against her will as she wondered how the other girls were able to live that lifestyle without it eating away at them. She thought about how they had stopped at Envy's house to use the bathroom while they were getting a ride home. She expected it to be laid out like Cry's house. Envy had an air mattress and a sectional couch that looked like it had come from the Salvation Army. The apartment was large and spacious with wooden floors that ran throughout, but there was nothing in it. She wondered if Envy had a drug problem as she tried to understand how she could travel all over the country selling pussy and still not have shit. When she left, she gave Envy a big hug and looked over her shoulder to see her son asleep on the floor in front of a laptop computer that he had been watching a movie on. The image stung her brain as she processed the sadness of it all.

Ke-Ke had decided right then and there, before she had even walked out of the door, that she would never live like that. She figured that if she reached a point in her life where she had to support herself with sex, she would at least have something to show for it besides a few outfits and some jewelry.

She slid the washcloth off her face and glanced over at the green and white sweatsuit that one of the firemen had given her to wear home. He had made a point to tell her not to wear it around because it was only issued to firefighters and the wrong person might see it and start asking questions. She played with the drawstring and laughed to herself, knowing that it was the only thing that saved her from coming home completely naked. She pictured her shredded, beer-soaked outfit in the bathroom's trash can.

Shantelle still charged her fifty dollars for it though and twenty-five more for the matching sandals. She charged an extra eighty dollars a head that she called her finder's fee for hooking the girls up with the party. Ke-Ke couldn't even hate on her though; she knew how to get money. The next time, if there was one, she would make sure to pick up her own outfit before she got there.

She turned the shower off and sat there waiting as the tub slowly began to fill up with hot water. She knew she needed to "soak the funk and sin off" as she had heard her grandmother put it so many times before. Her plan was to bathe, go get her hair done, and try to push the memories of what she had done out of her head forever. She glanced down at her phone, picked it up, and searched her list of recent calls to see if Cry had tried to reach her. She nodded and winked as she saw her number and a "3x" next to it. "That's my bitch," she said aloud as she settled into the hot water and relaxed with her eyes closed.

SEVENTEEN

KE-KE STOOD IN FRONT OF HER CLOSET, wrapped in a towel. She really wasn't in any mood to get all dressed up. She had gotten all the attention she would need for a while at the firehouse. She had only planned to go to the salon; however she already knew that a phone call or a chance encounter could change the course of her whole day, and she wasn't about to be caught out there looking busted. She looked down at her nails and thought about getting a manicure from the Koreans when she was done at the salon, but quickly decided against it. She always got the feeling that they were talking about her in their own language, no matter how much they smiled and bowed like servants.

She jumped as the phone rang and Misha knocked on the door at the same time. "Damn, Misha! A bitch can't even play with herself with you around!" she yelled, hoping it would be enough to keep Misha from coming in, but it wasn't. She found her phone under a pile of clothes and answered it with her sexy voice as Misha sat down on her bed and rolled her eyes.

"I'm at home, I just woke up," Ke-Ke spoke into the phone.

"Oh my God!" Misha shook her head and sucked her teeth. She was all too familiar with Ke-Ke's characters.

"Oh, okay, well I'm going to get my hair done and then I'll call you back." Ke-Ke finished her phone routine with a smile and hung up the phone.

"What, Misha?"

"Don't what me!" Misha answered back like she was the older sister. "Where you was at last night?" She stared up at her with a look of suspicion. Ke-Ke thought about telling her the truth, but she was already dealing with a certain amount of guilt from sharing too many of her previous exploits that most likely had given her little sister a warped perception of love, relationships, money, and sex.

"None of yo' damn...!" Ke-Ke answered waving her hand at her sister and letting the towel fall off her body as she walked to the door and closed it. She had hoped that Misha would take her cue and leave, but that didn't work either. Misha just laid on her back and stared up at the ceiling.

"You was getten some, huh?" she looked over and smirked as she asked.

"Maybe I was," Ke-Ke said as she danced in front of the bed like she had the night before.

"You is so nasty!" Misha laughed as she threw a pillow and pretended to cover her eyes.

"You know you love it, bitch!" Ke-Ke laughed and threw the pillow back at Misha. She turned to find an outfit in her closet, hoping that Misha didn't have any more questions. "When you get an ass, you can do this too!" Ke-Ke said as she stood in place and made her ass cheeks wiggle, sticking her tongue out at Misha.

"I *DO* got an ass! But I *don't want* to do that!" Misha lied on both counts. Ke-Ke felt the pillow hit her in the back again and laughed at her sister's attempts to hide her jealousy. "I'ma tell Ma you was out doen the do last night!" Misha threatened.

"She know what I do already. Whatever!" Ke-Ke dismissed her comment without turning around.

"Daaaamn! Where you get all this from?" Ke-Ke looked over to see that Misha had found the Crown Royal bag hidden underneath her clothes.

"Put it down!" Ke-Ke ordered as she crossed the room and snatched the bag from her as Misha sat with her mouth open and her eyes as bright as headlights. "That's why I don't let you in here, you always into shit!" She pushed Misha in the forehead with her finger and walked back to the closet. She selected an outfit and was surprised that Misha had gotten so quiet behind her.

"Whoa!" Misha said, as Ke-Ke had just turned to see what she was doing. She had found the gun in her jacket pocket that was laid across the top of the bed. "This is real?" she asked in a voice a little louder than a whisper.

"Yeah, and it's not a toy. Stop playen wit it!" Ke-Ke battled with how to approach the situation and kicked herself for not having the gun hidden somewhere where Misha would not have found it. She watched as Misha's eyes lit up as she looked back and forth at the gun and at her. Ke-Ke crossed the room, took the gun out of Misha's hands, dropped the clip out of it and removed the bullet from the chamber in one quick motion. Misha stared in amazement, like she had just seen a magic trick.

She placed the gun and the clip in her sock drawer, while she thought of a better place to hide it when she left for the day.

"I need money for a dress to wear to Tamera's funeral," Misha said flatly. The words sent a chill through Ke-Ke's body as the memories of that night flashed through her head again all at once. She knew Misha had her where she wanted her. One word about the gun and her mother would waste no time throwing her and her things out into the driveway. She knew she hadn't stacked enough money to deal with that situation, plus for the most part, she was still trying to be nice to Misha while she went through her grieving process. Ke-Ke fumbled through the bag and handed Misha a few of the crumbled bills.

"Here, Misha, and what happens in Vegas stays in Vegas, right?" She held onto Misha's hand and stared her directly in the eyes. She had heard the phrase on TV and had adopted it as a code that meant, "Keep your mouth shut."

"I swear, Ke, I'm older now. I wouldn't even do you like that... just don't get caught with that!" Misha said with more sincerity than Ke-Ke ever realized that she had. The words made her smile and sent a warmth through her body as she felt the bond between her and her little sister grow a little stronger.

"You growen up on me?" she said as she straightened Misha's hair then poked her in the side playfully. The room fell silent for a few moments as Ke-Ke walked back to the dresser.

"I'm sorry about Tamera too, Misha, I tried to stop it that night but I was too late." Ke-Ke finally took the time to speak to her about what had happened that night.

"I know... well, I didn't know, but I had a feeling." Misha thanked her sister for the money and left the room, slowly closing the door behind her. Ke-Ke noticed the yellow strings from a pair of her panties sticking out of Misha's robe pocket. She sat on the bed shaking her head and smiling as she lotioned herself.

Thoughts of Misha and the phone calls she had received from Cry earlier battled for supremacy in her head as she finished applying the lotion to her body. She caught a glimpse of movement out of the corner of her eyes. "Showtime," she whispered to herself.

Her bedroom window was positioned across from the bathroom window of the neighbor's house. Jack and Lettie, an older couple, had lived in the house since creation. The neighborhood kids would refer to him as Ol' Man Jack when he drove by in his rusted-out pickup truck that he sometimes used to tow cars and run cans back to the supermarket. However, when Ke-Ke had gotten older, she had found out that he was a known trick and a bona fide pervert. She had always heard stories of when Lettie would leave town to visit family, Jack would pay young girls to come clean his house in their underwear while he watched, drank, and talked dirty. Jack was the first grown man to comment on her body when she was walking to the store after a huge argument with her mother. She had brushed it off, figuring that he was just trying to cheer her up, but from that day on the comments and offers never stopped. "She may run the house, but you the *only* woman I see!" he had said as he winked and his gold tooth showed through his smiling lips.

Not too long after that, Ke-Ke had a couple of friends sleep over. They were in their T-shirts and underwear preparing for bed when one of them noticed that Jack was at his bathroom window, looking over into Ke-Ke's bedroom. The three of them took turns at the window lifting up their shirts, showing their asses and laughing at the shocked and pleased reactions on his face. Ke-Ke never knew how long he had been peeping on her, but ever since then he would flash the light in the bathroom and, if she was in the mood, she would give him a little show. She figured, *Old people need love too!* and for some reason got excited that this married man could never get enough of seeing her naked. A day or two after her "shows," he would innocently give her her "allowance" in front of his wife or her mother as compensation, and nobody had ever caught on to the fact that she was really getting paid for "services rendered."

That was officially her first hustle, but as she had gotten older, the little twenty dollars here and there didn't mean as much to her and she wasn't as committed to him signaling her. Young dudes would talk that "stay with you forever" shit and that "if I fucked you, I would fall in love" shit, but after they got what they wanted, they either started acting funny or were gone. After all the lines and all the compliments, they would disappear in a puff of smoke. Ol' Man Jack was a sign of hope to her. She smiled as she grabbed the bottle of lotion and rubbed the lotion on her titties in front of the window as he watched. She laughed as she thought of giving his old ass a heart attack one day. She ended her performance by slowly putting on her panties and slapping her ass as she walked away from the window, letting the curtains close behind her. She smiled as she finished getting dressed, feeling a sense of accomplishment, knowing that next time she saw him, she would at least have some weed money.

She paused and looked at herself in the mirror as a thought crawled into her mind slowly. It saddened her and made her heart feel heavy as she worked it over in her mind. The truth of if struck her in a way that she couldn't just brush off, like she usually did. *It may be sad, but it's true!* Her uncle's words always seemed to land in her head when she least expected them to. Ol' Man Jack had so far been the only man that had never gotten tired of her. He was her first and only long-term relationship. The thoughts became a feeling that made her skin feel prickly. She found herself forced to look away from her own reflection in the mirror.

"Sad, but true," she sighed to herself as she turned off the light and left the room.

EIGHTEEN

"YEAH, GIRL, YOU KNOW THEM NIGGAS AIN'T SHIT!" Ke-Ke could hear Tiff's voice coming from the open salon door as soon as she stepped out of the cab. She smiled as she walked towards the shop and checked her reflection in the shop windows. When she walked in, Tiff gave her that look and a smile like she had something to tell her. She made her way to the waiting area, grabbed a magazine, and looked to see what talk show was playing on the large screen TV. The shop was packed as usual and the gossip filled the air as Tiff spun stories and jokes like the ringmaster at her own private circus.

"So anyway, girl, here she is wit this nigga. He's a corrections officer at the prison..." Tiff's voice trailed off.

"Mmmhmmm... okay..." the ladies responded as they sat on the edge of their seats, waiting to hear how Tiff's tale would tragically end.

"Yeah, well..." Tiff continued, as she paused to put the rubber bands at the end of some young girl's braids. "He worked at the prison and, from what I hear, he was real nasty to the inmates, or maybe they just didn't like his ass, but anyway, he doen his rounds or whatever and one of them niggas throws acid in his face!"

"Damn!" One of the ladies under the dryers covered her face with shock as she spoke.

"Where the hell they get acid from in prison?" another woman asked with her face wrinkled up in confusion.

"Girl, I don't know, you know they ain't got nothen but time to sit up there and think of ways to fuck people up!"

"That's true, that *IS* true!" another woman supported Tiff's logic.

"So the shit burns the hell out his ass. He gets shit in his eyes and goes blind."

"Damn, damn, damn," another woman said, holding her hand to her chest and shaking her head as she listened.

"Now, wait a minute now," Tiff pointed at her. "My girl stays with him! Helps him learn how to use his hands to get around the house, cooks for him, gets him to the doctor's appointments and everything!" Tiff rambled off the list of good deeds.

"Oh that's good!" The ladies smiled and cheered the efforts of a young, strong black woman. Tiff smiled and nodded and allowed her listeners to have their moment before she continued. Ke-Ke had seen this routine too many times and knew that the hammer was about to drop on this story at any second. She braced herself for the ending, knowing that there was no way she could concentrate on a talk show while Tiff had the floor.

"Bruh man was about to get paid! He sued the state *AND* he's getting disability checks for the rest of his life, guaranteed. So my girl pulling all the bills and rent by herself, cooking and cleaning and waiting for the first part of his settlement to come. "

"That's what a woman is supposed to do! That's what a strong black woman does. Stand by your man!" said some woman who obviously hadn't been around enough times to know that none of Tiff's stories had a happily-ever-after in them.

Tiff dropped her head and smirked at the lady, "Hmpf. Come time that check was about to come, he talken about he gotta go home to get the check cashed cause it's coming to his momma's house. So my girl gets him together, puts him on the train, and waits for him to come back in two days cause that's what he says he's gonna do. He gonna come back, buy her another car, get her out of debt, blah, blah, blah." Tiff rolled her eyes and stopped talking. Ke-Ke smiled as she recognized Tiff's technique that had worked a hundred times. She knew what was coming.

"And... what happened?" The ladies began to ask in scattered voices as they stared at Tiff, seeing that she was making no effort to finish the story.

"Ohhh," Tiff said with an innocent and shocked look on her face as she glanced around the room. "Y'all wanna hear the words? The nigga never came back!"

"Nooooo!" a few of the ladies spoke at the same time. The look of shock on their faces was satisfaction enough for Tiff. They stared at Tiff as if they were waiting for her to tell them that it was a joke or she had made the whole story up. Tiff just continued putting rubber bands on her client's braids as if she hadn't just told them a story at all.

"Girl, you lyen...after all she had done for that man?" One lady had stood up in disbelief as she asked the question, clenching an *Essence* magazine.

"Yep!" was all Tiff answered with, leaving the woman standing there with her mouth open in disbelief before she finally sat down slowly.

"She got played by a blind nigga?" another lady asked.

"Yep!" Tiff said again.

"Why she ain't go down there or call?" another lady asked as if she was the first one to ever come up with that solution.

"She did call! His cell phone was turned off and she never knew where his momma lived." Tiff explained like she knew all these questions would be asked before she even started the story.

"He never called again? She never heard from the nigga again?" another lady asked, searching for some sort of closure.

"Nope, neva again! After two years with the nigga," Tiff said and continued to do hair like she didn't have a room full of people in suspense. Ke-Ke laughed as she watched Tiff hold all the cards while she skillfully fed the background information to them bit by bit.

"She should've taken her ass down there with him!" one lady finally said with anger in her voice. Tiff just nodded and pointed a comb at the lady in agreement.

There were some mumbles and the shop started to quiet when, with perfect timing as usual, Tiff spoke out of nowhere. "So when she told me, you know I *HAAAD* to ask the burning question." She stopped talking again and went back to concentrating on her client.

"What's the burning question?" The lady in the chair next to Tiff asked the question that everybody in the shop wanted to. She glanced over at Tiff out of the corner of her eye as the perm was being applied to her hair by another stylist.

"How the hell is he the one that went blind and *YOU* the one that didn't see that shit coming?" Tiff said in a booming voice as she pointed and smiled. The shop went crazy, as even people that seconds before were annoyed with Tiff couldn't help but laugh. One lady fell on the floor holding her stomach as the tears started to run down her face. The stylist next to Tiff was bent over the hair washing station, stomping her feet. Tiff had done it again.

"You ain't right!"

"You dead-ass wrong, bitch!"

"You goen to hell, girl." The shop threw the comments at her like they were rotten vegetables. Tiff just smiled, shrugged, and accepted them as if they were a dozen long-stemmed roses.

"I'm just sayen!" Tiff tried to win her audience back, but it was too late. She smiled and stuck out her tongue. "Y'all can get the fuck out!" she laughed as she jokingly kicked her patrons out for the second or third time that day.

Ke-Ke fought to keep herself from laughing but couldn't. The bag she had brought with her from the hair store fell off the couch and she pulled herself together long enough to pick it up and make sure the glass jar that her hair grease had come in hadn't broken or cracked. The ladies were still laughing and cursing Tiff when she finally called Ke-Ke to the chair.

"I'ma be right back," Tiff whispered in her ear as she grabbed her purse and ran out the door. Ke-Ke watched her cross the street and go into the Jamaican restaurant. She spun around in the chair and placed the hair and the contents of her bag on the counter so they would be ready when Tiff got back. Five minutes later, she was walking back in the door with a foam container full of oxtails and a Champagne Cola. She set the food on her station next to the curling irons. "You want some? It'll make your booty grow!" she offered as she bit into a fried plantain and looked around the shop, smiling.

"Naw, I'm good," Ke-Ke laughed as she looked at the dinner. "It smells good though, damn," she said, hoping Tiff would offer again, but she didn't.

"What's it gonna be today?" Tiff asked as she rinsed her hands in the sink and dried them with the napkin that her plastic fork had come wrapped in.

"I want some pink Iversons going into a blonde Mohawk," Ke-Ke said proudly, knowing Tiff was going to have something smart to say about it.

"You and that pink shit! You gonna get enough of that," Tiff said as she smacked her teeth and went through the supplies that she had brought for her to use. She smiled, knowing that she had annoyed Tiff with her decision, but knew she wouldn't try to talk her out of it. She had tried too many times in the past to convince her to go with a more mature or natural look, but Ke-Ke would have no parts of it. Tiff had soon stopped bothering altogether. She reached in her pocket and dug out the money to pay Tiff for her work plus a twenty-dollar tip.

"Damn, bitch! What you won on a scratch-off ticket?" Tiff asked as she took the money and stole a glimpse of the wad that Ke-Ke was struggling to put back into the pockets of her tight jeans.

"Something like that. You know I gets mines!" Ke-Ke answered back, as if having a pocket full of money was nothing new to her.

"Whatever, all money ain't good money. Know that, while you out there *getten mines,*" Tiff mocked her tone and made it a point to sound unimpressed as she knew it would only encourage her.

"Oh, Tiff, if I get somethen in the mail here, just hold onto it for me okay?" Ke-Ke spun around in the chair to make eye contact with Tiff so she would know it was a serious request.

"Don't be senden your bills to me, girl. I got more than enough of them already." Tiff said and rolled her eyes as she bit into an oxtail that she was holding on a fork.

"Naw, I had stopped by the clinic to get some free rubbers and they tricked me into taken a full exam. They senden the results out in the mail and I ain't need my moms to see that shit," Ke-Ke explained.

"Ohhh, okay, well you might as well did it all, it was free! Like my momma used to say, 'Any bitch with self-respect makes sure to get her coochie checked!'" Ke-Ke laughed with her as she tried to wonder where Tiff got all of her little sayings from. They were endless!

"Oh girl, I knew it was something I had to tell you," Tiff sad as she grabbed Ke-Ke by the shoulder and spun her around in the chair.

"What?" Ke-Ke asked, knowing that it had to be good by the way she had said it.

"You talked to your cousin Ti-Ti? What happened with her the other night?" Tiff asked, trying to sound concerned but laughing at the same time.

"I don't know, I ain't talk to her in a day or so. Why, whatsup?" Ke-Ke asked, wondering why Ti-Ti hadn't called her if something had gone down.

"Giiirl, lemme tell you!" Tiff said as she patted her on the shoulder and tried to hold in her laughter. "We was at the dollar store and I'm waiting for my son to come out with his ice cream, and who come running around the corner of the store naked as a jaybird?"

"Nooooo!" Ke-Ke said as she covered her face with her hands and tried to picture the sight in her mind. She knew the rest of the story would be like the train wreck that she wouldn't be able to pull her eyes from.

"Yeeessss! Yo' cousin! Runnen and tryen to cover up her goodies all at the same time!" Tiff spun Ke-Ke around in the chair to face her before she burst into laughter.

"You lyen, Tiff!" Ke-Ke said, hoping that it was all a big joke.

"If I'm lyen, I'm flyen, and you don't see no muthafucken wings on my big ass!" Tiff said like she was waiting on Ke-Ke to doubt her. "But wait, then a car pulls out from behind the building and the nigga driving throws out one of her boots and her panties and pulled the fuck off!"

"Damn, Ti-Ti, damn!" is all Ke-Ke could say as she dropped her head and laughed. She kept her face covered while she shook with laughter. "It was a lot of people out there?" Ke-Ke asked, hoping that her cousin had that much luck.

"PACKED!" Tiff said as she laughed and shook her head. "Fuck Victoria's Secrets! Especially since Ti-Ti out there tellen all of hers." Tiff leaned back on the counter and slid down to the floor in a fit of laughter.

"That shit ain't funny," Ke-Ke said with a smile on her face as she threw a plastic fork down at Tiff, which only made her laugh harder.

"So what happened after that? Where'd she go?" Ke-Ke had to know and hoped that Tiff wouldn't draw too much attention over to them. She knew that the other women in the shop would've begged to hear that story too.

"Whoo girl! I tried to call her to the car, but she hopped in the back of a cab so quick, she didn't even hear me. I know that man was happy!" Tiff shook uncontrollably. "What I been tryen to figure out for the life of me is how she paid the fare!" Tiff was lying all the way down on the floor now, wiping the tears off her face and trying to catch her breath.

"That's soo fucked up!" Ke-Ke couldn't help but laugh as she said it and tried to figure out what she would've done in the same situation.

"And what the hell is up wit that design or whatever she got in between her legs? Looked like she had a baby clown in a leg-lock!" Tiff went into more convulsions on the floor as Ke-Ke playfully kicked at her.

"I don't know…" is all Ke-Ke could answer as she knew that the "art" had to look even more crazy to someone who didn't know what they were looking at.

"Call her! Girl, you gotta call her and find out what the hell that was all about! I swear, I will give you half-off today if you can do that for me. I *HAVE* to know this one!" Tiff begged between her laughter and tears.

"Naw, cause you gonna laugh and she gonna hear you!" Ke-ke said, knowing that Ti-Ti would see that as a major violation.

"No, no, I promise… I'll be good, I'll be good!!" Tiff wiped her tears and sounded like a little kid as she made the sign of the cross on her chest and nodded sincerely. "Girl, matter of fact, take this back!" She took Ke-Ke's money off the counter and handed it back to her. "I'll do you for free!" she said as she upped her ante with a sneaky smile on her face.

Ke-Ke shot her an untrusting look as she put her money back into her pocket. She held her finger to her lips and pulled out her cell phone. She struggled to pull her own self together as she scrolled through her contacts and found Ti-Ti's number.

"Shh! It's ringing," she whispered to Tiff, as she looked down and noticed her holding both of her hands over her mouth.

NINETEEN

WHEN KE-KE FINALLY LEFT THE SALON, it was starting to get dark and Ti-Ti's unbelievable and twisted tale of betrayal mixed with Tiff's laughter were still holding any other thoughts she wanted to have hostage. Tiff was crazy as hell and Ke-Ke always ended up staying in the shop longer than she planned to. She was standing outside the shop smoking a cigarette when the yellow cab pulled up to the curb and honked. She signaled to the driver the she would be a minute and quickly pulled on the Newport, wodering why the cigarettes that tasted the best were always the ones you didn't have a chance to enjoy. She flicked the filter into the sewer and began walking to the car when Tiff stuck her head out of the door behind her.

"Hey!" Ke-Ke looked back, thinking that maybe she had forgotten something. "Stay yo' ass off them seesaws too!" Tiff stuck out her tongue and pointed as she held the door open and laughed. Ke-Ke stuck up her middle finger with a smile and got into the cab. *That bitch finds out everything!* she thought as she slammed the door and settled into the back seat.

"Where ya gwan?" the driver asked in a thick accent as he checked his mirror and pulled into traffic. Ke-Ke was still stunned. She racked her brain trying to figure out where Tiff got her information. She figured that one of the girls must have come by the shop before her and spilled the beans unknowingly.

"Miss Ladee," the cab driver asked her again, as he stared at her through his rear view mirror.

"Oh, 278 Champlain Street," Ke-Ke finally answered as she glanced up at his reflection then looked out of the window. She went through her phone to check her missed calls. She had learned that the less conversation she gave the driver, the less possibility there was for him to try and talk to her. She figured she would head to the Ave and try to run into Cry and find out what kind of deal she had hooked up for her.

The cab rode smoothly through the streets back to the West Side of the city, and Ke-Ke was relieved that the driver had driven in silence while he played reggae and answered his cell phone. The whole car smelled of weed and oils he had used to mask the smell and she figured the driver blazed in between fares. She fought the urge to ask him for some, thinking that he might take it as some sort of invitation. Niggas were like that, even the foreign ones.

They rode down Reynolds Street and made a right on Champlain. The car squeaked to a stop and rocked and the motion and noise snapped Ke-Ke back to reality. She was lost in her thoughts of the horror that Ti-Ti had experienced and everything they both had gone through since dropping out of school a year and a half ago. She paid the fare and hopped out of the backseat.

"Keeeeeee-Keeeeee," a female voice called out in a long exaggerated tone. She looked up to see her homegirl Muffy rolling a blunt under the dim light over her porch. Muffy was Cry's little sister and was know for being a drama queen on the Ave. Her public fights with her baby's father always escalated into an outrageous scene and the spectacles usually ended with family members being called to either break it up or make matters worse, depending on the day.

"That's my bitch! Whatup, Muff?" Ke-Ke acted happier to see her than she really was so Muffy would have no problem offering her some of the weed she was rolling.

"Shit, just getten my mind right!" Muffy answered as she licked the blunt to seal it. Ke-Ke climbed the four steps to the porch and noticed a small bottle of Hennessey in a brown paper bag at Muffy's feet.

"You got you a little personal?" she asked, gesturing down at the bottle.

"You can get a couple of shots, you know I gotta keep it low though, all these beggen-ass niggas out here," Muffy said as she rolled her eyes and dried the blunt with a pink lighter.

"Yeah, I know how that go," Ke-Ke agreed as she handed her a ten-dollar bill to pay for her share of the drink.

"Naw, you good, I wasn't talken about you, girl," Muffy said, as she waved away the bill casually. "Just get me next time," she said as she looked up at her to see if it was a deal. Ke-Ke sat down and sighed as she watched Muffy light the blunt and exhale the thick smoke. She took her phone out of her pocket and sat it on her leg so she wouldn't miss any more calls.

"Yo, you heard about Troi?" Muffy asked as she inhaled the smoke and sat back in her seat.

"Yeah, I heard." Ke-Ke kept it short, not knowing what all Muffy knew or had heard. She wasn't going to volunteer any information.

"That shit crazy! How you gonna kill your own little sister? What the fuck part of the game is that shit?" Muffy asked no one. "They say that bitch down there on suicide watch in the butt-naked cell, talking to herself and shit," Muffy added as she smiled and shook her head.

"Word?" Ke-Ke asked as she listened to the new update. She hadn't really heard anything about the incident since the news broadcast the story the night it had all happened.

"Hell yeah," Muffy continued. "You know they put you in that cell by yourself wit no clothes on when you get to talken about killen yourself. You ain't got no shoes or nothen. They don't want you to have no strings or nothen to hang yourself wit is what I heard." Muffy punched her fist into the palm of her hand to punctuate what she knew to be a fact. Ke-Ke just raised her eyebrows and shrugged her shoulders at the new information, as the image of Troi pacing back in forth in a dark, cold jail cell, ass-naked and mumbling things to herself, played in her head.

"It's a cold world," she said in a low voice as she took the blunt from Muffy's hand and inhaled.

"You said that shit! That shit is deep!" Muffy smiled and tapped her on the shoulder as she reached for the Hennessey. Ke-Ke looked down when she felt her phone vibrating on her leg. She checked the screen and saw the name "Cry" blinking against the light blue background.

"Yo!" she answered as she attempted to balance the bottle Muffy had handed back to her while she tried to sound unexcited.

"Where you at? I'm tryen to come see you. I need to run some shit by you," Cry said in a hurried tone, like she was preoccupied with something else.

"I'm at ya people's house. We smoken out," Ke-Ke said as she took a sip from the bottle. She figured she should get her buzz on in case Cry came to get her and had something freaky on her mind.

"Where on Champlain?" Cry's voice came through the phone and caught Muffy's attention.

"Yeah, I'm wit Muff," Ke-Ke said as she glanced at Muffy out of the corner of her eyes, knowing that as soon as she hung up the phone the questions would start.

"Yo, tell her to bring me some Mojos," Muffy said before Ke-Ke could end the conversation, referring to the local pizza and wings restaurant.

"Muffy said bring her some Mojos," Ke-Ke relayed the message.

"Tell Muffy to get a muthafucken job!" Cry half-shouted through the phone loud enough for Muffy to hear her.

"What she say?" Muffy asked, but Ke-Ke shook her head, like the last message wasn't intended for her to hear.

"Aiight," Ke-Ke said, hoping Cry wasn't waiting for her to say it while she was still on the phone with her.

"Aiight, love, I'll be through," Cry spoke in a soft tone that sent a chill through Ke-Ke's body, but she held in her smile.

"What she say? She on the way over here, right?" Muffy asked with a suspicious look on her face.

"Yeah, she on her way," is all Ke-Ke could find the nerve to say.

"So, what's good wit y'all two? I'm hearen thangs," Muffy asked as she bit down on her tongue and looked at Ke-Ke with a sneaky grin on her face.

"Here *you* go." Ke-Ke shook her head and handed the blunt back to her.

"Damn, my sis done got another one! I ain't know you got down like that, girl!" She spoke in between coughs and laughs.

"Shit ain't even like that." Ke-Ke made sure not to sound too mad about the teasing so as not to give herself away. "We just on some hustle shit, she said she got some work for me," Ke-Ke tried to fill in the blanks enough so Muffy wouldn't be left to her own very vocal devices.

"Mmmmhmmm," Muffy laughed. "That's what they call it now?" she laughed and leaned over the railing over the porch. "That's how it starts. She got some work for you, and then she *WORKING YOU!*" Muffy spoke the words and made thrusting motions with her hips to illustrate her point.

"Girl, stop it! That's how fucken rumors get started." Ke-Ke tried to sound more annoyed than mad.

"Naw, I'm just playen, girl. I know you strickly dickly, like me. I'm just fucken wit you," Muffy said as she stopped laughing all at once. Ke-Ke wondered silently if she really believed that or not and wondered if Cry would keep their secret from her own family. She couldn't do anything about it either way, so she took the blunt when Muffy handed it back and pushed the thoughts out of her mind completely.

"And if ain't no dick around, I mean ABSOLUTELY none can be found... Muffy will do Muffy by herself! You know they say can't nobody do you like you!" She reached down between her legs and rubbed herself playfully.

"You crazy as hell, girl!" Ke-Ke said and looked away quickly when she caught her eyes following Muffy's hand. She focused on the street and the cars passing on the Avenue as she tried to get the snapshot of Muffy's pussy lips showing through her stretch pants out of her head.

Muffy was the youngest of the three sisters in her family. She was thin, but had a nice tight ass and a cute face. She shared the same flawless complexion as Cry and always dressed well. What she lacked in physical dimensions she seemed to more than make up for with a natural sex appeal and style. She had small but perky tits and could easily go without a bra and not look tacky. Judging from the visual, she kept her pussy shaved and opted to go without panties as well. Ke-Ke was high and couldn't stop her mind from wandering.

I'd do her! Ke-Ke thought to herself. *If she didn't have such a big mouth!*

Muffy had turned to yell at someone up on the corner and Ke-Ke caught a smell of fruit coming off of her as she glanced down at her ass. She didn't know if it was the weed or whether she had turned full-fledge lesbian at that moment, but she was actually admiring how the stretch pants clung to her ass and left nothing to the imagination. She could see the little dimples on the small of her back, right above her waistline. It was almost as if Muffy was standing there completely naked. She watched her ass as it flexed when she moved and turned her head quickly before Muffy turned back around. She played a fantasy out in her head of Muffy bent over the railing of the porch while she plunged a strap-on sex toy in and out of her with no mercy. She would be talking shit and gripping her ass at the same time as Muffy's tight, bubble butt slammed against her pelvis harder and harder with every thrust.

The thoughts sent butterflies loose in her stomach and chest. She tried to hold the feelings down, but it was too late. The warmth had already spread to the middle of her legs and she could feel herself getting wet.

Damn, I'm fucken trippen, she thought as she wiped her face and tried to force her thoughts in another direction.

"Um... hello?" Muffy said with her forhead wrinkled in confusion as she held the remainder of the blunt in her outstretched hand. Ke-Ke shook her head and passed on her turn. She wondered if Muffy had caught the way she had been looking at her as she tried to get ahold of her high before she did or said something that she would regret later.

"Damn, you must got some *shit* on your mind, you all quiet over there and shit!" Muffy said as she sat on the railing in front of her with her legs open. Ke-Ke knew her judgment was off as she tried to figure out if Muffy was teasing her, fucking with her, or hitting on her. All the thoughts seemed to pile up in her mind at the same time like a car crash as the weed made her paranoid and horny at the same time.

"If only you knew," Ke-Ke said with a smirk, knowing that the truth was sometimes the hardest thing for people to believe. "Where you got that? That shit is fire!" Ke-Ke said quickly before she slipped and said too much.

"Ohh, you like that, huh?" Muffy smiled as she jumped down from the railing and did an erotic little dance. Ke-Ke couldn't tell whether she was talking about the weed or not. She decided to be slick and stood up and stretched and "accidentally" rubbed the back of her hand against Muffy's ass as she did.

"Oh, my bad," Ke-Ke said as she looked away and played it off, waiting to see what Muffy's reaction would be.

"Huh?" Muffy turned around with her eyebrows raised like she hadn't even noticed. Ke-Ke decided to push it a little further and said "Excuse me" as she lightly palmed both of her ass cheeks and moved her to the side as she scooted past her to the other side of the proch so she could stretch her legs. She felt it was still a subtle gesture that she could deny the intent of if Muffy tried to flip on her over it.

'You good!" Muffy said, like Ke-Ke had only tapped her on the shoulder. Ke-Ke could feel the fire building inside of her as she thought about slamming Muffy against the side of the house and having her way with her. Muffy unzipped her hooded sweatshirt and stretched, revealing a half shirt that displayed her flat stomach and a belly button piercing that dangled and sparkled as if it were winking.

"You know, in life, what I learned, Ke... is that if you *really* want something, you just gotta take it, you know? You just gotta reach out, grab it, and take it," Muffy said as she turned around again and stared off the porch into the night. She looked over her shoulder and their eyes locked as Muffy licked her lips and smiled.

Ke-Ke felt as if her body was vibrating with sexual energy, but she just could not get past her thoughts that Muffy could be setting her up and how the news would travel through the hood like wildfire. She licked her lips the same way Muffy had and stared into her eyes while in her fantasies she had already ripped her clothes off and forced her to the ground in an uninhibited fury of passion.

They both looked away as Cry pulled up and honked, snapping them out of their trance.

"There she go," Ke-Ke said as she moved back to her seat.

"Big ballen ass, sis!" Muffy yelled out as Cry turned the engine off. The car gleamed underneath the streetlights and the tires shone as if they were coated in clear nail polish. Cry took her time getting out of the car.

"I like your hair though, girl, you went to Tiff?" Muffy asked, trying to start a whole new conversation.

"Yeah, you know she the only one I fuck wit!" Ke-Ke answered and played along as she tried to act like she wasn't moved by Cry's presence and stared down the block in the opposite direction.

"I been wanten to go see her too, but my money been funny!" Muffy said as she stared down at her nails.

"I'd pay for some," Ke-Ke said underneath her breath.

"What you say?" Muffy smiled and acted like she hadn't really heard her.

"I ain't say nothen," Ke-Ke said as she decided not to push her luck any further.

They both stopped talking as they heard the car door slam and watched Cry walking to the house as she talked on the phone. She managed to look in every direction as she walked without appearing scared or paranoid. Ke-Ke smiled and tried not to seem excited. She admired how smooth Cry always was and how she never seemed to be worried about anything. She walked and handled herself with the confidence of a man, but still had all the grace and sexiness of a woman.

"Big Cry!" someone yelled from halfway down the block. Cry turned and held up her hand as if she knew who it was. She finished her conversation on the sidewalk before she looked around some more and climbed the steps to the porch.

"Whatup, Sis?" Muffy spoke first and rose to give Cry a half-hug before offering her the bottle that Ke-Ke was holding. Cry waved away the offer and handed Muffy another blunt to light. "Yo, where my Mojos at?" Muffy asked with a confused look on her face when she noticed that Cry wasn't carrying anything.

"Girl, please!" Cry rolled her eyes at her little sister.

"Okay." Muffy's voice trailed off as she tried to act like she really didn't want the food that bad anyway. She lit the blunt and sat down without saying anything else. Ke-Ke could tell that it was her version of pouting. Cry waited for the perfect moment when Muffy turned away to look up the street and stuck her tongue out at Ke-Ke and made a slow licking gesture, then winked. Ke-Ke smiled and gestured a kiss with her lips in Cry's direction, feeling a chill run down her spine.

"Damn, I thought I lost that bitch!" Muffy said as she bent over and grabbed her lighter before turning around and searching the faces of her company, realizing that all of a sudden it had gotten quiet. She glanced back and forth at their faces, but couldn't detect anything, so she sat back down and continued to smoke.

"Pass that shit!" Cry demanded as she noticed Muffy taking more than her turn on the freshly lit blunt.

"Aiight!" Muffy returned her attention to the blunt before handing it sideways to Ke-Ke. Cry leaned on the railing with her back to the street as she waited for her turn in the rotation. The three of them stared down the block at the hooded figures that occupied the corner a half a block away.

"Y'all heard about Forty?" she asked finally, never taking her eyes off of the corner.

"Naw, what happened?" Muffy froze with the bottle halfway from her mouth as she asked the question.

"You thirsty!" Cry laughed as she pointed and shook her head at Muffy.

"That nigga got bodied!" Cry spoke without ever changing her tone.

"Word?" Muffy half-asked, half-stated as she stared up at Cry with her mouth open. Ke-Ke glanced at Cry with a shocked look on her face, waiting to hear the whole story. Forty was from the hood and was well-liked by everybody on the West Side. Ke-Ke remembered when she was in junior high school and she and Forty had called themselves going together for a couple of months. They were forced to break up when Forty had fingered her on the back of the bus and the news traveled through the kids to the bus driver to the school and then back to her mother.

"Hell yeah!" Cry said as she nodded slowly. "Niggas came to rob his spot, he standen outside with his cousin and some other niggas drinken, the niggas walked up and pull out on them, and his cousin and boys ran into the house and left him outside."

"Get the fuck outta here!" Ke-Ke had said aloud before she realized it, not believing what she was hearing.

"That's fucked up!" Muffy added, still frozen in time, holding the bottle halfway from her mouth.

Cry nodded slowly before she continued. "The fucked up part about it is, all the money and dope was in the house. They end up killen Forty for seven dollars." She punched her palm to emphasize her point. "That's all that nigga had in his pockets."

"That's fucked up!" Ke-Ke and Muffy chorused. They looked at each other and then back at Cry. They sat silent on the porch for a few minutes, trying to digest the news before Cry spoke again.

"It's getten hectic out here! Niggas getten back on that stick-up kid shit!" Cry said.

"It's these young niggas," Muffy chimed in. Cry just shrugged and reached for the blunt when she noticed that Ke-Ke was just holding it and letting it burn.

"Word though! These young niggas is wilden," Muffy continued her campaign against a whole group of people that were only two to three years younger than her.

"Y'all heard about dude that killed on the East Side over the curry chicken dinner?" Muffy asked as she looked back and forth at Cry and Ke-Ke. She was visibly happy that she had center stage and smiled when she realized no one was familiar with the story. "Man, dude chillen wit his boy and I guess he leaves his dinner in the room with him to go the bathroom. His boy takes some of the chicken and when dude comes back, they end up getten in a fight over it." Muffy paused to drag out the story. "Anyway, dude leaves to pick up his girl and the curry chicken dude follows him, catches him at a stoplight and blows his head off with a shotgun!" Ke-Ke and Cry both shook their heads for Muffy's benefit, not sure how true the story was. "Over some curry chicken though!" Muffy repeated the detail, like they hadn't heard her the first time. "They say his girl had to go to the crazy house," she added as she puffed on the blunt that she had just taken back from Cry.

"Word?" Ke-Ke asked as she glanced over at her.

"Yeah, she went into shock, all that blood and brains all over her. She was sitten in the passenger seat. She lost it, I guess!" Muffy exhaled the smoke and coughed. "She was just sitten there, shaken wit his blood all over her until the police showed up!"

"Goddamn!" Cry said as she stood up, stretched, and began looking through her phone. The mood shifted as the three of them sat in silence for the next few minutes with their thoughts in different places.

"You ready?" Cry glanced up from her phone towards Ke-Ke as she turned to make her way down the porch steps.

"Aiight y'all," Muffy said with a grin on her face as she watched Ke-Ke and Cry walk away. "Don't do nothen I wouldn't do," she teased and laughed as she was left on the porch to get high by herself.

Ke-Ke got into the car and was overwhelmed by the strong smell of leather as she glanced around the interior. Cry's cars always looked and smelled like she had just driven them off the showroom floor minutes earlier. She smiled as the dash sprang to life in bright blue and white lights and the Infiniti logo popped up onto the navigation system like a movie screen. Cry pulled the car away from the curb and accelerated up the street smoothly. Ke-Ke reclined in the seat and enjoyed how it felt like they weren't even moving, as she relished the luxury and tried to push the images of death out of her mind.

Since as far back as she could remember, someone was always losing their life in the street. Ke-Ke struggled to remember names and instances and felt guilty because it was all a big, black, disorganized blur in her mind. The thoughts were like the garbage bags and dusty boxes in her grandmother's basement. You knew they were there, but what was in each individual one, you didn't remember until you opened them. A street sign or a particular corner was usually enough to spark your memory and send you back into the past as you vividly recalled the sordid and twisted details of one tragedy after another.

She remembered a Kwanzaa celebration where the speaker challenged her and her classmates asking, "What's it all about?" Of course there were all types of answers and smart remarks, but the question always stuck with her. What WAS it all about? Money? Reputation? Respect? She had even heard some boys in her class blame it on women or, more specifically, pussy. She could hear them in her head as clear as day speaking to the older black woman, adorned in a kente robe with a matching headwrap. She was extremely patient and tolerant as she listened to them profanely describe the self-destructive nature of a lost people.

"Niggas do what they do, cause that's what bitche— I mean females—like! Females like the jewelry, the cars, the rims, the clothes, and the money. Niggas just doen what they gotta do to impress them or get them half of the time."

Ke-Ke remembered the lady nodding as she walked with bare feet and smiling before she asked him, "Why would you want a female that only wanted you for what you had or for what you could do for her?"

She stumped him for a few seconds before he blurted out, "That's just the way it is, ma'am!"

Ke-Ke remembered the look of hurt in the woman's eyes as she looked down at them. She had a dark, rich complexion that seemed to glow and shimmer in the light with a seashell necklace that matched her earrings. She wore thin dreadlocks that came out of the top of her headwrap like a crown. She spoke in a low but strong tone and Ke-Ke remembered thinking that she must've been a queen that had traveled to America from Africa. She was beautiful, but in a totally different way that Ke-

Ke couldn't put her finger on, and for some reason she commanded a respect without yelling or threatening.

Her long, colorful dress flowed down to her feet, and it almost appeared as if she was hovering above the floor when she slowly walked from one side of the room to the other as she spoke. She told stories filled with animals that talked and spoke of faraway lands with funny names. She had asked the girls in the class to stay after when she dismissed the boys from the room.

"Your black man needs you, ladies," she said in a low tone as she searched their souls with her eyes. She made them stand in a circle and hold hands and prayed an African blessing over them. Ke-Ke could remember the power of the words even though she didn't understand what she was saying—the current of electricity that shot through her and the power she felt as the woman and the girls in her class "stood as one."

"You are all queens and mothers of the Earth. With that comes power, and with that power comes a great responsibility!" She closed their meeting and requested that everyone squeeze the hands of the person next to them seven times. Ke-Ke never forgot how that woman's words had made her feel and forgot the question that she had never come up with an answer to shortly after they had all gotten back on the bus.

"What she kept y'all for? Why she wanted to talk to y'all without us? What she say?" the boys asked as they climbed back on the bus.

Ke-Ke remembered looking back and seeing the woman watch them through the window with a look of sorrow on her face. Their eyes had locked just before she boarded the bus.

"She said pussy is power and we run the world, niggas!" somebody answered, and all the kids roared with laughter.

Ke-Ke thought about the whole conversation again as she rode in silence. What *was* it all about? She remembered the woman's words, all at once, about having the power to create your own reality and having the power to accept or reject what you decide is good or bad for you.

"Why would you accept such a self-destructive and superficial set of laws to live by?" The woman's words echoed in her head. Ke-Ke sat and thought about the ways that she and everybody around her seemed to just go with what they thought they were supposed to be doing. She never had really stopped to ask herself why. When people she knew started getting killed or were old enough to be locked up, she had just learned to accept it. Nobody ever asked why or ever even wondered what it was all about. People would just be like, "That's fucked up!"

When she was in grade school, a girl was stabbed to death in the bus loop at the end of a school day. The news reported that it was all over some boy who was in their class. She was only twelve. *"And the band played on!"* her Uncle James had yelled from the kitchen in response to the news report.

"Shut up, James!" her mother had yelled at him from the couch in front of the television.

"It's true," he said, and continued to make sandwiches and steal food out of the refrigerator.

Although she had thought about it before, she now completely understood what he was saying. The band does play on. Nobody gives a fuck or pays any attention to anything for too long. Reality was so different from the movies like that. No one she had ever known or even heard of had changed their life or moved away because of what was going on. They just continued to do what they always did and if they changed, they changed for the worse.

The band definitely plays on, and it gets louder and louder and louder.

"That shit fucken wit you?" Cry looked over at her, yanking Ke-Ke out of her thoughts and back into the present.

"Naw, that shit's just life," she answered coolly as she stared through the windshield like she was born without a soul.

TWENTY

CRY TURNED THE RADIO UP. WDKX was in slow-jam mode and playing love songs one after the other. The songs made Ke-Ke nostalgic and emotional as she thought about when Lee's funeral would be and whether she would have the strength to go. She knew she was never good with funerals and there would be too many people from the hood there for her to be breaking down and getting all teary.

"You heard when Lee's funeral is?" she asked.

"I heard they doen it at Metropolitan over on West Ave, but I don't know what day it's on," Cry answered as they stopped at a red light and watched an old man struggling to get his shopping cart full of cans over the curb and out of traffic.

After a short drive, they pulled up in front of a grey house in an area of the city known as Ghost Town. Ke-Ke observed how Cry's oversized watch sparkled as she reached down and pulled the keys out of the ignition.

"You ready to get your hustle on, or you still depressed about your dead homies?" Cry asked, as if she was doubting her.

"Hell, yeah. I told you I was tryen to get on," Ke-Ke said with no hesitation as she reached for the door handle.

"Aiight then killa, c'mon," Cry smiled and motioned with her head as she climbed out of the car. Ke-Ke followed her to the door as she looked around the dark neighborhood. Ghost Town was a run-down neighborhood that sat on the West Side. The houses looked haunted by night and it had earned its name by the amount of people that had been killed in that area, usually over something that had to do with drugs. The area, though not far from the hood, had its own eerie vibe, and the people from that area always seemed to have a look in their eyes that was a veil to a world full of dark secrets that only they knew. The niggas from that area were not as flashy as the ones from Ke-Ke's neighborhood. They wore big jeans and hoodies and the only way you could tell that they had any money was to look down at their hundred-dollar sneakers. There was a police sub-station that sat on the edge of the neighborhood, but it didn't deter or stop all the shootings, murders, and robberies that made the area notorious.

A girl in her class who lived in the neighborhood had invited her over when she was still in school and Ke-Ke remembered the large mice that scurried across the kitchen floor and disappeared under the stove or the refrigerator. They were EVERYWHERE. Ke-Ke's skin crawled. She hesitated to sit down while her friend would just stomp her foot on the floor and continue talking like they were house pets. That memory was the source of many nightmares for years to come. She would dream of falling asleep on their couch and waking up with mice crawling all over her.

"Don't get scared now," Cry looked over and smiled when she noticed Ke-Ke looked like she had caught a chill that shook her body.

"I'm good," Ke-Ke laughed as she tried to make it look like she was just brushing herself off.

"Whatup though!" P-nut answered the door in his boxers with the dumb smile on his face that had made him famous. P-nut was a used-to-be-big-time baller who lost it all somehow, drank too much, and was generally more tolerated than liked by those he came in contact with. He was commonly referred to as Nut and was harmless for the most part. His saving grace was that he favored the rapper Ludacris and kind of acted like him. He had tried to hit on Ke-Ke or one of her friends a million times before when he was drunk, saying off-the-wall comments and flashing money. He would never remember his antics when he sobered up, which kept him in petty squabbles with boyfriends and husbands citywide. The majority of the time, no one touched him though, out of respect for his cousins. They would always be there to bail him out like, "Man, that's just Nut. He ain't mean no harm. You know how he is."

"Whatup, Ke?" he greeted her and gave her a half-hug as Cry pushed him away when he tried to reach around her neck. Nut stumbled and ended up holding onto her for balance.

"This is the new recruit?" he asked with a sneaky smile as he glanced over at Cry.

"Yeah, she gonna grind wit y'all for a minute. See how she like it," Cry responded as she glanced around the room.

Ke-Ke looked up to see a naked girl walk past the doorway that led to the kitchen and into the bathroom.

"What, y'all in here tricken off again?" Cry asked with disgust in her voice as she handed him a large Ziploc bag. Ke-Ke stared at the bag and noticed all of the small, individual bags that filled it contained what looked like little pieces of soap. She never understood why people went so crazy for that stuff.

"You know how we do." P-nut did a little dance with his arms raised. "Shorty gonna have to get used to that, or join in, it's her choice." He shot a look at Ke-Ke and stuck his tongue out.

"Don't fucken play yourself!" Ke-Ke said as cold as she possibly could. She watched the smile disappear from his face as she stared him directly in his eyes. She wanted to make sure that niggas knew that she was here for business and not entertainment. She decided right at that moment that she would not be drinking at this house and she would try to keep her smoking under control as well. She knew that she was a whole lot easier to convince when she got smoked out or was saucy. She figured she would have Ti-Ti over to watch her back and take the edge off things.

"Fall back off her like that!" Cry said as she sat up on the couch. "I told yo' dumb ass that this was strictly business." She stared at P-nut with fire in her eyes as she spoke. Ke-Ke tried to hide her smile as Cry defended her honor in a way that no one had before.

"My bad," P-nut smiled with his hands up in surrender. He glanced back and forth at them with a grin, like he was mentally puttting two and two together.

"Where the fuck your boy at?" Cry asked as she sat back on the couch but kept the serious look on her face.

"Oh, he in the back doen his thang. He should be out in a minute. I'ma go get him, hold up." P-Nut walked through the kitchen to the back bedroom and knocked on the door before he opened it and disappeared inside. Ke-Ke heard the bathroom door open and the girl come out. It was Asia! She didn't look into the front room though and headed back to the bedroom.

"You gonna have to grow some thick skin up in here. These niggas be on some wild shit, and they gonna try you!" Cry warned. "You can handle it though," she nodded at Ke-Ke as she made eye contact.

Ke-Ke nodded back as her mind raced and she felt a nervous energy come over. She wondered what other girl was in the room with Asia and what they would say when they saw her. All she needed was for *that* story to get out and she would have hell trying to keep P-nut and whoever else from thinking she was just a ho playing hard to get. That would be bad for business.

"You good, right?" Cry asked as Ke-Ke stared ahead and wondered how things were going to play out.

"Yeah, I'm straight," she nodded as she tried to come up with a way to handle the situation if she did get called out.

Cry sighed impatiently as she stood up and walked into the kitchen. She was halfway to the door when it opened and Co-Co walked out in a white G-string with sweat dripping from her naked chest. Ke-Ke watched from the other room as she crossed the kitchen and ran her fingers through her mangled hair.

"Damn, y'all bitches comfortable, huh?" Cry asked with a smile on her face as she watched Co-Co from behind.

Lotto emerged from the bedroom finally, wiping himself with a towel, smiling.

"You know we be putten in that work," he said as he glanced around Cry to look at Ke-Ke in the other room.

"Can I get me?" Cry asked as she held out her hand and leaned against the doorway. Ke-Ke watched as she looked into the bedroom like she was trying to catch another glimpse of Asia.

"Oh shit, yeah," Lotto wiped his face again, went back into the bedroom, and came out with an oversized pair of Coogi jeans in his hands. He reached in the pocket and pulled out a wad of bills held together by a rubber band and handed it to Cry. She casually flipped through the bills with one hand as Lotto tried to keep his balance while he slipped his jeans on.

Lotto was a dude that Ke-Ke had heard about on many occasions, but had never really met. She had heard of females fighting over him on several occasions and had wondered in the past what females seemed to find so amazing about him. He could dress and was always in matching outfits but seemed really quiet and reserved.

"I gave Nut the next pack. Let me holla at you for a minute." Cry gestured for Lotto to follow her into the front room where Ke-Ke was sitting, after she closed the bedroom door.

"Yo, this my girl I told you about. She gonna hold it down here with you and Nut and make some paper," Cry said with her arm around Lotto's shoulder as they stood in front of Ke-Ke. Lotto crossed the room, holding his pants up with one hand and casually slapped Ke-Ke's hand. Ke-Ke could tell already that he was the brains of the organization by the way that he carried himself.

"I seen you on the Ave before," he commented as he reached for a pack of cigarettes that sat on the table in front of her.

"Yeah, I seen you before," Ke-Ke responded. "It's strictly money though. I'm here for business. What y'all do is what y'all do, just respect my gangsta," Ke-Ke had spoken the words so sharply and quickly that she surprised herself.

"Aiight, shorty!" Lotto smiled as he held the cigarette to the flame of his lighter. "Ain't nobody tryen to disrespect nobody, that's what it is," he said as he exhaled the smoke and looked over at her. Ke-Ke looked over at Cry and saw a smile forming on her face like she was proud of her.

"My bitch hold it down," Cry said with a smile on her face. "So y'all work it out. As far as shifts, show her all the regulars and cut her in even," Cry instructed Lotto as she patted him on the shoulder.

Ke-Ke was instantly turned on at how a female could run two niggas the way Cry did. She had heard the stories in the past about her, but to see her in action was a totally different thing altogether. Lotto and Nut respected her as if she was a nigga twice their size and they were afraid to piss her off. Ke-Ke loved that and wondered what Cry had done in the past to commad that kind of respect. She thought back to the way she and her friends had always managed to get men to do things for them, by being cute, giving up ass, or catering to them to make them feel important. Cry's style of handling business made her regret every second of it.

She watched as Cry walked to the door and noticed how Lotto didn't even stare at her ass or try to make some veiled sexual comment the way that men always did. He just did as he was told and respected every word that came from the "Boss Bitch."

Ke-Ke felt herself falling in love as she inhaled one last image of Cry standing by the door with her hand on the knob. She stared her up and down from the chain that glimmered under the collar of her long-sleeved Polo shirt, to the bulge on her wrist where her diamond encrusted watch and bracelet were concealed, to the baggy, dark blue jeans that partially hid her shapely body and stopped in small cuffs above her white-on-white sneakers. Ke-Ke felt high as she stared at "Daddy." When she glanced back up, she noticed Cry had been following her eyes again. She winked and disappeared out the door. Ke-Ke gave a quick wave, which was a weak substitute for the fantasy she played in her head of crossing the room and shoving her tongue down her throat.

"Hold up for a second," Lotto said as he locked the door behind Cry and jogged out of the room. Ke-Ke sat back on the couch and looked around the front room. There was a small fourteen-inch television with a DVD player and a large stack of bootleg DVDs on top of it. She figured that crackheads had probably traded the goods for product and that Nut and Lotto came across good deals on stuff like that all the time.

The paint on the walls was a faded yellow that began to crack when it reached the ceiling at the corners where she could see watermarks from the apartment above. There was a coffee table that looked like it probably came with the apartment, years before Lotto and Nut ever set up shop there. Four ashtrays cluttered the table, overflowing with cigar tobacco and empty wrap packages. She moved a magazine with her hand to reveal another bootleg X-rated DVD with big-booty women posing in nothing but fishnet stockings and heels. She shook her head as she noticed the flattened box of Magnum condoms and rolled her eyes, remembering what her grandmother would always say: "If these walls could talk...the things they would say!" She smiled at the thought of her grandmother, but was interrupted when Co-Co emerged from the bathroom, glanced over at her twice, and stopped in her tracks.

"Hey, girl!" She waved and walked around the kitchen table and into the room with Ke-Ke as if she was fully dressed.

"Whatup?" Ke-Ke answered, trying to keep it short.

"You worken over here too? These niggas is some major tricks girl, you gonna make some paper once you figure out what they like. We been here two days now!" Co-Co whispered as she kept glancing over her shoulder, making sure no one had walked up behind her. She sat down across from Ke-Ke and found the cigarettes on the cluttered table and lit one.

"Naw, not like that. I'm tryna do something different." She gave Co-Co a serious look that said, "Don't blow up my spot, bitch." She prepared herself for battle as she waited to see what Co-Co's reaction would be.

"Ohhh, okay, I hear that shit! This hoen shit ain't for everybody. You gotta get your paper though," she said casually as she exhaled the smoke towards the ceiling. Ke-Ke was relieved and relaxed herself. She could tell immediately that Co-Co wasn't the talking type. She glanced down and noticed how her nipples were rock hard, even though there wasn't a draft in the room.

"Dope ain't never been my thang though." She spoke again before she took another long pull on the cigarette. "Too much drama, too many cutthroat niggas, too many snitches, too much time, and I love dick too much to be locked up with a bunch of stanken-ass bitches!" She ran down the list like she had spent some time alone, arranging it in order of importance.

"I feel you." Ke-Ke laughed as she continued to sneak glances at Co-Co's body. She had a cute belly button piercing that worked well against the complexion of her skin.

"Me, I'd rather just lay on my back for mines. I get the best of both worlds, good dick and good money," Co-Co spoke the words rapid-fire with no shame in her tone.

Ke-Ke nodded and smiled, but deep inside wondered what happened in a girl's life to make her just accept that she was a ho. Co-Co sat there in front of her and said it no differently than someone would say that they had worked for the phone company for the last ten years. She had to respect it though, at least she was being real about it. The world was filled with too many bitches that dressed up and played professional or high-maintenance. They would lie to your face forever about how they didn't suck dick or do this and that, but when the lights went out or they were out of your sight, they got down with the best of them. The same girls would fight you to the death if you ever called them a ho and deny shit until they were blue in the face, but Co-Co was at least a stand-up bitch about hers.

"At least you real about it," Ke-Ke complimented her, breaking the silence that had fallen between them.

"Ain't got no choice. I was born into this shit pretty much," Co-Co said as she stared off into space. She looked over at Ke-Ke and must've noticed the confused look on her face, then sat up straight in her chair. She glanced over her shoulder again, making sure the coast was clear. "Look, a bitch like me was like thirteen or fourteen." She squinted and looked up at the ceiling like she was trying to remember exactly. "Moms was on that shit since I was young and it just got worse and worse. We started noticing our toys and games coming up missing and then our clothes. She used to blame it on the people that stayed underneath us."

Co-Co hit the cigarette again and smiled as she shook her head at the memories.

"Anyway, I guess after a while she had gotten herself into some debt and them peoples wanted they money. She told me she was dropping me off at a friend's house while she went to look for a job. She drops me off at this Puerto Rican nigga's house. He was like thirty at the time, I guess."

She paused again and stared into Ke-Ke's eyes like she was debating on whether or not to finsh the rest of the story. "Yeah well, let's just say she never came back and that nigga, his brother, and his friends put they dick in every hole I had for like a year."

A silence fell over the room that Ke-Ke was afraid to break. She could feel her heart ripping slowly in her chest, but for some reason couldn't find the strength to cut Co-Co off.

"That nigga raised me though, taught me this game. He said the way I took dick at that age, I was born to do it. I came back to my mother when I was seventeen. She was still smoking that shit, but I had a car, clothes, my own place, and a bunch of niggas that was old enough to be my daddy or uncles that knew my name, in a way that..."

She stopped and looked up at Ke-Ke again. "Well, you know what I'm sayen, girl." Ke-Ke nodded to let her know that she did as she stared into her eyes. She could hear the pain in Co-Co's voice and didn't dare try to make her explain something that was hard for her to deal with, even if she hadn't completely understood what she had meant.

"Yeah, well that's my story." Co-Co had obviously cut the story short when she felt herself about to become emotional. She stared off in space with a glazed look in her eyes and rocked back in forth in her chair. Ke-Ke found herself lost in her eyes and knew they were windows to a world full of pain that no one could ever fully know or understand. The deep, dark brown circles encased in ice were tunnels that led to an underground chamber where room after room exposed a horrible secret and a terrible memory that haunted her. "This is what I do. I ain't been to school since the summer of my eighth grade year when she dropped me off. Shit, I ain't got no choice but to claim it. This is who I am, what I am... shit... I am what I am, like Popeye be sayen. You feel me?" She smiled to try and lighten the mood as she offered what was left of her cigarette to Ke-Ke. Co-Co stood up and stretched with her palms facing the ceiling while she tried to find a place to extinguish the cigarette that Ke-Ke had waved away when Lotto walked back into the room.

"Damn, somebody died in here?" he asked, feeling the somber vibe that hung in the air. He smiled and slapped Co-Co on the ass and sat down with a half-empty bottle of Paul Masson. Ke-Ke fought back the tears as she watched Co-Co smile and give her a wave before she walked back through the kitchen towards the bedroom. "Make it clap for me one time, Co-Co," Lotto ordered with a smile on his face.

Ke-Ke dropped her head as Co-Co grabbed the back of a chair in the kitchen, stood on her toes and bounced up and down. Her ass clapped loudly as Lotto laughed and stomped his feet.

"Damn, I think you got shorty in here checken you out too!" Lotto continued to laugh as he took a sip from the bottle he was holding. Ke-Ke glanced up one more time and made eye contact with Co-Co as she winked, blew her a kiss, and disappeared into the bedroom.

"Soo, you ready to be a hustler?" Lotto asked as he put the bottle on the table and dashed into the kitchen, returning with two short glasses that he had put ice cubes in.

"Yeah, I been ready," Ke-Ke sighed. "I need the paper right about now," she said, trying to establish a homeboy relationship with Lotto so she wouldn't constantly have to deal with him trying to get some pussy from her.

"Aiight, I hear you, you came to the right place then," he said as he poured two double shots into the glasses and handed one to her.

"You ain't got no chaser?" Ke-Ke asked as she stared at the amount of liquor that he had generously poured into her glass.

"Oh shit, my bad." Lotto bounced off the chair, into the kitchen, and returned with a two-liter generic cola. "I always just take mine to the head," he said and sat back down smiling. Ke-Ke shot him a distrusting look that told him that she knew the game.

"I ain't tryen to get you drunk, shorty! I just want you to be comfortable. We party around here and get money. Ain't no reason for you to be all uptight. The shit pretty laid back, you gonna see." Lotto spoke like a big brother or a mentor in a halfway house.

Ke-Ke poured the cola into her glass and noticed how it had no fizz in it before she leaned back on the couch. "So how this shit work?" she asked as she looked over at him.

"It's like this," Lotto sat forward and made small hand gestures as he spoke, like they were in a football huddle. "Cry drop off the packs, we get em off, she pay us at the end of the week. Everybody eat, everybody happy." He made it sound simple. Ke-Ke knew that there had to be a lot more to it.

"We make extra money 'coonen' and 'piggybacking,' but she don't need to know about that as long as our drop to her is always right and we don't run no business away."

Ke-Ke squinted like Lotto was speaking a foreign language.

"Aiight, you know what 'coonen' is, right?" Lotto made eye contact as he tested her.

"Hell naw," Ke-Ke shook her head and looked at him like he was crazy. She had to learn the game, but she felt uncomfortable having to reveal already how much she didn't know. "We probably call it somethen different," she lied, hoping that he wouldn't catch on.

For the next half hour, Lotto gave her a crash course in crack dealing. No matter how nonchalant she looked on the outside, she was hanging onto his every word and secretly appreciating the fact that he was trying to school her. No one had ever really explained how drugs worked to her. She knew what a dime was and what it went for and she knew some prices for weight amounts in weed, but outside of that she really didn't know how the whole drug dealing world worked at all. Lotto explained tricks of the trade, clues on how to tell if someone was an undercover, what to do if they were robbed or in a raid, and where to stash dope where K-9 dogs would have an impossible time sniffing it out.

She soaked up the information like a sponge, the whole time acting it was something that she already knew. She traded stories with Lotto to convince him that she was a seasoned vet from bits and pieces of other people's conversations she had heard on the Ave or in school. By the time Cry texted to see if she was okay, she and Lotto were talking and joking like old friends. She felt like she could relax around him a little bit, even though she had followed his eyes down to her crotch more than once while they were talking. He warned her about Nut not being able to take "no" for an answer but followed up with, "But he harmless though, he harmless though."

The only part that she was uncomfortable with, after everything had been explained, was the fact that there was no trapdoor or window that they served customers out of. Lotto and Nut would have to open the door completely, day or night, to let the fiends in the house in order to make transactions. She wasn't feeling that part of it at all. She secretly hoped that at least one of them would always be in the house with her.

She watched a few rounds of the door being opened when there was knock and it made her heart skip every time. She had met most of the regulars after an hour or so, according to Lotto, when her buzz set in and she told him that she was ready to handle things alone. He handed her the Ziploc bag, slapped her hand, and returned to the bedroom.

She was in the game and on her own.

TWENTY-ONE

THE FIRST NIGHT RAN SMOOTHLY. SHE had learned the regulars by name quickly and the games that they tried to play as well. They always had a story and after a few hours Ke-Ke felt like she had heard everything. The females usually wanted to speak directly to Lotto or Nut in private so they could offer pussy for product. She paid close attention to those "deals" and learned the fine art of cooning.

Cooning was a method where Lotto and Nut would empty three or four of the larger bags of dope onto a table. They would shave pieces of the larger rocks with a razor, combine the shavings, and create a new bag of dope that wasn't on the count. The original bags stayed uncompromised in appearance by taking just a little from each one and they could easily create one hundred fifty to two hundred dollars of side profit off each pack they moved. The process was a win-win in that Cry still got her money, the fiends never complained, and Lotto and Nut stayed knee-deep in an endless sea of pretty-faced fiends that sucked dick and gave up pussy like it was ice water.

There was an art to it though. You had to have a good eye to know which bags to shave, and finding the exact same bags that Cry used proved to be a challenge, especially if you waited too late to start the process. Lotto had it down to a science and Ke-Ke watched him skillfully shave rocks of crack with a steady hand any time he felt the urge to trick off or just wanted extra pocket money for liquor, weed, or to buy food for a cookout.

The operation ran like a regular business. Cry would drop off a thousand dollars' worth of dope, come pick up the money, and drop off another one. She paid them on Saturdays and also gave them a fifty to a hundred dollar allowance off each package to eat, drink, smoke weed, and purchase entertainment like bootleg DVDs or video games. The allowance was a saving grace, seeing as you needed things to do or watch being cooped up in a house for days on end. Lotto and Nut took shifts and during the day, either one of them was usually gone blowing money or getting drunk somewhere, which left Ke-Ke alone with one of them by herself. She enjoyed running the operation by herself the most because once she had mastered the art of shaving down bags, she was able to pocket all of that profit without having to share it.

Hustling was working out all right and she stayed at the house around the clock for three days straight before leaving to go home so she could take a shower and change clothes. She now knew the true meaning of "on the grind" and had a whole new respect for dudes who seemed to only change their clothes once a week and always offered that response. She remembered she and her friends, back in the school days, making fun of those dudes, calling them dusty for always having the same clothes on. The niggas would smile and pull out wads of money wrapped in rubber bands and say, "I'm on the grind." The whole time they would be wondering why "on the grind" meant you didn't wash your ass. Days in the spot had given her an education. You couldn't and didn't want to leave to take a shower or change clothes because you could miss out on a lot of money.

She had learned that when Nut and Lotto were gone. They were missing out on hundreds of dollars and she was cleaning up. The other thing she remembered was someone saying, "Don't ever get too comfortable in the spot." That had proven to be a fatal and embarrassing mistake for many people in the past.

Ke-Ke thought back to the time they were coming home from church and there had been a raid on Reynolds Street. White men with bulletproof vests and

213

helmets, dressed like a football team, holding large military weapons, crowded the street and directed traffic.

"Oh, they is so wrong for that!" her mom said as she pointed to the porch where a door that led into an apartment had been knocked off its hinges.

There stood a girl completely naked with soap covering half of her body and shampoo still in her hair. They had obviously hit the house when she was in the middle of taking a shower. They cuffed her and brought her outside butt-naked while she squirmed, screamed, and tried to cross her legs. They drove through the scene slowly and Ke-Ke remembered feeling so bad for the girl whose goodies were on display for the whole world to see. They passed a man being shoved into the back of a black van who kept yelling, "Let my fucken girl put some clothes on!" but no one seemed to be the least bit interested in honoring his demands. They turned the corner to their street and Ke-Ke remembered two of the officers slapping hands and laughing as they stared at the girl and pointed.

"That's what happens when you choose that life," she remembered their mother saying as they pulled into the driveway. Ke-Ke had never agreed with that logic. They could've let the girl get dressed before they brought her outside.

With that memory branded on her brain, Ke-Ke didn't care if the neighbors upstairs could smell her stank ass, she would NEVER take a shower at the spot. She called a cab that would take her to the safety of her own bathroom as she left the package with Nut. She climbed in the backseat of the cab with nine hundred dollars in her pockets, feeling like a superstar. She tried to arrange the money in some sort of order as she rode but stopped when she noticed the driver was watching her through the rearview mirror. She decided to wait until she got home. There was no reason to invite a problem.

"Look like somebody robbed a bank. I ain't the getaway driver, am I? I can speed up if you want me to." The woman spoke with sarcasm as she grinned at her through the mirror.

"Naw, nothen like that," Ke-Ke answered, mad at herself for attracting unwanted attention. She hoped deep down that this wouldn't be one of those talking, tell-a-story cab drivers who got on her nerves.

"Yeah, well last I knew, there wasn't no bank in *this* neighborhood. Anyway, you must know something everybody else don't, huh?" She giggled and winked at Ke-Ke as she drove and kept glancing up in her mirror. Ke-Ke mentally ran through the faces of fiends in her head and tried to see if the woman was a match to someone she had sold dope to in the last three days. She couldn't place her face so she just smiled in response and sat back in the seat, anticipating a hot shower as soon as she got in the house.

"Tell me something. Maybe you can help me with this," the lady continued, obviously not able to take a hint.

"What's that?" Ke-Ke answered without looking up at her.

"Why you think folks be out here tryen to sell drugs?" Her voice cut through the air.

Ke-Ke took her eyes off the street and glared at the woman's reflection in the mirror. "I don't know. I guess that would be *THEY* business!" Ke-Ke snapped back, wondering if she would be able to find the energy to curse this woman out if it came to that.

"Oh, I wasn't tryen to piss you off, I was just asken a question." The woman spoke in a soft and steady voice. "I mean, you see people going to jail and getting killed over it time and time again, yet it don't seem to be a shortage of young fools lining up for that one-way ticket to hell."

She spoke the words in a way that caused Ke-Ke to get an uneasy feeling in her chest, like when her grandmother ran guilt trips on her.

"I don't know," the woman continued as she steered the car effortlessly with one hand and crossed underneath a bridge that led back to the hood. "It just seems like people would learn from other people's mistakes, you know? I don't have to jump off a cliff to know that I'm going to die when I hit the ground in the canyon below, you feel me?"

Ke-Ke smiled and nodded in agreement, without trying to give the woman the satisfaction of knowing that the conversation was fucking with her head. "But then again, you know you young folks know EVERYTHING! You can't tell y'all nothing." She shook her head as she slowed to allow a car to turn in front of her. "Maybe they feel they know something about the game that thousands before them didn't know. Shit, maybe I'm crazy. Maybe they really are smarter than everybody else." She brought the cab to a stop across the street from Ke-Ke's house and hit the power locks. Ke-Ke reached in her pocket and tried to pull out one bill without revealing the whole wad as she had mistakenly done before.

"You good." The woman waved her hand and reset the meter. "The ride was free and so was the advice. After all, it was an honor being in the presence of such intelligence and greatness!" She turned around in her seat, looking Ke-Ke directly in the face. "Don't sell your soul, girl," she half-hissed in a low voice.

Ke-Ke reached for the door handle but stopped when she noticed the look in the woman's eyes. She moved her hair behind her ear to reveal a scar that started from her temple, ran down the side of her face and disappeared under her chin. Ke-Ke couldn't help but stare. The woman smiled and continued to pierce Ke-Ke with an emotionless, glassy-eyed stare. "I wasn't always a cab driver." She forced a smile across her face as she spoke the words slowly and her cheek quivered. "Yeah, I was young, dumb, and beautiful too! But them butch bitches in Bedford and Albion Correctional... I guess they only liked the young and dumb parts of me!"

She stared at Ke-Ke for a few more seconds and winked before she turned back around in her seat.

Ke-Ke hopped out of the cab and walked around the back of the car as a chill shot through her entire body. She didn't look back until she had reached the porch and had the front door open. The car was gone without a trace, without a sound. She tried to calm herself as she realized her heart was beating hard and fast in her chest. She knew she would never be able to get the sound of her voice or the image of her disfigured face out of her head.

"Look everybody, it's the Queen of the Damned!" Ke-Ke was greeted by her mother's smart-ass remark as soon as she had closed the door.

"Ma, don't start." Ke-Ke sighed as she took her shoes off and left them by the door.

"We was just waiten for the call, so we could go identify the body," her mother continued as she walked into the kitchen. Ke-Ke ignored her, punched Misha in the back, and made her way up the stairs. She found her charger under a pile of clothes, plugged it in, and waited to see all the calls she had missed. Nut and Lotto had newer phones and their chargers were different, so her phone had been dead for the past two days.

She lay down on the bed and tried to relax her body, feeling like she hadn't slept in a week. Sleeping in the spot wasn't the same. She could only take short naps that were always interrupted and the slightest noise or sound had her up on her feet and looking out of the window. The constant traffic and stress of the environment, combined with thoughts that became a paranoia about being raided or robbed, prevented a person from getting any real rest.

"And you need to tell that dyke to stop comen through here. I'm starten to hear the rumors myself!" her mother yelled from the foot of the stairs. Ke-Ke rolled her eyes and turned over on her bed, using her foot to slam her bedroom door shut. She turned onto her back and tried to figure out why Cry would stop by the house, if she knew where she was. She rolled over again and covered her face with her hands when she heard Misha scratching at the door.

"What?" she answered. Misha pushed the door open and closed it behind her.

"Where you been?" Misha asked with the cute sound of concern in her voice. "Ma was about to call the jail and everything!" she whispered.

"She wasn't about to do shit," Ke-Ke said as she stood up and walked to her dresser to check her hair in the mirror.

"She acted like she was serious," Misha responded with a look of sincerity and doubt in her eyes. Ke-Ke looked over at her and shook her head. She had years more experience dealing with their mother and this was one of the times that it showed.

"You wanna go shopping wit me?" She pulled the wad of money out of her pocket and flashed it at Misha.

"Daaaamn, where you get all that? Again?" Misha's eyes looked like they were going to fall out of her head. Ke-Ke smiled and put the money back in her pocket without answering her.

"Just get ready to go, and tell Ma wit your big-mouth ass!" Misha moved faster than Ke-Ke had ever seen her move as she rushed into her bedroom to get dressed.

She sat back on her bed as the image of the cab driver's face floated through her head again. She wondered who and what had left her with a scar like that. She sat in a daze as she remembered her face and her hazel eyes. She had probably been pretty when she was younger. She looked like one of those people her mom would say, "Life beat him or her down." Ke-Ke pictured a younger version of the woman in prison, on the floor bleeding, holding her face as a huge man-looking chick kicked her repeatedly. Somehow she knew that the scar had been one of the reasons, if not the only one, that the woman had changed her life. Ke-Ke convinced herself that the woman had probably fucked with someone, or stole something, or maybe had even been a snitch. *Sheep get slaughtered.* Her uncle's words, as always, shot through her head.

Ke-Ke brought herself back to reality thinking this woman had lost the game and that's the only reason she was speaking against it. She stood up, thinking that if anyone had put a scar on her face like that, she would STILL be in prison. She would've gotten a life sentence for murder. That bitch *had* to be weak.

Twenty minutes later she was out of the shower, feeling like a brand-new person. Standing at her closet, an image of Cry on her front porch ringing the doorbell, looking flawless, ran through her head.

"What you smiling at?" Misha had slipped back into the room without her noticing.

"Nothen. You ready?" Ke-Ke turned and pushed pause on the movie that was about to begin in her head.

"You probably haven freaky thoughts," Misha responded and gave her a look like she was toxic waste.

"Shut up before I leave you here and you don't get shit," Ke-Ke snapped at her, knowing that the threat would be enough to keep her mouth shut for a little while anyway.

"Where y'all goen to?" their mother said after she climbed the stairs and caught her breath.

"We just walken to the store," Ke-Ke lied on cue so she wouldn't have to explain and answer a whole string of questions.

"Mmmhmm, y'all better not be up there tryna steal them folks' stuff, cause I ain't comen to get y'all out of jail!" their mother warned as she rolled her eyes and walked to her room.

"We know!" Misha mumbled under her breath and waved her hand as a signal for Ke-Ke to hurry up.

"Don't rush me!" Ke-Ke said as she pulled on her sweatpants and reached for a hoodie.

"Eww, you ain't even put no panties on," Misha pointed out with a look of disbelief on her face.

"Shut up, little girl," Ke-Ke pushed past her and ran down the stairs.

The two walked down the street towards the strip mall where Ke-Ke usually visited the hair store alone. There was a clothing boutique that specialized in all of the newest hip-hop fashions next door to it, with mannequins dressed in skimpy clubwear standing in the large picture windows that framed the entrance. Ke-Ke felt a sense of confidence, knowing that she had enough money to get whatever she wanted and then some, so when they finally got there, she swung the doors open like she owned the place.

Misha broke off from her almost immediately and walked towards the jewelry counter, where they carried the large, hollow earrings that Ke-Ke always bought on her trips to the hair store. Ke-Ke walked to the back of the store to look at the jeans and tops while she checked the time on the wall. She laughed as she thought about how she had never been on time for school, didn't ever care to be on time for a job, yet she was checking the clock to make sure that she got back in time to sell dope.

She picked up a Gucci wrap for her hair and tried on a tight pair of jeans that she was undecided on until she saw a girl walking through the store with her boyfriend and he mouthed the word, "Goddamn!" behind his girl's back as she walked in front of him. Misha picked out a piece that was too colorful by Ke-Ke's standards, but if she chose to walk around looking like a box of crayons, that was her business. She wasn't going to waste her time trying to talk her out of it.

She had to smile when she saw Misha grab a see-through pair of thong panties and hide them under the pile of clothes they had brought to the register. She decided to act like she didn't notice them and turned around as if she was looking at something when the old Arab man scanned them and put them in the bag. She played it out in her head, how Misha would get caught with them in her room or laundry and she would lie and say, "Those are Ke-Ke's." She laughed to herself.

"One hundred fifty," the man announced from behind the register as he finished bagging the last item. He looked down at Ke-Ke and Misha suspiciously, like he thought they were up to something. He stepped to the side and pointed at a sign that read, "NO CREDIT CARDS WITHOUT PROPER ID."

"What, you think I ain't got money? You think I got a stolen credit card?" Ke-Ke was pissed off instantly.

"No, no, I don't say nothing. I want no problems." The man spoke through a thick accent with his hands raised in the air as if Ke-Ke had pulled a gun on him.

"You want shoes, Mish?" Ke-Ke asked without taking her eyes off of the man behind the counter.

"Hell yeah!" Misha raced to the shoe section and picked up a pair of Jordans that matched her outfit. Ke-Ke walked to the shoe display and selected a pair of suede high-heeled boots that she thought would take her new jeans to another level and returned to the counter. The man rang up both pair and added them to the total. Ke-Ke counted out the money and dropped it on the counter like the bills were napkins. She grabbed her bags and turned to walk out the store in one motion. Misha pointed and laughed at the look of shock on the old man's face as he counted through the bills again.

"We get money, Ha-beeb!" Misha said as she stuck her middle finger up and skipped behind Ke-Ke, flipping the "open" sign to "closed" as she left.

***

Ke-Ke and Misha had made it halfway home holding bags and laughing at the look on the old man's face. They had gone through a dozen things that he must have been thinking and probably saying about them when they left. Ke-Ke offered to buy Misha a steak sub and they were waiting outside in front of the store when two police cars sped by with their lights flashing. A few moments passed and three gunshots rang out as people screamed and yelled a block away. They looked at each other and ran down the sidewalk towards the commotion. When they neared the corner, Ke-Ke grabbed Misha's arm and held her behind her as she looked down the block, making sure the coast was clear. They turned the corner and saw a crowd of people gathered in front of an apartment.

"They done shot somebody!" Misha whispered as she held on to Ke-Ke's sweatshirt. They made their way up to the crowd and saw two pit bulls lying on the street, bleeding from their heads.

"Oh shit," Ke-Ke said as she took in the scene and watched two police officers wrestling with a large, shirtless man, trying to get him in handcuffs. They finally tased him and he fell to the ground shaking.

"Y'all ain't have to shoot the dogs. Those is twelve-hundred-dollar dogs," a man yelled from an upstairs window at the police officers carrying the man to the patrol car.

"Control your fucken pets!" one of them yelled over his shoulder.

"C'mon, Mish," Ke-Ke nudged her sister and then pulled her by her collar, dragging her away from where she stood frozen with her mouth open.

"I can't wait to go to college and get the hell away from here," Misha said, sounding like she was getting ready to cry. Ke-Ke just looked over at her and smiled. She was happy to hear Misha finally admit that she couldn't stomach what happened around their neighborhood on a daily basis.

They picked up their food and headed back to the house in silence. The whole scene had shaken Ke-Ke up as well, but she pushed it out of her mind the way that she always did. That was life as she knew it. Constant ups and downs, literally "Laugh now, cry later" all the time. She searched her mind and couldn't remember a time that she had felt an extended period of peace, happiness, love, or compassion. The good times were only served in small doses and were no match for the tragedies that were always lurking in the alleyways. The insanity that life had forced her to believe was normal.

When she was younger she had overheard a conversation her father had with her Uncle James when he had come home from prison one time. She could remember them sitting on the porch drinking beer out of green bottles when her father looked over and asked him what it was like in prison. Her Uncle James just smiled, hung his head and exhaled a thick cloud of smoke from the cigar he was puffing on. He looked over out of the corner of his eyes and said, "It's amazing what a human being can get used to."

TWENTY-TWO

"WHAT DUMB-ASS NIGGA DONE GAVE YOU SOME MONEY?" Their mother must've seen them coming and opened the door. She looked back and forth at the bags and then stopped and waited for answer.

"Where mines at?" she asked as she reached out her hand. Ke-Ke reached in her pocket and counted out her first rent payment. Her mother made her way up the stairs, singing the gospel remix to her favorite saying: "Something strange for a little change, something straaaange, for just a little change!"

Ke-Ke listened as she began laughing before the door to her bedroom closed. She ran up the stairs, emptied the shopping bags on her bed, and checked her phone. Six missed calls.

"Shit!" she said out loud as she got herself ready to head back to the spot. She was sure that two of the calls were from Cry or Lotto, wondering where she was. She put her phone on speaker while she got dressed. One message was from Cry checking on her, asking how things went, and telling her that she had stopped by the house. The second message was from Lotto, wondering where she was and when she was coming back and letting her know that they were cooking out that day. The third message was from Ahmed.

She deleted the messages and called Ahmed back, figuring that he would be good for a ride back to the spot and she could save money that she would've spent on a cab. She had looked for his truck outside of the hair store earlier, but didn't see it parked on the sidewalk the way it usually was.

"Hello?" Ahmed answered the phone with no trace of an accent.

"Hey, baby, you wanna come get me?" she asked in her cute voice that she reserved for when she wanted to pry things out of a nigga.

"Yeah, I'll be through there," he answered. Ke-Ke could tell that he was speaking through a smile and was relieved to find out that he was still into her. She dressed quickly, admiring how her new jeans hugged her shape in the mirror. They had no back pockets and fit like a second skin, with a gold zipper that ran from the front through her crotch area and stopped underneath a snap at the small of her back. The zipper separated her ass cheeks like a thong would and actually made her ass look bigger, so she decided to go without panties after she had checked how they looked both with and without them. She picked out one of her thicker belly chains and fastened it around her waist. The golden heart charm hung over the front of her jeans and matched the zipper perfectly. She picked out a hoodie and looked over to see her phone vibrating on the bed.

"Yo," she answered in a laid-back tone, without checking the screen.

"Yo, you goen back to the spot? I'm around the corner," Cry spoke as she inhaled and the music bumped loudly in the background.

"Yeah, yeah, I'm comen out right now, hold up," Ke-Ke said as she grabbed her things, hid the rest of her money in a shoebox, and ran down the steps, hoping Ahmed wouldn't pull up at the same time.

The cold air smacked her in the face and wrapped around her body like the arms of a corpse before she could put her sweater on and zip it. A white Lexus with white rims pulled over to the curb with its parking lights on and Ke-Ke just smiled when she saw Cry reclined behind the wheel. She felt a sense of pride as people watched and then realized that the car was waiting on her. She stuck her middle finger up at Pam, who was standing at the end of the block staring at her as she walked to the passenger side of the car.

"You own a dealership or what?" she asked as she closed the door and looked around the car before glancing over at Cry.

"Naw, nothen like that, love," Cry smiled and handed her the blunt before she shifted the car into drive and pulled off.

"Your little tight ass looken right in them jeans though," Cry smiled as she reached over and ran her hand across her thighs. Ke-Ke's heart skipped a beat when she felt the warmth of her hand. Cry knew how to touch her and her body wouldn't let her deny that fact.

"You know what it is." Ke-Ke couldn't stop herself from grinning as she watched Cry's hand slide up her thighs and rest in between her legs.

"I know a little." Cry winked as her eyes crept up and down her whole body. The way her eyes moved up and down her body made Ke-Ke feel like she was sitting in the passenger seat naked. The attention made her heart beat faster as she tried to play cool, reclined in her seat, and stared out the window. There was a way that Cry made her feel desirable, wanted, and sexy without being too pushy or aggressive. She made Ke-Ke *want* to do things without even asking. Her eyes and hands seemed to be able to speak to Ke-Ke in a way that no man's words had ever been able to, and she fought to keep control of herself.

She focused her attention on the street as they cruised through the neighborhood. She loved the way people would stare at the car, even when they tried to act like they weren't. They pulled up at a light and a few people waved as they noticed who was driving while Ke-Ke watched the distorted reflection of the car in the glass doors of a storefront. Cry pushed the car through the gritty streets like a sterilized sword. The car turned corners and reflected life off of its paint job. Ke-Ke felt high, knowing that for most people it was the closest they would ever come to "seeing themselves" in a car like that. She nodded and smiled when all at once she noticed something in their faces that hid behind the smiles and the waves. She had always referred to it as people "hating" because everybody else did, but for the first time, she saw something else.

The people looked sad. Ke-Ke inhaled the smoke and blew it out in a thin stream while she cracked the window. She realized that the majority of them realized no matter what came out of their mouths in the form of "game" or how much of a "hustle" they had, they would probably never know what it was like to own a car like that. They were standing on the street and on the corners dreaming. That car that passed in front of them represented everything that either they had and lost or would never have the chance to obtain. Yeah, they were staring at the car and looking at the rims, but deep down in the depths of their eyes, they were watching a better life pass them by. The only thing that they hated was how that vehicle reminded them of how they felt stuck, trapped, and forced them to accept that as a reality.

Ke-Ke caught herself nodding to people that she didn't know. She remembered standing on the corner when a nice car drove by and somebody in her group would be like, "That's my cousin," and wave at the car. Sometimes the car would honk and sometimes it wouldn't. She figured that people felt that being able to say they knew somebody that actually had something made them stand out as well. She started seeing it as an act of charity as she nodded and held two fingers up at somebody they passed on the street.

"You know that nigga?" Cry asked, pulling her from her thoughts.

"Yeah," Ke-Ke lied as she sat back in the seat and stared straight out of the front windshield, feeling the eyes watching her. They began to burn a hole in her heart.

"Hello, hello." Cry was snapping her fingers in Ke-Ke's face. "Damn girl, there you go off into the land of make-believe! What's on your mind? Snap out that shit and pass the weed back." Cry looked irritated as she took the blunt and inhaled it while she looked over at her. "You know you do that shit way too much. I'm bout to get you counseling or some shit. You be going off into your own little world." Cry laughed and nudged her.

"Naw, I'm good." Ke-Ke couldn't help but be embarrassed. "I just be thinken bout shit, that's all." She tried to make it seem like nothing as she wondered how many times Cry had noticed her doing it.

"Aww, you be stressen." Cry said as the light turned green and she accelerated through an intersection. "I got somethen for that." She turned onto the expressway and stomped on the gas as she signaled and switched all the way over to the fast lane. "You ain't the scared type, is you?" she asked with a sneaky smile appearing on her face.

"C'mon man," Ke-Ke said as she stretched and heard her back crack.

"Okay, we'll see." Cry steered the car with one hand and Ke-Ke felt her other hand sliding in between her legs. Ke-Ke unsnapped her jeans in the back and slid the zipper down through her legs, feeling the cool leather make contact with her skin. She sat with her legs open, revealing to Cry that she wasn't wearing panties.

"Damn, girl, like that?" Cry watched the road but took several quick glances down at her exposed pussy. Ke-Ke smiled as Cry's fingers delicately found their way inside of her, one at a time. She moaned and leaned back to make it easier for her to work. Cry sped past other cars and plunged her fingers into Ke-Ke's now dripping wet pussy and worked them in and out of her with precision. Ke-Ke moaned louder and dug her heels into the floor, feeling the floor mat shift underneath her feet.

"Goddamn!" was all she could whimper as Cry's soft touch manipulated her body like she owned it. She closed her eyes and felt her teeth grinding against each other as she was stroked and penetrated. Ke-Ke managed to glance up at the dashboard to see the car had reached a speed of one hundred miles per hour, but she was nowhere close to being in a place where she could say something about it. Cry's fingers inside of her body were like a bow that ran across the strings of a violin, forcing Ke-Ke's body to create a song that she didn't even know existed. Her body shook and trembled as her legs vise-gripped Cry's hand in between her thighs.

"OH MY GOD! Shiit!" she screamed out in a voice she didn't recognize as being her own.

"Shut up, bitch! Shut the fuck up." Cry playfully dominated her and forced her over the edge in dramatic fashion. Ke-Ke twisted in the seat and lost all control of herself as she gripped Cry's arm for support. She prayed that Cry could control the car with one hand as the image of her naked ass hanging out of a shattered windshield on the news made her giggle to herself. Her body finally relaxed and she fell back into her seat, sweating and gasping for air as a fluttering sensation ran through her body. She ran her hand across the fogged up window then let it down and glanced over at the dash to see that Cry had just begun to slow the car down from a speed of one hundred thirty miles per hour. The strong breeze hit her face as she began to catch her breath, thinking that if she was going to die young, that would be the way that she would've wanted to go.

Cry patted her pussy playfully and licked her fingers. "That's mine now!" she said as she turned on her blinker and steered the car off of the expressway.

"You got that," is all Ke-Ke could say as she wiped her forehead and closed her eyes. She wondered how it was possible that Cry could touch her better than she touched herself.

They were back on the expressway and headed back to the city when Ke-Ke heard a loud horn honk. She opened her eyes and looked out the window to see a man driving a truck, looking down into the car. She realized that her jeans were still wide open. He gave a thumbs up sign as Ke-Ke squirmed to run the zipper back through her legs and up the backside before snapping the button in the back. Cry laughed and waved her hand out of the moonroof as she accelerated past him while Ke-Ke punched her in the arm.

"What, you tryen to cause accidents out here?" Cry laughed as she avoided more of Ke-Ke's punches.

"Oh *NOW* you worried about accidents?" Ke-Ke smiled and then had to laugh at herself.

***

They were pulling up in front of the spot as they both checked themselves to make sure they were looking normal. Cry followed Ke-Ke as they walked up to the house and made comments in a low voice about how good her ass looked as she walked. Ke-Ke was still smiling and trying to hold in her laughter when Nut finally opened the door, holding a plate of food.

"Damn, I know you missed me," he said with a smile and reached out his one free arm like he expected a hug. Ke-Ke pushed his face away and walked past him into the house. She fell onto the couch, still feeling the vibrations running through her body, as Cry walked into the kitchen to speak with Lotto.

"Where y'all comen from?" Nut sat on the chair across from her and asked as he chewed on a chicken bone.

"Ya momma's!" Ke-Ke answered as she laid back on the couch and stared up at the ceiling. She heard Nut mumble something then get up and leave the room. She let her head fall to the left just in time to catch eyes with Cry, who bit into a piece of chicken and licked her fingers slowly.

"That chicken good, ain't it? I can cook my ass off!" Nut blurted out and ruined the moment.

"Yeah, it's straight," Cry answered as she slapped Nut's hand. "I think it's the special sauce though. I'm loven that!" Cry said as she winked at Ke-Ke and kept licking her fingers. Nut stood in the kitchen with his arms folded, basking in the compliment that wasn't directed towards him. Ke-Ke could feel the butterflies in her stomach and chest all over again.

"Yeah, nigga! Told y'all I could burn!" he walked around the kitchen with his arms in the air as if he had just won a title fight. "I'm bout to open my own restaurant. I'ma call it the *Nut House!*" he announced. Cry and Ke-Ke both laughed as he unknowingly fueled the fire of their inside jokes.

Cry hung around for about half an hour before she said she had to go. Ke-Ke tried to act like it didn't bother her, but on the inside she was dying to ask if she could go too. She walked past her, slapped her hand on the way out the door, and was gone, without even looking back. Ke-Ke let out a long, loud sigh and then stared back at the ceiling.

The thoughts and feelings that had overcome her were too many for her to organize. *Damn, am I gay?* Her body seemed to respond and answer the question as clips of the high-speed orgasm from earlier shot through her mind. But she also thought back to the conversation she had with Tiff. "*STIM-U-LA-TION.*" The word rang in her ears as if Tiff were standing in the room with her. She smiled at the thought of Tiff but knew she couldn't discuss the issue with her. Ke-Ke tried to tell herself that it was a physical thing and that Cry just knew how to find her spots, but that didn't explain her thinking of her all the time and wanting to be around her constantly. She thought about the look on her mother's face and wondered if it would change the way Misha saw her. She thought about her grandmother calling it a demon as she hummed and chanted then placed blessed oil on her forehead and prayed.

Her mind played her encounters with Cry in slow motion as she compared them to her dealings with men. Was it better? It wasn't as if she had never climaxed with a man, but it was just something about the way that Cry touched her with an erotic understanding, like she knew exactly what her body needed. There was always a high level of intensity and passion that she had never before experienced. She let her mind drift as she recalled countless encounters with men where it had just been mechanical with no connection whatsoever. She could even remember telling men to hurry up or get off on more than a few occasions. Cry's touch seemed to speak to her body in a pulsating whisper. Men never paid attention, they broke into routines, and either didn't care if you enjoyed it or automatically thought you did because some girl somewhere had lied to them or faked so well that they believed they were sexual stallions. The others seemed to want to impress, as if they could force an orgasm out of you whether you wanted it or not.

Cry's touch was the exact opposite. Her hands were experienced and gentle. She wasn't forcing anything onto you. Her touch beckoned the insides of you to come out and play and there was no way your body could resist the invitation. Ke-Ke had never felt that before, and she had never felt as comfortable or safe with anyone. She thought back to the early days when niggas would try to get her to take all her clothes off and she never would. She had always kept her shirt and bra on. Those feelings didn't exist at all with Cry and she looked forward to the day when she could and would give all of herself to her.

Ke-Ke bounced thoughts around of her and Cry actually having a place together and going all out with it on a serious level. Could she really do that? It was one thing to be creeping around, but for everyone to know? Then she thought about what Cry might be into sexually and whether she would be willing or even able to keep up with her on that level. There were certain things that she just couldn't see herself doing on a regular basis. Would that cause a problem? Would that lead to Cry becoming unfaithful? The more she thought, the more questions arose and the more confused she got.

Ke-Ke laid across the couch with her leg hanging over the armrest, staring into space, trying to jigsaw the whole situation in a way that would result in a happy ending for once in her life. The feelings and thoughts she was wrestling with made her feel like she was out of control, like her body was a vessel flying through space with Cry behind the wheel.

She struggled to figure out where they were going. The only thing that she seemed to know for sure is that she still craved dick and couldn't see herself walking away from it forever. Toys and vibrators were fun, but there was no substitute for the real thing. Would Cry have a problem with her messing with men every once in a while? The questions rained in her head, creating a perfect storm of doubts and uneasiness.

She turned on the couch in frustration, torn between loving the encounters with Cry and the reality of knowing that there probably wasn't much of a future in the best feeling that she had ever felt in her life. Ke-Ke smiled as she thought about it in the way that she was getting back at men for all the bullshit they did. When she was riding in the car with Cry, she would catch herself looking at niggas and thinking, "Yeah, you dumb muthafuckas, all this good pussy coulda been yours, but you fucked up!"

Whether anyone knew what she was doing or not, for some reason she got some sort of satisfaction out of the two experiences she had shared with Cry. Ke-Ke wondered why men had to be the way they were. The few times she had opened up to one, she had gotten crushed and she swore to herself a few years back that she would never trust one of them again.

She thought back to the time that she had incredible sex with Guns, a local block nigga who drove a Honda with custom interior and a banging system. He had tried to get at her for months before she finally gave in and agreed to smoke with him. The night was unforgettable. He took her out to eat then to the beach before they ended up going back to his apartment to "watch movies." The sex was unbelievable. He licked, massaged, nibbled, tongued, grabbed, pulled, and penetrated like a dream. Ke-Ke remembered how they seamlessly switched positions as if they were dancing, and how he held her close and whispered softly in her ear as she came all over his dick and dug her nails into his back.

The next day, she woke up before him and just stared at him while he slept. She rehearsed in her head all the things she wanted to tell him, how she wanted to try to have something with him for real and how she was going to convince him that it was not just another night to her. When he woke up though, he acted like it was nothing to him and got dressed without speaking. They would catch eyes from time to time, but he would look away quickly and bring up something stupid so they weren't forced to talk about what they were both probably feeling. He took her by a fast food place and bought her a breakfast sandwich then dropped her off. Ke-Ke remembered waiting for him to call for two weeks, but he never did.

A month later she had heard he was fucking her home girl NayNay and the rumors were confirmed when she saw his Honda parked in front of the corner store with NayNay grinning from ear to ear in the passenger seat. She related the whole experience to being at the pool in the summertime. She would stick her foot in the water, it would feel too cold, and she would take forever to walk down the stairs in the shallow end so her body would get used to the water a little bit at a time. People would always say, "Just jump in" but she could never do it that way. She knew she and Guns had both been afraid of the water and they were both too timid to jump in. They both had felt something but their own fears had prevented them from admitting it to each other. That would mean leaving yourself wide open, feeling vulnerable, and everybody knows, "That ain't hood!" It was the first and last time she had ever felt that type of connection with a man.

A year later, Guns had walked in the house to find NayNay fucking his cousin. He stabbed his cousin eight times. NayNay even testified against him at trial and he was sentenced to fifteen to twenty years in prison. Time had passed but Ke-Ke had still not gotten over him and she secretly blamed herself for what had happened.

She closed her eyes as the thoughts and memories had begun to make her head hurt. She sighed as she thought about how her life was like one of those amusement park rides designed to make you dizzy as she drifted off to sleep.

***

The next morning Ke-Ke woke up to the sun beating on her face through the dingy curtains and heavy breathing coming from across the room. She turned her head and slightly cracked her eyelids to see Nut sitting in the chair jacking his dick like he was trying to pull it off. She felt a draft around her waist and realized that her pants had slipped down while she was sleeping and the top half of her ass was exposed for the world to see. That had been enough to push Nut over the edge.

"What the fuck?" She sat up and pulled her pants around her waist at the same time.

"I ain't touch you!" Nut jumped as he covered himself and tried to act like he hadn't been doing anything.

"You a sick, perverted muthafucka!" Ke-Ke yelled at him while she continued to straighten her jeans.

"Why it gotta be like that, Ma?" he answered with an embarrassed look on his face.

"What the fuck you mean, why it gotta be like that?" Ke-Ke stood up, stretched her legs, and glared at him while she debated whether or not to rush him and hit him with something. Then a thought crossed her mind. Nut was a big-time trick and she figured she could juice this nigga without even giving up the pussy if he was into her like that.

"What the fuck is on your mind, Nut?" she asked with a lowered voice, looking him directly in his eyes. She glanced around the corner to see that Lotto's door was wide open and realized that they were in the house alone.

"Nah, I'm just sayen, Ma, you sexy as hell!" He tried not to look as embarrassed as he was. "Yo, fuck it, just don't say nothen about this shit." Nut got up, crossed the room, and dropped a fifty-dollar bill on the table in front of her. Ke-Ke glanced down at the bill for a second before reaching down, folding it, and slipping it into her bra.

"I'm sayen... it's all good, you just freaked me out wit that shit!" Ke-Ke smiled at him and tried to turn on her charm. "I'm sayen whatever happens between us is between us! I'll let you see what you wanna see, you do what you do, just don't touch me!" Ke-Ke pointed her finger at him as she spoke.

"Word?" Nut asked with his eyes wide in disbelief. Ke-Ke couldn't stand the way he always said "Ma" but she winked at him to make him feel like she was feeling him. She had learned in the salon that the promise of pussy was sometimes more powerful then giving it up at all. Nut was the perfect subject to test the theory out on.

"What you wanna see?" she said as she smiled down at him. "Just know it's gonna cost you a few more of these." She patted her chest where she had placed the fifty-dollar bill.

"Oh, that's nothen, Ma." He stood up and produced a wad of crumpled bills from his pocket. "You know how I be getten it. I couldn't front on you if I wanted to!" he said as he tried to straighten the bills in his hand.

"Cool, so we gotta deal then. What you wanna see, baby?" Ke-Ke asked as she concentrated on the money in Nut's hand.

"Let me see that ass!" he said, staring down at her jeans like he could see through them.

"Aiight," she answered as she turned around and unsnapped her jeans in the back. "You better show me the money too, Nut. I ain't one of these cheap, dusty bitches you used to fucken wit!" she warned him over her shoulder.

"I got you," he answered, as she could hear him starting to breathe harder behind her. She figured if he got that excited before she had gotten a chance to slide her jeans down then this would be over quickly. Ke-Ke bent over and unzipped her jeans then slid them down to her thighs.

"Damn, Ma! Damn..." was all she could hear, as Nut panted behind her like a puppy. She wondered how she would explain herself to Lotto or someone else if they just happened to look through a window. She had to encourage him to speed up the process.

"Get it, Nut! Get it, Daddy! Get this tight ass baby!" Ke-Ke cheered him on as she tried not to bust out laughing.

"Yeah, Ma, I'ma fuck the shit out that tight ass. Damn!" Ke-Ke could hear him breathing harder and harder behind her. She made sure to listen for any attempt he could've been making to come closer to her as she talked dirty and moaned like she was really into it.

"Oh shiiit! Oh shit! You freak bitch!" Nut screamed as he reached his peak and fell back onto the chair that he was standing in front of. Ke-Ke forced the smile off of her face before she pulled her jeans up and zipped them.

"You straight?" she asked, like he was one of the fiends that had come to buy dope.

"Hell yeah, I knew you was a freak," he said as he tired to catch his breath. He smiled and reached into his pocket. "This is a down payment on the real thing, right?" he said as he held her hand when she reached over to take it from him.

"I'll think about it, boo." She winked and stuck her tongue out. She knew all too well how to play Nut. She had dealt with his type before. She watched as he went through the bills in his hand. "Oh, and you know you gotta give me a little extra for calling me a bitch," she said with a serious look on her face.

Nut laughed and placed three fifty-dollar bills in her hand then went into the bathroom to clean himself up. Ke-Ke stuffed the bills in her bra and shook her head. "Easy money," she whispered to herself.

Moments later, Lotto was at the door with two females. Nut and Ke-Ke were busy acting like nothing had happened. Business picked up around noon. They were all running back and forth to answer the door, making sure that the money was right for when Cry made another drop-off. Nut grabbed her ass twice as he passed behind her on his way to answer the door and she "taxed" him forty dollars for "misbehaving in public." She had him wrapped around her finger.

Cry came back to make the swap at two, but Ke-Ke had run to the store for blunts and missed her. She didn't want too sound to obvious about being upset that she had missed her, so she didn't ask too many questions. The money was flowing. She had managed to coon two hundred dollars once Nut had gotten drunk and fell asleep. Lotto was busy entertaining his company and in no time had them high enough to feel comfortable walking around the house in their underwear.

Ke-Ke laughed in her head as she watched these chicks do and say anything to impress Lotto like he was some millionaire nigga. They actually thought they were going to get something, but time and time again, all they ever got was high, drunk, and dicked down. She sat on the couch and counted money while Lotto sat in the kitchen and tried to talk them into having some sort of private hot body contest. They would be lucky if they walked away with fifty dollars for their efforts. Lotto seemed like he was way more willing to spend money on the professional girls than the random, around-the-way girls that were in and out of the house on a daily basis. When they would leave, Lotto would make his announcement, "I ain't given up nothen but hard dick and bubblegum and I'm fresh out of bubblegum!"

Ke-Ke would laugh because the saying always reminded her of Tiff. Inside she would feel guilty and a few times she had wanted to pull the girls to the side and have a talk with them. The thoughts were always erased from her mind when she thought about all the times she had played the fool for a nigga and no one ever told her anything. Those bitches would just have to learn the hard way like everyone else did.

The spot always seemed to stay alive with the customers, the groupie females, and the fiends who were always trying to sell movies, steaks, clothes, cologne, or something. She took advantage on a few good deals on jewelry and bought a couple of movies for the long nights she would stay awake to answer the door when Lotto and Nut were gone or passed out or "busy."

The atmosphere was something that took some getting used to and you definitely had to learn to stomach the gritty visuals. She would come into the house sometimes and not be surprised to see a fiend on her knees in the kitchen or in the corner of the front room, sucking Lotto's or Nut's dick, and she had gotten used to random girls walking around the house naked.

The one thing that always blew her mind was when she was offered sexual favors by some dope fiend who didn't have the money. She had begun to see why niggas that hustled had so much confidence and felt like they could pull any female. They lived in a world where everything was offered to them and placed at their feet.

The outrageous became boring quickly. Lotto and Nut were always coming up with ways to break the monotony of the day or night. One time they had the sexiest strip dance contest. Four or five female fiends who didn't look like they smoked engaged in a dance battle where they had to take off their clothes. Ke-Ke laughed and actually took part as a judge in the competition where the winner was awarded two free bags. She never ceased to be amazed by what people were willing to do to get high. Lotto made three grown men have a skipping contest down the middle of the street in their boxers in broad daylight, Nut hosted a contest to see who could steal the best, and Ke-Ke had laughed uncontrollably when two crackheads came racing around the corner with a lit grill they had stolen from someone's yard, full of meat! They actually gave them extra bags when they noticed the burn marks on their legs and hands. The possibilities were endless, and the question started to become what *wouldn't* they do for a free couple of bags. The games brought on a whole new level of entertainment and comedy and helped to pass the time.

There were always those who took things too far though.

Lotto finally pulled Ke-Ke to the side and explained in detail, the art of piggybacking. She figured she had earned his trust. The hustle worked one of two ways: either Lotto and Nut would go in on a separate package that they didn't get from Cry, hustle it out of the spot like it was the same dope, and keep all of the profits, or they would let someone come to the spot and move their own dope and charge them rent. Lotto explained it in terms of food. "It's like if McDonald's let you sell your own burgers out of their drive-through for a limited time."

Occasionally Lotto and Nut let their cousin and his friend come through and piggyback. They were not really cut out for hustling and, for the most part, Lotto felt sorry for them because their spots never seemed to take off, or they lost dope or dropped it or spent their re-up money. They always had a story. The one night they came over, they brought a bottle of cheap brandy, claiming they were going to pull an all-nighter. Ke-Ke rolled her eyes at the sight of them. They were basically trying to ride off of the little clout that Lotto had. They thought they were major hustlers because they had made a couple hundred dollars here and there and that the sixty-dollar ten-karat rings they wore with the bullshit outfits they had pieced together from the corner store were supposed to impress people.

"Whatup, shorty?" One of them grinned at her as he sat in the kitchen drinking from the bottle like he was a superstar. "You all quiet, come talk to me." Ke-Ke looked over her shoulder at him like he had lost his mind and continued to watch television. She would be damned if she was caught dead talking to a nigga named Poppy or Butchie. She just couldn't see herself doing it.

"I'm good, you good too!" she said without taking her eyes off of the television. She prayed he would give up without it turning into a major ordeal.

"Damn, it's like that?" he said as he slammed the bottle down on the table beside him. Ke-Ke just shot him a look and ignored him. She saw him as one of those dudes who NEVER looked clean. He could have on a new outfit and new boots and he would still have that dirty look to him. Some people were just cursed like that. He could have a mink coat, a hundred-thousand-dollar watch, and be driving a Bentley and he would still look like he smelled.

The night went as planned. Lotto let them move their dope and they made a quick three hundred dollars in less than an hour. Their egos were through the roof and they seemed to forget that without Lotto's help they would still be walking around the neighborhood in circles with a pocket full of dope and no money.

"Yo, let's smut the next bitch that comes through," Poppy said as he sipped on a Heineken.

"Word, I need my dick sucked," Butchie agreed as he nudged Lotto to see how he felt about the idea.

"Man, I get pussy," Lotto said like he was above tricking off with a fiend. Ke-Ke sat in the other room like she wasn't listening to the conversation, but she had heard too many horror stories about girls alone in a room full of men drinking to not stay on point. She had tried to text Cry but had gotten no response.

A few minutes went by and there was a knock on the door. Poppy rushed into the front room to answer it. Lettie, a regular, walked into the house with her niece and began trying to talk Poppy into crediting her for two bags. She was pitching him some story about getting a check the next day and saying how she would come and give him his money back as he guided her into the kitchen with a sneaky smile on his face. Their voices dropped in the kitchen so Ke-Ke turned her attention back to the movie she was watching. She knew Butchie and Poppy were out of dope, so she figured that Lettie would be walking back out of the door with a sad look on her face any minute.

"I'm bout to lay down," she heard Lotto say as his bedroom door slammed shut, leaving Lettie in the kitchen alone, holding her niece's hand. Ke-Ke got up quietly and crept to the doorway of the kitchen when she didn't hear any conversation and peeped around the corner to see what was going on. She saw Poppy hold up a ten-dollar bill and rip it in half. He handed one half to Butchie and told Lettie that in order to get both halves of the bill, she would have to suck both of their dicks. Lettie protested about having to do it in front of her eight-year-old niece, but Poppy had already stated the terms and they were non-negotiable. Ke-Ke watched as Lettie looked at the bill and fidgeted nervously.

"You know you need that money, girl," Poppy teased with a devilish smile plastered across his face.

"Aiight, shit!" Lettie dropped to her knees and began to perform the services requested as if her niece wasn't there at all. After Poppy, she moved over to Butchie who was already holding his dick in his hand. Her head bobbed in and out at a quick pace, as Ke-Ke watched in shock as he gripped her hair while her niece stood there crying and confused.

"You ain't know your auntie was a freak like that, huh?" Poppy asked as he zipped his pants and patted the girl on her head.

Lettie snatched the two pieces of the bill from their hands and put them in her coat pocket. She went to the sink and stuck her mouth underneath the faucet. Then without any words, she picked her crying niece up and walked out of the kitchen. When she passed Ke-Ke, who was standing up against the wall by the doorway, she had tears running down her face. She left the house without looking back and slammed the door.

TWENTY-THREE

TWO MONTHS HAD PASSED since Ke-Ke had begun her hustling career at Cry's spot. The money was good and she had managed to stack close to ten thousand dollars. The majority of the time, she was looking for apartments and furniture, but she quickly realized that she had expensive taste and wanted to save more money before she made her move. Misha had figured out what was going on, so Ke-Ke was forced to give her a weekly stipend to keep her mouth shut. The whole hustling thing was a total change in lifestyle and she only saw Misha here and there. She actually missed her asking her questions and following her around. Their mother didn't seem to notice or care, as long as she got her rent payments, and Ke-Ke definitely didn't miss having to hear her mouth all the time.

Ti-Ti had become a regular at the spot, smoking weed and talking shit. She called herself having a crush on Lotto, and Ke-Ke watched the train wreck of a relationship blossom into a dysfunctional, talk show-worthy mess.

Her routine stayed the same though. She would stay at the spot for a couple of days and then go home to shower, rest, shop, and bullshit with Misha. Her mother had threatened to sell all her clothes on several occasions when she suspected that she was spending the nights with a new boyfriend, but Ke-Ke would slip her a few extra dollars and the threats would cease.

She stood in front of her mirror in a towel deciding what to wear. Her wardrobe had more than doubled and it was really becoming a process. She stopped for a moment as she stared at her reflection in the mirror and wondered if her mother really knew what she was up to and just wasn't saying anything. She would just grunt and roll her eyes when she came in the house with bags of clothes or shoes that she bought with the profits from her job.

Cry had taken her to an auction, where she had bought an Audi A6 that she kept covered in a blue tarp behind the spot. She had made plans to paint it pink and customize it after she got her driver's license. Ke-Ke wondered how her mother would react when she pulled into the driveway on chrome wheels, seated in white leather, and honked the horn for Misha to come out. She figured by that time, she would be moved out of the house completely and there was not much that she would be able to say. Her imagination played a short film of her mother begging her to come back home and help her with the bills because Kent had left her and she was lonely. She and Misha would pull out of the driveway, leaving her on her knees on the sidewalk in tears and a white cloud of exhaust smoke. She smiled at the thought of that scenario as she checked her hair in the mirror.

She reached into the back pocket of her pants that she had taken off before her shower and pulled out a small roll of bills. She counted it and saw that it was four hundred dollars. The whole tricking thing with Nut had been going better than she had ever planned. He was constantly trying to pay her to see her naked or watch her play with herself. The trick was to make him believe that he was getting closer and closer to actually getting some pussy. She had managed to slowly go up on the prices and it had become a steady side hustle. Whenever they were alone in the house, he would start in by asking, "Whatsup?" and that would lead to some indecent proposal that she would grant once he had sworn on his children that he wouldn't try to touch her. Men were fucken stupid.

She counted the money again and sat down on her bed. There was no way on Earth she would drop the kind of money Nut did and not even get a whiff of the pussy. In his mind he was controlling her with money, and in her mind, she was so fine that she could charge a nigga just to look at her. For some reason, it worked out for the both of them. She thought about the dumb look on his face just before he would come, the way his body would spasm and the way he would struggle to catch his breath. She opened her towel and stared down at her freshly shaved ATM machine. Pussy was power.

There was a slight knock on the door and Misha came into the room. "Can I wear your earrings, Ke?" she asked as she headed to the jewelry box on the dresser and began to go through it to find the pair she wanted. Ke-Ke started to say no when she noticed what Misha was wearing.

"Where the hell you going dressed like that?" she tried to sound more concerned than nosy.

"Ma said I could go to this party. Can I get the earrings?" Misha said without turning around.

"Don't get nasty!" Ke-Ke said and waved her hand as she stared Misha up and down. She had on a light blue silk button-down shirt that stopped an inch below the bottom of her ass and some white lace leggings. Ke-Ke watched as the fabric settled on her frame and hugged her thin shape.

"I bet Ma ain't see you wit that shit on." Ke-Ke stated the facts as she went to her closet to pick out her own outfit. She had to admit that her sister had put the outfit together well, almost too well, but she would never say it out loud and give her the satisfaction.

"And she ain't gonna know! I'ma be gone by the time she gets back," Misha answered in her grown tone that had gotten her slapped in the mouth by her mother countless times in the past.

Ke-Ke already knew that when Misha was allowed to go somewhere or do something, that her whole attitude changed. She usually ended up taking it too far, which always resulted in her being grounded for another century.

Ke-Ke turned around and took another look at her as she stood at the mirror and put the earrings on. She had to admit that her little sister was growing up and she was happy to see that Misha wasn't still depressed about the whole incident with Tamera. Her whole performance had reminded her of herself when she was younger and she had to smile as she turned to face her closet again. "I done created a monster!" she laughed and clapped her hands as she stared at Misha.

"Yeah, a better monster!" Misha snapped her fingers and swished her hips as she walked out of the door. Ke-Ke could smell their mother's "good perfume" on her as she passed and yelled, "Ma gonna whoop your ass for fucken wit her shit!"

"Whatever," Misha's voice trailed off as she ran down the stairs.

Her phone rang loudly on the bed so she crossed the room, checked the screen, and then answered it.

"Hey girl, what's been up with you?"

Ke-Ke rolled her eyes at the sound of her father's voice.

"Nothen, how you get this number?" she asked, knowing that she had never given it to him.

"Who else?" he answered with a laugh. Ke-Ke knew he was talking about her mother.

"What, you didn't want me to have it?" he asked as if his feelings were going to be hurt if she answered yes.

"Naw, it's not like that," she lied, for his sake.

"Oh, okay." He laughed again as Ke-Ke got up off the bed and continued trying to find something to wear.

"I was thinken... You wanna come to Germany?" he asked and paused to catch her reaction.

"Germany? What the hell I'ma do over there?" Ke-Ke snapped back at him.

"Live," he answered, and for the next hour, her father tried to sell her on Germany. How it was such a wonderful place, and how the taxicabs were Mercedes-Benzes, and the men had all types of money and were single. Ke-Ke listened to him as if he was one of the men on an infomercial.

"I can't see it," she said when he finally paused to take a breath. She was trying to figure in her head why he out of the blue wanted to have her live with him again. There had to be some sort of hidden reason.

"You there?" she could hear her father's voice ask through the phone after she sat silent in her own thoughts.

"Yeah, I'm here," she said with an attitude as she thought about the reality of how her father treated her and her sister. He went on and on, talking about how he was leaving his wife and how he moved to Germany to make it official. Ke-Ke half-listened and matched outfits in front of the mirror at the same time.

"Well, at least think about it," he ended the conversation quickly as he explained that he was getting a call from his "new flame" on the other line and that he would call her back later in the week.

"Aiight," Ke-Ke pushed END and threw the phone on her bed without saying goodbye.

She half-entertained the idea of actually moving away and living in another country. She had to admit that it was an exciting idea. Her father would still be her father, no matter what country they lived in, and she wasn't looking forward to round two with that man anytime soon. She thought about his new woman and figured that she was just after him for his money. He seemed to attract that type, despite the fact that he swore he was a player. She had tried to warn him about his soon-to-be-ex-wife, but he never listened. She felt herself becoming angry as she thought about all he did for his women. He would've been father of the year in a magazine if he jumped through half of those hoops for her and Misha.

Then a thought hit her out of nowhere.

He was always complaining about how much money he had to pay their mother in child support. He would often use it as an excuse as to why he never sent anything. He wanted her and her sister to move to Germany so he could claim full custody of them and not have to pay anything. He was constantly trying to work some angle then call it love, and Ke-Ke had become skilled in seeing through them and uncovering his hidden agendas.

Niggas was fucken snakes! ALL NIGGAS! She pulled her hair back in the mirror as the thoughts came together in her head like magnets. Ke-Ke sighed, knowing that he had at least taught her that one thing. Her father was officially the first nigga to fuck her over.

***

Ke-Ke was dressed and on her way out the door when her phone rang again. She was reminded to change the ringtone as the Mary J. Blige song was now starting to get on her nerves. She glanced at the screen and saw UNKNOWN in bold letters flashing on the screen.

"Who dis?" she answered, as she tried to balance the phone on her shoulder while she reached for her coat.

"Where you at?" A voice spoke like it was confident that she already knew who it was.

"Who the fuck is this?" she asked again as she tried to place the voice that sounded vaguely familiar.

"Yo, this Chop man, stop fucken playen wit me," the voice answered.

"Yeah, yeah," Ke-Ke answered, preparing herself to hear more bullshit. When it rains, it pours. She wondered how many more unwanted phone calls she would receive before the day was over.

Chop was a nigga she had fucked a few times who had sold her a dream about how he was a rapper and he had a major record deal and he was going to be famous and so on. She figured out way too late that all he had said was either an outright lie or greatly exaggerated. He did hustle though and made decent money, so she used him to support her weed habit and to ride around when she had nothing better to do.

She remembered breaking it off with him when she found out he was into the group sex thing and was constantly trying to get her in a situation with another female or one or more of his friends or cousins.

She caught a chill when she remembered the time that they were having sex and she looked up to see two niggas on the side of the bed with their dicks in their hands. She thought she was going to get gang raped. She remembered getting dressed as fast as she could and walking all the way home in the rain at four o'clock in the morning. She figured he had to have had them hiding in the closet or something, because they had come out of nowhere.

She told Ti-Ti about the situation and remembered her laughing and saying, "He was tryen to get that DP shit goen wit yo' ass!" as she laughed and fell on her bed.

Ke-Ke sat confused as she watched Ti-Ti tear up from laughing so hard.

"What the fuck is DP?" she had asked and felt stupid when Ti-Ti sat up on the bed with a shocked look on her face.

"Girl, you don't know about that?" Ti-Ti said as she stared up at her in disbelief. An hour later, after watching one of Ti-Ti's many porno DVDs that were all labeled "cartoons" she had been schooled to a whole new world of perversion. "Now you know what it is?" Ti-Ti looked over at her as Ke-Ke watched in amazement while two men penetrated the woman on the muted television at the same time. "That's that double penetration shit!" Ti-Ti said as she basked in the fact that for once, she had known about something before her cousin did.

Ke-Ke remembered staring like she was watching a circus act, wondering how any woman could do that and make it look so easy! She had thought back to the time when Chop had tried to ram his dick in her ass and how it hurt for days anytime she bent over or sat down too hard. She shook her head and wondered how the chicks in the movie did it. They made it look simple and painless *AND* they were taking another dick in their pussy.

"That shit do look kinda fun though," Ti-Ti said. "All the attention on me!" She clapped and nudged Ke-Ke, who was still in a state of shock.

Ke-Ke remembered silently thanking God that they had just let her leave the house that morning.

"What you want, ol' nasty-ass nigga?" Ke-Ke said into the phone with the images from Ti-Ti's movies still stuck in her head.

"Aww, you still on that?" he asked, like he couldn't understand why she would still be mad.

"You be on some super freak shit! I ain't wit all that!" Ke-Ke said in a cold tone.

"Aiight, aiight, my bad, love!" Chop apologized like he really meant it and Ke-Ke couldn't deny that she had always like the sound of his voice over the phone.

"So whatup, stranger?" Ke-Ke asked, trying to change the subject and let him know that she wasn't really that mad anymore.

"You," Chop answered in his deep voice that always sent chills down her spine.

"Well, why don't you come scoop me? I gotta go to work," she suggested.

"Work, where the fuck you worken at?" Chop asked with surprise in his tone. "If you had acted right, you would have never had to work again," he stated like he was the president of some major company.

"Shit, if acten right means becoming a human pincushion, I'll work forever!" she stated with a laugh. "Hurry up, I'm at the house." She hung up the phone, confident that he would be there in a few minutes.

For the first time ever, Ke-Ke had stolen a fashion tip from her little sister and went with no panties underneath stretch pants and a black hoodie that barely covered her ass. The outfit was sexy, but comfortable enough to wear at the spot for a couple of days. She finished the outfit with gold earrings, grabbed the few things she would need and ran down the stairs to wait for Chop.

She sat on the good furniture and peered out the blinds waiting for him to pull up when she noticed the newspaper her mother had saved, folded on the coffee table. The paper was on the obituary page and she felt strong guilt all over again as she looked at Lee's black and white photo staring back at her.

She wasn't trying to be nasty or act like she didn't care about what had happened to him, but she knew she wouldn't have been able to hold herself together at his funeral. Lee was one of the few niggas that had entered her life who she actually cared about and she knew she wasn't ready to see him in a casket. She thought about Misha and how she had changed after Tamera was killed. She couldn't put her finger on it, but Misha had a little more edge to her. She had actually gone to Tamera's wake and funeral and the whole ordeal must have broken something inside of her.

She remembered back to the first time that one of her close friends was killed and all the anger she had felt. She walked around for a year, looking for people to take that anger out on. She hoped that her sister didn't go through the same thing.

Headlights shining through the window broke her chain of thoughts and she grabbed her charger and made her way out the door.

"Whatup, sexy?" Chop greeted her as she got into the passenger seat and closed the door.

"Whatup, my shoulda-been nigga," Ke-Ke answered, hoping it would lure him in.

"Damn, you still looken right!" Chop said, not at all trying to hide the fact that he was staring down at her crotch. Ke-Ke humored him and stretched as she reached for the seatbelt, watching his eyes get wider as the material revealed the imprint of her shaved pussy. She finished her routine and let her hoodie fall back into place while Chop still stared down in between her legs.

"What?" she asked innocently.

"Uh, nothen," Chop answered as he quickly turned his head and tried to shake it off while he shifted the car into reverse and backed out of the driveway. Ke-Ke looked out of the passenger side window thinking, "Mission accomplished." She set her unimpressed attitude on high as she stole glances of the interior of the new BMW 750 he had bought since the last time they had talked. She had already decided in her head to act like she hadn't noticed if he asked about it.

"Where you worken now?" he asked as he flashed his high beams to allow a man carrying a mattress to cross the street. She gave him the directions and settled in to play her nonchalant role for the duration of the ride. She had learned years ago at the salon that the best way to get money from a nigga was to act like you didn't want none, or weren't impressed by it.

"Ohhhh, you hustlen now?" Chop asked, fishing for information. "When I asked you to work for me, you was all like, 'That ain't me.' Whatsup now?" Chop asked, mocking her voice. "Some nigga done put that thang on you and got you worken, huh?" Chop asked with a hint of jealousy in his voice.

Ke-Ke just smiled as she stared out of the window thinking, "If this nigga only knew." She tapped him on the shoulder and responded, "Things change, boo! Don't take it to the head." She could tell that her not filling in the blanks for him was pissing him off. He lit the blunt that he was holding behind his ear, barely hit it, then handed it to Ke-Ke. She made a mental note of it as she took the blunt. If Chop thought he was going to smoke her out and fuck her, he had another thing coming.

"So, you like the ride or what?" Chop finally got around to asking.

"Ain't this the same one you had before?" Ke-Ke answered as she looked around the car with a confused look on her face.

"Man, stop that shit," Chop called her out and she couldn't help but laugh at her own bad acting.

"Naw, it's cool. I like, I like," she said, still laughing.

"Wait til I come out though. It's game over," Ke-Ke said as she took the Audi key out of her pocket and waved it proudly.

"Oh, you got it like that now? You rollen like that?" Chop slapped her hand, congratulating her on her success. Ke-Ke felt proud, like Chop saw her in a different way, like he respected her as an equal.

"You know how I do." Ke-Ke slipped the key back into her pocket then felt ice water run through her body as she glanced out of the window.

Cry's black Infiniti was parked outside of a green house across from a corner store. She watched as a dark-skinned female climbed out of the passenger side and walked around to the driver's side window. Chop was saying something, but Ke-Ke raised her hand to silence him as she homed in on what she was seeing. Chop pulled off from the stop sign and they passed just as Cry was reaching out of the window and grabbing the girl's ass as they kissed. Ke-Ke sunk low in the seat as she noticed the smile on Cry's face. She felt a familiar sickness beginning to fill her stomach.

"Damn, what you get all quiet for?" Chop asked as he kept looking over at her. She was shaken up and couldn't even answer. They rode the next couple of minutes in complete silence.

"I'm good," she finally pushed the words out, wondering if it even sounded convincing.

"I told you about fucken wit these bitch-ass niggas," Chop offered, like he had figured out what was going on.

"You're right!" Ke-Ke answered, knowing that she wasn't about to share that truth with Chop or anyone else. Chop wasn't the talker type by nature, but he did spend a lot of time in the barbershop and she wasn't going to chance having her business put on the "ghetto internet."

He pulled the car to a stop across the street from the spot and turned his headlights off.

"You can't spend no time with a nigga tonight?" Chop asked, as he tried to capitalize on her moment of weakness with a smile on his face. "You know the best way to get back at him is to fuck wit me!" he said, like it was a healthy solution to her problem.

"You crazy as hell!" Ke-Ke said as she laughed at his creative approach to getting some ass. She played the image in her head of fucking Chop in the car, right in front of the spot. Cry would pull up and she would let the fogged-up windows down "by accident" so she could catch a glimpse of her fucking the hell out of Chop and moaning. The thought almost amused her as she wondered what Cry would say or do. The idea dissolved in her mind when she pictured Cry shrugging and walking into the house like she didn't care and the sick feeling returned to her stomach with twice the intensity.

"Yo," Chop nudged her and brought her back to reality. "There you go off to your special place." He laughed.

"You got work on you?" Ke-Ke asked like that was what she had been thinking about. "Why you don't let me make you some money for old time's sake. Then we'll go from there," she said as the wheels began to slowly turn in her head.

"You gonna make some money for me?" Chop laughed, but he sat back in his seat and rubbed his chin like he was in deep thought. "Aiight, shorty, let's see what you can do," he said once he had checked his rearview mirror four or five times. Chop reached down the front of his pants and pulled a plastic bag out of his boxers. He handed Ke-Ke a rock that looked like two bars of hotel soap stuck together.

"It's about time you started fucken wit Daddy," he said with a smile on his face. "Make it do what it do, shorty," he said as he checked her face for a reaction. "And don't go disappearing on me either."

"C'mon, boo, you know me better than that." Ke-Ke waved away his warning. She placed her hand on his face softly and kissed his lips. She put the rock in her pocket and leaned back in the passenger seat, pulling her hoodie above her waist. "Go ahead, rub it for good luck," she said as she spread her legs and looked over at him seductively. Chop smiled and patted her pussy three times then licked his fingers. They both burst into laughter and Ke-Ke climbed out of the car.

"Call me wit your number unblocked, so I can let you know when to come through," she instructed him as she crossed the street. When she got to the porch, she smiled as she noticed he hadn't pulled off yet and was watching her walk. She climbed the short flight of stairs and disappeared into the darkness of the porch.

"Still got it!" she thought as she performed the coded knock on the door and waited for someone to answer.

"Whatup, though." Lotto answered the door in jeans with no shirt on. The smell of weed and alcohol rushed out of the house. Ke-Ke passed him without speaking and sat on the couch. She reached into her pocket, got her charger out, then passed the rock she had just gotten to Lotto for him to inspect. She crossed her fingers, hoping that he wouldn't say it was garbage and they couldn't work with it.

"Oh shit. This that whip! Where you get this?" He asked with his mouth open, like he was in a daze. He sat down on the couch next to her sniffing the rock and turning it over in his hands.

"I got peoples," Ke-Ke answered proudly as a feeling of relief came over her that she didn't show.

"If you had peoples like this, you shoulda *BEEN* said somethen!" he said, as he stared down at the rock and shook his head. "Damn, this shit gonna move like asses in a strip club!" he said as he began peeling off the plastic wrap. "This shit gotta be like twenty-five hundred to the good, maybe more!" he said as he laid it on the table in front of them. Ke-Ke tried to not look surprised at the number he shot out, like she knew what it was worth the whole time.

"Let's get it off then, I'll cut you in" she whispered, as she locked eyes with him to let him know that the deal was only between them.

"Bet," he slapped her hand with a huge smile on his face and walked into the kitchen to get the extra bags they kept hidden under the sink. Ke-Ke sat back on the couch and thought about everything that had happened in the last twenty minutes. She had caught Cry in the act, had her heart broken, and somehow found a whole new supplier at the same time. She thought about how her life seemed to be in a constant state of extremes.

She thought about Cry and felt stupid for even thinking that things could or would be different with her. She had been played by niggas for years, so why would she think things would be different with a bitch that thought she was a nigga? The logic of it all appeared out of nowhere and ripped her two-month fairy tale to shreds. The only thought that comforted her was that she had caught it early enough. She knew in her heart if she had actually told her family, claimed the lifestyle, moved in with Cry, given up dick, and THEN found out that she was getting played the whole time? That would've ended tragically with her or Cry in jail, and she knew it. Her mind drifted and she thought about all the times she had texted Cry and she never responded or she had called and there was no answer. The thoughts of her riding around with another bitch or having another bitch at her house were like hot coals burning in her chest.

She had noticed that lately there hadn't been a whole lot of interaction between them, but she always told herself that Cry was handling business and she wasn't ever comfortable playing the role of the "nagging wife" type. Ke-Ke sighed as she thought about Cry's hands and how they could bring her to ecstacy within seconds. The memories almost made her smile until she thought of the dark-skinned girl who she probably made feel the exact same way. Ke-Ke was mad at the fact that she had let her feelings get the best of her so quickly, mad that she had allowed her spirit to be touched, and mad that her hopes and imagination had again been led on a journey to nowhere.

The whole time she had worked at the spot, she had always felt a sense of disloyalty when they brought in someone else's product, passed it off as Cry's, then pocketed the profits behind her back. She had even thought about telling on Nut and Lotto for doing it to the extremes that they did, because in the end it had to cost Cry thousands. Her not being there all the time led to her not knowing the actual worth of the spot. That "not knowing" was going to cost her even more, as Ke-Ke planned to exploit that ignorance to the fullest. All bets were off, and loyalty, as her uncle had told her one night, *Was a song that only the victims ever learn the words to.*

She glanced in the kitchen and watched Lotto and Nut bragging and pulling out wads of money to impress the two girls they had in the kitchen frying chicken. The night was in full swing and Ke-Ke watched as the two acted like they were not giving up any money to fuck, and the girls acted like they weren't all about fucking for money. They were just walking around in their tiny underwear because they were "around good people" and "comfortable." The end result would be the same: Lotto and Nut would have a little less money and the girls would have a little more dick.

She watched the show from the other room and wondered why they both just didn't come out and say what they were really after. The whole scene was like some poorly written movie where you figured out what was going to happen long before it ended. You stayed in the theater though, because you had already spent your money.

She lay across the couch with a sense of accomplishment. She watched the festivities, knowing that she was looking at her past, a past that she had managed to escape. She used to be one of those girls, laughing at dumb jokes and begging for handouts, but now she was on another level. She had gotten some real money and, from the looks of it, was about to make even more and hadn't laid on her back to do it. A warm feeling came over her body as she basked in a freedom that she knew most girls her age would never know.

***

Ke-Ke woke up the next morning to the sound of Ti-Ti's voice coming from the kitchen. She stretched and sat up, wondering why Ti-Ti wasn't screaming about the girls that were there.

"Ohhh, Sleeping Beauty is up," Ti-Ti laughed and skipped into the room with a blunt in her mouth. She hugged her neck and Ke-Ke pushed her away when she tried to kiss her on the cheek. She noticed Ti-Ti was in her bra and panties. She glanced over her shoulder and caught eyes with Lotto, who just winked and stuck his tongue out to signal he had gotten the other girls out of the house. Ke-Ke just shook her head and rolled her eyes.

"We family, bitch! Stop acten like that. I seen you naked a million times," Ti-Ti said as she caught herself from falling.

"Heyyy," Lotto called out from the kitchen as he stared at them with a playful suspicion. Ke-Ke stuck her middle finger up at him and smiled. She always thought Lotto was cute, but seeing how he got down with females was a turnoff. Deep down she knew that other niggas she had fucked with were probably the same way or worse, but there was something about seeing it up close and personal that made it different. Lotto always kept his flirting on a playful level, but Ke-Ke knew if she offered he would "fuck the back off her" as the old ladies at the salon would say.

"Yoooo, you heard? I know you heard, right?" Ti-Ti began her broadcast before Ke-Ke could ask her why she was walking around the house with no clothes on.

"What now?" Ke-Ke asked as she reached for the pack of Newports on the coffee table.

"Y'all boss locked up! They won't let her out. They won't let her out!" Ti-Ti told the news as she sang the song by Akon.

"What they hell you talken about now?" Ke-Ke lit the cigarette and rolled her eyes at Ti-Ti. Lotto stepped into the room and did the honors officially.

"Cry got locked up last night," he said as he shook his head with a look of doubt on his face.

"For real? Y'all bullshitten. I just seen her last night." Ke-Ke was wide awake now as she checked her phone for the time. She glanced back and forth at Lotto and Ti-Ti, waiting for them to say "gotcha" or something.

"Naw, man, I guess her mom's boyfriend had jumped on her and she called Cry." Lotto told the story with his hands in his pockets. "Cry goes over there and pistol whips the nigga and the nigga run around the corner and call the boys on her." Lotto told the story like he had witnessed it first hand.

"Geeet the fuck outta here!" Ke-Ke said, still waiting for both of them to start laughing.

"So they bagged her wit the pistol."

"And she had like two ounces of dope on her," Ti-Ti finished the sentence before Lotto had a chance to.

"Real shit!" Lotto said, as he nodded and reached for the cigarette.

"Daamn, for real?" Ke-Ke's mind spun as she played the story out in her mind.

"That shit was on the news and everything. It might be in the paper too," Lotto added to the story as he came in the front room and sat down across from them. Ke-Ke felt a sense of panic as all of her future plans seemed to be derailed in a split second.

"Y'all gonna have to shut down shop," Ti-Ti said as she shrugged and pulled on her blunt. Ke-Ke's eyes danced around the room and then landed on Lotto, who sat across from her with a smile beginning to form on his face. She could read his thoughts and knew where this was going.

"Unless," he said and nodded at her. "I mean I ain't even close to where I'm tryen to be, and I know you want to get your shit painted back there, right?" Lotto pointed towards the back of the house where her Audi sat parked and covered. "We gotta keep our doors open somehow. It ain't personal, this is business!"

Lotto sounded like one of those actors from the B movies they sold behind the liquor store. You bought it because the cover made it look like it was going to be good.

Ke-Ke nodded slowly as she worked the thoughts over in her head and tried to ignore the stupid-ass comments Ti-Ti kept making.

"That shit you brought in here last night is gone." Lotto went to the kitchen and pulled a brown paper bag out of the oven. It was stuffed with cash.

"Whoever you got this shit from is gonna know this spot is jumpen. I bet they ain't gonna have no problem filling in." Lotto ran down the facts like he had been role-playing the speech with Ti-Ti before she had woken up. "Cry ain't comen home! I'll tell you that right now. This her second pistol charge." Lotto broadcasted her criminal past and sounded like the district attorney himself. "Shiit, the way I see it, she looken at like three felonies at least! The pistol charge, assault with a deadly weapon, possession..." Lotto counted the charges out on his fingers like he was in math class. "Her fucken bail gonna be through the roof, IF they even give her one. Ain't no tellen what else is on her record that we don't know about. Shit, I don't even know her real fucken name to be able to look the shit up."

Ke-Ke weighed everything in her head as she stared at Lotto, knowing that he was speaking the truth.

"Shit, even if..." Ke-Ke stopped as she tried to organize her tangled mind. "Cry got paper though, she might get bailed out, then everything goes back to normal. There ain't no problem really." She spoke her thoughts out loud without really weighing them.

"Man, having money and being able to get to it is two different things," Lotto answered quickly. "And how you gonna pay a bail if they don't give you one?"

"If she do got the paper to post bail, only she knows where it's at, so what good is it?" Ti-Ti finally said something that made sense. Lotto pointed at her to cosign the point.

"This the game, and the game don't stop," Lotto offered another punchline from a movie.

"Oooh, that's deep!" Ti-Ti said as she smiled over at him.

Ke-Ke thought about not wanting to be tied to Chop in that way. She knew enough about him to know that the business deal would only be as good as their personal relationship, and that could go sour at any time. She pictured everything being good and then him deciding to cut them off because she wouldn't agree to one of his freaky requests. She could already hear how that would go over when she came back to try and explain what happened to Nut and Lotto. "Take one for the team," she was sure they would probably say, or something like that.

"Hell naw!" she had said out loud, before she had even realized it.

"What you mean?" Lotto said throwing his hands in the air and stomping off into the kitchen like a little boy having a temper tantrum.

"Naw, I mean, let me see! Give me the money. I can ask, but I ain't promising nothen." Lotto handed her the bag and she was shocked by the weight of it. "I ain't no fucken pincushion. I'm tellen you that right now though," Ke-Ke said as she opened the bag and sat back down on the couch.

"What the fuck is a pincushion?" Lotto stood in the doorway with a confused look on his face.

Ke-Ke had to admit that she wasn't close to her goal and she wasn't ready to give up. She grabbed her phone and selected Chop's number from the list of her missed calls. She was glad he listened when she'd told him to unblock it.

"Yo, who dis?" Chop answered the phone with the music too loud in the background.

"I got you, Daddy!" Ke-Ke flirted with him. "I need to see you ASAP too!"

"Yeah... already?" Ke-Ke could hear the music in the background had quickly disappeared. "Where you at? The same spot?" he asked with doubt in his voice.

"Yeah, where you dropped me off at?" Ke-Ke answered, not wanting to say too much over the phone.

"I'm on my way," he said and hung up the phone. Ke-Ke looked into the kitchen at Lotto who was nodding, smiling, and giving her the thumbs up.

Twenty minutes later, Chop was outside honking the horn. Ke-Ke tucked the bag full of money under her hoodie and jogged out to the car, looking both ways.

"Whatsup, baby?" she asked as she slid into the passenger seat and closed the door. She looked down to see that Chop had his pistol on his lap and wasn't smiling. "Whatsup wit all that?" she asked as she noticed the size of the barrel and then looked back up at Chop.

"My daddy taught me that when something sounds too good to be true, it usually is," he said with no emotion in his voice as he watched the street through the windows. Ke-Ke handed him the money with no further hesitation. They sat in silence as he took the bag, dumped the money on his lap, and began to count it. He stopped after he was a little more than halfway through and looked over at her, still holding his gun. "There's a first time for everything though!" He glanced down at the remainder of the money and looked over at her again. "That spot is jumpen like that?" He looked past her at the rundown house across the street.

"I told you," Ke-Ke said as she tried to settle her nerves while she kept her attention on the gun. She had never seen the serious side of Chop; he was always smoking weed and telling jokes. She figured he was acting so serious because of the amount of money that was involved and she was glad that she hadn't tried to play him.

In the back of her mind, she was still thinking about the possibility that Cry would post bail and the whole situation becoming ugly with her and Chop bumping heads over who would run the spot. She knew that she would be in the middle of it and Cry would see it as a sign of disloyalty. The other side of it was if she didn't post bail or wasn't offered one, then she couldn't really blame them for finding another way to get money, could she?

"Yeah, a little birdy told me that you lost your sponsor last night," Chop spoke after a moment, letting her know that he knew the situation she was in. Ke-Ke never ceased to be amazed at how fast bad news traveled in the streets.

"Yeah, well we don't know how it's all gonna end up, but at the same time we tryen to keep our doors open while we wait." Ke-Ke spoke Lotto's words that seemed to flow much better than anything she would've thought of on her own.

Chop pulled on his chin as he nodded and digested her logic.

"Either way it goes, you gonna get your money, the only question is for how long."

"Cry done! It's a wrap for that bitch. She ain't getten out!" Chop said, like he knew it for a fact. The car fell silent as his words hit Ke-Ke like a brick.

"Aiight, aiight, I'ma put you on. But everything is on you. Shit ain't right, the money ain't right, it's on you. I don't know them other niggas up in there and don't really want to. I'm dealen wit you and you only." The way Chop spoke reminded her of her track coach back in junior high. He was dead serious though and she wasn't at all trying to see the monster that he would become if his money came up short. She figured she would take the first front and cover it with the money she had already stacked if something went wrong. The next round she would buy outright then make Nut and Lotto think that they were still getting the dope fronted. They would never even know that they were really working for her. The real bonus was that if Chop tried to come at her on a sexual level, she could easily just tell him that it was bad for business and he wouldn't cut them off as long as he was getting money.

The plan came together in her head so fast that it surprised her. "Can I get our cut from that?" she said as she pointed to the money in his hands and on his lap. "I gotta pay my crew." She winked as she formerly announced her own promotion.

"Oh shit, you already talken like a boss! I knew you would catch on. You always had good instincts, that's why I like you," Chop admitted as he counted out the money and then slipped a few extra bills in her pocket.

"Oh, you tryen to take care of me, huh?" she winked as she took the money out of her pocket and hid it in her sock.

"Just a little somethen." He smiled. "Tell ya peoples whatsup. I'ma be back wit the work. I gotta go cross town," Chop said as he unlocked the doors for her to get out.

"We gonna be here, but hurry up, we almost out," she informed him with a serious look on her face.

"I got you," Chop said as she stepped out of the car and watched him pull off.

Ke-Ke walked back to the house, sorting through the reality of what she had just negotiated as her heart beat out of control. If Cry stayed locked up after this second round, she would officially run the spot. She was shocked at how quickly it all happened and how it really had just fallen into her lap. She looked up at the sky with a smile before pulling herself together to walk back into the house.

Somebody up there loved her.

TWENTY-FOUR

KE-KE STEPPED INTO THE HOUSE with her head down. She had decided to pull one of Tiff's routines and make Lotto and Ti-Ti sweat for the details. When she walked in the door, Ti-Ti and Lotto's eyes were glued to the television and they hadn't even noticed her walk in.

"Yo, that shit is crazy," Lotto said as he nudged Ti-Ti, who was smiling and shaking her head. Ke-Ke crossed the room and walked into the kitchen, waiting for them to ask her what had happened. She checked the refrigerator to find a plate of fried chicken covered with a paper towel and foam takeout food containers. She sighed and opened the freezer to find two bottles of gin and a can of soda. "This shit worse than home," she said as she closed the freezer door and her phone fell out of her pocket. She debated on whether she was hungry enough to warm up the chicken when she felt her phone vibrate in her hand. The screen flashed an UNKNOWN so she pushed the ignore button and decided to check her voicemails and texts.

"Yo, that *is* that nigga!" Ti-Ti shrieked from the front room and started laughing. "Yo Ke, you know this dude right?" Ke-Ke walked into the front room and caught a glimpse of a familiar face in a small square in the middle of the television.

"Oh shit, turn that up," she said, as she rushed towards the television and turned up the volume.

"He is being charged with rape in the third degree, sexual abuse, and sodomy," the woman reported on the news. Ke-Ke's mouth dropped as she focused on the picture and realized it was Ahmed from the hair store. "Apparently, he approached young women that frequented the hair store he owned and operated and solicited them with free merchandise and cash," the woman reported from the colorful news studio.

"Now, is this something that they are saying has been going on for some time?" the male anchor asked, encouraging the woman reporting to offer more details.

"So far that's all the information that is being given. Understandably there are confidentiality issues, four of the victims are underaged and from what we've been able to find out, more have come forward after the arrest was made. The suspect in this case, Ahmed Mohammed, allegedly engaged in various acts on the premises using the stockroom and fitting rooms, we're being told," the woman answered shortly.

"Yo, that nasty muthafucka! He used to always look at me funny when I went in that bitch," Ti-Ti said as she shook her head and pointed at the screen. "Ke-Ke, I know you gotta know that nigga as much as you be up there."

"Yeah, I seen him before, he ain't never come at me like that though," she said quickly as she felt Ti-Ti's eyes glaring at the side of her face. "He tried you?" she shot the question back before Ti-Ti had a chance to start in on her.

"Hell naw! Them Arab muthafuckas stank! I woulda told him from the door to get the fuck out my face," Ti-Ti said, as she tried to play the tough role in front of Lotto. Ke-Ke rolled her eyes, knowing that Ti-Ti wasn't the type to turn down anything she could get for free, but didn't want to call her out in front of her man.

She took one last glance at the picture of Ahmed before it disappeared from the corner of the screen and the newscasters began to talk about the weather. She was still in shock as she played back her encounter with Ahmed in the fitting room that they had just mentioned on the news. Her mind raced as she wondered how many girls he had done that with and what the actual details were.

"Damn, they got that nigga on sodomy too!" Lotto said, as he turned the television down with the remote and pulled on his cigarette.

"That mean he was fucken girls in the ass," Ti-Ti blurted out. "In the store. In them fitting rooms!" she laughed and clapped her hands. "Damn, I'm glad I ain't never tried shit on in that store," she continued.

"That ain't what that shit mean!" Lotto said as he looked over at her like she was an alien.

"It do mean that! Ke-Ke, don't sodomy mean you fucked someone in the butt?" Ti-Ti tried to pull her into the middle of the debate.

Ke-Ke's head was still spinning as she thought about Ahmed. She knew there was something about him that turned her off, but she could never put her finger on it. She thought about how things could've gotten out of control if they had been in the shop alone. She remembered the old lady that sat by the door. She could picture her face in her mind perfectly for some reason, the look in her eyes and the sound of her voice. Her mind focused on her face as the details seemed to become sharper and sharper, like someone was drawing a sketch in front of her. She could see the creases in her face, the wrinkles around her eyes, her coat and then her eyes again. She felt a chill run through her body as the woman's left eye winked at her then disappeared.

"KE-KE! HELLO! COME BACK TO PLANET EARTH!" Ti-Ti was standing up across from her.

"Girl, I don't fucken know, I ain't no fucken lawyer!" Ke-Ke yelled as Ti-Ti had startled her back into the land of the present.

"Yeah, yo' cousin just don't wanna tell you you wrong." Lotto laughed as he continued to smoke his cigarette.

"Whatever, nigga. Ke, let me hold ya phone." Ti-Ti reached out for her phone and tried to hit Lotto at the same time.

Ke-Ke thought fast and scrolled through her phone, deleting Ahmed's number from her contacts. Ti-Ti was nosy as hell and if she saw that, she knew she would never hear the end of it. She handed the phone to Ti-Ti and watched as she performed her "sexy walk" into the kitchen to make her call.

"So yo, what's good wit the connect?" Lotto asked as soon as she was out of the room. Ke-Ke looked up at him and let a smile slowly form on her face.

"I knew that shit!" He jumped up like he was watching a football game.

"What? What I miss?" Ti-Ti dashed back into the front room with the phone to her ear.

"Take yo' nosy ass back in the kitchen!" Lotto ordered, but Ti-Ti just stood there looking back and forth at their faces. "Ain't you supposed to be on the phone?" Lotto asked as if he was annoyed at the sight of her.

"Nigga, shut up! I'm just checken my voicemail! You getten all jealous and shit!" Ti-Ti said as she winked and blew a kiss at him.

"Jealous, my ass! I'll pay that nigga cab fare if he come take you somewhere," Lotto said.

"Ooh I love you too, boo!" Ti-Ti said, as if she had no idea how serious Lotto really was.

Ke-Ke laughed as she watched them go back and forth. She took the blunt from Ti-Ti and focused her mind back on her plan. She wondered whether she could really pull it off without Lotto and Nut catching on.

"Ke, that shit worked out?" Ti-Ti asked, invading her thoughts again. Ke-Ke nodded and rolled her eyes, knowing that her cousin wouldn't leave it alone until she knew all the business.

"Hey! We bout to be poppen champagne at the concert. We gonna be the shit up in that bitch!" Ti-Ti did her world-famous catwalk strut across the front room as Ke-Ke caught Lotto's eyes and laughed. She tried to do the math in her head of how much money they could make in the short period of time before the concert and entertained the chances of being able to pull up in front of the Armory in her pink Audi, dressed to kill. Her heart sank again as she remembered she had planned to hit Ahmed up to find out who had done his truck, but that option was out of the question now.

"But yo, was that that nigga Chop you was talken to?" Lotto asked as he sat on the couch, looking up at her.

Ke-Ke felt her heart drop as she realized that Lotto already knew who he was. That might ruin her whole plan.

"Yeah, why?" Ke-Ke asked as she took her phone from Ti-Ti's hand. Lotto stood up and banged his head up against the wall in mock disgust with a look of disappointment on his face.

"What?" Ke-Ke asked, trying to anticipate anything that he might be thinking as an objection to working with Chop.

"Yo, on the low, I heard that nigga was on some other shit!" Lotto sat down and began talking in a low voice, like he thought Chop could be standing right outside of the door.

"What you mean, some other shit?" Ke-Ke asked as she glanced up at Ti-Ti to see if she knew what he was talking about. Lotto stood back up and paced back and forth.

"Yo, you know that nigga was down in the city worken for the Jamaicans, right?" Lotto asked the question with a serious look on his face.

"Yeah, I heard somethen about him bein in the city," Ke-Ke answered. She thought back to the time when Chop had called from Brooklyn with reggae music blasting in the background.

"Well, I heard that nigga robbed them and came back here to set up shop wit they product and they been looken for that nigga!" Lotto told her with his eyes wide as he waited to see her reaction.

"C'mon, as tight as he was wit them damn Jamaicans, I thought he was half-Jamaican when I met him." Ke-Ke shook her head in disbelief. "He just gonna up and rob his own peoples for no reason? They the ones that put him in the game." She tried to argue down the information with everything she could remember. Lotto just dropped his head and walked past Ti-Ti towards the kitchen.

"I'm tellen you what I heard and I been hearen it from a bunch of different people," Lotto said as he stopped in the doorway.

"So what you sayen now? You don't wanna fuck wit him?" Ke-Ke asked, as she tried to gauge how strong Lotto's feelings were.

"*AND* that nigga a homo-thug," Ti-Ti interrupted the conversation and pulled it in a whole new direction.

"What?" Ke-Ke spun around to face her.

"I heard that shit too," Lotto said as he stood in the doorway and nodded. Ke-Ke stared back and forth at their faces like she was watching a tennis match.

"Man, y'all fucken trippen! You say he robben his own people, you sayen he fucken niggas! What the fuck is *really* goen on?" she said and laughed, trying to lighten the mood.

"The streets talk," is all Ti-Ti would say as she made a face like she smelled something funny. Ke-Ke recognized her act and knew that someone had sworn her to secrecy and she wasn't going to give up any more information.

"Y'all really fucken me up right now." Ke-Ke moved across the room and sat on the couch. She tried to sift through the information and figure out how much of it she was willing to believe.

"All I know for sure is I ain't tryen to have no beef with them Jamaicans. Especially over some shit I ain't have nothen to do wit!" Lotto announced as he glanced over at her.

"Man, that shit probably ain't even true. This nigga riden a brand new 750. He ain't hard to find!" Ke-Ke tried to reason with him as Lotto threw his hands in the air and disappeared into the kitchen. "I'm just sayen!" Ke-Ke called after him, as she looked over at Ti-Ti who was playing with her nails like she wasn't absorbing every word of the conversation.

Lotto returned to the front room with his jacket on and said he would be back. Ke-Ke watched as he walked out of the door and wondered whether he was really going to come back or was that his way of resigning. She sighed loudly and stared up at the cracked, water-stained ceiling.

"Niggas don't fuck wit them dreads!" Ti-Ti laughed, as she tried to cover for Lotto leaving the house.

Ke-Ke's head was throbbing. She felt her phone vibrating and glanced at the screen, then threw it on the couch next to her.

"I'm wit you cuz, ride or die!" Ti-Ti said, like the situation wasn't as serious as it really was.

"If that nigga quit, you gonna have to be, Ti. I need someone else besides Nut to help run this shit." She looked over at Ti-Ti to see if she realized what she was actually agreeing to.

"I got you," Ti-Ti said without looking up from her nails. "Shit, I need some paper too. This shit go good. We can ride up to the concert in Audis back to back!" She smiled and nodded at the thought. "Lotto on some paranoid shit anyway. He been looken out the window, talken about he be seeing cars parked out there and all types of shit. I think the weed is getten to him." Ti-Ti added as she rolled her eyes and held her hands out in front of her face.

"What kind of cars?" Ke-Ke asked as she remembered seeing a black car with its blinkers on parked a couple of blocks down from the house.

"Shit, I don't know, I think he said some black car. He ain't say what kind it was though." Ti-Ti kept inspecting her nails. "Now what? You seen the shit too, right?" Ti-Ti said as she looked up from her nails and rolled her eyes again.

"Naw," Ke-Ke answered as she tried to find a logical reason why a car would park there. But she was drawing a blank and started to feel a nervousness come over her as she weighed the information Lotto had given her.

"When Chop get back, you can hold it down for me? I'm gonna run to the salon and holla at Tiff. I'll bring you some food back." Ke-Ke tried to sweeten the deal, knowing that Ti-Ti hated to be left alone anywhere.

"You know I got it!" Ti-Ti said, putting her hand in the air. She bounced up and down in her chair like music was playing as she continued to stare at her nails.

"Ti-Ti, for real. Don't be in here bullshitten and talken on the phone. You gotta hold it down until me, Lotto, or Nut get back. Nut should have his drunk ass back here in a few anyway, but you can't be in here playen." Ke-Ke raised her voice so Ti-Ti would know she was serious.

"I got it, damn!" Ti-Ti looked up finally and made eye contact with her.

Ke-Ke felt her phone vibrate and looked down to see Chop had texted her. "Hold up, he's here," she said to Ti-Ti, who just nodded and kept bouncing in her chair. Ke-Ke jumped off the porch and ran over to the car as she made a point to look up the block but saw no other cars.

"Yo, whatup," Chop said as his eyes were locked in his rearview mirror like he was looking for something. Ke-Ke turned around in her seat and looked through the back window to see if she could catch a glimpse of what he was looking at.

"Don't do that shit! You all fucken obvious," he said, as he hit her leg. He unzipped his coat, removed a plastic grocery bag, and handed it to her.

"What the fuck is all this?" Ke-Ke asked as she felt the weight of it and tried to guess how much was in it.

"Hustle that off, like you did before, I'm just tryna get rid of it ASAP so I can pick up this new package," Chop said as he glanced back and forth at her and his rearview mirror. Ke-Ke's heart sank as she could hear Lotto's words in her head and knew all at once that what he had told her was true.

"Just hold it down for me. You ain't on the clock, but the sooner the better!" Chop spoke quickly like he had somewhere to go.

"Aiight, but on some real shit, we need to talk, cause I'm hearen things," Ke-Ke said, hoping that Chop would volunteer more information.

"I got you on the come around," is all Chop said, as he continued to check his mirror. "That's big money you holden, and Fed time if you get caught. You don't know me," he said as he made eye contact with her.

Ke-Ke sat, confused, as she stuffed the bag underneath her hoodie. She felt the sweat starting to form on the palms of her hands, the way it did when she got nervous while she stared over at the side of Chop's face.

"Fifty-fifty split on that shit, shorty. You rich! Just get rid of it for me," Chop said as he unlocked the doors and shifted the car into drive. Ke-Ke thought to ask him another question but decided against it as she climbed out of the car and speed-walked back across the street. Chop sped off down the block and she could hear his tires screech as he turned the corner.

Ke-Ke got in the house and bolted the door. She walked to the windows and peeped through the blinds, wondering if she would catch a glimpse of a car that might have been following Chop.

"What the fuck you doen? You ordered a pizza?" Ti-Ti asked from the other room. Ke-Ke waved her silent as she moved to another window and waited to see if anything looked out of the ordinary. She walked back to the front door and checked the locks again then pulled Ti-Ti by her shirt into the kitchen.

"You gotta see this shit!" she said as she placed the bag on the kitchen table.

"Damn, what the fuck is that, a brick?" Ti-Ti asked.

"I don't even fucken know," Ke-Ke whispered as she dumped the contents of the bag on the table.

"Jackpot!" Ti-Ti screamed as she patted her on the shoulder. Ke-Ke could feel the sweat starting to form on her forehead as she stared down at the two rectangular packages wrapped in tape that sat on the table in front of them. She placed them side by side and looked up at Ti-Ti, who was still celebrating.

"Yo, you got two fucken bricks here," Ti-Ti said, as she picked up one of the packages and turned it over. Ke-Ke watched as the smile disappeared from her face as quickly as it had appeared. "Oh shit!"

"What?" Ke-Ke asked as she stared at Ti-Ti who was holding the taped package in her hand. "What? Why you say that?" Ke-Ke asked, knowing that her nerves couldn't take much more.

Ti-Ti flipped the package over, set it on the table, and backed away from it with her hands in the air.

Ke-Ke looked down at the package and dropped her head. "Fuck."

TWENTY-FIVE

KE-KE SAT DOWN in one of the chairs that surrounded the small glass table as she felt her legs beginning to feel weak.

"That's they shit!" Ti-Ti pointed at the stamp on the back of the package that was staring them both in the face. There was a lion painted red, gold, and green, wearing a crown and holding a flag in its paw. "How much you think this shit is worth?" Ti-Ti asked without taking her eyes off of the stamp.

"I can't even guess that shit," Ke-Ke said. "I ain't never seen this much in real life, only on TV," she said as she stared up at Ti-Ti and forgot all about trying to lie as she usually would. "That nigga *did* do that shit," she whispered.

"Yeah," Ti-Ti answered as she ran her fingers across the stamp like she thought she could erase it. "This ain't good!"

"Okay, let's think about this," Ke-Ke struggled against everything inside to pull herself together. "Don't nobody know about this but me, you, Lotto, and Chop. We in the clear. It ain't like them fucken Jamaicans know who we are!" She reasoned it out loud for herself as much as for Ti-Ti. She felt a wave of excitement run through her body as her own words gave her a sense of confidence. "It ain't like they gonna come looken for us," she finished as she stared over at Ti-Ti to catch her reaction.

Ti-Ti's eyes moved around slowly, the way they did when she was caught in a lie or thinking. She began to nod slowly as a smirk began to form on her face.

"Riiiiight?" Ke-Ke tried to sell her on the idea and pull her to a conclusion quicker than it was happening. "Shit, all we gotta do is break it down and get it off. Who's gonna know where the hell it came from? They just gonna know it's good!"

Ke-Ke's mind started to put everything together as she spoke. "This is brand new Benz and a house in the burbs money!" Ke-Ke said as she pictured a castle-like mansion that sat on a hill, surrounded by grass and trees. Ti-Ti grabbed a knife off of the counter and began scratching at the stamp on the package, until it started to flake up and the image of the lion was no longer visible. She scratched off the image on the other package and then looked up at Ke-Ke with a smile.

"I think we rich, bitch!" she said as she reached across the table and the two slapped hands. "But wait, shit!" Ti-Ti said as the smile disappeared from her face again.

"What? What now?" Ke-Ke asked as she watched the doubt come back into Ti-Ti's face. "Bitch, who gonna cook this shit? You know how to cook?" Ti-Ti asked.

Ke-Ke looked confused as she stared at Ti-Ti and wondered what the hell she was talking about.

"Guess you *don't* know everything, huh?" Ti-Ti smiled and pointed as she spoke the words that she knew would sting. "Bitch, this shit is powder. It still gotta be cooked! This ain't no powder spot. There's soft and there's hard. This is soft," she said as she made a small cut in the top of the package and dug the white crumbs out with the blade she was still holding. "This shit gotta be made hard, and if you don't know what the fuck you doen, you can fuck *ALL* this shit up!" Ti-Ti waved her hands over the table like one of those models on a game show that gave away appliances.

"Fuck," was all Ke-Ke could say as the nervousness rose in her chest again. "You don't know how to do it?" she asked Ti-Ti, already knowing the answer.

"Hell naw! You gotta be like a ghetto chemist to do that shit. All I know is you need baking soda or some shit like that," Ti-Ti said. "So now what?" she asked as she sat the knife on top of the package and stared at Ke-Ke.

There was a knock on the door and the two of them scrambled to put the packages back in the bag and hide it underneath the sink.

"Who the fuck is that?" Ti-Ti asked as they made their way into the front room and tried to act as normal as they possibly could.

"Yoooo hooo!" Nut's voice called from the other side of the door.

"Don't tell that nigga shit!" Ke-Ke ordered as she unbolted the door and let him in.

"Whatuuup!" Nut said as he stumbled into the house and collapsed on the couch with a bottle of Hennessey that had no top on it. "Where Lotto at?" he asked as he laughed at nothing and threw his hat across the room.

"That's *your* cousin," Ke-Ke answered, as she looked down at him and wondered if he knew anything about cooking. She knew he had been around dope his whole life, but she also knew he had a big mouth and everything ceased to be a secret once he found out about it. Ti-Ti snatched the bottle out of his hand and took it into the kitchen. She returned with two glasses and handed one to Ke-Ke.

"You a fuck-up Nut!" Ti-Ti said as she poured his liquor and stared down at him.

"I know, I know!" Nut said and laughed as if there were another Nut that Ti-Ti was talking about that wasn't him.

A million thoughts ran through Ke-Ke's head as she drank and stared down at Nut. Her thoughts bounced around uncontrollably as she tried to make sense of everything that had happened in such a short span of time. Her whole world had been turned upside down within the course of a few hours and it was now a place where the ground moved, like when she got off the tire swing in elementary school. There was a moment when she even thought about running to Germany after all. Selling everything, not giving a fuck who knew or found out, and then disappearing off the face of the Earth. She would bring all the money, Misha, and Ti-Ti, and they would party like rock stars in a whole new world. If her father got stupid, they would have enough money to buy a house or an apartment over there. They would figure something out. She was forced to only think about the things and people that really mattered to her as her mind snatched things like a person whose house was on fire. The people that mattered the most to her were Ti-Ti and Misha and she would definitely pack them if she had to resort to a plan B that she was still constructing.

"Ti-Ti, I'm bout to be out!" she yelled out from the kitchen as she stuffed one of the bricks in her hoodie to stash at her house. She figured that it didn't make sense to keep everything under one roof and she would have an easier time convincing Lotto and Nut that it was coming from Chop if they saw her bringing it in the house. Ti-Ti saw her walking away from the area and winked.

"I was thinken that same shit," she whispered and smiled as Ke-Ke made her way to the front room to wait on the cab she had called.

"Just run it how you seen us do it. Just don't let him know nothing!" Ke-Ke said as she nodded to Nut passed out on the couch.

"I got it. Just hurry back. I'm hungry as hell and you know I get bored when I'm by myself," Ti-Ti spoke the words fast, in a nervous tone.

"I'ma be right back, I just gotta holla at Tiff and drop this off by the house. I got something I wanna run by you when I get back anyway," Ke-Ke said as she tried to guess what Ti-Ti's reaction would be to leaving the country.

"Aiight, there go the cab." Ti-Ti pointed as she looked out of the window, over her shoulder.

Ke-Ke gave her a quick hug. "Keep the door locked, cuz," she instructed as she slipped out of the door with her own words echoing in her ears.

"Where to?" the driver asked as she slowly sat down in the backseat.

She checked her phone for messages and gave the address of the salon without even looking up. The thought of Germany came back in her mind as she glanced out of the window at the house and noticed her car covered in the blue tarp behind the house. She remembered a show where movie stars had their cars shipped overseas for vacations and wondered how much it would cost to do if it came to that.

Ke-Ke put her phone back in her pocket and sighed as it began to rain and the drops formed a warped view of the people, lights, and storefronts that they passed. Her mind jumped from subject to subject like it did when she was high. Why did everything in her life seem to go bad? Why did Chop put her in such a fucked-up situation without telling her? Why hadn't she taken school more seriously? The more she thought, the more questions arose as she wondered was she cursed like people in the Bible had been a long time ago. She thought about selling everything and not giving Chop shit, but the thought of having to duck and dodge him until she could make it out of town forced her to change her mind. She thought about bailing Cry out if she could and played a fairy tale ending in her head where her act of loyalty won her over and the two of them lived happily ever after.

The thought of her walking back and forth in a dark, cold cell with those ugly jumpsuits on forced her to push Cry out of her mind and almost made her tear up. She thought of Ahmed and still couldn't believe the story that she had seen on the news. She wondered how many of the girls were really just fast asses that got caught in their own lies or got scared and then threw him under the bus to save themselves. She had seen it happen in high school half a dozen times at least. A lot of girls had written checks with their mouths that they knew their bodies and nerves couldn't cash and ended up in a scary, uncomfortable situation with a grown man that they had been leading on for months. The courts would never know that side of the story of course. For some reason, part of her felt sorry for Ahmed. Those girls would go to court, cry, and tell on him, then go home and put on those grown-women panties and clothes they had been given free of charge and be at it again. *Don't play the game if you ain't got the chips.* Her uncle's words rang in her head, framing the complex nature of her thoughts.

The cab came to a stop in front of the salon and jerked Ke-Ke from the web of thoughts that pinned her mind down.

"I'm comen right back," she said as she jumped out of the cab and put her hoodie up as she walked away. Tiff would tell her what to do and she decided to just spill everything to her and see what she said. She couldn't be concerned with who Tiff told when she left.

"Hey, girl, hold up. I just talked you up," Tiff waved and went back to entertaining the ladies who sat underneath the hair dryers.

"So um, yeah girl, that's what it is. These niggas out here ain't got no role models. Even when you think you getten a good man, he end up sooner or later doing some bullshit. Then you stuck there asking yourself, 'What the fuck did I ever see in this nigga?'"

The ladies laughed, clapped, and held up their hands. Ke-Ke found herself mad that she hadn't gotten to the shop a little earlier to catch this "episode" from the beginning.

"Yeah, I be tellen these young girls, they be comen in here with they feelens all hurt up, broken hearted and shit. I mean, just look at the facts, and the truth shall set you free. Half of these niggas' daddies is crackheads, locked up, wanna-be players, or dead. You got a nation full of niggas raised by women then you be all surprised when he do some bitch-ass shit."

"Amen!" A woman stood up and spun around in a circle as Tiff delivered another one of her deathblow punchlines with perfect timing.

Ke-Ke got that creepy feeling she did when she was in church and felt like the pastor was talking directly to her. She looked up at Tiff and wondered if she already knew why she was there. The lady seemed to know a little bit about everything. She watched as Tiff made her rounds in the shop, slapping hands and soaking up the applause, but her thoughts prevented her from being able to fully appreciate the comedy.

"C'mon back here, girl," Tiff nodded and Ke-Ke followed her to the back of the salon where her office was.

"Give us a minute, girl." She tapped her secretary on the shoulder. Once they were alone, Tiff closed the door and sat behind the desk, grabbing a bottled water out of the cooler.

"So this is backstage?" Ke-Ke looked around the room and noticed the art on the walls next to Tiff's licenses and hair show awards.

"Yeah, somethen like that. I'm thinken about putten a star on the door." Tiff laughed. "Whatsup? I can tell you got some *shit* on your mind. And why you don't wrap your hair, girl? You throwen your money away!" she commented as she got up and touched up Ke-Ke's hair with her fingers.

"Shit, I been on the run," Ke-Ke answered as she sat down and allowed Tiff to bring the flair back to her hairstyle. "I got in some shit, Tiff, and I don't know how the fuck to play this shit," Ke-Ke started as she looked at the wooden African animals that were arranged across the front of the desk.

"What you do now, girl?" Tiff asked with her hand on her hip. She looked at her with a smile like she expected a "young girl" problem to come that she would be able to solve in record time, like she always did. Ke-Ke reached in her pocket and placed the brick on the desk in front of her.

"I got *THIS* type of problem," she said, as she felt Tiff's hands stop teasing her hair all at once.

"Girl! What the—?" Ke-Ke put her hand up and interrupted her question. She sat and slowly explained the whole situation for the next ten minutes. Tiff looked like she was watching an action movie for the very first time. She told Tiff what she had planned to do and even about her thoughts of leaving the country with her cousin and her sister. Tiff just listened and nodded without making eye contact. For the first time ever, Ke-Ke felt like when she was finished, Tiff would have nothing to say.

"So wait, this nigga just dumped this shit on you like that?" Tiff asked as she crossed the room and made sure the office door was locked.

"Yeah, basically," Ke-Ke answered as she looked up at Tiff, hoping she would be holding the keys that would free her from her situation.

"Girl, I done seen and heard a lot of shit in my day, but this is some NEW shit here," Tiff said as she shook her head and picked the brick up off the desk. "The first thing that comes to my mind is a set up." She spoke the words hesitantly, but they hit Ke-Ke cold and hard. That was the one thing she hadn't figured.

"I mean, why would a nigga rob the Jamaicans, and then just give you all of this? It don't add up. But then you say you don't even know the Jamaicans he was dealing wit? You ain't never met them and they don't even know who you are?" Tiff asked with her eyebrows raised, like she was beginning to doubt her story. "This that same nigga Chop wit the BMW I be hearen females talken about? The one that dropped Ti-Ti off over here a couple of times?"

Ke-Ke snapped her neck as she looked up at Tiff. She nodded and tried to play off the new information that shocked her whole system. She thought back to the house and how Ti-Ti had called Chop a homo-thug and those scattered pieces came together and clicked.

"And you say this had a stamp on it. The lion holding the flag?" Ke-Ke nodded again as she tried to stop her mind from running wild with thoughts of Ti-Ti fucking Chop behind her back. "Then you know for *SURE* that this is their shit?" Tiff asked the questions like she had missed part of the story and was still trying to play catch-up.

"Pretty much," Ke-Ke said as she rubbed her hands together and waited for Tiff's instructions. Her mind landed on thoughts of the black car that she had seen that one time and she kicked herself for not looking for it again when she left the house.

"I ain't gonna lie to you, girl, you know them damn Jamaicans don't play. They like the Haitians down in Florida. The thing you got worken for you is that there ain't nothen really connecten you to this nigga. If they catch him, they kill HIM and you still walk away wit like six figures in dope, free and clear!" Tiff spoke the words slowly, like she was thinking of every angle possible. "But who says that nigga Chop don't give you up? What if they catch him and he tells what he did wit they product? That brings them DIRECTLY to you!" Tiff pointed at her as Ke-Ke felt her heart sink. Then she remembered a detail she had forgot to mention.

"Tiff, can you cook?" she asked, hoping that Tiff would say yes and she could cross that off her list of impossible tasks for the day.

"Grits, yeah! Cocaine... hell to the naw!" Tiff laughed and slapped her thick thighs before she clapped her hands. Ke-Ke dropped her head again, but couldn't stop herself from smiling. Tiff could be in the depths of hell and she'd still be cracking jokes. "But hold up, I got someone that do!" Tiff said as she hopped off the desk and unplugged her cell phone from its charger. Ke-Ke fell silent as she watched Tiff going through her phone and dialing a number. She hoped with everything in her that Tiff would be able to put something together.

"Hold up, I gotta check the cab," Ke-Ke said, as Tiff nodded and put the phone to her ear. Ke-Ke walked to the front of the salon to see the cab was gone."Damn!" They probably figured she had walked out of a back door and wasn't coming back. She made her way back through the shop of gossiping woman and into the office.

"Close that door, girl," Tiff ordered as she placed her hand over the mouthpiece of the phone. Ke-Ke closed the door and slid the lock into place. "Yeah, girl, yeah. This will be a solid for me. I'll owe you. Girl, I know you ain't in the life no more, but I need you on this one, just one time. If I could think of someone else I could trust, I wouldn't be on this phone wit you!" Tiff spoke in a serious tone as she held one finger up at Ke-Ke. "I'ma text you her address. Her name's Ke-Ke. Y'all can discuss how y'all wanna do it then," Tiff said.

Ke-Ke wondered how comfortable she felt having a total stranger in on the action, but she hadn't come up with a better solution yet. Tiff hung up the phone and sighed loudly. "Girl, you lucky I love you. I ain't *NEVER* gonna hear the end of this favor. I'll be doen her head for free, her daughter's head, her boyfriend's kids' heads, and if she die before me, I'll be doen her hair in the casket!" Tiff ran down her burdens as she shook her head.

"Yo, you can run me across town real quick, Tiff? The cab left me," Ke-Ke asked, wondering if there was any more love to withdraw from Tiff's account.

"Yeah, come on now though. I got one more appointment comen later tonight," she said as she grabbed her phone, coat, and purse in one motion and the two of them walked through the shop without saying anything.

"Awwww shit! Don't hurt nobody, Tiff!" someone called out behind them, but Tiff didn't respond. When they got in the car, Tiff looked over at her.

"Girl, you got a *grown-woman* problem on your hands right now. You gonna have to grow up, like right fucken now."

Ke-Ke nodded as she listened and could hear the stress in Tiff's voice. "You gonna learn from this shit, or it's gonna kill you!" Tiff continued in a way that Ke-Ke had never heard her speak before. "On some real shit, I seen some Jamaicans at the bar last night and they didn't look like they was from around here. I just figured they was here early for the concert. Then you show up with this shit." She steered the car and glanced over at her at the same time. "You gotta stay focused now. Do what you been doing, keep your mouth shut, and get rid of that shit. I *would* say throw it away, but then you could have two problems and that's just too much money to throw away anyway."

Ke-Ke had to appreciate her honesty. Tiff wasn't the type of person that would tell you to do something that she wouldn't. "Just get that shit off as quick as you can and yeah, it might be a good idea to get out of town for a few months at least. Let shit cool down." Tiff spoke the words like she was talking to herself.

"That's what it is then. That's what I'm gonna do." Ke-Ke agreed with everything that Tiff said.

"And stay away from that nigga! Don't *ever* be seen with him. Right now you ain't connected to him and you don't *want* to be connected to him. You don't even want them Jamaican muthafuckas to know what you look like," Tiff said. Her voice quavered with nervous energy as she looked over at her.

"I got you." Ke-Ke kept agreeing, hoping it would help to calm Tiff down. "If he asks for money, I'll drop it off somewhere. He don't need to see me no more."

Tiff nodded while she waited for the traffic light to change.

"If you want, you can drop it at the shop. He can come there and pick it up. That way it won't be no bullshit about it not being there or whatever other games he might try to play wit you. Shit, I feel like I'm already in this shit, so fuck it." Tiff spoke her level of commitment to her in coded words.

"Good looken, Tiff." Ke-Ke grabbed her hand and held onto it for a minute when they pulled up in front of Ke-Ke's house.

"What's that number?" Tiff asked as she leaned over and tried to see the number on the front of the house. "I'm senden my girl Sin to see you. She used to be heavy in the game, and she said she gonna help you wit the cooken part," Tiff said as she texted on her phone. "She ain't the type to play, so don't try to get over on her in *any* way, and remember she only doen it cause I asked her. Don't make me look bad," Tiff said as she pointed her finger at Ke-Ke for the second time that night.

"I got you, Tiff. You know I don't be on no bullshit anyway," Ke-Ke said as Tiff reached out and hugged her neck and held her close for a few seconds.

"Sin will be here soon, so be ready," Tiff informed her after she checked her phone. Ke-Ke nodded and opened the door when Tiff grabbed the sleeve of her hoodie.

"Hold up." Tiff sighed and said, "I can't believe I'm bout to do this," she said as she reached for her purse that sat on the floor in between her legs. She unzipped a side compartment on the inside of the bag and pulled out a chrome revolver. "You know how to work one of these?" Tiff asked as their eyes met.

"Yeah, what's this, a .380?" Ke-Ke asked as she turned it over in her hand. "This shit is pretty," she said with a smile as she watched how the light skipped across it whenever she moved it.

"It's a .32, but it will do the job. My brother gave it to me when I first got up here. I got another one though," Tiff said quickly.

"Aiight!" Ke-Ke said as she hugged Tiff again and could no longer stop the tears from running down her face.

"Wipe them tears! You gotta be a big girl on this. It's gonna be okay." Tiff rocked her back in forth in her arms. "I'm wit you and I know if anybody can pull this shit off, you can."

Ke-Ke sat back in the passenger seat, embarrassed, as she wiped the tears off her face with her sleeve. The pressure had been building up in her the whole day. "When life deals you lemons... you know the rest!" Tiff said as she handed her a few napkins out of her purse. Ke-Ke nodded and forced a smile across her face.

"Call me if you need *anything,* girl! You know I'll come get you or whatever. Just stay in touch." Tiff sounded like she was begging as Ke-Ke stepped out of the car.

"I love you, Tiff!" Ke-Ke didn't know where she even found the courage to say it as she closed the door and ran up to the house before Tiff could answer back.

Deep down she knew what Tiff would say anyway.

TWENTY-SIX

KE-KE STEPPED IN THE HOUSE and closed the door as softly as she possibly could. She wasn't in the mood to hear her mother's mouth on top of everything else that was going on.

"Why you creepen?" She jumped as Misha came out of the kitchen eating a sandwich.

"Damn, girl! Why you in the kitchen with the lights off, like you a fucken vampire?" Ke-Ke whispered as she walked towards the stairs.

"I'm not," Misha followed her with "nosy" written all over her face. She followed Ke-Ke into her room, closing the door silently, without having to be told to. She was learning, Ke-Ke thought to herself, as she plugged in her phone and sat down on the bed. She looked at Misha then thought "fuck it" and pulled the gun out in front of her and laid it on the bed. She was surprised that Misha reacted so coolly as she hopped on her dresser and continued eating her sandwich like she hadn't seen anything.

"Damn, what, you starten a collection?" Misha asked as she chewed and rolled her eyes. "What the hell is you doen out there?" she asked with a look that was already prepared to hear a lie.

"Nothen," Ke-Ke answered as she walked to her closet to look for a change of clothes. Her phone vibrated and she answered it when she saw it was Ti-Ti.

"Yoooo, this shit is bubbling!" Ti-Ti's voice came through the phone, sounding excited. "This shit is that whip! The same muthafuckas done came back three times already. This one nigga came back and copped eight of em! This shit is sellen itself. We rich!" Ti-Ti screamed through the phone as she inhaled weed at the same time.

"How the fuck you get it to cooked? You was the one talken about it was soft that needed to be hard. I been out here goen crazy tryen to find someone to cook that shit!" Ke-Ke was still mad about the information she had gotten from Tiff, but knew she couldn't let it get in the way of business.

"I broke off a little and said it was from my cousin and he whipped it up for me. We almost out though. He passed out in the back now, called himself tryen to get some pussy, but I shut him down. I'm drinken his Hennessey right now!" she bragged and laughed.

"Aiight, I'm on my way." Ke-Ke ended the call and threw her phone on the bed.

"Y'all swear y'all some hustlers!" Misha said as she rolled her eyes and looked around the room unimpressed. "I heard her dumb ass, she talk too loud." Misha never really cared for Ti-Ti and they always ended up arguing and then wrestling any time they were around each other for too long.

Ke-Ke rushed into the bathroom. She pulled the brick out of her pants and began the process of breaking it into two halves. She wrapped the two halves in old T-shirts from her closet and then did a quick birdbath with warm water in the sink before she came back to her room. Misha had picked up the gun and was cocking the hammer back. Ke-Ke quickly stashed one half of the brick in a shoebox while Misha was distracted.

"How you knew how to do that?" Ke-Ke asked as she watched her hold the hammer and pull the trigger without, allowing it to strike the bullet with enough force to make it go off.

"I ain't stupid!" Misha said as she handed her the gun. "I know things!" She rolled her eyes again and picked her half-eaten sandwich back up off of the dresser. Ke-Ke stared at her, wondering how much she really knew and who had taught her. She didn't have the time to question her. She got dressed without saying anything.

"Well you *know* to keep your mouth shut, right?" Ke-Ke finally asked to see if their understanding was still intact.

"Yeah, yeah..." Misha waved her hand casually and rolled her eyes again.

"Yeah, yeah, my ass!" Ke-Ke said as she silently wrestled with the guilt of exposing Misha to so much at her early age. She knew Misha looked up to her, but half of the time she was so consumed with doing what she was doing that she didn't have the time or energy to break things down for her. She reached in her pocket and handed Misha a crisp hundred-dollar bill. Misha slipped it into her pocket without missing a beat.

She grabbed her phone and the charger just as a text was coming through.

SIN: IM OUTSIDE.

The message sent her heart into overdrive as she slipped on her boots and ran through a mental checklist of what she needed to take with her. Misha pulled the bill out of her pocket and realized all at once what she had been given.

"Damn! Thanks, Ke!" she said with that dumb look of wonderment written across her face. "Why you given me all this?" she asked as she held the bill up to the light to make sure that it was real.

"Bitch, it's real!" Ke-Ke spat at her as she sat on the bed and laced her second boot. "Misha, we gotta have a talk about something serious. I'ma come see you tomorrow, okay? I gotta plan for us, I think it might be a good idea," she said, trying to read whether Misha was going to be open to her idea without knowing what it was.

"What plan?" Misha asked with a confused look on her face.

"I said I'll tell you tomorrow!" Ke-Ke repeated herself as she stood up and made sure the brick was concealed in her jeans underneath her sweatshirt.

"It's gonna be your choice in the end, but whatever you end up doing, don't ever be like me, Misha, okay?" She ignored the blank look on Misha's face and hugged her, then kissed her on the cheek before she left her in the room and ran down the stairs.

A truck pulled up in the driveway and turned its lights off then honked just as Ke-Ke heard her mother's bedroom door opening. "Right on time," she thought. She felt her stomach feel uneasy as she stepped towards the passenger side and opened the door.

"Sin?" she asked as she climbed in the seat and closed the door. There was a moment of silence, as she stared at the side of the women's face behind the steering wheel and tried to remember where she knew her from.

"Yeah, I'm Sin. My real name's Cynthia, but like I told you before, I used to be young and dumb too!" the woman spoke as she slipped off her hood and stared Ke-Ke directly in the face. Ke-Ke felt a chill wash over her body as she recognized the scar that ran from her temple and disappeared underneath her chin.

"I told you I wasn't *always* a cab driver... remember?" she asked as her glassy eyes pierced Ke-Ke's heart the way they had done before. "I see you didn't take my advice about not selling your soul. Now you in the Devil's playground!" she said as she shifted the truck into reverse and backed out of the driveway. Ke-Ke sat frozen in the passenger seat as Sin drove down the block. She could feel the hairs on the back of her neck standing up and couldn't find words that would break the block of ice that had formed in her throat. Sin glanced over a few times and smiled like she knew that she was the last person in the world Ke-Ke was expecting to see.

"How, how... you... how you know Tiff?" Ke-Ke finally found the words after they had turned a few corners.

"I didn't think this was one of those social calls. I'm not really tryen to get to know you or like you," Sin spoke with a hiss that made Ke-Ke uncomfortable. She was the type of woman that you knew had been through it all, but the stories were only told in her eyes. Ke-Ke was trying to put on her nonchalant act, but nothing was working. She knew that Sin could see right through her, so she sat there, riding in silence feeling afraid and vulnerable. She noticed the open Bible on the dashboard and the rosary beads that swung from the rearview mirror.

"How much you need done?" Sin asked again in her whisper of a voice as she came to a stop at a light.

"Bout half a brick," Ke-Ke answered as she looked over at her, hoping that it would get some kind of human response out of her. It didn't. Sin nodded and continued to drive with gospel music playing low on her stereo. They pulled up in front of a grey house with an enclosed porch. Sin pulled into the long driveway and parked behind it in front of the detached garage.

"We here, c'mon," she instructed as she turned the ignition off and got out of the truck. Ke-Ke followed behind her to the side door and was led into a large kitchen. "You can have a seat," Sin said, as she took off her hoodie and threw it on a chair in the dining room. Ke-Ke passed through the kitchen and sat at the wooden table.

"Let me see what you got," Sin said as she rolled up the sleeves on her thermal. Ke-Ke stood up and pulled out the package that was wrapped in a shirt. She handed it to Sin and watched as she removed the shirt and laid it on the counter top. Sin dipped the tip of her finger in the white powder and tasted it, rolling her tongue around in her mouth slowly, then shook her head.

"What?" Ke-Ke asked as she prepared herself to hear that something was wrong.

"I'm not even gonna ask where you got this from. The less I know, the better," Sin said in her low voice as she walked towards the stove and turned a knob. The blue flames sprang to life on the front burner while she pulled a pot out of the sink and began filling it with water. She reached into a cabinet and pulled out a large glass measuring cup that had red lines and writing that ran down its sides. She placed the pot on the stove and then turned to face her.

"You don't need to be tryen to learn something that's only gonna get you into more trouble. Wait in the other room," she said as she pointed in the direction of the dining room.

Ke-Ke turned around and sat down at the table again. Sin came in the room after a few minutes, sat down across the table from her, and lit a cigarette. "Little girls," she said, as she shook her head.

Ke-Ke sighed and prepared to hear a speech.

"Oh, don't worry, I ain't gonna preach to you, you already got everything figured out, right?" Sin laughed as she spoke and continued to stare at her. "From what I can tell you in deep water though, and that water got a whole bunch of sharks in it." Sin spoke slowly and the words sent another chill through Ke-Ke's body. "And you out here splashing around in the water, but you don't know how to swim," Sin added as Ke-Ke watched her place the cigarette down in the ashtray and fold her hands. "I got a secret for you, Ke-Ke. The sharks don't care what you know. They never do," she said in her low voice as she pointed across the table at her.

Sin walked back into the kitchen without saying another word. Ke-Ke sat and tried to figure out the point of what Sin had just told her, but she gave up on it when she heard dishes clanging and Sin humming. She looked around the room at the pictures on the wall, of Sin at some sort of graduation dressed in a prison uniform and hugging an older woman that looked to be Spanish. She figured it had to be her mother as she noticed her in other pictures where they were standing in front of a church. Ke-Ke turned and looked behind her at a picture of a tall, dark-skinned man in overalls, holding a straw hat. Sin was standing by his side smiling and looked to be in her late teens, with no scar across her face. She was gorgeous. Ke-Ke's eyes followed the wall and noticed that there was a time-gap in the pictures. The pictures were either of Sin when she was a teenager or younger, or they were of how she looked now in a prison outfit, with the scar on her face. She figured that the picture that was taken in front of the church had to be one of the most recent.

"That's my parents." Ke-Ke jumped when she realized Sin had walked back into the room behind her. "My mom is Dominican and my father..." she paused and gave a sneaky giggle as she looked down at Ke-Ke. "My father is Jamaican." Ke-Ke felt her heart skip a beat. Their eyes locked as Sin nodded and smiled at her with a wild look in her eyes.

"Ya still tink I'm just a bloodclot cabbie star?" Sin spoke with a perfect Jamaican accent. Ke-Ke felt a rush of panic overcome her as her heart pounded in her chest. "You still think I don't know what I'm talken about?" Sin spoke in her regular voice as she smiled and backed into the kitchen. Ke-Ke realized that Sin was just fucking with her and relaxed as she watched her walk out of the room. She tried to figure out how much Sin had put together on her own and how much of the story Tiff had told her.

"This will be done in a few," she called from the kitchen. Every minute alone with Sin felt like an hour, so Ke-Ke pulled out her phone to text Ti-Ti and held it in her hands while she waited for a response. "I'm gonna have to do the other half of this and bring it to you later," Sin said. "You probably need to be getting back now, and I don't want to hold you up."

Ke-Ke grabbed her jacket off the back of the chair and walked into the kitchen as Sin stood over the counter with her back to her. She watched as Sin placed a large rock in a piece of aluminum foil and handed it to her. "It's still wet, so give it a few," she said as she reached for her own coat and picked up her keys.

Sin drove using back streets and avoided all traffic lights and busy intersections. Ke-Ke tried to figure out the process of cooking, from the tools and ingredients she saw still laying around in the kitchen when they left. She couldn't figure it out and had given up by the time they had hit West Main Street. She checked her phone but had no text message from Ti-Ti yet and then remembered she was supposed to be bringing food back.

"Can you make a quick stop for me?" She hesitated to ask, but Sin nodded like it wasn't a big deal. "I gotta grab somethen to eat. You can just stop at Menezes." She directed Sin to the closest spot she could think of.

"You want somethen?" she asked, in a final effort to break the thick ice between them.

"You got a heart in there after all, huh?" Sin smiled as she turned into the restaurant parking lot and parked. "I'd be stopping your blessings if I said no, so just bring me a steak sub."

Ke-Ke felt relieved as she got out of the truck and walked through the glass double-doors to place the orders. She stepped outside and tried Ti-Ti's phone again, and heard it ring four times and then loud music. It was her voicemail message. Ke-Ke started to feel worried as she walked back inside to see if her food was almost ready. She leaned against the wall and watched the workers answering phones and filling orders in a frenzy as more customers crowded into the small space.

"Ke-Ke!" the short man yelled as he held up bags and placed them on the counter. She paid him and walked back towards the truck. Her mind focused on the conversation with Tiff from earlier and she began to seriously think about leaving the country.

"You'd be surprised how a little good can go a long way," Sin said as Ke-Ke climbed back into the truck and handed her the sub. She noticed how her mood had seemed to change, but she didn't have the energy to figure it out. "I'm starten to think you might turn out all right after all. I had you figured as just a taker," Sin said as she pulled out of the parking lot and turned her lights on.

"Naw, I look out for people that look out for me," Ke-Ke said as she tried to figure out how Sin had come up with her first opinion.

"Well, I guess that's a start." Sin nodded and gave Ke-Ke the same look that pierced her every time. "I'll let you know when the rest of that is ready, it won't be long," she said in a whisper as she pulled up in front of the spot and Ke-Ke stepped out of the truck. Ke-Ke nodded, waved, then closed the door. She looked up the block to see if the black car was anywhere in sight, but the street was clear once Sin had pulled off.

She walked towards the house trying to manage the bags but slowed down when she noticed that she didn't see any lights on. Great. All she needed was for the power company to come through and shut the lights and gas off. She had never even thought about that expense.

She balanced the food on her knee and performed the knock. The door swung open quickly, and Ke-Ke dropped the food on the porch. "Damn, Ti-Ti," she said as she reached down and picked the bags up. She froze when she felt a strong, cold hand grasp the back of her neck.

TWENTY-SEVEN

SHE FELT HERSELF BEING DRAGGED INTO THE HOUSE and thrown across the room. She could hear the door slam behind her and the sound of feet walking towards her as she scrambled to get to her feet. She squinted and winced in pain as her eyes tried to become accustomed to the darkness of the house. Then the lights clicked on, blinding her again. Ke-Ke looked up to see a tall, dark-skinned man with dreadlocks that stopped just above his waist standing over her. He paused for a moment and she watched as four of his dreads waved back and forth in front of his chiseled face like a curtain that she could barely make out his bloodshot eyes through.

The smell of weed filled the house and Ke-Ke could hear more footsteps coming from behind her and the sound of muffled voices. She wanted to turn around to see the person coming from behind, but she couldn't break the hypnotic gaze on the face of the man that stood before her. His eyes swirled with a fire and insanity that she felt all at once, like she did when she was younger and wasn't sure if she was going to get an ass-whooping or not.

She watched as he brought a blunt to his lips and inhaled deeply as the light illuminated parts of his features that were hidden before. Ke-Ke tried to catch her breath as she figured that this man had to have thrown her across the room with one hand. Her mind struggled to place his face when she realized that he closely resembled the man in the oversized pictures of a black Jesus that they sold in gold frames on West Main. They could've been twins, she thought as she held her ribs and climbed to her feet.

"So you da one, star?" he asked in a steady voice and an accent that wasn't as thick as she had anticipated it to be. He held out his hand and shook his head, as a signal to whoever was standing behind her.

"The what?" Ke-Ke asked as she tried to figure out what he was asking. The man seemed to be staring right through her then began to pace back and forth in silence. Ke-Ke felt like the two words she had spoken were the wrong answer, as the man stopped in front of her and mumbled something that she couldn't understand.

"You know what me talk bout, star!" he said as he sighed, like he was losing his patience. "You like me stuff, eh? You like take money from me, star?" he asked the questions back to back as he walked towards her and raised his voice. Ke-Ke stood frozen as she tried to come up with something to say. The muffled sound got louder and she could recognize Ti-Ti's voice. She spun around and came face to face with another dreadlocked man wearing shades. He reminded her of a professional football player as his massive frame completely blocked the doorway that led to the kitchen. He held a spoon wrapped in a dish rag from the sink in his right hand and Ke-Ke could feel the evil coming off of him as she stared at his emotionless face. She turned back around just as Jesus was saying, "Let her g'wan see."

The man with the shades and the spoon stepped to the side and Ke-Ke rushed past him into the kitchen, making sure not to brush against him.

Her mouth dropped and the tears began to flood her eyes as she saw Ti-Ti and Nut bound to chairs with grey duct tape. They were both bleeding from their mouths and noses and were gagged with cloth that was tied in knots in the back of their heads. Ke-Ke shrieked and made an effort to run towards Ti-Ti but was lifted off of her feet and held up against the wall. She struggled to break the grip, but it was too strong and he laughed at her efforts as he held her with one hand.

"What the fuck is y'all doen?" she screamed and continued to struggle. The kitchen smelled like someone had burned something as she noticed the blue flames on the stove and the control knob on HI. She looked back over at Ti-Ti and Nut who were both crying when she noticed the oval burn marks on their faces and necks. She flailed with her arms and screamed louder when she realized it was their burned flesh she was smelling.

The man released her and pushed her back into the front room as he sniffed the spoon and laughed. She wiped her tears and tried to pull herself together when she noticed Jesus was sitting on the couch casually with his head cocked to the side, watching her.

"Me 'ave story ti tell," he spoke in a low, controlled tone as he pointed towards the chair.

"Okay, okay..." Ke-Ke stammered as she followed his directions, hoping it would help all of them get out of the situation alive. Her hands trembled as she brought them to her face and she shook uncontrollably.

"Easy, star," he said as he reclined on the couch and waited for her to pull herself together.

"Just don't hurt my cousin. I'll tell you whatever, just don't fucken hurt my cousin no more, this shit ain't even..." her voice trailed off as she looked up and saw that he had placed his finger to his lips and glared at her, shaking his head back and forth.

"Me 'ave story ti tell!" he said again as he sat up on the couch and rubbed his hands together. Ke-Ke put her hands up in front of her in a sign of surrender and waited for him to speak. The whimpering sounds that Ti-Ti and Nut were making and knowing that there was nothing she could do for them was tearing her heart to pieces.

Jesus began telling a story about how he was raised poor in some part of Jamaica. He took his time and described the conditions and made sure she understood that it was a totally different level of poverty than what spoiled Americans with food stamps and Section 8 complained about. He grew up in what he called a shantytown with his mother, two brothers, and one sister, who was later killed in Miami. He spoke of how he had come to America and made his way up north and eventually ended up in Rochester, New York, helping his cousin run restaurants, which Ke-Ke took as code for selling dope. The story went on and he spoke of women he loved and lost, money he made, the violence he had seen, and parts of the world he had been to. Overall, he had done well in the business and he spoke of how his mother enjoyed a beach home in Jamaica complete with servants who cooked, cleaned, and cut the grass. He slowly changed the subject and began speaking about how his cousin and other family members had to believe in him, had to trust him, and had to give him a chance in order for him to make it to where he was. He had never forgotten their kindness and generosity. Years of running drugs and enforcing their territories had resulted in one of his cousins doing life in federal prison and another one that was found in a dumpster in Toronto with a bullet to the head.

Ke-Ke listened intently as he talked about his life and death, murder and torture, like it was politics or sports. She found herself mesmerized at the way his voice and mood could go from a soft, caring place when he spoke of his mother to cutthroat ruthless when he talked about people who had crossed him and his family over the years. She sat captivated as she listened to him eloquently display this dance between beauty and the beast that existed within him.

He stared off in space as if he were watching a mirage of the events that he spoke about on the table in front of them. He had even smiled once when he spoke of the women he had loved. Ke-Ke had figured that he had to be the sole heir of his family's drug empire, which spanned from cities on the east coast to Canada and even England.

Her mind drifted against her will and she thought back to the time when Ti-Ti was going to get jumped by some girls for messing with one of their boyfriends. She had called Ke-Ke crying and she remembered running all the way to her grandmother's house without stopping. The girls pulled up in front of the house in a pickup truck and hopped out of the back, calling Ti-TI outside. Ke-Ke remembered running out of the house with the aluminium softball bat that their grandmother kept behind the front door. She swung wildly and knocked two of the girls out while the other three ran, tripping over themselves as they tried to get away.

She remembered tossing the bat to Ti-Ti and then straddling one of the girls and punching her repeatedly. "You know who you fucken wit?" she screamed as she pounded the girl with no mercy until she felt herself being lifted off of the girl. She spun around to punch whoever it was that had grabbed her, but felt herself get hit and she fell to the ground. She looked up to see that it was her grandmother.

"Child, don't you ever in your life raise your hands to me!" She pointed down at her with a look on her face that Ke-Ke had never seen. Ke-Ke remembered holding her face and trying to blink off the stars she was seeing as her grandmother stood over her with her purse in one hand and the other still balled in a fist. Ke-Ke sat up on the lawn, stunned, as her grandmother snatched the bat from Ti-Ti and walked into the house. She had pulled up in the middle of the fight and neither she or Ti-Ti had seen her coming.

Later that night there was an awkward silence at the dinner table and when it came time to do the dishes, Ke-Ke had taken the time to apologize to her and let her know that she didn't know that it was her. She remembered her grandmother smiling and looking at her over the top of her reading glasses. She set her knitting needles to the side and pointed her finger at Ke-Ke and spoke softly. "Girl, one day... one day, you gonna meet your match out there."

Ke-Ke started to walk away when her grandmother grabbed her arm and pulled her back. "One day you gonna meet the Devil face to face. We'll see how bad you are then."

"You wit me, star?" Ke-Ke snapped out of her flashback as Jesus snapped his fingers.

"My bad," Ke-Ke said as she could see he was annoyed with the fact that she wasn't giving him her full attention. Ke-Ke stared into the darkness of his eyes and knew in her heart that the day her grandmother had spoken about had come.

He continued his story about how he traveled to different cities and met different people. He had met rappers and singers in New York and partied with movie stars in Canada. Ke-Ke had begun to wonder where all of this was going until he started to talk about a young soldier, as he put it, that lived in the neighborhood one of his dope spots was in. He had gone to the supermarket and seen the boy running from security with a bag full of steaks and other food. He was eventually tackled in the parking lot and the security guards were attempting to drag him back into the store. Jesus told of how he had intervened and paid for the food right there in the parking lot.

He took the boy home to his mother and his heart went out when he walked in the boy's house and found three children in the home alone with no food in the refrigerator. Their mother was strung out and would leave them alone for days to fend for themselves. He spoke of how he walked through the house, looked through the cabinets one by one, and only found a stale box of cereal that rats had chewed through the bottom of. He had taken the boy under his wing, respecting that the young teenage kid was assuming grown-up responsibility for his sisters and brothers, much like he had when he grew up. From that day on, he taught the boy everything about the streets and everything about selling drugs. He had named him Chopper.

302

TWENTY-EIGHT

KE-KE'S MOUTH DROPPED as the story was now coming full circle. Jesus looked at her and smirked when he saw that she realized where he was going. She listened as the laundry list of contradictions started coming out and she compared what Chop had told her in the past to what she was hearing now. Jesus had given him the name Chopper because of the way he always shot off at the mouth. She caught herself smirking as she remembered how Chop had told her it was because of the way he liked to use automatic assault rifles when he had problems with people.

The next ten minutes Jesus spent exposing Chop. He wasn't the gangster, hustler nigga she had come to know, but an ungrateful, thieving coward. Jesus explained how Chop was supposed to supervise a network of drug houses in New York City while he was across seas. Chop had come up with a plan of his own, which had resulted in Jesus' nephew being thrown out of a tenth-floor window and Chop vanishing into thin air.

She listened as the reality and seriousness of the situation she had been thrown into finally sank in. She thought back to the conversation she had with Lotto and wished with everything in her that she had left while she still had the chance. She searched her mind for anything she could say to convince Jesus that she had nothing to do with what Chop had done, knowing that the fact that they had been caught with his product told another story. She could still hear Ti-Ti and Nut squirming in their chairs and trying to speak through their gags and wondered how long it would be before she ended up in a chair right beside them. Tears began to from in her eyes again as she thought about her face being disfigured with burn marks from a hot spoon until she was ultimately tortured and beaten to death. Ke-Ke sat there shaking as the room fell silent, afraid to make eye contact with the man who held her life in his hands.

"You could just let us go though. We ain't have nothen to do wit that shit. Chop ain't tell me nothen about that shit in New York." Ke-Ke felt like she was pleading her case to a deaf judge and jury. She looked up quickly, just in time to see Jesus make a nodding motion to his friend who disappeared into the kitchen. He grabbed her by the arm and pulled her close to his face.

"Don't ya lie, star!" he spoke in a whisper as she heard footsteps in the kitchen and then Ti-Ti's muffled scream. She felt another wave of fear crash over her as she tried desperately to come up with something that he would believe. She remembered the gun and reached for it but was knocked to the ground before her hand touched the handle. The salty taste of blood filled her mouth as she spun around to see him holding the pistol in his hand. She figured it must've fallen out when she was thrown across the room earlier and all at once felt stupid for even trying to reach for it. Jesus smiled as he stood and looked down at her. Ke-Ke thought about closing her eyes, the way people did in the movies when they knew they were about to get killed.

"Me tink me 'ave a plan," he said as he yanked her to her feet and dragged her into the kitchen by her arm.

Here it was. This was how she was going to die. She tried to prepare her mind and body for what was coming. She knew that she was tougher than Ti-Ti, but she figured she wouldn't be able to withstand a scorching spoon to the face any better than she had. Ke-Ke felt her body starting to go limp as he stood her in front of Nut and Ti-Ti and gave another silent command to his partner. He whispered in her ear about how creative he could be when it came to getting information that he needed. Ke-Ke struggled to turn her face away as

304

his partner unsnapped Ti-Ti's pants and pulled them off of her. Ti-Ti screamed. Her face was already a bright red and Ke-Ke could see that the tape that bound her wrists was cutting off her circulation. She felt Jesus grab the back of her neck tightly, forcing her to look forward and watch.

"You love... eh?" he asked as Ke-Ke cried and braced herself to feel the hot spoon on her face. He jerked her back into the front room, pushed her hard against the wall, then placed his hands around her throat. He explained his plan, slowly and softly to her, as he tighthened his grip. When he was finished, he stared into her eyes with a smirk and waited, as if he expected her to resist. Ke-Ke nodded frantically in agreement—whatever it would take to get Ti-Ti out of that kitchen, even though she wasn't sure his plan would even work.

Jesus made sure she could recite his plan perfectly first, then she was in the backseat of a car headed across town. He sat in the passenger seat while another man, who had showed up with the car, sped through the streets. She learned from their conversation that they had tracked Chop back to Rochester from some female and they had been following him around but had lost him. She figured that it had to have been them that she had seen in the black car earlier that week but didn't have the nerve to ask. She wondered why they hadn't just killed Chop as soon as they found him, but she answered her own question in her head. *Why kill someone for revenge, when you can kill them AND get your money back?*

She listened to Jesus and the driver speak a combination of Jamaican P\patois and broken English. She could only piece together that Chop had switched vehicles at some point and that's how they had lost him. Ke-Ke knew that if Chop had skipped town, that would mean certain death for her, Nut, and Ti-Ti, so she tried to convince herelf that he was still around. Jesus had left the man with the spoon behind to "babysit" and she was desperately trying to keep the thoughts of what he was doing to them out of her head.

"Make the call, star," Jesus ordered over his shoulder to her. She took a deep breath and reached for her phone that he had been holding for her. She dialed Chop's number on speakerphone and heard it ringing just as the driver had turned down the stereo. The phone rang four or five times and then the voicemail picked up. Ke-Ke's heart sank as she redialed the number.

"Yooo," Chop answered in a low voice. Ke-Ke tried to sound normal, although her insides were doing flips.

"Whatup, baby?" she asked, trying to mask the fear in her voice, hoping that he wouldn't be able to pick up on anything.

"Nothen, whatsup?" Chop answered. Ke-Ke turned the volume on her phone to the max as he spoke.

"You!" Ke-Ke answered. "I figured I should thank you for putten me on like you did," she said, realizing that acting like she wanted dick was harder than when she really did and everything just seemed to flow naturally.

"Word, shorty?" She could tell he was smiling, she just had to reel him in.

"I was thinken bout letten you get that too," she said as she watched Jesus nodding at how she was playing it.

"*Word?* Where you at?" His whole voice changed as he asked the question. Ke-Ke had to roll her eyes at how simple niggas were. A second ago he sounded like he was about to go to sleep, but the possibility of getting some pussy was like a splash of cold water on his face.

She fed him a story about how she had gotten kicked out of her house and gave him directions to a hotel just as they were pulling into its parking lot. She hung up the phone and waited to see if her performance had met their approval.

The driver stepped out of the car and slammed the door. The car fell silent. Ke-Ke had come to the conclusion that Jesus was not a talker as the car remained silent until the driver had returned with two keycards and handed one over the seat to her. She handed her phone back to Jesus, who texted the room number to Chop's phone.

"Ya wa'an live? No mistakes!" he spoke softly as he pointed her towards the room and lit another blunt.

Ke-Ke ran up the outside stairs towards the room on the second level. She opened the door and was shocked by how cold it was. She turned the heat on full blast and ran the shower hot to heat the room. She didn't want Chop to have any reason to be suspicious. She laid the covers on one of the beds back, turned on the TV, then waited. When she went to the window and looked down, the car was gone. A feeling of fear came over her when she thought that they couldn't have gone far and she knew in some way they had to be watching the room.

She sat on the bed and ran through all the different reasons she'd had sex with people and concluded that this was definitely a first. The thought of her cousin being tortured and raped across town was more than enough motivation for her though. She would fuck the hell out of Chop if it meant her and Ti-Ti getting out of this.

She fell back on the bed and felt her world spinning. She thought about asking Ti-Ti to leave with her and Misha if they made it out of this whole thing. The option of leaving the country seemed like a free ticket to heaven now. She thought about the course her life had taken, everything that had happened, and everything that she had been through in the past few years. She had watched those real-life homicide investigation shows and always wondered what the victims had thought about right before they were killed. The thought scared her to death and she jumped when the phone rang.

"Hello?" she anwered, figuring that it had to be the front desk calling for something.

"No funny shit!" the voice came through the phone and, before she could answer, they had hung up. She put the phone down and kneeled at the side of the bed, praying that God would see her through this. She stood up with a sigh and sat back down on the bed, nervously rubbing her palms together. It had taken a man she had named Jesus to put the fear of God back into her.

TWENTY-NINE

SHE HAD JUST GOTTEN OUT OF THE SHOWER when she heard a knock on the door. She dried herself off quickly and crept towards the window, letting her towel fall off of her as she walked. Chop stood at the door holding a brown paper bag and looking around. She flicked off the room's overhead light and opened the door.

"Damn, you wasn't playen, was you, shorty?" He smiled as he stood in the doorway looking her up and down.

"Close the door, nigga. I ain't tryen to share!" she said as she pushed the door closed and walked over to the bed and got under the sheets. She watched as he took off his leather jacket and pulled a tall bottle of Cîroc from the bag. Ke-Ke smiled as she thought about how Chop didn't have a problem spending money as long as he knew he was going to get some ass with his receipt.

He removed the plastic from the hotel cups that were stacked on the table and poured a double shot in both, then handed one to her. She turned the cup up and felt it burn on the way down, knowing it would take a few more for her to really relax. She tried to act natural, even though she wasn't at all feeling that way on the inside. She thought back to the times that she had gotten high before going to school. You spent so much time wondering if you were looking and acting high that you started to do things that you thought would throw people off, that in the end made you look higher than you really were.

Chop didn't seem to notice though as he had downed two shots and was working on his third. Ke-Ke smirked as she figured that he was trying to give her that everlasting drunk dick and really put it on her.

The mood was interrupted as a sadness swept over her while she looked over at him and knew that he had no idea what he had just walked into. She would be the last piece of ass he ever got in his life. The depth of the whole thing was too much for her and she shifted her thoughts and distracted herself with the television.

"How's that flow over there now?" he asked as he slipped off his boots and continued drinking.

"Shit, it's better than ever. I shoulda *been* got down wit you!" Ke-Ke winked as she looked over at him.

Chop finished another two shots and stood up to take his clothes off. Ke-Ke slid over to make room for him in the bed. She felt a weird sense of obligation in making him enjoy everything, figuring it was the least that she could do.

Chop climbed into the bed and kissed her as she clicked the TV off with the remote. She remembered instantly that he had always been a good kisser as she felt her body responding to his touch.

He climbed on top of her and looked into her eyes. "You know I'm really feeling you, right?" he asked as he held himself up and looked down at her.

She couldn't help but feel the butterflies in her stomach, knowing that most niggas wouldn't take the time to lie to her if they had already gotten that far. She stared back into his eyes and for a second she could see the thirteen-year-old boy who had stolen steaks to feed his younger siblings. She felt sick. She was still mad at him for what he had gotten her and her cousin into, but at the same time she felt a sense of understanding, knowing what it must've been like to try to make it out here on your own. He had definitely had a rough life, like everyone else she had known, and she wanted to hear his side of the story at least. But there was no way she could get him on the subject without showing her hand.

He was just like everybody else, running around trying to figure out this whole life thing all by himself, lost, a fraternal member of a fucked-up and misguided generation that sought instant gratification by any means necessary. The game they played was the same, but everybody seemed to be on their own team. They ran around an asphalt field, colliding and bouncing off each other, headed for a goal that they most likely would never see. They each inevitably would be tackled, injured, end up running out of bounds, or somehow or other be taken out of the game completely. Years later they would end up on the sidelines, nursing old battle scars, drinking themselves to death, and sharing stories from their "glory days." Battered and bruised they would watch and place bets on the next generation as they took to the field and, maybe out of spite, maybe out of fear that they wouldn't be listened to, refuse to share the secrets of the game.

Ke-Ke cherished this connection she was feeling in her chest, although she struggled to find the words to say what she was feeling in any sensible manner. She wanted to talk to him, maybe even tell him what was going on and form a plan to run away together. The thoughts clouded her mind and she fought back the tears for what was going to happen to him, her, Ti-Ti, Nut, and everybody like them. She embraced him tightly as he pushed himself inside of her, intoxicated by the smell of his cologne. His body weight formed a blanket of security on top of her as she remembered all at once why she always preferred grown men. They made her feel like a woman; the fact that they desired her and she could satisfy them was beyond the understanding of the older women who said she was "fast."

Ke-Ke had played this moment out at least a dozen times since she was shoved into the car, but was totally unprepared for what had quickly become the intense passion of a moment. She thrust her hips in unison with his and moaned as she felt the feeling, the connection growing inside of her like a ball of flame. She closed her eyes and imagined a world where the sky was purple and the air was warm, where birds changed colors as they streaked across the sky like tiny comets and disappeared—a place with waterfalls and scenic views, a place far away from the brutality of a world that she had come to know.

Chop thrust himself in and out of her in a strong circular motion and she dug her nails into his back and gasped as the hot tears started running down her face. She wished that she could fly away with him and this feeling, make him believe that such a place existed. The imagery of her fantasy made her feel like she was outside of her own body. She struggled to understand how the worst experience of her life had seemed to join hands with the most beautiful feeling in the world, allowing her to catch a short glimpse of a place she would remember to name "hope."

She had heard of girls talking about making love but always figured they were exaggerating to make their boyfriends seem more romantic. Now she found heself lost in Chop as she wrapped her legs around his waist and breathed heavily underneath him. She felt herself beginning to shake as Chop pulled out of her, began to lick down her neck to the middle of her chest, and then made circles with his tongue around her belly button. She placed her hands on either side of his head and pushed it down, in between her legs—

"Bloodclot!" Ke-Ke's eyes sprang open. Jesus and his driver stood at the foot of the bed, looking down on them. They both froze. The covers were snatched off of them and the barrel of a shotgun was pressed up against Chop's face. The driver walked him to the front of the room and sat him down in front of Jesus. Ke-Ke balled herself up at the head of the bed and put her head down as Chop glanced back and forth at the two men in front of him, then back at her. She couldn't bring herself to make eye contact with him.

"I was tryna get in touch with you," he stuttered, which only led the driver to smack him in the face with the barrel of the gun. Blood squirted from his face as he fell to the floor, holding his head. "Look, I was gonna call you. I was tryna get the money back!" He tried to block himself from being hit again with an outstretched arm. Chop sounded like a little kid, trying to explain something to his father.

There was a light knock on the door and two more men entered the room. Ke-Ke noticed the latex gloves on their hands as they gripped what she figured were guns in their waistbands. They closed the door and moved quickly, removing their jackets and sliding machetes out of the front of their pants. Ke-Ke stared in shock, then covered her face with her hands, knowing she wouldn't be able to watch what was going to happen.

"Dun him!" Jesus ordered to the men as they dragged Chop to the back of the hotel room and into the bathroom. The driver snatched the pillowcase off of a pillow that sat next to Ke-Ke, smacked the side of her ass, then headed for the bathroom. A few moments later, she could no longer hear Chop talking, just the sounds of a struggle as the men cursed him in patois and laughed.

She heard more banging then a gurgling sound that she knew she would never forget. It reminded her of when she went down south to a family reunion and watched her grandmother kill a pig for the cookout. The sounds of the machetes hacking and clanging against the floor and tub sent goosebumps all over her naked body. She jumped at every noise and tried not to imagine what the scene in the bathroom had to look like. She could only hear the loud, angry voices speaking fast and asking questions that they didn't really seem to want answers to.

It seemed like hours had gone by since she had heard Chop's voice and she knew he was dead. Against her will, her mind pictured his body in bloody pieces all over the floor. She heard the water running and then more laughter as the door swung open. The two men with the machetes emerged, wiping the blood off of their faces with their shirts before taking them off. One of the men winked at her as he noticed her staring at the blade in his hand that dripped thick drops of Chop's blood onto the carpet. She felt light-headed and then her stomach churning like it did when she was about to throw up.

Jesus spoke to the men, barking more orders in words that Ke-Ke couldn't understand. The two of them returned to the bathroom and came back with the blades on their machetes washed clean of any traces of blood. They put their coats on and disappeared out of the room as quickly as they had appeared.

She inched away from the head of the bed, feeling like she was moving in slow motion. Everything she had heard and seen had her in a dreamlike state, but she was trying not to show it. She knew her face was telling on her as the tears fell and her guilt consumed her. She told herself that she had done what she had to do, but it wasn't enough to stop her body from shaking.

"Me see you 'ave heart, star."

She was relieved to hear him speak again in words that she understood. She was positive he was standing right behind her, watching her pull her pants up over her ass. She jumped as he spoke though and tried to play it off, as she reached down to pick up her shirt and bra.

"Me 'ave what you say... dilemma," he spoke in his soft voice and seemed to struggle with the word. She could hear him moving towards her as she clipped her bra together and was adjusting the straps when he said it.

"Me like you, star... but me caaan't leave dem witness!" The words felt like a winter breeze that wrapped around her half-clothed body. She spun around to see him lifting the gun he had taken from her earlier at the house.

She heard a shot, saw a flash of light, and felt her body falling.

***

MISHA AWOKE TO THE SOUND of her mother screaming. She sat up in the bed instantly as an uneasy feeling shot through her body. She ran to her closet and grabbed the aluminum softball bat that Ke-Ke had given her with instructions of where and how to hit Kent if he ever put his hands on their mother. Her heart raced as she swung the door of her bedroom open and headed down the hall towards her mother's bedroom.

The sound of unfamiliar, low voices coming from downstairs stopped her in her tracks. She crept down the stairs with the bat gripped tightly in her hands, reached the landing at the bottom quickly, and turned the corner to find two tall white men with badges and guns clipped to their dress pants standing over her mother. Her mother was screaming hysterically with her hands covering her face.

Misha dropped the bat and ran across the room, startling the two men, who half-spun and reached for their weapons. They stared down at her with fire in their eyes before they relaxed and allowed her through to her mother. "She still alive?" her mother mumbled through her hands as her tears leaked through her fingers and she shook as she rocked back on forth on the couch.

"Yes, ma'am. We tried to reach you last night, but there was no answer." Misha watched as her mother held up her hand to cut the young officer off.

"Misha, get your things and call your grandmother. Tell her we are on the way to come get her."

"What happened—"

"Just go, Misha!" Her mother screamed and almost pushed Misha off the couch as she cut her off.

Misha ran upstairs and got dressed in a daze. Everything in her told her that something had happened to Ke-Ke. She jogged down the hall and burst into her mother's room to find Kent snoring in the bed and the phone off the hook. She quickly dialed her grandmother's number, but the phone rang with no answer. Misha figured Ti-Ti was probably on the phone, ignoring the beep coming from the other line. She slammed the phone back on the receiver and ran down the stairs to find the officers apologizing and trying to console her mother.

A moment later, they were in the car, speeding through the streets as her mother cursed Kent for taking the phone off the hook so they could have "alone time." The tears ran down her face in a steady stream as her hands shook on the steering wheel. Misha watched her unravel in small pieces but couldn't think of anything to say to make her feel better or calm down.

They pulled up in front of their grandmother's house and found her sitting on the porch in her housecoat speaking with two uniformed police officers. Her eyes looked glazed over and she just stared up at the officers as if they were speaking a different language.

They were all seated in the waiting room that had the word "Emergency" painted in bold red letters above a circular desk. Nurses and doctors appeared and then disappeared down a long white hallway before her grandmother spoke a word.

"They say Ti-Ti was in a burning house," she said slowly, but it sounded like a question, as if she expected Misha or her mother to have more information or details. Misha looked over and watched her mother shake her head and attempt to wipe the tears that had drenched her face with a balled-up tissue. A short man in a blue uniform and a white coat approached them and asked "Ketasia?" as he squinted and looked down at the three of them.

"Yes, that's my daughter," Misha's mother spoke with her eyes fixed on the man.

He sat down across from them, removed a pen from his coat pocket, and opened a steel clipboard that he was carrying. "Ketasia and Tionne are cousins, correct?" he asked slowly as he flipped back and forth between two sheets of multicolored papers and glanced back up at them with a curious look on his face.

"Yes, I'm the guardian of Tionne," Misha's grandmother spoke as she gripped Misha's hand tightly.

"I'm Dr. Kates." He offered his hand and then retracted it when he saw that the people that sat before him were too distraught to offer a return to the gesture.

Misha listened closely for the next ten minutes as the doctor spoke softly and used big words to describe the condition of her sister and cousin. He spoke of how Ke-Ke had undergone surgery the night before and was in critical condition. She tried her hardest to understand but found herself lost in a sea of words that he seamlessly linked together, like "trauma" and "hemorrhaging." He spoke of how lucky Ti-Ti had been, but there was a moment of awkwardness when he asked about the significant amount of cocaine found in her system.

"She's lucky to be alive," the doctor finished, focusing on them with a sincere intensity. "Her friend that was in the house with her wasn't so lucky." He discreetly nodded towards the group of people that sat across the room from them who were also crying and speaking softly amongst each other.

Misha noticed the two officers from the house enter through the automatic doors and head for the circular desk that sat in the middle of the room. They spoke to the woman behind the computer screen and headed over to where Misha sat with her grandmother and mother once she had pointed in their direction. Misha felt a lump in her throat as her mind began to process everything she had heard so far.

"I want to see my baby," Misha's mother said out of nowhere, without even looking at the doctor.

"That's not usually allowed with people in her condition, but I will see what I can do."

He replaced the pen in his pocket and informed them that he would be back to speak with them shortly.

"I want to see her!" Misha's mother spoke in a louder voice as the doctor stood, pursed his lips, and nodded in understanding before walking away from them.

Misha watched as he placed his clipboard on the counter of the desk and took a deep breath before approaching the family that sat across from them. He sat down in the same way that he had with them, but this time he did not bother to extend his hand. Misha couldn't make out his words from where she sat, but she watched as the family erupted into tears and cursed loudly while a middle-aged, overweight woman slid out of her chair and onto the floor as if her body didn't have bones. The other members of the family struggled to pull her to her feet as she flailed her arms and shrieked in a tone that ripped through the air and gave voice to her broken heart.

Misha had gone numb after an hour of the police asking them questions that for the most part they answered with one "I don't know" after another. The police coldly filled in the details in plain English that the doctor had left out or spoken too complexly for them to fully understand.

Ke-Ke had been shot multiple times—once in the face—and was found half-dressed and bleeding on the floor of a hotel room by housekeepers that heard the gunshots. In a different part of town, fire rescue personnel arrived just in time to pull Ti-Ti and another man out of an abandoned house that had been set on fire. They had both been severely beaten and burned with a foreign object.

Misha stared ahead with no emotion as she tried to picture and piece together for herself what had happened. The investigators asked the same questions in different ways, as if they believed that they were being lied to. They left their business cards and walked away, shaking their heads as they approached the grieving family members across the room.

Misha's mother nudged her and asked her something about Ti-Ti being on drugs, but she could only bring herself to shrug and shake her head back and forth.

A petite Asian nurse appeared before them out of nowhere with a concerned look on her face. She instructed them that they could have a few minutes with Ketasia and warned them that she appeared to be slipping in and out of consciousness.

Misha tried to prepare herself for what she was about to see as they followed the nurse halfway down the long hallway before she pointed to a room on the right and nodded without speaking.

Misha turned to see Ke-Ke lying in the bed with a large, white bandage wrapped around her head that completely covered one of her eyes. There were tubes running into her nose and mouth and a machine that beeped on a stand next to the bed.

Misha felt her mother let go of her hand as she fell to the floor screaming and crying. The nurse returned quickly with a large security guard that escorted her back in the direction of the waiting room. She watched her mother's body go limp as they half-carried her around the corner while she screamed "My baby!" Misha felt her grandmother's grip tighten on her other hand as they entered the room and slowly got closer to the side of the bed. The nurse reappeared in the room, pushed some buttons on one of the machines, and whispered, "She can hear you," before she left the room, giving them their privacy.

"She looks dead," Misha said as she noticed all the wires that seemed to come from underneath the bed sheets in different directions. She felt the tears welling in her eyes but managed to fight them back.

"Your sister just resting, girl," her grandmother said as she squeezed her hand. Misha looked up at her grandmother when she released her hand and began humming, making her way to the opposite side of the bed, never taking her eyes off Ke-Ke.

"Lord, who did this to my child?" she asked aloud with a sense of anger that sounded unfamiliar. She raised her head to the ceiling and rocked back and forth. "Lord, Lord, Lord..." Her voice trailed off.

Misha turned as one of the investigators had slipped into the room behind them and stood there with his hands in his pockets. She watched her grandmother's heavily wrinkled hands touch Ke-Ke as she asked, "Baby, who did this to you?" Her voice was barely a whisper that trembled with pain.

Ke-Ke coughed and stirred as the officer moved closer and they all stared down at her, expecting some sort of miracle. "Who would do this to you?" her grandmother asked again as she rubbed the back of Ke-Ke's hands.

Ke-Ke stirred again and the pain registered on her face. Her mouth opened and Misha stood in shock as it appeared that she was trying to speak. She glanced back and forth at her grandmother, then at Ke-Ke. "Tell me who, baby," her grandmother coaxed.

Ke-Ke's head slowly turned in the direction of their grandmother and in a cracked, soft voice whispered, "Jesus."

THIRTY

TIFF UNLOCKED THE DOOR TO THE SHOP and paused as she reached down to grab the mail. She walked in and closed the door behind her and crossed the room to her station without bothering to turn the lights on. The shop was closed that day, but she needed to be somewhere quiet where she could be alone with her thoughts. The past few days had been torture on her.

She had been to the hospital to visit Ke-Ke but was not allowed in because she wasn't an immediate family member. The scattered details of the shooting and the house fire were plastered all over the news and she was struggling to get the images out of her head. Her mind traveled against her will back to the last time she had seen Ke-Ke. The night she had shown up to the shop with stolen cocaine and fear in her eyes. Tiff played their conversation back in her head word for word, searching for anything that she could've or should've said differently that might've changed the outcome of what everybody in the city seemed to be talking about.

She sat in her chair, swaying back and forth, lost in her own thoughts. She rode her chair around in circles as the guilt and feelings of regret crashed down on her all at once. She looked away from her reflection in the mirror, "Damn that little girl!" she said aloud as she dropped her head and stared at the floor.

She stood up, holding herself against the counter cluttered with hair grease and brushes when her eyes settled on the letter at the top of her stack of mail.

ATTN: KETASIA M. SINGLETON
QUEENS SALON
ROCHESTER, NY 14612

Tiff stared down at the letter, confused, until she remembered Ke-Ke had said she was having something sent there. Tiff searched around her station, found a rat-tail comb, and ripped the letter open. She said a short prayer, hoping that whatever news the letter held would be something that she would be able to handle. She prayed that, on top of everything else, Ke-Ke hadn't contracted HIV or some other STD.

She took the letter out of the envelope with a long sigh, glanced up at the mirror, and unfolded the letter slowly, hoping for the best. She smiled and pumped her fist as she immediately noticed a column on the right-hand side of the letter that read, "Negative" repeatedly.

"Good girl," she said aloud, relieved. Her attention was taken away from the letter as she heard raindrops beginning to tap on the front window of the salon. People were beginning to run to their cars and destinations to avoid it. Tiff reclined in the chair and let her eyes fall back to the letter in her lap. "Positive" was written in blue at the very end of the list. Her heart sank as she glanced to the left of the page to find out what Ke-Ke had tested positive for.

She bit down on her upper lip and the tears flowed, uncontrollably now. She was mad at life, mad at herself, and mad at God all at the same time. She threw her curling irons, combs, and hair products off the counter in one motion as she sobbed loudly and paced the floor.

She tried to force-feed herself the saying "God works in mysterious ways," but she just shook her head. Tiff was certain that the one thing that would have slowed Ke-Ke down was the one thing that she didn't even know.

She thought back to how she had once talked to Ke-Ke about becoming a stylist and going to Continental Beauty School. Ke-Ke had always been receptive to the idea but was always saying she didn't have the time. Tiff imagined how it would've been to see her have her baby, graduate, and work in the shop alongside her and the other ladies. The thought made her smile: the alternate ending where Ke-Ke fire-walked through hell but landed on her feet, the same way she had done herself a decade or more earlier. Life obviously had other plans.

Tiff stood in the middle of the dark shop, watching the rain fall harder and harder. She walked over to the waiting area and sat on the arm of the leather couch with a million thoughts and emotions running through her that she had accepted she wouldn't be able to control.

For some reason the memory of the first time she had seen Ke-Ke popped in her head. Ke-Ke had to have been only twelve at the time. It had been raining that day too. She remembered Ke-Ke asking her, "Tiff, when it rains, is God crying?"

Tiff remembered laughing and telling her that she was being silly as she slipped her apron around her neck. More than anything, she wanted that one moment back as she stared out the window and watched the rain turn everything grey.

"Yeah, baby, He's crying. He's crying for all of us," she said as the tears began to run down her face again. "He's crying for all of us."

ABOUT THE AUTHOR

JULIAN FOSTER is a novelist from Rochester, New York. He began his writing career as a spoken word artist under the stage name Tearz, performing with his group The Vagabonds. Julian has been in gangs, gone to jail, and has now come full circle, hoping to bridge people from different walks of life through the power of the written, visual, and performance arts. He also hopes to develop a community outreach center for at-risk people of all ages.